Praise for *Solimeos* and Rhoda Lerman

"*Solimeos* is an astonishing novel of epic sweep in which The Third Reich is reborn in the forests of the Amazon—singular in its exquisitely detailed, bold re-imagining of the aftermath of the darkest chapter in twentieth century history. The most astonishing and original book I've read in years, this tale of adventure and intrigue is as horrifying and shocking as it is sublime and beautiful."

–**Jay Neugeboren**, author of *The Stolen Jew*

"Lerman's is a unique voice—wildly funny, achingly spiritual, profoundly Jewish and feminist at the same time."

–*The New York Times Book Review*

"The very opposite of a minimalist, Lerman proves herself mistress not only of side-splitting one-liners but also of pregnant perception about faith and virtue."

–*Publishers Weekly*

"Reality is canted through Lerman's slyly irreverent sensibility, one of the most idiosyncratic in contemporary prose."

–*Village Voice*

Also by Rhoda Lerman

.

SOLIMEOS

Rhoda Lerman

WICKED SON

A WICKED SON BOOK
An Imprint of Post Hill Press
ISBN: 978-1-63758-763-8
ISBN (eBook): 978-1-63758-764-5

Solimeos
© 2023 by Rhoda Lerman
All Rights Reserved

Cover Design by Cody Corcoran
Interior Design by Yoni Limor

Post Hill Press
New York • Nashville
WickedSonBooks.com

Published in the United States of America
1 2 3 4 5 6 7 8 9 10

To my husband Bob

And the whole earth was of one language,
and of one speech.

Genesis 11:1 (KJV)

Prologue

My father stood on the parade grounds between the castle and our home, between the past and present. The only animal we hadn't eaten was his beloved giraffe, Violet. Papa gazed up at the fortress and sighed. *"Where will it sink to sleep and rest, this murderous hatred, this fury?"* Then he turned to me. "Who wrote that, Axel? Do you know?"

I was fourteen and half his size. Of course I didn't know.

The Pappendorf castle, our castle, built on the ancient foundations of a Knights Templar fortress, loomed above our house, sinister, archaic, toothless, collapsing into the dark arms of the Black Forest. A fortress, a stronghold that was no longer strong; it was our history. Its shadow crept over us, blocking our house from the sun until noon. In winter storms, criminal winds blew through the castle's windows and turrets, shrieking a terrible symphony. Sometimes a stone crashed into the silences of our forest, a crumbling block of wall shattered the night. From the weapon windows, shafts of musky sunlight, quivering with their ashes of stone and death, drew stripes on the stretch of pavement that lay between our house and the castle. This pavement had once been the parade ground for the Pappendorf armies.

Our house, a turreted, buttressed solidity, itself built by my grandfather from Templar rubble, was a few hundred feet distant from the castle. Where once banners and flags fluttered in the forest winds, now a rope line fluttered with diapers and bed linens.

To our left, on the shoulder of our mountain, my great-grand-father had built foundries with stones from the Templars' great stables. For the last generations of Pappendorfs, these foundries had belched black smoke into the forest and fortunes into our pockets. Below the foundries in the valley was a chocolate factory. Now abandoned, but before the war its sweet smells had wafted through the windows of our house into my childhood. A railroad ran along the valley to the chocolate factory, then up our mountain, stopping at the gates of our foundries. Sprightly birches followed the railbed to the forest but stopped, dismayed by a wall of dark firs made darker by the smoke of the foundries, which, up until the last few months, had burned day and night. No longer.

The Baron von Pappendorf, my father, Dietrich, beaten and despairing, carried a rifle. I had always imagined him in another time, handsome on a great horse, wearing the suit of armor that now lies rusted and crushed in the castle, slashing at his enemies with the sword that hung over his bed. I had never imagined him like this.

Papa said, "I don't know when or how, but we must leave all this."

"Where will we be going?"

"I have no idea."

Chapter One

Back when the war first thrust itself upon us, it didn't seem real. I was eleven, but a very young eleven. I would hear adults speaking in hushed voices about my father having to leave for war. They said Uncle Wolf would take over the factory and we would have to be frugal. All I knew was that Papa and Uncle Wolf now wore handsome uniforms to the factory and carried pistols. With my father's binoculars, Mama watched the skies above Pappendorf Castle, praying the war would end quickly. But for the bored boy that I was, it spoke of a distant excitement; nothing seemed imminent.

Occasionally a visitor with medals and ribbons would arrive and leave after long private conversations in the library. Trains screamed as they strained up the steep rails to our factories while trucks rumbled down the roads. The older son of Volker the barn man left to join the war, at which time Papa presented him with a watch. I complained that it wasn't fair. I invariably complained things weren't fair. When I moaned about an injustice of one sort or the other to my mother, Mama would respond, "Life isn't fair."

It wasn't fair that I did not receive a watch. Just because I was too young to go to war. And on and on. Papa gave me a watch that had been his great grandfather's. It had a sapphire, and Roman numerals in gold. It was magnificent and didn't yet fit the bones of my wrist.

"It will fit. In time. You must eat well and eat your vegetables, and your bones will grow. And your member will be like mine. In time. Everything in time, Axel."

❧

Shteinberg the cook grumbled more than ever. Mama cried, snapped at us all, and carried on about shortages. Papa scolded them both, assuring them the war would soon be over as we were winning everything: Austria, Poland, Czechoslovakia. No one could stop us. Even so, Shteinberg—who had worked when she was young as a nanny in New York City—taught me English in case we didn't win.

We were safe and ignorant. My mother thought it was perfectly stupid to learn English. If anyone could beat us, she insisted, it would be the Russians, and we certainly wouldn't have time to argue with them before they slit our throats.

❧

I may have been ignorant, but I was overwhelmingly curious. One night I lay in my bed, the featherbed pulled tightly around my neck. I wore Mama's white fox coat and my winter boots under the cloud of puff and warmth.

Papa entered my room and sat on the edge of the bed. He wore his uniform and a great coat of thick black wool and gold buttons embossed with eagles and the SS runes of lightning strikes on his arm.

"Why are you wearing your uniform, Papa? Are you going to the war? Will you be a pilot again?"

"No. I'm here for a while. I'm going out tonight because a train arrives."

"Can I go with you?"

"Absolutely not. You are never to go near the factory. You know it is forbidden."

I was accustomed to hearing the trains' screeches as they approached our lands, grinding lower as they arrived at the factory. When a train was arriving, Papa always put on his uniform and drove to the factory. I would hear men shouting, people screaming, then gunshots, followed by a terrible quiet. Papa explained to me it was just workers arriving from the city to make more steel and they had very bad manners.

I didn't believe him. Why at night? Why gunshots?

He smiled, never answering such questions. Mama rolled her eyes, shook her head, muttered, "This is not our business," each time. Finally, that night after he visited me in my bedroom, I too went to meet the train.

Perspiring in my mother's fur coat, I heard the engine of Papa's car, threw off my featherbed, and climbed from the bed, tip-toeing downstairs and out of the house. All the lights were out. Against the windows, snow was blowing in fistfuls. Outside, I made my way to the barn, where I harnessed goats to my goat cart.

The road was bare, the forest deep in snow, the wind playing the trees in a terrible orchestration of cracking and groaning. Wolves sang in the forest around me, and Papa's bellowing hounds answered. The light in the snow-tipped forest was cold and pink. Billows of dark smoke hung and swelled over the factories. Trucks loaded with ore shifted gears as they climbed the mountain. In the white of Mama's coat, in the white of the snow, I was almost invisible. In my pajamas and the fur coat, riding the two-wheeled goat cart down the road, I felt strangely powerful.

I pulled the goats into the dark under the trees. Pink smoke, meat roasting, the pine trees, Papa's factory. A train arrived, its long shrieks slicing the night. Then came the cries of people as they poured from the trains, looking into the searchlights, rubbing their eyes, stunned.

Two SS troopers with upright bayonets stood in front of the growing crowd. Troopers pulled men from women, children from parents. In the yard of the factory, I saw my uncle Wolf marking a clipboard. He counted workers one by one as they were pulled from the train. Many wore nice hats. Searchlights flashed on gold teeth, illuminated them, eyeglasses, wedding rings, the extraordinary bone, satin, rubber undergarments of women.

A frantic woman shouted, "Wait by the gate, girls. Don't let them touch you!"

Uncle Wolf whistled Viennese waltzes with a clipboard and a whip. Weeping women were undressing. A pile of clothing, of coats, hats. Women naked, men naked, children naked, freezing. Snow on the ground. Two soldiers jumped from the train, stuck corsets on the points of the bayonets, and, as if they carried flags,

paraded around in goosesteps. Other soldiers laughed. Uncle
Wolf snapped a whip at them and their foolishness. They shook
the corsets from their bayonets, dropped them into the pile. A
soldier wrenched an infant from a woman, tossed it into the snow
near me. It howled.

I crept toward the baby, wanting to lift it into the warmth of
my mother's coat. A soldier loomed over me, grabbed me by the
neck, and shoved me into the crowd of naked children. Two beautiful girls with black hair down to their waists, with masses of black
hair between their legs, hit me, beat me to the ground, ripped off
my coat and at my pajamas. I'd never seen nakedness before. Never.
On anyone. I was terrified. I yelled, "Papa! Papa!" But everyone was
yelling "Papa! Mama!"

My father's long black car roared up, into the crowd. Papa
stepped out. All the soldiers froze, saluted him.

"Wait for me. Wait at the gate. Wait!" The mother's screams
grew into one continuous scream, the scream of a pig as Volker slit
its throat. The scream filled me.

I yelled, "Papa. It's me, Axel!" I broke loose.

A trooper shot at me as I came near my father. A man fell next
to me, clutching his forehead. His face was red as blood. I fell at
Papa's knees.

"What are you doing here? You are never to come here." He
raised his hand and slapped me across the face. "Stupid. You endanger
yourself." My face burned and pounded with pain, shame, fear, and
the mothers' screams. At last, he threw me into the arms of a massive
trooper, who wrapped me in a rough blanket and carried me to Papa's
car. Over the trooper's shoulder I saw one of the dark-haired girls
who had hit me covering her sister with my mother's coat.

My father also saw the girl in Mama's coat. He returned to the
crowd of children. They fell back except the girl. She stood frozen,
a rabbit swallowed by my mother's white fox fur. I saw the intensity
in Papa's eyes as he looked at her, lifted her up, and carried her into
the factory.

"Luba!" her sister cried out.

"Dorie! Help!"

Through the window of Papa's car, I watched as a soldier
smashed my goat cart and let our goats loose in the woods. A
mother, many mothers, screamed, "Wait at the gate!"

❧

By next morning, my goats had found their way back to the barn. And I followed Shteinberg so closely she finally swung around and snapped at me, "What? What do you want?"

I wanted to know if I'd had a bad dream. I wanted to hide in her skirts. I wanted her to soothe my wounds. Instead, I asked her why my mother hated the factory.

A silken screen slid over her face. She was behind it, no longer there. "Oh, people have to work hard there. She feels sorry for them." It had to be a lie.

"Why do they have to work so hard?" I shivered with the cold and the memory of fear I had experienced the previous night.

She shrugged and mumbled into her soup pot. "War is hard work, Axel. Some fight. Some work. For the war. All hard. All sad," was the most she would offer me. "Now, go. I also work."

Lies. I took her hand and laid it on my hot and swollen cheeks, where Papa had struck me. She drew a sharp breath, shook her head, cleared her worktable, and pressed dishrags soaked in cold water against the swelling. Tears ran down her face. "You went there, didn't you? So that's why the Baron was so upset at breakfast. He told you not to. You don't know that other people might be smarter than you. Especially your father. Don't take chances, Young Baron."

❧

Hanging on the walls of the great room were dour portraits of kings and emperors, of Papa's forefathers with piercing blue eyes and flamboyant walrus mustaches. In this central hall, Mama, as she often did, sat by a weak fire and quilted boiled wool vests, red and hideously ugly.

Many months after that terrifying night at the factory, Papa was leaving. Earlier, in my bedroom, holding me by my thin shoulders, he had told me not to worry. "I am not going away to fight or fly planes, Axel. I am going to learn."

Now, as I often did, I hid and spied from the heavy, dark mahogany silences: the great fireplace, the deep window seats, the shutters. After my stern Norwegian tutor had fled because of the war, there, in the alcove of the window seat facing the forest, I read volume after volume from our library, some forbidden. I'd already studied English, French, and Latin, but now I sought out books in other languages, decoding and translating their contents.

Shteinberg gave my mother a cup of steaming tea and shuffled back to the kitchen.

In our house, which was almost two hundred years old, twisting stairwells curved upward four floors and then dropped downward to the servants' quarters in the rear. The kitchen was behind the stairwell on the first floor to the rear of the central room and the dining room to the far side of the great room. That room was divided from the front hallway by two massive mahogany columns. More mahogany columns embraced the stairwell and the floor-to-ceiling mirror. The mirror was framed in gilded carvings of animals, intricately woven among each other. A gold eagle rode its crest. It had once been Napoleon's, that mirror. The glass was silvered with age and moisture. Window seats draped with musty brocade and bookshelves filled with leatherbound collections lined the walls of the great room.

Apparently, Mama knew I was hiding in the window seat. As my father packed to leave upstairs, she said, "Axel, run to my bedroom and bring me another spool of red thread."

I remember examining myself in Napoleon's mirror on the first landing of the long and curving stair and wondering who I would be. I was blond, knobby, narrow, not unlike Papa's giraffe. My eyes had dark rings. Mama's were even darker.

My father was in his bedroom, sorting books and documents. I watched him from the other side of the bed where he had laid out his notebooks and glass boxes of fragments.

"I shall study languages," he said. "I will be entirely safe." He closed the suitcase with a finality, rubbed my head, and kissed my forehead. "What do you want from India? A pair of peacocks?" He knelt, looked steadily into my eyes, held my shoulders tightly, as if squeezing something out of me.

"I want to go with you to India."

"Perhaps on the next trip," said Papa. "Come with me to visit Violet so we can tell her that I am leaving." On the way to the giraffe's barn, he put his arm around my shoulders. "Don't worry about war, Axel. War is the fire that tempers the steel in mankind."

Violet had been saved from the Nuremberg Zoo when people in the city began to eat the animals. She lived in an igloo-shaped barn with heat and a walkway at the second story. Up there we could stand and look directly into her huge limpid eyes. With Papa, I entered her barn and stood on the platform high above the floor.

"Axel, pride of my loins, you will be the man of the house, yes? That is asking a great deal of such a young man, but I ask it of you. You will obey your mother and show respect to the servants and be a model for them." It would not be easy, but I would try. Small for my age, I sometimes had difficulty making sense of my surroundings. It wasn't clear to me if I stupidly misunderstood or if the people around me were forever hiding secrets. Maybe both. All too often I was in some sort of trouble.

"I do not want to hear that you climb on the roof," Papa said. "And you will visit my Violet morning and night, as I do. Give her a biscuit and stroke her ears. You will make certain Volker feeds her well. There is enough lucerne and enough hay cubes for two giraffes for a year! Don't let her eat too many cubes. She'll get the runs."

I giggled at the idea of a giraffe with the runs. Papa's face tightened. "If she wants more cubes, you must soak them first. I leave her in your care. If Violet becomes ill and will not get up, you must ask Volker to...to put her to sleep gently and swiftly. Everything gently. Everything. Make certain Volker and his sons keep her floor clean. And she must be fed from up here, not from the floor. Uncle Wolf, he will bring you whatever you need from Berlin. Don't be afraid to ask."

Violet brushed my face with her eyelashes. Her tongue was immensely long and black. Eighteen inches? Two feet? I held a biscuit in my mouth, and she lifted it out, licked me, drowning me in her rough-tongued giraffeness. She curled her tongue around my neck and pulled/sucked me to her. She examined my nostrils. I felt her warm breath all over me.

She nuzzled my father as he spoke to her about a gentle world and how he was working to make it a perfect world so even giraffes could be happy and have full stomachs; he assured her that he would come home again and make her happy. He clasped her neck and wept into it.

I thought he was really talking to my mother, or maybe, I hoped, even myself.

"Dear, dear, sweet, patient Violet. How can I love you as much as you love me? Forgive me."

☙

Papa, shoulders stiff with duty and sorrow and pride, always pride, climbed the stairs to finish his packing. I again hid behind the musty green–gold curtains in the window seat. Not daring to gaze through the split in the drapery, I leaned back and listened. Uncle Wolf arrived, whistling the same Viennese waltzes he had whistled while counting the workers arriving at our factory. He was a narrower, younger version of his brother Dietrich: handsome but not as substantial, slightly effete.

"Oh, gardenias. How exotic, Wolf. How very lovely," I heard my mother say, her voice tinkling like crystal in the heavy room. Then I heard Papa's heels hammer on the stone floor of the great hall.

"Wolf, so you've come to see me off."

"India, Dietrich? Why are they sending you to India?"

"Research. My languages. The Indus Valley. I am to live on an isolated tea plantation in Kashmir, far from the British, and study the old languages of India."

"Oh, yes, all that Indo-European stuff you do. They have you looking for the Aryans too? Himmler has already sent three expeditions into Tibet looking for Aryan giants." Was he joking? He must have been joking. I could hear the humor in his voice. Or not joking. "They think the Tibetans are our ancestors. They measured Tibetans, who must have been seriously amused. Hermann is focused on the Indus Valley for traces of the Aryans, their genes, their blood. Himmler actually had some Tibetans brought back and made them German soldiers. I've seen them in Berlin."

I heard teacups rattle, chairs scrape, pillows exhale.

"Yes," my mother answered softly. "Foolish business. Himmler is mad. And Manfred Hermann.... Protect us from Manfred Hermann and his insanity."

Uncle Wolf cleared his throat. He was not joking. I think he was belittling, for Papa's benefit. "The official position of the SS Occult Bureau is that the Aryan race, the blood of the gods, came from Atlantis. There was a great flood. The Atlanteans fled to India and then to Tibet. Some arrived in the Nordic realms. The Atlanteans came...their knowledge and their blood...came from the star Sirius. That is Himmler's position and, of course, the position of his astrologers and his mystics. And Hitler."

"And you, Wolf? What is *your* position with this madness?" Papa asked.

"I find it interesting. I have no position."

"Perhaps you should. As for myself, I'll do my duty. I'll examine language and look for its origins—the phonetic fossils, so to speak. The Hermanns and the Himmlers, they can examine blood and do their experiments, play with their black magic. Not I."

I heard Uncle Wolf pacing the stone floor. "Poland, Holland, Belgium, France, Luxembourg, the Netherlands, Norway."

"Enough, Wolf." Mama spoke softly, swallowing her words. She often disguised strong opinions by using a weak voice. "He wants to rule the world, Wolf. To enslave it. He is very dangerous. And mad. Astrologers, Tibetans, stars, Atlantis."

Uncle Wolf didn't respond to that. Instead, he said, "Dietrich, I assume you are aware of the great success of our submarine packs. Do you know how we find the Allied ships?"

"No, I don't."

"The Occult Bureau assembles a room filled with mystics and magicians, maps, and pendulums, which are used for divination. They roll out the maps of the Atlantic, suspend a crystal pendulum, here, there. If it swings counterclockwise, they move it to another place until it swings clockwise; they then send the submarines to that spot." Uncle Wolf snapped his thumb and forefinger. "And there they find the Allied ships. You may consider all this madness, but it is working. The Fuehrer has split the atom, Dietrich. Soon he will have a bomb that will destroy a city. But there is another atom he wants to split. The atom of heavy matter. If he can retrieve heavy matter from the dwarf star Sirius B and split that, in a few years his bomb will be able to destroy the world. He is on the cusp of destroying the world if he wishes.

Certainly, he will conquer it. He leads the Germans to become a race of god-men and himself as Messiah. I don't know if he is mad, but he will probably succeed."

Uncle Wolf again cleared his throat. "The goal of the Occult Bureau is to send a rocket ship to Sirius to collect heavy matter, split its atom, and create a great biological mutation: the new man."

Papa's voice rose. "Sirius? The star? What are they talking about?"

"Wernher has designed the rocket ships already. His goal is Sirius, because that, the Fuehrer believes, is the origin of Aryan divinity. This is the historic marriage of science and philosophy."

My father's voice took on a staccato of impatience. "You sound far too much like one of Manfred Hermann's madmen. This is black magic, Wolf. Science and madness. Back to the primitive. I've heard nothing like this from our industrialist friends. Wouldn't Krupp know? Wouldn't Thyssen know? There's no talk of Sirius or heavy matter. Wolf, it's all propaganda, sword-rattling, occult smoke tricks. As for myself, I am off to India to do my own work. Wolf, you'll run the factory, of course, until they call you up. Berthe, I trust you to run the house, the farms."

I heard the swish of Mama's dress, the soft padding of her shoes as she approached my hiding place. I held my breath. "Be still," she whispered, almost hissing, terrifying, terrified. "You have heard nothing." Then she sighed and returned to her chair.

My father's voice dropped, placating, decidedly insincere. "Listen, Wolf, I believe anything. If Hitler can put bread on everyone's table, butter in their cupboards, and pride in their hearts, let him be the Messiah. Let him go to Sirius. The Germans are starving. If the Germans can become a race of god-men…why, that's…that's wonderful. A great nation once again. But forgive me my doubts. Please assure me, Wolf, that you will take care of my home, my family, and our business while I am gone. Until and unless, of course, you are called to join the fight. And so, dear brother, to victory, to the future of Germany."

I imagined them raising their teacups. I heard the rattle of a teacup in a dish, and I thought my mother's small hands were shaking as well. Mine were. I twisted a knot in the velvet of the drapes to keep my hands still.

Mama rang the bell for Shteinberg. I heard her slippers shuffling into the room. "Put these flowers in water, Shteinberg. Trim the ends. Don't forget: at an angle."

Peeking through the edge of the drapery, I saw Uncle Wolf shake Papa's hand. He wished him good luck and a safe return. Papa nodded. Uncle Wolf left the waxy gardenias, left my mother. I watched their eyes meet, slip away. Uncle Wolf gave my mother a quick nod of assurance, and a rosy blush bloomed on her cheeks. I sat in the alcove of my window seat, hidden, frightened, holding myself.

Papa's footsteps hammered on the stone floors: determined, deliberate, powerful. From my vantage point behind the drapery, I watched my mother in her chair. She didn't look up at him. My father wore his uniform: the greatcoat, the gleaming brass, the medals. My heart stopped. Would he die in the war? He crossed the room, opened the drapes of an alcove window overlooking the road to the factory, the barns, the icehouse, the planting fields, the church on the hill, the ruins of the chocolate factory behind it, and across the courtyard, our grandfather's collapsing castle. Light fading, our lives fading. Chickens ran back and forth.

Berthe spoke to his back, alarm in her voice. "Dietrich, are you leaving now for Berlin?" The dread in her voice slid into my stomach and became pain.

Papa was tall and thin, a slant of light himself, electric. He folded his hands behind his back, stood ramrod straight, cleared his throat. "I leave in the morning."

"So why do you wear your uniform?"

"The train is coming in."

"Oh, yes, your train. God help us. God help them."

His voice turned sharp and mean. "Berthe, put your sewing down."

"Yes, Dietrich?" Her voice was small and narrow as if she were threading it through the eye of her needle. I moved the curtains slightly so I could see them both at once. Papa turned to her, stood straight, cleared his throat. "As I am off to war, I want to establish certain issues between us before I leave." Suddenly, he leaned over her, pulling her from her chair, up and off the floor. Her face was inches from his. Her fur slippers swung under her. She made small sounds but did not struggle.

I could not move. I knew I should not move.

Suspended and held so tightly, she screamed out and held her stomach. "The baby, Dietrich. I beg you." Papa did not stop shaking her. I was confused. This was the first I'd heard about my mother having a baby.

"Berthe, your son has asked me a few questions that I am unable to answer fully."

"Please, Dietrich," she croaked.

"Your son has inquired as to why I don't kiss you, but his uncle Wolf does. A pretty question, is it not?"

"Dietrich, please. My pains. My pains begin."

I held my breath. Papa wasn't telling the truth. I had not asked those questions.

"I will enlighten you, Berthe. My little brother kisses you because he burns with jealousy. Because *I* am the gifted one. Because *I* am the heir to the lands and the title. He only wants you because you are mine. Because my father loved me and not him. He was fortunate, Berthe." His voice rose. He shook her. She hung limp and whimpering. "My father's love was…demanding. Brutal." His voice rose. "Violent." He shook her again. "Painful." He shook her again and then dropped her like a stone into her chair. He fisted his hands and held them tightly by his sides. "Wolf was fortunate our father didn't love him the way he loved me. Do you understand, Berthe? I loved my father. In return, he gave me terrible pain. And now you give me pain. Do you understand? Look at me!"

"Yes."

"Don't be fooled, Berthe. Wolf just wants you because you are mine."

"I am no longer yours, Dietrich," she said softly. "No longer."

He drew himself up, considered her, examined his fingernails, cleaned one with another. "So be it!" He strode to the great oak double doors retrieved long ago from my grandfather's castle, flung them open, with stiff arms held them open against the wind, and shouted into the night. "If it's a boy, I disown him. You hear that? So be it!"

And he left, my heart pounding to the cadence of his footsteps, my jaw locked in horror. The great doors stood open. The cold wind of the forest filled the room. The drapes billowed and lifted to the ceiling. The trees cracked and screamed.

My mother stood, struggled to close the doors against the winds, walked toward my window seat, tore the curtains open, exposed me.

"Get out, you little spy. You and your questions. You and your questions."

"Mama, I didn't…. It's not my fault, Mama. It's not fair."

"Get out of my sight. Maybe you should go with your father and watch the trains come in again, watch him count the Jews. Maybe you should remind yourself who your father really is, who you will one day become."

And there it was: my mother's curse.

Chapter Two

Papa left the next day.

At dawn, from my bedroom window, I watched a long and gleaming black car drive into our yard. I would forever after have nightmares about long and gleaming black cars. The hounds barked wildly at the intrusion. Small flags fluttered on either side of the car's hood. From its roof, a searchlight beam flooded our fields.

Soldiers opened the trunk and stood by, smoking cigarettes, as Shteinberg directed the servants to load boxes and suitcases. Later I heard the soldiers' heavy boots on the stairs leading to the attic, where they would sleep.

Papa walked into my room, his footsteps heavy. He sighed, shook his head, sat, and spoke to the ceiling, not quite to me. It was as if he were saying his prayers or reciting his lessons. His voice had lost confidence, its cadence had quickened. "Stay away from the factory and stay off the roof. Respect your mother. Be kind to the servants. Take care of my hounds and Violet, especially Violet. You understand?" He slapped his knees with his hands and pushed himself heavily from the bed. "So, then, Axel, goodbye." I leapt up to hug him. I felt him recoil. He was correct: When you love, you receive pain.

❧

Hours after Papa left, as if the baby had been waiting for his departure, Shteinberg thrust her head into the alcove. "Quickly. Your mother's baby comes much too early. Tell Volker to go to the factory. He should tell Wolf it is time to bring the girl Luba to feed the baby. Tell them to wash her before she comes."

When they brought Luba into the house, I recognized her as the dark curly-haired girl who had taken Mama's fur coat from me on that terrible cold night so many months ago, the girl who Papa had lifted up in his arms and saved. She was even more beautiful than I remembered. She wore striped prison pajamas with a gold star on the pocket.

Silent, frantic, furious, beautiful, dark, and distant, Luba had moist, sullen eyes and long, wet lashes. She didn't look in anyone's eyes, just at the floor. Always at the floor.

Immediately drawn to her, I tried to be friendly, but she ignored me. When she wasn't crying, she looked angry. When she wasn't angry, she was frightened. I thought she was perhaps three or four years older than me. When we first started to speak and I asked her how old she was, she answered, "Very." Once I found her crying in the nursery, and she told me it was her sister Dorie's birthday, and they should be having a wonderful birthday party with a cake and candles and clowns. But she said she would never see Dorie again. Luba was mystery itself.

Shteinberg called her "the Jew." "You, Jew," Shteinberg would yell, "get over here." I think now my mother's milk must have been as bitter as my mother. And Luba's milk must have been bitter as well. Even so, I loved Luba from the moment she walked into our home. She was frantic and terrified and beautiful.

My sister Cecilia was born on a night of screams and running and towels and rags and boiling water. I was imprisoned in my room for days after until at last they allowed me to see her. She didn't look like a human, but seemed, to me, a chicken. She cried and screamed, and Luba was with her all the time. I was unimpressed, and jealous of the attention she was receiving.

We carried the squalling baby one afternoon up the hill to the little church to be baptized. Uncle Wolf came with us. The church had been in the Pappendorf family as long as the castle. My ancestors—the archdukes, heroes, barons—were buried in the cellar in stone caskets, on which the turnips were stored.

Father Damien was a small, gentle, and stooped man with an enormous forehead, to whom no one turned except for christenings and funerals. Sister Gerlinde, who was twice the size of Father Damien, never spoke. Silent as a cow, with burning red cheeks and a blue nose, she would wait every morning at the back door of the great house, holding out her pail and basket for bread and milk. Sister Gerlinde attended to the church's cleanliness as well as Father Damien's needs, like tea and sauerkraut and cabbage rolls. Whenever I was sent up to the church with eggs or a fresh cinnamon cake, she was on her knees polishing the pews.

Sister Gerlinde looked into the blankets at Cecilia and scowled. Luba cried. My mother cried. The skin on Uncle Wolf's cheeks twitched.

Shteinberg walked beside me on the way back down the hill. "You, my Axel, you were a beautiful baby. I was young. I was your wet nurse. Your mother never had good milk. I had very good milk, plenty. Look at you."

"Is something wrong with the baby?"

"I don't know. We have to wait and see."

"Why does Luba have milk? She doesn't have a baby."

"She had a baby in the factory. It died. So she still has milk."

"How did it die?"

"Oh—" She searched for a good explanation. "She won't tell me. Perhaps it died at birth. Perhaps they killed it because babies can't work."

❧

As Mama grew more distant, sitting from dawn to dusk in her chair by the fire, forgetting, quilting the ugly red vests, not speaking, I felt more and more responsibility for the household. I didn't mind. At any rate, I had nothing to do except read and dream. And worry. One morning I smelled smoke, an acrid smell from the nursery. In no time, I heard shouting and screaming from the kitchen.

At first, I didn't know which way to run, and then I remembered it was Cecilia's nap time. I burst into an empty room and found something odd on the changing table: a rough piece of lumber a foot or so long with eight fat candles and one tall thin candle. They were no longer burning, but that is what I had smelled. The screams

and shouts ascending, I raced down the stairs to the kitchen where
Volker was holding Luba down on the worktable, her skirt pulled
up. Shteinberg was beating her bare behind with a belt.

I pulled Volker from Luba. I think he was relieved. Shteinberg's arm froze in the air. "The Jew stole candles from the church.
She lit a fire in the nursery."

"Get out of here. Both of you. Get out." As the Baron's son, I
was, after all, in charge, even if I was still a boy and young for my
years. "Get out." I astonished myself with the level of authority in
my voice.

"No one steals in this house," argued Shteinberg.

"It's my house. You are the servant. Get out! Luba, come with
me. Volker, back to the barn."

Luba pulled her skirt down, sat on the edge of the table,
looking defiantly at Shteinberg. "I was celebrating a holiday, a
Jewish holiday. What's wrong with that?"

"You stole candles from the church."

"They have enough. I only took a few."

"You stole."

"What's a few candles?"

"We do not steal in this house."

I took Luba's hand and pulled her from the table. "Luba, come
up to the roof with me."

Shteinberg followed us out of the kitchen, still haranguing. I
looked over my shoulder at her and jerked my chin in the direction
behind her. She turned back into the kitchen. It was the first time
I had ever given her a command.

"It's Hanukah," said Luba. "I wanted to light the candles. We
always lit the candles on Hanukah. I like Hanukah…a party. I
wanted a party. A little party for me and Cecilia. I lit the Shamash
candle and the first night candle—"

"What's that?"

"The Shamash? The other candles are the planets. He's the
leader of the planets. You light him every night and use him to
light the others, one by one until they are all burning. Eight days.
He's like the god of the planets."

"Shamash? And it's a party?"

"It always was every year…a holiday, a religious holiday, like
Christmas."

"You're religious?"

"We were, before…before God turned against us."

I put my arm around her shoulder and let her cry. I didn't have a handkerchief, so I pulled my shirt from my pants and let her blow her nose into it. "You just can't steal, whatever you wanted them for. What if the servants stole?"

"There's food at the church and lots of gold. And boxes of candles. I took eight."

"Weren't they there? Father Damien and Sister Gerlinde?"

"They were digging turnips."

"Alright." I felt so like a man. "Alright, if there's something you want or need, Luba, you ask me. You come to me. You understand? No stealing. Don't get into trouble."

She mumbled something.

"You understand?"

"Yes. I have no place to go. Where can I go?"

"That's why you have to stay out of trouble. And you can bring that thing into my room, and I'll watch it for you."

But Volker had already destroyed it and returned the unlit candles to the church. After a few days, Shteinberg stopped grumbling when she saw me.

Chapter Three

It had been two years since that night when I took my goat cart to the factory, more than a year since Papa left for India. Now and then, Luba silently climbed into my bed, buried herself next to me. At thirteen, I was still very much a boy. In the mornings, I heard her in the nursery singing Schumann's "Träumerei" to the baby, Cecilia, who was central to everyone's life except my own. Luba, however distant, silent, and withdrawn, was central to mine.

Uncle Wolf slept in our house, in the attic. Some nights I watched Mama climb those stairs and carry a bottle of wine up to him. In the mornings, he would walk to work. Trucks loaded up in the foundry and roared past our gates. Trains howled in the night, shaking the house's foundation. Uncle Wolf taught me how to load and shoot Papa's guns. For months my mother struggled up the attic stairs to Uncle Wolf, then finally he slept in her room with her—until he too went to war in another long, black car.

Months passed. It was bitterly cold. Snow covered the roads. I climbed up to the roof and sat in the shapeless night under the stars. I watched workers from the foundry now wandering in the forest. Some lay down in the snow. In the day, from my bedroom window, I watched dirty, bloody, starving, ruined men, all too young, the dregs of the German army, stumble across our barren fields, emerge out of our forests. Some died in our barns where they'd sought shelter. Volker carted their bodies into the woods. At night I heard crying. Mama would not let me out of the house.

Luba rocked the baby and wept. I watched when she nursed the baby. She closed her eyes, her face softened, and was beautiful. She was food, resource, safety. Her eyelashes were long, like Papa's giraffe. She walked as if she were dancing, graceful and strong. I wanted to drink her milk. She was life itself. When she was angry, her eyes flashed at me with black fires. She was secretive; she was mysterious. Sometimes she snapped at me, ordering me to stop staring at her. In my bleak life, she was pure beauty, and I was afraid, always would be. Although she wasn't supposed to leave the nursery, she crawled into my room, and with her back to me, slept in my bed when I was frightened. In retrospect, I realize she was also frightened. I was too young to understand love, but I knew what I felt for Luba. She told me her mother taught philosophy and that her father had been shot in the head at the gymnasium in the university where they both taught. Late one night, Luba told me that hundreds of Jews were slaves in Papa's factory. I pounded her back with my fists.

"Yes," she insisted. "When the Jews are not working in your family's factory, they are sleeping or dying in the long houses. But now the soldiers sleep and die there too." I didn't want to believe her—about the Jews, about the desperate soldiers—but of course I did.

Once, she turned over and said to me, "German boy, I know you feel bad that your papa is gone."

"How do you know?"

"I just know. Dorie, my brothers, my mother, your papa, all gone. All gone."

❧

As birds darkened the sky, swarming, soldiers came begging, were turned away. Every time there was a knock on the door, Luba flew up the four twisting flights of stairs to the attic with the baby. Volker accompanied me to the barn to visit Violet. She had sores on her neck. Volker said she needed greens; there were none, but soon would be. He held me by my shoulders.

"Spring will come. You will see. It will come, no matter what your father and his friends do." Together, Volker and I went into the deep snow, into the forest, and dug under tree roots for old grasses and weeds.

I rubbed Violet's velvet horns, the little tassels at their tips. "In the spring, Violet, we'll take a walk in the forest and you can eat fresh leaves at the top of trees." I thought she looked over my shoulder, looking for Papa, whom she truly loved. Every day her sores spread. I no longer wanted to touch her. I did, but only on the ears.

One morning, at a pale-yellow winter dawn, under a reluctant sun, Volker and his sons had gone up to the factory to tear down shelves for firewood. Standing at the kitchen door, I heard something unusual. I didn't know what the sound was. Perhaps it wasn't a sound at all, but a silent cry for help. I grabbed a shotgun and ran to the barn.

Four soldiers, ragged and filthy, had a rope around Violet's neck and were struggling to drag her from the barn. I raced upstairs to the walkway above and, just as Papa would have, got off a shot at them. Three of the desperate men ran away.

The fourth stood his ground, gazing up at me defiantly from the floor of the barn while struggling to pull away Violet, who fiercely resisted, but with diminishing strength. Though starvation made him appear older, I realized Violet's tormenter—in a ragged, torn uniform—was perhaps just two or so years older than me. When his frantic eyes met mine, I pulled the shotgun trigger.

He dropped to the ground, struggling momentarily before falling still. Violet panicked and fled to the corner of the barn. I ran down from the upper platform, cooing soothing words and managing to coax her back into her pen. To get there, she had to step over the soldier's body.

I had killed a man—more of a boy. At thirteen, I had killed. I heard my father: "A man must do what a man must do." I had.

Outside, I heard Volker, just back from the factory, swearing at the fleeing men. More shots. And they were gone.

Volker entered the barn and examined Violet. The giraffe was fine. He stood over the dead boy, shook his own head, exhaled. "War." Then he dragged the body into the forest. When he came back, he folded me into his stinking, blood-soaked arms and held me while I sobbed.

"I don't have to tell nobody." From then on, whenever Volker left the barn, I kept my promise to Papa and stood watch on the balcony. I did what I had to do.

I sincerely contemplated that such an act of violence might have biological effects on my body—which refused to grow its member, to put it politely. I was slow to mature. I'd seen Volker pee unashamedly in the horse stalls. His member was enormous. And I'd seen the horses'.

I found Shteinberg and asked if she'd had children. When she answered that she had four sons and they were all married and had their own children, I then posed my question.

"Why am I so small in my private parts? Aren't I old enough? Volker's is huge."

She hugged me. "Sure, sure, you're old enough. But we starve now, and you need meat and plenty of fat to be a man. Don't worry. You will grow. You have plenty of time. When this is over...." She shook her head, patted my behind, and sent me from her kitchen.

ɛ♫ɔ

One night at dusk, Mama sat, wetting thread with her tongue, threading the needle, squinting under a faint light, biting her lower lip. Every night and most of the day, she sat under the lamp, sewing tiny stitches into red flannel vests, quilting them. She said softly to me, "Dusk, Axel. The hour between dog and wolf. If Americans come, they'll burn the house. If Russians come, they'll rape me and then burn the house." I asked what rape was. She said, "It's making love with someone you don't like." I could not understand the difference between the Russians and Papa.

I secretly climbed the roof and around the turrets of our house and dreamed of flying. My mother instructed Volker to beat me when she found me climbing on the roof, but still, I sat for hours watching the stars. The sides of the chimney kept me warm. The night sky was my coloring book. I played connect the dots with the constellations until I could make out animal shapes in them. Night after night the moon rolled through the constellations of stars until the next month began.

I had my own zodiac, inaccurate as it might have been. I found shapes in the constellations of stars and matched them to letters in my father's books. There was a new letter for every night of the moon. The moon gave me an alphabet.

I watched as the moon rolled through the shapes I imagined. I told myself the story the moon told. Here is a house. Here is a little dog. Here is a lady. Here is a man. Here is a child, a bull, a goat. I read the letters again and again and made up words and sounds and stories. This roof-climbing, I could not help. The sky was my book, the stars my letters.

☙

I sat one day in the safety of the window seat alcove, behind the drapes, a leatherbound book on my lap. The huge volume of things male and female—dreamy, wet, sepia—was one I should not have been reading. Its edges cut into my thighs.

I heard the muffled "Halloo!" of my uncle Wolf, arriving as he often did from Berlin with food and money. I was about to leap from my hiding place when Mama flew down the curve of the stairs and threw herself at Uncle Wolf in a way I had never before seen. I watched them in the silvered glass of the mirrors on the landing. He stood with his arms stiff. She clasped him with the ferocity with which Papa had clasped Violet. She wept against his chest. There was something happy in her sobs, something in the mirror that was in the pages of my purloined book. Uncle Wolf's boots gleamed. His chest was covered with medals. He wore a long, black leather coat lined with red fox fur. Double exposed, the two of them loomed larger than life; something about their whispers was the same sepia color as the book on my lap.

Two proper soldiers arrived with tins of hams and cakes, bags of oranges, rice, flour, and potatoes, which they took under the stairs to the kitchen from where I heard giggles, even Shteinberg's deep, rolling laughter.

When the soldiers were gone into the kitchen, Uncle Wolf said, "He's in Kashmir. He is hiding in a cave until he can cross the border. The English are nearby. Hermann is back in Berlin.

The natives burned his laboratories after he put two of them in freezing water to see how long they could live in outer space, in the atmosphere. He's really going for rockets, isn't he? When the natives found out, they killed two of our men and burned the place down." Uncle Wolf kissed my mother's forehead, then her nose. "And when he does come back, he has orders to report to Berlin. A big honor. He will be a pilot for..."

The soldiers' laughter rippled and rose from the kitchen. I smelled coffee.

"Where's the boy?"

Mama shrugged. "Probably in the barn with the giraffe." In the mirror, I saw Uncle Wolf lift her in his arms and carry her upstairs.

Just as I sprung from the draperies to follow, Luba appeared.

She grabbed my arm. "Stay here. No." She ducked into the alcove with me, drew her knees up under her chin so there would be room for both of us, our feet touching, and sat rocking, her arms around herself, eyes closed, breathing too fast, shaking with fear.

We stayed in the alcove until the light failed. After I heard Cecilia crying, Luba tiptoed upstairs. At last, I saw the lights flash on Uncle Wolf's truck as he departed. The soldiers left the kitchen, and the incredible aroma of meat and onions cooking drew me out of hiding. It was the last we saw of Uncle Wolf for months.

વ્ર

One day, Luba asked me to go into the courtyard to help her hang bed linens and diapers. She was afraid to be outside alone. Starving animals and even more dangerous humans roamed the surrounding forest, which itself seemed more overgrown and wilder every day. I was in the courtyard, shaking out linens and handing them to Luba to hang when a pebble fell at my feet.

And another. And another.

"Luba! Luba!" Three young men and a girl emerged from behind a pile of fallen logs at the woods' edge; they were thin, pale, terribly thin.

Luba stiffened, then hid her reaction, moving carefully, slowly up the length of the clothesline; Shteinberg could be watching from the kitchen window. I hung diapers at the far end.

Luba started weeping but struggled to hide it, whispering into the woods without turning her head, "Dorie, where have you been?" I realized this was the naked girl I had seen with Luba at the factory railhead that horrible snowy night.

"After the foundry closed, I had nowhere to go," said Dorie, "but then Frederick, Daniel, and Ruben came for me."

"And Mama?" Luba's voice uttered.

Dorie shook her head, then said, "We've been living in the woods. Luba, we need food, money, weapons, clothes. Can you help?"

Luba finished hanging the diapers as quickly as she could, walked slowly back into the house so as not to raise suspicion. A few minutes later, she returned with another load of diapers. Under them in the bottom of the wicker basket were butcher knives, the Baron's socks, sweaters, wool hats, guns, and boxes of bullets. Luba laid the basket just where the clothesline ended and the woods began. "There is no food. But there are turnips at the church…and gold things and clothing. Two old people." She pointed up the hill.

"Come with us, Luba," Dorie begged. "We're going to cross the Alps."

"I can't."

"Why not?"

"I just can't."

"Come on," her brother Daniel said. "We don't have time to argue. Come on."

Dorie dared to break out of the woods and approach. She hungrily kissed her sister all over her head and face and hands. "We'll find you, Luba. We'll come get you."

They disappeared behind the trees, headed toward the church.

From the kitchen, Shteinberg was yelling. "Jew girl, what's taking you so long? Move."

"Say nothing of this," Luba said. Standing in the shadows of the castle, she blew her nose into a clean diaper. I was pleased that she trusted me.

Upon hearing Luba crying in her room that night, I knocked on the door of the nursery. "Luba, do you want to come with me and find cake?" I would have sold my soul to give her comfort.

"Cake?" she repeated, opening the door. Stepping into the hall, she closed the nursery door softly behind her, then said, "Take off your shoes, stupid."

In the great room, Mama snored lightly in her chair by the fireplace. Uncle Wolf had left her his fur-lined leather coat, and it lay on her lap. I pulled it up to her shoulders and made a great and noisy event of tucking her in and patting the coat into folds of her body while slipping the ring of pantry keys from her pocket.

The house was dark and freezing, a cave of imagination and warrior ghosts. My teeth chattered. We held hands and felt our way, Luba and me, along the cold and familiar walls to the hallway, then toward the kitchen, and to the pantry door. I fumbled with the lock. Even our breathing was thunder in our ears. The key was an odd shape, long, with a notched square at the bottom and a round circle at the top. The lock opened easily. I patted the shelves until I found the cake tins I'd seen the soldiers bring in.

I pried one open with the key. It was filled with stones.

I took another tin, a heavier one, to the hallway. There Luba lit a match against a button on my trouser fly, startling me so with the action that I dropped the tin. It made a terrible echoing crash in that silent house. There was no cake. The tin was painted with beautiful women in long dresses, with elephants under bowing palm trees. Dried peas or pebbles, something hard, fell and rolled along the sloping floor of the old boards. We heard footsteps, bare-foot footsteps running toward the pantry from someplace behind the kitchen.

Luba blew out the match, sniffed her hands. "It smells of sandalwood from India," she whispered. "Put it back."

I ran to the pantry, put the cake tin on the shelf, crept along the walls toward my mother, and slipped the keyring back into her pocket. She smiled in her sleep as I tucked the fur around her neck. I followed Luba up to her room.

"What was in the tin? Nuts? Dried fruit?"

"You are so stupid." She closed the door and wouldn't let me in. And through the door she whispered, "Diamonds, stupid! Your uncle Wolf brought diamonds from Berlin. Your father was able to send them from India to Berlin. They are so well-organized, the bastards."

"Tomorrow," I promised the closed door. "Tomorrow I can take you to see the giraffe."

"No, thank you. My heart is already broken." I heard the lock turn.

❧

In the morning we sat in the dining room and waited for breakfast, but none came. Mama rang her little bell again and again.

"Shteinberg, where is everyone?"

There was no answer. She sent me into the kitchen. It was empty. The cake tin, sitting on Shteinberg's table, was open and also empty. My mother unlocked the pantry, returned. I slid down into my chair. I could not become small enough.

"The cakes are missing," she reported, her mouth as small as her wedding band.

Luba dared, "So what is cake? A week more of life?"

"Don't be stupid," my mother said to Luba, and I felt a nasty pleasure.

Mama ran into the kitchen and beyond, shouting and cursing. She examined all the servants' beds. She returned with none of the servants except for a young chambermaid she dragged into the dining room.

Ulla, wrapped in a rough blanket, rubbed her eyes, shook her head, sucked on her knuckles. She knew nothing. Shteinberg was gone.

How could she have left us? My mother fell into her chair and buried her face in her hands. Luba and I sat in frozen silence. At last she looked up and down the table at Luba, at me, at Ulla the chambermaid who had somehow orchestrated the wringing of hands with the sucking of knuckles.

"Axel, tell Volker and his sons to bring their things in here. They will sleep in the dining room. Go to your father's study." Mama handed me the keyring. She had become someone I didn't know. "Bring down four of his rifles. Then you and Luba will go up to the church and bring Father Damien and Sister Gerlinde here. Help them to carry their things. It's safer for them. And you, what is your name—*aah*, Ulla? Put on some clothes and wash your hands. Then go slice ham and bread. You will sit with us and eat. We must all stay together until this is over," she added, but the determination had already left her voice. There was no ham.

Luba didn't want to go with me to the church. Her face was white. I thought she was afraid to go because she was Jewish. But Mama told Luba she would starve her if she didn't go. She had no choice. Luba took my hand, and we struggled up the hill to the small stone church.

Ice coated the trees, each limb, each leaf, and the stubble of the fields. Elm trees moaned and creaked. Weeds chattered in the wind, "Don't go. Don't go." Luba held my hand so tightly it hurt. The church's heavy front doors swung and squealed in the wind.

"I can't go in," she said.

"It's just a church. It's alright."

"No. You go."

It was not alright. Things were missing; things were broken. Sunlight danced on amber and red glass in pieces from the windows.

"Father Damien? Sister Gerlinde?" I moved slowly through the chapel to their rooms. The door to Father Damien's bedroom was open. Two sets of feet, small and large, utterly pale white, naked, stuck out from a cloud of a featherbed. The pillows under their heads were crimson with blood, their eyes open in large O's as were their mouths. Sister Gerlinde's large gold and ruby cross that had always swung between her saddlebag bosoms, that too was gone.

"Luba!" I was unable to move.

She stood behind me for a brief moment, yanked me away, pulled me down the hill. My chest heaved with fear and the icy air. "I didn't know they were married," I said.

"What?" she yelled through the wind, which howled in my chest.

"Married."

"Don't be stupid." That word again.

❧

Uncle Wolf arrived in a battered truck with his two soldiers. Blood-less, his hands shaking, he sat before the fireplace in an armchair, his head in his hands. He told my mother that it had been difficult to come as some roads were closed, that the Russian campaign was a disaster, that we'd lost thousands of men.

She stood up from her chair and put her hands on his shoulders while he wept into her hair. The red corner of the sky that I thought must be the war had moved closer to our house.

Papa had somehow managed to leave India, that was all he knew. He did not know under what circumstances or when or how. One of his men installed a shortwave radio in the rear end of the wooden Madonna in the basement of Father Damien's church. Another carried boxes of hay cubes to Violet's barn. Papa was supposed to radio Berlin as soon as he returned here. Uncle Wolf placed my father's orders on the mantelpiece and a fresh uniform in his closet. Uncle Wolf gave me a pistol. He had brought a much smaller amount of food for us, mostly oatmeal, tea, and stale biscuits. He directed Volker to build a stockade of half timbers adjacent to the front of the house, next to the doors.

The dogs' little cabins were pulled down from the barns and installed next to the front doors of the house. Loosed one by one, the dogs cautiously left the stockade enclosure, looked behind themselves once, confused, realized they were free, and raced joyously into the woods. We didn't feed them from that day forward. Even so, Volker whistled them in at night, and they slept in a pile in the stockade. I watched them from the window of the nursery. At first they lost weight and then, within a week's time, they fattened.

One night I saw a bitch bring in a man's boot, a soldier's boot; the next night, a hand. I followed some of our hounds into the woods and, while I counted to three thousand, watched as they devoured an entire soldier. I heard a woman calling for her children in the forest. "Children, children, where are you?"

Volker's oldest son returned from the war with only a few inches of his arm left. He didn't remember how he found his way home or what had happened to his arm.

We did not bury Father Damien or Sister Gerlinde because the ground was too hard and the task was, as my mother expressed it, too abominable. I asked Mama if the dogs might not eat Father Damien and Sister Gerlinde. She sighed. "We will either eat the dogs or they will eat us. At any rate"—she patted my head to comfort me or perhaps herself—"the priest and his lady are quite safe in the icehouse."

I begged Luba to let me sleep in her bed. She would not allow it. Neither would my mother, but I knew that without having to ask. Luba came into my room late one night, sat at the edge of my bed, wrung her hands.

"What?" I asked.

"Maybe we should talk about something."

"Maybe."

"You think because I am Jewish and it was a church, that's why I wouldn't go in?"

"I saw their feet," I said. "I saw pillowcases scarlet with blood."

She turned, searching for something in my face. "I already knew they were dead. I knew who did it. I know what happened. That's why I didn't go in."

"Who did it?'

"My sister and my brothers."

I took her hand. "Is this okay?"

"For now." Her hand was limp and cold. We settled in my bedroom's window seat until we heard Cecilia crying. She must have been hungry.

We were all hungry and running out of food. The red corner of the sky drifted closer every night. There was no sign of Uncle Wolf. We dared not eat the chickens. Luba was always given more food than me. She had biscuits in tins and sausages in her room. Mama told me Luba must eat so Cecilia had enough milk. Luba told me that her breasts hurt from the baby's teeth. "Cecilia," she predicted accurately in a low voice, frightening, "will be a mean person. Already, she bites."

Sometimes Luba shared a bit of sausage, a miracle of taste, but not often.

One morning Volker and his three sons sat at the kitchen table. Shteinberg would never have allowed such a thing. They carried gunnysacks and baskets. My mother sent Volker, his sons, and myself to find the room in the old wing of my grandfather's castle where partridges nested.

I followed them into vast, looming, shredded darknesses

with slippery mold and droppings on the castle floors. The castle had many rooms—Papa said three or four hundred, but nobody really knew. He told me a clay pot filled with gold coins minted in Egypt had been found under the entry floor. Mama had said the old wings were filled with the ghosts of soldiers gone mad. I suspected she told me this to keep me from exploring. She said rats and birds lived there, and the dance hall was filled with nesting partridges. Now the danger of starving took priority over the danger of exploring.

Volker had an ax. He broke open one door after the other. I leaned against a cold wall. A light flashed on in the room. An old woman carrying an umbrella stepped in the hallway, cleared her throat, and disappeared. No one else had seen her. I was alone with my illusions.

Floorboards splintered. Plaster crumbled. Rats scurried across my feet, a feathery feeling. I refused fear. Fear refused to be refused. It rose in my throat. Hunger swallowed it.

"Someday we'll be eating you," the one-armed son yelled to the rats who sat on their haunches and audaciously watched us from a windowsill.

At first we saw no partridges. Finally, we climbed to the fourth and most dreadful floor. Stink and dust filled our lungs. Volker and his sons grumbled and stood back. I took my place ahead of them and led. It was not because I was the Baron's son and must show courage that I climbed ahead. It was because I didn't want them to see that I was crying as I worked my way up the broken stairs, fell, tripped, urged them on, grabbed walls that dropped away into emptiness below. I followed the stink until we came to a huge ball-room filled with partridges.

They squawked and flapped at us. Even so, we filled baskets with their eggs. Volker and his sons grabbed as many birds as they could and twisted their necks. I could not. When we returned with our haul, Mama fell on her knees and thanked God, whom I thought, by then, after my having seen the crimson pillows and the slit throats of Father Damien and Sister Gerlinde, was not with us in the forest.

The last servant left in the kitchen—Ulla—plucked feathers day and night. Volker took the birds to the icehouse. We cooked a few

with milk pods. To eat more slowly, we used our left hands. Luba
and I dug potatoes and turnips from the kitchen garden behind the
church. We chopped and hacked at the ground. Our hands blistered,
our shovels bent. We were overjoyed with our good luck.

I followed Volker to the icehouse. He carried a gunnysack and
a meat cleaver.

"Don't think you should go down here. Your mama said—"

"She's sleeping." I stood well behind him as he unlocked the
door of the icehouse, helped him pull it open as it was tremen-
dously thick and heavy, stepped into the dome of rock, clutched
a wooden railing. Looking into the deep pit of ice, I saw Father
Damien and Sister Gerlinde hanging on meat hooks. I vomited.

"Go on. Get out. I told you not to come."

I backed out. I heard Volker grunting with effort.

In a few minutes, my vomit pooling, steaming in the snow
at my feet, my pants fouled, Volker emerged with his gunnysack
heavier. I waited until he was out of sight, then ran back to the
house, to my bedroom, threw off my clothing and flung myself into
the safety of my bed.

On the night that we ate slices of Sister Gerlinde's fatty breast,
my mother said the meat was pork, that Volker had trapped a boar
in the forest. I knew better for I had seen the saddlebag breast
upright, brown nipple in the air, melting on the kitchen stove,
watched Ulla gag as she sliced it and threw it into boiling water
with turnips.

After the supper I could not eat, I climbed into Luba's bed.
Sitting up, she rocked and breathed fast, her arms around her
knees, eyes closed. In Luba's bed, I felt her belly. It was soft
and spongy, wobbly, a world unformed, yeasty, like Shteinberg's
cinnamon cakes that once rose magically on the kitchen table
where I had seen Sister Gerlinde's breast.

I said, "Luba, you smell like cake." We clung to each other.
"Aren't you frightened?" I asked.

"Not yet. Not until they eat Jews."

"I killed a man. He was trying to steal Violet. I had to."

"So?"

I took her hand. "Tomorrow night, if you'd like, I'll take you on
the roof with me and show you how to read the stars."

Chapter Four

We climbed a ladder and pulled ourselves onto the roof through a transom on the fourth floor.

I had counted this dreary day's many hours, urging them to move faster while awaiting this ascension with Luba from the labyrinth of gloomy rooms and repulsive realities below. The night seemed more alive to me. Here I was not weary or weak.

She shivered, and I showed her the chimney to lean against. She sat and rocked and held herself, breathing too fast.

"Things will be better when my father comes home," I said.

"He has blood on his hands."

"How can you tell from here?"

"You are so stupid, Axel. I don't know why I come up here anyway."

"You won't tell, will you, Luba?"

"I didn't tell about the cake tins, did I?" She looked up at the sky, appearing unmoved by the brilliant display of stars, which offered me both inspiration and consolation. I longed to comfort her, and be comforted myself. I dreamed of an escape, destination unknown, with her at my side.

When I settled against another side of the chimney, she reached around and took my hand.

"Luba, do you ever dream of flying?"

"I dream of being dead."

"You can't dream if you're dead."

"So, maybe, German boy, I'm already dead. And I dream of a meatloaf with a whole egg in its center. With onions."

"I dream of flying so close to the stars I can hear them sing."

"Stars don't sing."

"I hear them sing. Every night. In my head."

After giving it some thought, she said, "I want to go back down."

"I'm making an alphabet from the stars. I'm learning to write. The sky is filled with letters." I lifted her hand and pointed to a cluster low on the horizon. "See those stars? You take three stars and make triangles. Then you play connect the dots and make letters from them. Draw...." I pulled her hand from one star to another, as if Luba were the moon rolling through the heavens of knowledge. "Triangle means three angels. Angels, angles. Same word. You draw a line from one to the other, and it is a letter. See? I have my own alphabet. Over here, a little house. Over here, a cow. Each picture is a letter and the moon goes from one to the other and makes stories. They make a triangle. The first triangle...there. That's a lady with a slit between her legs."

She pulled her hand from mine. "That's disgusting. I'm going to tell your mother."

"I know that from Papa's books. So don't dare say my father is disgusting, or I'll tell that to my mother." I suppressed angry tears, desperate for her to travel with me in the stars, angry that she insisted on remaining tethered to the scorched earth. "So that's the lady," I said, summoning my strength and again directing her to look above. "She meets another triangle with only two sides, and they slide down a tree to Earth. That's a B. Then they climb into a cave, that's a C. Then they have a baby. That's a complete triangle with a bottom because he is on Earth. That's how people learned to write. They drew the pictures of the constellations and made them letters, and the moon moved, and then they had an alphabet that repeated itself every month. One day for each letter."

"You are crazy. Where did you hear such things? Angels, angles."

"I hear them in my head. They make me feel better."

She grunted, dismissing the idea. "What's that constellation?" She took my hand, moved it into another shape.

"That's two triangles on top of each other: an 8."

She dropped my hand. "Eight is a number, stupid." Luba shoved her sleeve up toward her elbow, roughly. "This is an eight. Here is an eight for you."

In the moonlight, I saw a string of numbers riding up her arm. She pulled her sleeve down. "It makes no sense to have your own alphabet; then no one else can understand you. Here." She took my hand, moved it between three stars, drew a triangle in the air, then shoved my innocent hand between her legs, drew the same triangle. "That's the big secret. That's the triangle. That's your holy trinity."

I was frightened; now I too was tied to the world, and it was spinning. I might fall off the roof. "How do you know that?" I asked, wanting and not wanting to move my hand, afraid to do either.

She tossed it aside and pulled herself to her feet. "My mother was a professor," she said. "She told me." Looking down at me with contempt, she added, "I'm going back downstairs. You have a lifetime to think about all this. I don't. I have no future." She crawled to the transom.

"Axel, Axel!" I heard my mother's voice.

"I've found him," Luba yelled down to her. "He's on the roof again."

Her betrayal astonished me. While my mother's voice shouted and threatened, my eyes remained stubbornly fixed on the night sky. I finished my alphabet, tracing each star to the other to find the shape and sound. I shut out the rest of the world, searching to find my name written above in fiery letters.

Whenever I was found climbing on the roof, it was Volker's duty to take me to the barn and beat me. But he was my friend. That night he beat a saddle with a whip. I cried out appropriately. I heard Violet snorting great gusts of air in protest. But still I could not stop thinking of the stars and what was between Luba's legs.

The moon rolls through the constellations. Each shape is a letter, and the moon tells a story. Men write the story by drawing shapes of the constellations in the sand. *That's how*, in my head, I told stupid Luba. I hated her. I hated her so much because she would not love me.

చిం

Another winter. We ate partridge and partridge eggs. Ulla and my mother cut down the drapes and made featherbeds from the partridge pluckings. Volker and his three sons were afraid to go into the forest for wood, so the house was freezing. We ate rats.

And then one night while I was on the roof watching stars, a small plane sailed over our mountain and across the moon, back and forth above our house. I climbed down from the roof and warned everyone. We hid in the pantry. The engine got louder, softer, louder. It approached, left, then returned in the direction of the straightaway between the house and the factory.

The noise stopped. Mama gave each of the barn men a rifle and held one herself. Luba, white-faced, fled upstairs with the baby. In the front doorway, I held my pistol with both hands, directly in front of myself.

But when the dogs barked in an exultant hysteria, I knew Papa had come home.

I shoved my way out between the legs of the barn men and raced into his arms. He was dark and ragged and very thin. I threw myself at him. There was no blood on his hands. He was still able to lift me in the air.

"See that?" He showed me his plane sitting on the road. It was a small propeller plane, white, with a red cross on it. "I stole the plane. Look at you. Who feeds you?"

"Uncle Wolf sometimes brings us food. And we ate a lot of partridges." I didn't tell him about the other meals.

We were already on the porch. He kissed the doors of his father's house, the carved bears and mountains and swords of the Pappendorfs. Volker and his two sons bowed to him. He pounded them on their backs. "Go, good men, and hide the plane." Papa even kissed me on my cheek, then did the same with Luba after she rushed to him from inside the house.

He smelled the way the cake tins smelled. Sandalwood. Under his Army coat, he wore a long silken orange robe. My father was home: dark, grandiose, his faced chiseled in pain, bearded, much older, grim. He knew we were starved—as he was. His eyes were sunken in pale and yellow pools.

ری

Mama waited for him in her chair by the giant cold fireplace. They did not embrace. He touched her shoulder. I watched her draw back without moving, shrinking within herself the way a frog will if one pokes it.

He sank into the chair across from hers. "I rode out under a bale of hay on an oxcart. I walked, I swam. I stole a horse. I climbed a train. I stole a plane. And I am home."

"There are orders for you on the mantelpiece. There is a fresh uniform on your bed. There is a shortwave radio built into the backside of the Madonna in the basement of the church."

"Berthe, in a fourteenth-century Madonna, a treasure? Have you no respect?"

She shrugged.

He examined himself in the mirror, turned his head and examined his eyes. "Jesus!"

"When will it be over, Dietrich?" she asked with no emotion.

"We are taking a monstrous defeat." He took the envelope of his orders from the mantelpiece above my mother's head.

"Why do they want you, Dietrich?"

"I'm not sure. I don't know what I can contribute any longer. But someone requires me, and I must go."

That night I saw him go into the nursery. I saw Papa's shadow slip along the wall of my room. I heard Luba crying. I leaned on my elbow and listened. The following night, he waited in front of the house. A car came without headlights, and he was gone again.

ری

Mama, Luba, and I dragged my mother's mattress into the nursery, and we all slept together. We slept in our coats and shoes.

One night Luba tugged at my sleeve. "Axel, wake up. Wake up!"

My mother woke up. She hissed, "Listen!"

Ping ping. My heart stopped. *Ping ping.* I slid the pistol from under my pillow. I was, after all, almost fourteen. I rolled from the bed. "Someone's throwing stones at the window."

Mama put her arms around me. "The barn men hear nothing? What good are they? Wake Volker up. Don't go out there, Axel."

Luba already had the baby in her arms, ready to run. "How can they hear over their snores?"

"Hide in the fireplace," I told them.

"But the dogs don't bark," Luba argued, and she was correct.

I slowly moved along the wall next to the window, knelt, looked down over the windowsill. The moon hid behind the clouds. *Ping ping*. A cloud released the moon.

Shteinberg's round face, a shadow, a shape.

I raced outside to the front of the house.

"Shteinberg!" I threw myself at her vast safety.

"Look what I bring you for your father's diamonds." She smelled of cinnamon. Somewhere under her coat there would be a cake.

I didn't understand her at first because I was able to distinguish a strange sight: tethered to each other three pigs and a cow, a quartet of food and life.

"For your diamonds," she repeated, and suddenly I understood the cake tins, the quilted vests, and the disappearance of the servants. Dietrich was sending diamonds home from India, and my mother was sewing them into the vests. Due to my stupidity, the servants had found the remaining tins of diamonds, stolen them, and left. "Here, Axel, give these to your mother. There's nothing more to buy in Germany. Is that rotten girl still here?"

Berthe and Luba had remained upstairs in the nursery, but I woke Volker, who first pissed like a horse in the front yard, then lit a kerosene lamp and prodded Shteinberg's agreeable animals toward the barn. A small pig hid under the long skirts of Shteinberg. She shooed it out to follow with its family. "*Shah*. Go. *Shluf*."

I hugged Shteinberg, and she hugged me and from under her coat drew out the cinnamon cake, flat, round, coated with sugar— which somehow looked like her sweet face.

Soon we sat in her kitchen. She lit candles, boiled water. Volker came in, removed his shoes and hat.

"Wash your hands and sit with us." Shteinberg pulled coffee from a sack, and sugar. "I had to move at night. The roads are filled with desperate people. They would kill me for my animals. We hid during the daylight." Shteinberg reached for me, as large as I had become, and pulled me onto her lap. I felt her bury her nose in the back of my neck, heard her whisper, "My baby is so big, almost a man. What's to become of you?"

"Shteinberg, we had to eat Sister Gerlinde's breast."

"*Ach.*"

Volker laughed. "It was good. Greasy. Like pork."

Shteinberg reached over me and walloped him across the face.

"It was a terrible thing to do, I think. Wasn't it?" I asked, hoping for absolution.

Volker said, "Her ass would have lasted longer."

"Cow, chicken, pig. Who are any of us to eat each other? This war." Shteinberg kissed my head and pushed me from her lap. "I have to clean this kitchen." She rubbed her hands. Very politely, Volker helped her off with her coat.

"I counted as the dogs ate a big soldier in the woods," I told Shteinberg. "It didn't take that long."

"And how long can we last?" Volker asked her.

"It's almost over," she answered.

Neither of us left. Volker and I sat in the kitchen, watching the joy of Shteinberg. We both drank coffee with sugar. I felt grown up. My mother never allowed me to drink coffee.

All at once, Volker started blubbering into his coffee. He wiped his nose on a rag.

"Why do you cry, Volker?" I asked.

"Coffee."

Shteinberg stood over him, placed her hands on his shoulders. "Volker, ask me why I came back."

"Yes. Why?"

"I went to my son's house in Nuremberg. No one was there. There was no house. A stranger living with many children in the basement told me everyone and my son had died months before. I gave him a diamond. A big mistake. But it was all I had. He followed me, asked me for another. I told him they were in my boot. I bent down and took my knife and stood up quickly and slit his throat the way you kill your pigs. So, I came back." She took her hands from his shoulders and covered her eyes.

There was something unexpectedly courtly about Volker's answer. "We are happy that you are back with us." He blew his nose into his rag again. He was crying again.

So was Shteinberg. I ate her cake and cried salty snot into it. She wiped my eyes with the corner of her apron. "I go away, you are a baby, I come back, and you are growing a mustache. Look at you!" She pressed me to herself and rocked me back and forth. "Cry, little man. It's good to cry. You deserve to cry. Cry all you want."

Chapter Five

We knew the war had ended because the red in the sky came closer, swelled, flashed, and then vanished, leaving our forest world stunned, dark, blank, silent. This was confirmed a week later when Papa walked into the house without knocking, barefoot, gaunt, half of himself, collapsing in the chair opposite my mother. He was covered with mud. His uniform was in rags. The slice of a dueling scar in his cheek smoldered, a red moon in a dark night. His hair was stiff with dirt. Each strand stood upright as if electrified, as if receiving messages from the universe. His glorious mustache was greasy and embedded with bits of dirt. And still he was beautiful to me.

"Is it over?" my mother asked without looking at him. If she looked at him, it would have been with hatred.

"Yes. Start packing."

I sprinted to Luba's room. "It's over! It's over!" Luba had grown into a dusky, voluptuous beauty. Behind her stood the kitchen girl, Ulla, a flattened, sexless creature. I was still in short pants, skinny, knobby-kneed, a fourteen-year-old of, my mother said, "Teutonic perfection." The resemblance to my father was often mentioned.

Luba, Ulla, and I made a parade, marching up and down the stairs, shouting, exultant, banging wooden spoons against Shteinberg's big soup pots. "It's over! The war's over!"

At the foot of the stairs, Papa grabbed me by my collar and lifted me from the floor. "Stop! There is nothing to celebrate. Nothing!"

Muttering in fury, my mother, small and birdlike, with tiny feet and huge breasts, unbalanced in many ways, retrieved the dented pots and wooden spoons.

The next day, I followed Papa into the yard, beyond the empty dairy barns, into the giraffe house. Up on the second-story walkway, he looked into Violet's giant eyes, eyes that had grown more forlorn every day since he had left for the war. She had sores all over her neck and belly.

She leaned her long neck down to him, cleaned him with her tongue. He sculpted her bony face with both hands. He pulled on the velvet tassels at the ends of her velvet horns, stroking her ears, her horns. Violet rubbed his cheek with hers, licked his face, his hands, licked the butt of the rifle, and then my father shot her between the eyes.

Her legs folded. The floor ran red with Violet's blood.

He turned away. I thought him a terribly brave man, a responsible man. And he said what he always said, "A man does what he must do." Which was in direct conflict to what I always said: "It isn't fair." But I still wore short pants. As we rounded the walkway and descended the stairs, my father's hand squeezing my shoulder, I heard the hack and scrape of knives as Volker and his two coarse sons began the terrible butchery.

After our cook Shteinberg boiled Violet's flesh in the soup pots, the barn men dragged the pots to the workers' houses up by the foundry, where soldiers still came to rest or die on their way home from battlefields. And we, starving, ate Violet's tongue for supper. I choked and put my share into my pants pocket.

❧

On our last night at the house, the fortunate moon hid behind clouds. We heard a motorcycle in the forest, roaring toward us. It was Uncle Wolf. He was taking us somewhere, secretly, dangerously. "I have a truck coming. Get ready. The Russians are just ten or fifteen kilometers away." He wore an American officer's uniform with an array of ribbons on its chest and a bullet hole in its back.

"Where did you get a truck?" my father asked.

"Manfred Hermann."

Papa spat on the floor. "Why is that madman helping us?"

"He said your name was on the list."

"What list?"

"For South America." Uncle Wolf glanced over his shoulder. "You are wanted for the Occult Bureau. South America."

"The Occult Bureau wants *me*? What the hell are they doing in South America? Why is Hermann saving *me*?"

"Maybe he wants to give you a second head, so you can think twice as much. He's good at that sort of operation." Uncle Wolf joking a joke that wasn't a joke. Uncle Wolf was crazy. I had already heard in other conversations that Dr. Manfred Hermann was a butcher. "No time to question, Dietrich. All the roads are closed. Troops, tanks, everywhere. The truck is coming up the railroad bed. Please hurry."

Papa nodded a single curt nod. "Luba, get blankets, extra boots, any food you can find. Dress the baby in her warmest clothes. Where the hell is Berthe?" Luba raced to the nursery for Cecilia. Cecilia was no longer a baby, but she was unnaturally small for a three-year-old, so she seemed to all of us still an infant.

"The boxes outside in the driveway, please. Get the clothes from the attic. Berthe, where are you?"

Everyone shouted at each other until a dark truck covered in camouflage cloth and fir boughs slid into the road in front of our house. Luba, my mother, Cecilia, and I hid in the alcove. Papa stood at the open door.

Three American soldiers jumped from the truck. Boxes were stacked in the driveway. Luba stood next to me, rubbing her arms as if she would peel them. "Germans in American uniforms pushing a stolen American truck," she explained.

I pulled more boxes from the kitchen. Luba, Shteinberg, and Ulla dragged featherbeds to the truck. My mother, biting her lower lip, tears streaming down her face, took her chair before the weak fire, a cup of cold tea at her elbow, her knuckles white, frozen.

"Come, Berthe. Get moving, Berthe."

"Shoot me, Dietrich. Shoot me like you shot your giraffe. Kill me as you killed your Jews. I'm not going."

"We have no choice. I am a war criminal now. If we'd won the war, I'd be a hero." He knelt at her feet, laying his head in her lap. She stiffened, folded her arms across her chest.

My father wrenched her from the chair. "Pack food," he ordered.

He changed from his uniform into the black-and-gray striped pajamas of the workmen at the steel mill: dark, shapeless, patched with yellow stars. He gave similar clothes to my mother, Luba, and me. The clothing stank of metal and sweat. Luba, who three years before had arrived in our house in the striped pajamas with the yellow star, looked at us and broke into ugly manic laughter. I knew why she was laughing. We did not look like Jews. My first long pants were disgusting. We covered ourselves with the filthy factory clothes, hot, scratchy, heavy, stiff, stinking, and stood before Papa as he gave us money belts with American dollars, cyanide pills in silver containers, and small guns.

Uncle Wolf had his hand on my father's shoulder. He gave him a rifle, and they turned toward the hounds' yard. I was about to follow Papa, but Uncle Wolf grabbed me. "Stay here. You've seen enough already. Get over to the truck and help with the boxes."

When we heard the gunshots—six—my mother clutched her throat and whispered, "His hounds." They still came at his call.

Papa tracked blood on the entry stones, his face itself stone. He thrust his hand under Luba's blouse, pulled out a balloon of a breast, and from under his own Jewish clothes he retrieved a handful of vizsla puppy, which he shoved onto her brown nipple. "It needs milk."

Luba stood, circles of red fury painted on her quivering cheeks, weeping as the vizsla suckled viciously. "It has teeth!" she cried out. I didn't know how to help her. My father was a whirlwind. Everything happened too fast. Everything was an order. And everything was threatening.

Papa and Uncle Wolf knelt and kissed the hearthstone of our great fireplace. In disbelief, the two brothers shook their heads at each other, and then, groaning with the effort and the ache, unhinged the oak doors from their frames and carried them on their shoulders like crosses to the truck. These doors had come from the family castle. They were deeply carved with the Pappendorf coat of arms: pine trees, bears, and swords. My mother took her own ring of house keys and handed them to Cook Shteinberg, who covered her face with her apron. With the soldiers and Uncle Wolf hurrying us, we were bundled into the truck.

Ulla, Shteinberg, Volker the barn man, and his two sons stood on the porch. The house was now theirs. Running, my father led the soldiers to the little church beyond the orchards to pick up the ancient wooden Madonna from whose rear end the shortwave radio had been removed and replaced with diamonds from India.

He had his boxes of books packed next to my mother's boxes of dishes. He ordered the soldiers to leave my mother's boxes and take only his.

With fisted hands, my mother beat on the shield of his chest. "My dishes! How dare you?"

"We are not moving, Berthe. We are escaping."

Mama, porcelain herself, a network of small veins crackling her skin like old china, fought in whispers and hisses with Papa over the boxes while the soldiers turned their faces away and waited. The engine of the truck was running, the driver pacing around us. I considered asking him if I could sit up front. I'd never been in a truck.

When he turned away to study road maps with Uncle Wolf and the driver, Mama tore into his boxes, throwing books into the dirt. "I will not leave until I have my dishes."

I watched in horror as Mama ripped pages from notebooks, broke the backs of leather-covered dictionaries. Yellowed pages flew. She read a label from a notebook. "The origins of man's consciousness through phonetic fossils. Wonderful." She tore out a few pages, crumpled them in her fist and tossed the notebook at Papa's back.

At last, he realized what she was doing. "Berthe? Are you mad? Those are my notes, my ideas. Berthe, I beg you."

"You and your ideas. Look where they got us."

"The war was not my idea, Berthe."

Luba, somehow holding both Cecilia and the squirming puppy, moved behind the truck. Papa looked to Uncle Wolf for help. Uncle Wolf shrugged. I shoved books back into their boxes. More flew over my head.

"Herr Baron," the driver called from the truck. "The ship…" He waved his arm to Papa, tapped his watch.

"I want my dishes."

"My lifetime work, Berthe! My ideas are essential. Your dishes are not."

"The world can live without your *Is* and your *Og*, your words, your old gods. Your...your Platos." Deftly, she shredded an entire notebook. Uncle Wolf tried to calm his brother, who was simultaneously attempting to attack Berthe and give directions to the driver. Uncle Wolf held my father's elbow, whispering in his ear.

I didn't know what an Is or an Og was. I just patted Mama on the back. I loved my mother.

She elbowed me away. "Gods with tails. We give our life for his gods with tails."

"She's very upset, Dietrich," Uncle Wolf spoke softly. "Let her take a few dishes. We must go!"

"It's not about the dishes," Papa shouted as we chased papers in the wind. "It's about the war. She blames *me* for the war. Stupid woman!"

"Right now, Dietrich, it's about escaping. Now."

Hands trembling, my father's with anger, mine with fear, I helped him repack his books and notebooks. "Listen, Axel," he told me, "your mother is not herself." He was wrong. She was absolutely herself: angry, depressed, distant. It was he who was not himself. I sensed weakness and fear. Of course, we were all terrified. Escaping. And boy that I was, I hoped that wherever we were going, I would be able to wear more respectable long pants.

Uncle Wolf put his arm around my mother's waist, offered her a dessert plate and a demitasse cup, and led her gently into the back of the truck. Luba climbed in beside her. She carried baby Cecilia, the infant puppy, and dutifully, frantically covered them with a featherbed. The soldiers lifted the Madonna, the doors of our house, and Papa's books into the truck.

"Where are you taking us, Dietrich?" my mother asked.

Uncle Wolf laughed and snapped the camouflage cloth over the rear of the truck. "We're going to Paradise." Three soldiers climbed into the truck with us and immediately fell asleep. My father sat with the driver. The back of his neck was red and taut with fury.

"Origins of man's consciousness, *ha!*" Mama shouted to Papa in the front of the truck. "I spit on your word fossils. *Spit!*" But he couldn't hear her over the engine and the deeply drawn snores of the soldiers.

Uncle Wolf slid over to her and held her in his arms, at which moment she began the frantic unending recital of her china inventory, inherited from her mother, who had inherited it from the Empress of Austria, and she never stopped.

Uncle Wolf interrupted. "His work, Berthe, his Is and his Og, they are saving our lives, so mind your tongue." And then he kissed her on her forehead.

We passed a burning tank. The earth shook with explosions. Shells burst overhead. The truck jolted, shook, swung wildly around sharp curves and flaming potholes. Luba sniffled. I curled as close to her as I could.

Papa yelled, "Out of the truck. Everybody out." He dragged me out and pulled me into the woods. A plane buzzed above. I fell on my back. He fell on top of me. His bones were sharp, breath rotten.

"If we are caught, Axel, run, hide. Find a farmhouse. There is food at farmhouses."

Another bomb exploded. "Wolf, you there?"

"Be quiet, Dietrich," came his brother's voice. "There may be some on foot, from the tank."

"You won't be hurt, Axel. Don't worry. I won't let you die. Axel, listen to me." His words came from deep within, his mouth close to my ear, his breath hot and acidic, smoky. "I'm not like other men."

I watched his Adam's apple bobbing, as if he were gagging on his words, struggling. A tank rumbled past us toward the explosions.

"Russian," Uncle Wolf whispered from someplace nearby.

"They're after the tank, not us." Another bomb exploded. Dirt and stones showered upon us. My father pressed down on me. "Axel, if they find us, they'll kill me. Are you listening?"

"Sir." It was all I dared to say. He was squeezing the air out of my chest.

He kneaded my shoulders as if shaping dough. Tears or sweat, I couldn't tell which, were running down his cheeks into my ear. "If we are caught, remember who you are."

And who was that? It was an unlikely moment for a revelation of any kind, and this one was devastating. Suddenly I thought my papa was insane. Mama was too, and we were all going to die. I struggled, wanting him off of me. A plane buzzed overhead in circles, dipping and diving. The world was spinning off its axis. Cecilia screamed. Luba gently shook her quiet.

"Find a farmhouse," said Papa. "If they come, run."

Uncle Wolf whispered, "The bombs are farther away."

My father rolled off me. "Back in the truck, everyone. Back. Be quiet." He sprinted out of the woods, found the driver who lay crushed, dead, raw meat, next to the truck. Papa climbed into the driver's seat. He let me sit next to him.

"Hold on, Axel. We go over the mountain. A half mile back." The soldiers had never left the truck. They were still asleep. The gears screamed as he turned, backed up, and roared onto the mountain road. My father was two men—one of whom I wished to be and one who terrified me.

Chapter Six

Leaving the Black Forest, we raced through twilight into a night of fear, then a fog-thick morning on dirt roads, through woods and emptiness, empty towns, empty roads, an empty day, through a ghost city to the sea and to a dark dock. Yellow stars on our arms, the infant puppy hidden in a burlap bag. Luba, carrying three-year-old Cecilia in her arms, Uncle Wolf, Papa and Mama and I, at last, boarded a darkened destroyer. We were led down steps along freezing metal walls until we found our cabins and fell into cots. In one area, my mother and father occupied a cabin, Luba and Cecilia were in another, my uncle Wolf shared one with me.

Uncle Wolf stared at the ceiling and didn't speak.

The chains dropped, the engines turned, churned. The ship moved forward. As long as I could, I counted the slap of the ship's bottom on the waves. I thought about the time our hounds ate a dead soldier in the forest while I counted to three thousand, and I was happy to be going to Paradise, wherever it was, whatever it was.

By daylight, still in our factory rags, on the deck, we saw other families. Two men clicked their heels and saluted my father, despite his shoddy clothes. When my father returned their devotion with hot looks, they dropped their raised arms.

"It is over," he said, steely-eyed. "We are no longer what we were." They looked away from his madness. To their backs, he whispered, "And now we are criminals, suspended outside history, pariahs, but we will live in Paradise." My mother walked behind us, leaned over the railing, and stared into the sea.

That night, she summoned me to her cabin. She lay on a cot, wearing the striped shirt and pants with the yellow star we took from the factory, her cheeks sunken, eyes hollow. "Axel, find your father. Tell him we're not supposed to be on the deck after dark." Other than the unending frantic recitation of her Meissen collection of china, my mother hadn't spoken a word since we'd raced from our forest home to the sea, fleeing in a filthy truck from all things familiar to all things unknown. "Hurry," she urged.

I found my way past icy metal walls, stumbling up to the deck. Everything was dark but for the red eye of my father's cigarette. He leaned against a railing. Reaching down, he held my hand. "We're going south, then across the Atlantic Ocean. We escaped and are safe."

"Mama says we're not supposed to be up here on the deck at night."

"That isn't fair, is it?"

This was the father I loved. He was mimicking me, joking with me, the son who forever claimed things were unfair.

"It isn't fair that we lost the war, Papa, is it?"

I could feel the warmth of his smile. "We do what we can; we take what we must." He dropped my hand and flipped his cigarette into the sea. "Go tell Luba I want to see her. Go, run."

In their cabin, Luba and Cecilia were sleeping. I woke up Luba. "Dietrich wishes to see you," I said, feeling grown up as I used my father's first name.

"Goddamn him. Alright, you watch the baby." Though Cecilia wasn't exactly a baby anymore, that was how she acted. And how all of us treated her. "Ten minutes," said Luba.

Cecilia realized Luba had left and boiled into a tantrum that wouldn't stop, no matter what I did or promised. Finally, I knocked on my mother's cabin door with my squealing sister. "It isn't fair. Luba gets to go for a walk with Papa and I have to..."

Mama was instantly out of her bed, tossing a blanket over her shoulders. Uncle Wolf appeared in the hallway, taking Cecilia in his arms, rocking. She quieted. My mother threw her arms around Uncle Wolf and Cecilia, then wept with deep, wet sobs.

The ship's captain suddenly appeared in the doorway. Captain Friedrich Kroening brought with him a case of pears wrapped in yellow papers. He caught my mother by the arm. "Baroness von

Pappendorf, I am proud to welcome you to my ship and pray we can serve your illustrious family well. These pears and cigarettes are from friends and for you, madam. The Baron has also received cigarettes."

"I have to go on the deck. My husband..."

Captain Kroening was fat, much shorter than everyone but me. He adjusted the blanket over my mother's shoulders, took her arm and led her away. I ate the miracle of the pear, wiped my mouth with my sleeve, then licked my sleeve, counted to one hundred, and followed.

By the time I was on the deck and found my mother at the far end of the ship, Captain Kroening was gone and the ship lights were off. In the moonlight, I found Mama leaning on a railing. She held the vizsla puppy in her arms and was again reciting her inventory of Meissen dishes.

"...three dozen, gold-rimmed, two slightly chipped. Saucers with gold crowns, fourteen." She was on dessert plates, slowly smoking a cigarette while staring at something going on between the gun mountings: It was my father atop Luba, amid groaning and labored breathing and the slosh of seawater.

I don't know how long I stood there. As Luba cried softly, I watched, transfixed. When I turned around, Mama was gone. After hearing a cry and a splash, I swung about. My mother was gone.

Amid the faltering conclusion of the Meissen dessert plate recital, she had disappeared. She'd ended with the dessert plates. I ran the length of the ship, looking everywhere I could, even reluctantly at the dark waters roiling below. I bolted back to our cabin to find my uncle.

Bootless, barefoot, Uncle Wolf lay on his bunk, Cecilia sleeping at his side. His feet were pale and narrow. I woke him, saying, "I can't find my mother."

"And where is your father?"

I shrugged. I remembered the seawater sloshing between the gun mounts. Papa's breathing, pumping. I thought that he somehow controlled the beat of the ocean itself, the plow of this ship through the sea.

Cecilia started shrieking. Just as Uncle Wolf picked her up, Papa and Luba arrived. Luba rubbed her eyes with her knuckles, her dress dripping wet. Cecilia screamed, and Papa took her from Uncle Wolf's arms, thrust her at Luba. She dropped her bodice before both men and me, closing her eyes while Cecilia suckled.

"Luba, where is my puppy?" Papa asked.

"How should I know? I keep my eyes closed."

"Where is your mother?" Sensing something disturbing in my gaze, he shook me by my shoulders. "Tell me, Axel, where is she?"

"I've been looking," I said. "I can't find her."

Uncle Wolf slammed his hand against the wall so hard a burning kerosene lamp fell. Papa danced to stomp out its sparks. He stomped long after the flames died.

"If Berthe is hurt, Dietrich, it's on your head. I shall never forgive you."

My father made a fist, swung a half arc toward his brother, then stopped himself.

"Papa." I tugged at his sleeve. "I don't know where she went. Maybe Mama's hiding."

Uncle Wolf rushed to the captain, beseeching him to stop the ship and search the waters, but Kroening refused. The ship continued on its course as Uncle Wolf, numerous crew members, and I searched for Mama in its every corner: the engine room, the kitchen, and so on.

Behind nearly every cabin door, I heard weeping and quarreling. Pain was everywhere, I observed, but was my mother's so severe she'd leave me behind? Did a cold, watery grave offer her more solace than a loving son?

❧

Uncle Wolf moved from our cabin space to sleep in a hammock with the crew. When we docked in Spain, I watched a small army of men bringing on board meats, vegetables, fruits, bags of flour, sugar, salt, boxes of eggs. We were to eat like kings.

Dietrich, Luba, Cecilia, and I sat at the captain's table for three meals a day, noble and high-ranking as we were. Captain Kroening did not join us.

Uncle Wolf stopped once at our table and explained to me he'd moved to a bunk in the crew quarters because Cecilia was keeping him awake at night with her tantrums. From the way his eyes slid around, I knew he was lying. He did not sit with us but farther down a long table.

Dietrich's face had changed overnight. There was a film over it, a scab. I couldn't look into his eyes; they were so lifeless. It was as if he had gone blind. Now that Uncle Wolf was avoiding us, I had a cabin to myself, which allowed me to continue sneaking out at night, wandering the ship, looking for my mother. I leaned against door after door, listened, listened. It was cold. Two men slept in the hallway outside our rooms.

One night, Dietrich came fumbling and stumbling into my cabin. "Can you write? Do you have paper and pen? Get up. I don't want to forget this."

This was the first of my father's waking lectures. It was the beginning of my endless task of writing them out for him. He began: "Gentlemen of the Royal Astronomical Society, the relationship of blood to language is indivisible. It is the ultimate framework for the origins of consciousness. Words have a peculiar property. It is the same property in our genetics...no doubt you have heard of Friedrich Miescher's work." He strode up and down the deck. I ran after, back and forth, trying to write and keep up with him. He bumped into a woman who was watching the sea, a sailor who was watching us.

Another night. The engines were off again. The lights flickered, died. Captain Kroening stood next to Dietrich on the deck, whispering, squinting into the night. "I'm afraid there's a British ship nearby and at least one submarine. Please put out your cigarette."

"If there is a nearby submarine, possibly following us, why don't we race forward and lose them? We can't continue to delay like this. We'll run out of rations, water."

"No, no, let me assure you, Herr Baron, we *are* moving forward."

"I order you to turn on the engines and move at full speed away from the danger. Or I shall report you as soon as we land."

"This is my ship, Herr Baron. And you must realize there is no longer anyone to report to."

Dietrich wasn't finished. "And why didn't you stop the ship to search for my wife?"

Captain Kroening sighed, shook his head. "At the time, there was a British ship nearby following us. I could not sacrifice all my passengers for one."

"I see." Dietrich had given up his arguments.

"Right now, we drift, Herr Baron. On the current." The captain was a gentle man.

"The current takes us in the correct direction?"

"Oh, yes, from North Africa directly to Brazil. Below the equator, the passageway takes us to the west. Above, to the east, like a conveyor belt. We are on the conveyor belt, Herr Baron. We're fine. We'll slip through just like this. It will take a little longer. We may have to ration water, even fuel. But we'll get there, I assure you."

Dietrich squinted to the horizon. "How long has it been there, this current?"

"Forever, Herr Baron. As long as the sun shines. It is caused by warm water."

"A conveyor belt. *Aah*. That means in ancient times, anyone could sail from the Mediterranean Sea across the Atlantic to... to..."

"Brazil. The current ends at the mouth of the Amazon."

Dietrich grabbed Captain Kroening's arm. "Do you know what this means? This conveyor belt changes history. Anyone could cross the Atlantic to South America. Plato's River of the Ocean to the Lands of the West, the legendary Lands of the West. Perhaps, after all, to Paradise. Plato was correct. Anyone could have come here. Even Solomon...yes, Solomon's ships would have journeyed here for gold. And the Egyptians and...the Carthaginians, any of the seafaring...my God. This place in the Amazon actually *was* their Paradise...is it possible?"

The captain cleared his throat, shook Dietrich off, and spit into the ocean. "Perhaps Hell, Baron. Perhaps Hell."

❧

One night when Luba was seasick, Dietrich sent me upstairs with her to get fresh air. The ship rolled. She held my hand as we stood side by side on the deck, looking up at the stars. The moon sailed steadily through the clouds, followed us, led us. She asked, "What does the moon teach you, German boy?"

"It teaches me how the world began."

"German boy, ask your moon how my world ended."

"Let's not talk. Let's just watch and stay right here forever."

"All that you have seen, German boy, you must tuck it away and just go on. There is no other way."

We held hands as the ship rolled and pitched and the moon stayed steady until the engines of the ship stopped. As did our hearts. The quiet swallowed us.

A sailor ran toward us, saluted. "The captain believes there is a submarine nearby. Enemy. Please, below, life jackets, no lights. Please."

Except for the slap of waves and the creaking of the ship, we were nowhere. The engines had been comforting. We met Dietrich ascending the stairs. I whispered, "Submarine."

"Come along! *Macht schnell!*" Dietrich pulled us away from the railing, rushed us to our cabins. I heard Captain Kroening calling for everyone to leave the deck, return to their cabins, put on life jackets.

From my porthole, I watched the submarine approach on the water's surface. It was fog-wrapped on a clear, bright night. A small boat dropped from its side, and a dark man wrapped in a black cloak climbed into it. Another followed. The boat was rowed to ours, and, when it was next to us, the captain helped the two men aboard.

Hours later, locked into an existential fear of the nothingness, the emptiness we were in, the nowhereness, the engines finally started up again. I removed my life jacket.

The next morning, I was with my father in his cabin. Dietrich had piled his boxes on what had been my mother's cot. In his mind, she was no longer. Soon after, Uncle Wolf unexpectedly joined us, there was a soft knock on the door. A slip of paper slid under it.

Dietrich jumped backward. Until that moment, I had no idea how very frightened he was. No one bent to pick up the paper. More out of curiosity than bravery, I did.

I read. "It says 'Hermann.'"

"Manfred?" Dietrich whispered through the door, hesitating before opening it.

Dr. Manfred Hermann wore dark trousers and a thick black shirt. Another smaller man stood behind him, wearing the same.

"Baron." Dr. Hermann put out his hand.

Dietrich had no choice but to shake it. I instinctively didn't like Dr. Manfred Hermann. He had a baby face with a little turned-up nose, dark brows, rosebud lips, and violently blue eyes, all narrow parts, pinched and small, lost in the vastness of a round, fleshy, brutal German face with an enormous forehead.

"Yes, on behalf of my family, thank you. Who is your friend?" My father gestured at the man behind Dr. Hermann.

Stepping forward was a man we would come to know only too well as Willi. Dietrich did not offer his hand to Willi but instead saluted him: "Heil Hitler." Uncle Wolf moved toward the door. The two men sat heavily on Dietrich's cot.

Dietrich's eyes were agates, stony and cold.

Willi nodded, smiled a mouth filled with gold teeth, a cruel, sadistic mouth. He sneezed again and again. "This room is cold, Herr Baron, I'm sorry we couldn't have arranged better for you. My blood is thin, for I have lived in the tropics all these years." He looked my way and said in English, "I will need a coat. Boy, can you get me a coat?"

After glancing his way for permission, I quickly handed Willi a jacket of my father's.

Dr. Hermann said, "Please understand, we all speak English. Some in our Colony even learned by watching American movies. We tell people we are Boers, the Dutch, from South Africa. It is good that you and your brother speak English. And the boy also speaks English?"

My father nodded. "We had a cook who lived in America and returned to Germany."

Dr. Hermann nodded. "That saves us trouble. So." He slapped his knees. "Willi is our banker and spymaster in South America. He was creating our Occult Bureau Colony long before the war. We are well established, thanks to Willi. And because of Willi, we shall go on to triumphs. And, also, because of you, Dietrich."

Uncle Wolf left the room. I had the feeling this had been rehearsed, and that Uncle Wolf had been privy to it. I was sure these were the strangers who had boarded from the submarine last night in the middle of the ocean.

As he spoke, Dr. Hermann moved from the cot he sat on with Willi and began to remove Dietrich's boxes from my mother's cot, one by one. "We've come to escort you. You are protected and safe. We already have our men aboard the ship. They have been guarding your cabin, sleeping in the hallway." He puffed the pillows. I thought, with shock, that he was about to lie down. He sat on the cot. My mother's bed. Did he know she was gone?

"Many others were more valuable and loyal to the Fuehrer, Manfred," said Dietrich. "Why me, Manfred? What do you want from me?"

"This no longer has anything to do with Hitler. Now it is about us." He put his hands on his knees, leaned forward. "You are valuable to the Occult Bureau. Invaluable, in fact. It is the Occult Bureau that will raise the flag of the Reich again. You were on Hitler's list to protect, but we couldn't find you. Your brother helped. In Brazil, you will continue your work on languages."

Dietrich paced the small room, caged. "You saved me for my language studies?"

"From you, we need the alphabet of Babel."

"This is difficult to believe. My work is to find phonetic fossils, to trace back to the origins of consciousness. Finding what you want would take years. If, indeed, it exists."

I remembered what I had learned: Before Babel, mankind had one universal language. Was it even possible for Dietrich to discover that universal language?

Willi leaned forward as Dr. Hermann spoke: "But we have years, Dietrich. There are many areas to organize before we are ready to...move. And, of course, the Aryan language exists. The Ur language, before the Indo-European, at the dawn of civilization, the first language. The first Aryan language. Willi, read to the Baron."

From his shirt pocket, Willi pulled a folded page torn from a book. He squinted, turning to find light. "This is from the mouth of the Fuehrer." As if a schoolboy in recital, Willi cleared his throat. "'The power that has always started the greatest religions and political avalanches in history'...uh...'rolling from time immemorial has been the magic power of the spoken word. The broad masses of the people can only be moved by the power of speech. If I approach

the masses with reasoned'...uh...'arguments, they will not under-
stand me. In the mass meeting, their reasoning power is paralyzed.
What I say is like an order given under hypnosis.' Adolf Hitler,
Mein Kampf."

Dr. Hermann took off his boots, then his socks. Little white
clouds lifted around his feet, which smelled like Cecelia's baby
powder. "Thank you, Willi. You understand, Dietrich? If you find
the right language, we can hypnotize the entire world, not just the
Germans. The right word is an order given under hypnosis to a
blind and obedient world. You must find for us the right words.
This is your responsibility. Word by word, going back before Babel.
That's why we saved your family. So we could give an order with
your language. We need your alphabet."

He looked directly at me and my knees shook. When Dietrich
stepped a few inches closer to me, I looked into his face. There was
nothing in his eyes.

"The word, Herr Baron—that is our real weapon and you will
find it," said Dr. Hermann. "In the beginning was the word. Through
the word, Hitler won Germany. Through the word, we will rule the
world. The world will be under our spell, blind and obedient."

Willi echoed, "Blind and obedient, Herr Baron. You understand, Herr Baron?"

"And so you will find this language, letter by letter." Dr.
Hermann lay down with his arms behind his head, adjusting
my mother's pillows. It seemed sacrilegious, like taking a nap in
a coffin. He spoke to the ceiling. "Your family will be protected,
provided for. We are very well organized and have powerful friends.
There is a lot of money, much from the Jewish dead, much from
the American living who still give us their support. People who
believed. People who still believe. We have support from all over
the world. You will be safe, and we will remain hidden until we are
ready to...complete the Fuehrer's dream. And when you are ready,
the Occult Bureau will bring the Fourth Reich to life. With the
original language, we will hypnotize the world."

"What if I don't find the right words?"

Dr. Hermann sighed. "Oh, you will succeed, Dietrich. You will
look for the Aryan language, letter by letter. We know you were
working on this in India and before that, when you were digging

along the Indus, looking for…what was that, the Rosetta stone for the Aryan nation?"

"Am I to understand that you believe the language of Babel was an Aryan language? Not Semitic?"

"Of course. We have no doubt. You know," his voice dropped, shifted to dreamy, which we would come to learn was when he was most dangerous. "You know, since your wife is no longer occupying these quarters and your brother sleeps with the crew, Willi and I ask that you move into your boy's cabin for the few days remaining. Our men—" he jerked his head to the door "—they will help you with your things. Is that not a good idea, Dietrich? Everyone has a bed."

"Manfred, say I am able to give you the alphabet of Babel. I would like to ensure that I then have my freedom in exchange."

"Of course, of course." Dreamy voice. Not sincere.

Shaking his head, Dietrich led me to my cabin, then sat on my bed, his head in his hands. "We go to an insane asylum in a jungle. Well, what they do with my work is their business. They are madmen. They will never succeed." He fell backward on the bed. "How strange. That one spells words. And words cast a spell. How strange all of this is. If we find the correct letters, Manfred Hermann and his people will cast a spell on the world. What is the origin of the word 'spell'?" He stared at the ceiling a long time, then fell asleep. Dietrich often woke with a start, with a new idea. His naps were productive.

❧

Later that day, he led me to the place where I had last seen my mother. I found it hard to concentrate on him, feeling the urge to gaze out at the ocean and seek her out in its vastness. We sat directly on the deck between two guns. He said, "I already have three, possibly four words of this alphabet Hermann is looking for. I can find more. He's correct about one original language. Genesis reads: *And the whole earth was of one language, and of one speech*. But why do they differentiate between language and speech? Someone mistranslated. What is missing is the written language, the language of letters, of spelling: the letters of Babel Hermann wants. I need eighteen, perhaps twenty-four letters. Of those I'm certain. Of the rest…it will take years to complete. But even if I give him his letters, I doubt Hermann will be able to build the correct words. Vision is not his strength—cruelty, ambition, greed, but not vision. Vision is *my* burden. And, remember, Axel, I can always leave out something pivotal, the way Shteinberg would leave out the salt in her soups. Now, let me tell you how we do this, because this will now be your work too."

"Why did we take Luba and not Shteinberg?"

"Shteinberg will be fine. Please, don't interrupt."

A sailor bent over a gun and looked at us sitting on the deck. "Fresh air," my father explained. "We need nothing. You are dismissed." The sailor shrugged, left.

"So, Axel, stand, lean against the gun, keep an eye out. So, in Turkey, in India, I went to ancient sites, to museums, caves, looking for the language of Babel. Certain syllables, sounds, letters kept appearing in many languages, in words and place names, river names that held mysteries, suggestions, attractions. I found a way into that original language, just a keyhole, not a door. This is how we are to go about escaping, Axel. We will find the language of Babel. We will find the letters of that alphabet and give them to Hermann."

"What letters have you found?" I said, looking past the guns to the sea.

"You heard your mother shouting them at me in the truck, didn't you? Is and Og. And Sir, possibly Mus, but I'm not certain of Mus and have done little work on Sir since the war began."

"Those aren't letters."

"Of course not. They're the names of the gods. This is the foundation of the alphabet. Those are the diamonds we look for within modern words. What I seek is the Rosetta stone, the basic alphabet from Babel, the god list. You and I will give the Occult Bureau an alphabet, but no words. I am going to teach you to find the letters. It will be time-consuming, looking for a diamond in a hunk of limestone. *Chip, chip, chip.* Someday we'll have the entire necklace. Are you following?"

"I'm trying."

"Good. This is how we will get away, Axel, trading letters for freedom." He stretched out his hand to me. From the deck, I pulled him upright.

"What if they manage to take over the world?"

"They won't…and we'll be long gone. I can always leave out the salt. Let me tell you about the word 'hand' to give you an idea of the way we must think. Go back to the time before mankind knew the gods. Words and meaning and mankind evolved. Consciousness evolved. In many languages, the word 'hand' is found as *hend*, even *ghend*. If you examine the word 'prehensile,' it suggests time before hands. And 'reprehensible' implies something ugly and terrible before hands. That seems simple enough, but let's go back further. In Egypt, the ancient cuneiform shape of a hand means understanding, to grasp. It now may suggest that 'prehensile' means to capture. Letters are actions. 'Comprehensible' means that which the mind can grasp. You see?"

"I don't. But if you need me to, I'll try."

"I will most certainly need you to help me. When this nightmare is over, my work will be ready, Axel, and I will speak at the Royal Astronomical Society in London, taking my rightful place. I will be heard." This was Dietrich's dream: to speak at the Royal Society. Finally, to be heard.

❦

By the time we turned west from North Africa, I knew my mother was truly gone. Halfway across the Atlantic one night, I heard her crying at my door.

At first, I thought I was dreaming. But then I flung open the door and yelled, "Mama!" She was nowhere. I raced along the halls, the stairs, onto the deck.

I knocked on Luba's door. She understood. "I, too, lost my mother. Come." I climbed into Luba's bed and slept next to her until Dietrich came in, pulled me by my hair, and sent me to my cabin.

We did not see Dr. Manfred Hermann and his friend Willi again. They had their meals delivered and never left their room. As the days passed, the air grew warmer, hotter, thicker. Clouds boiled above us. Strong rains broke the afternoon heat. Sailors took off their shirts and worked bare-chested. The other travelers hid in their cabins below until dusk. Water was rationed.

On the last night before reaching shore, there was a faint knocking on my door. "Wolf? Wolf?"

I flew from the bed, flung the door open to the darkened hallway. There was the ghost of my mother, holding the vizsla puppy.

"Oh! Where is Wolf?" The ghost of my mother turned, whispering over her shoulder, "Take care of your father. Promise."

I could barely speak. "I will."

Take care of your father. Take care of your father. I will.

Later that night, while I cried in our cabin, my father held me in his arms. Then he brought me up to the deck, pointing to lights onshore. "Paradise."

The ship turned gently into the mouth of the Amazon.

Chapter Seven

If I hadn't told my mother that Dietrich was on the deck with Luba, would she still be alive?

That question loomed large in my mind along this long river journey, even as we sailed at last into the cauldron of clouds and clamor that was the inland jungle city of Manaus.

"Manaus," Dietrich announced. "More than a thousand kilometers from the mouth of the Amazon, built by European rubber barons at the turn of the century. Pay attention," he ordered. "Stand up straight. Smile."

The ship tied up to a floating river dock. The air was heavy with heat. Everyone here seemed to move slowly, heavily. The sun pressed down. Captain Kroening stood with us on deck. A band played German oompah marches. *Oompah, oompah. Thud. Thud.* Dietrich stood at the railing of the ship, swiveling his right hand as if screwing in a light bulb, a noble gesture to the crowd gathered on the dock. A shout went up. "Herr Baron! Herr Baron!"

I hid behind Luba. She hid behind me.

Heavy, thick people climbed aboard. The women wore hats with flowers on them, the men, white suits and war medals and white handkerchiefs under the brim of their hats. They bore crosses of perspiration on the backs of their jackets. These Germans who had come to greet us were dressed in beautiful clothes, but they were coarse and their speech unlike ours, unrefined, self-satisfied, preening. They had the high foreheads, narrow pig eyes, and fat cheeks of peasants. They looked more like Shteinberg and Volker.

None of us were as happy as they. The women curtsied, then couldn't raise themselves, were lifted by their husbands. They'd been eating for a long time. They had been here for a long time.

Dietrich smiled stiffly as men hugged him, slapped him on the back, pumped his hands. He looked as if he didn't want to be touched. Nor did I. I kept turning, watching for my mother to walk down the gangway, to appear as mysteriously as she'd vanished. Women lifted baby Cecilia, covered her with kisses. Cecilia kicked at their bellies. They put her down. I saw them looking at each other, questions in their eyes.

The men tousled my hair, slapped me on the shoulders, and shook my hand again and again, as if I had done something marvelous. And indeed, being the only son of the Baron, this marvelous man, seemed to have made me marvelous. Like a spider, Luba withdrew into dark corners.

I met Margaret, a girl my age. Although she looked nothing like him, she was introduced as the daughter of Dr. Hermann's sidekick, Willi. After she blushed, curtsied, and thrust a bouquet of baby orchids at me, Margaret nestled closer to pint-sized Willi. Dr. Hermann shook Captain Kroening's hand, then departed with Willi and Margaret in tow, without another word to us.

On the dock, a naked brown baby slept on a mountain of green bananas. Voluptuous dark-skinned women bursting from tight dresses of every color in the tropical rainbow beckoned and whistled for the sailors to come ashore. Dietrich cuffed me when he caught me looking. Cliffs of lumber rose near a city of warehouses. Oil lamps swung over the boats in the soft winds. Barges loaded with jute swung in the light tide. Dugouts, poor launches, ancient two- and three-level river boats moored to the docks were loaded with harvests of palm fronds, squashes, enormous fish larger than men, mighty turtles, baskets of strange fruits, bizarre shapes and colors, strange faces of as many shapes and colors as the fruits. I watched families of savages curled up in hammocks in their boats.

"Don't stare," Dietrich said. I couldn't help myself. Some native people looked up at us, staring back at me. On the arm of an Indian boy my age, I saw a baby sloth. Suddenly I could not live another moment without my own baby sloth. I made a fuss.

His fingernails in my flesh, Dietrich led me away from the visitors. "Axel, you are too old for this nonsense. Don't be like your mother, for God's sake." I stepped back into the corners with Luba. Her knuckles were white. She held my hand.

Back in our cabins, tailors from Manaus measured us for new clothes. "Long pants," I told them.

Luba refused to be measured.

That night, we remained on board. In the morning, the tailors returned with our clothes. Luba's new dress didn't fit across the bosom. Dietrich gave her one of the unappealing red vests my mother had quilted to cover herself.

Even as she knew it was stitched full of diamonds, Luba did not want to wear it. "I hate red clothes. They are the color of blood." But she had little choice; she put on the ugly red vest packed with gemstones, vowing to never wear red again.

We waited until nightfall.

⁓

When at last the city slept, Dr. Hermann drove yet another long, black car onto the dock. Our belongings would be shipped to our new house, but we proceeded to a dismal airstrip and climbed into a sixteen-seat plane: Uncle Wolf, Cecilia, Luba, Dietrich, and me. We sat in soft seats and ate candy bars. Dr. Hermann piloted the plane. Dietrich sat beside him. I wore long pants: white linen with cuffs, pleated, with a zipper instead of buttons at the fly.

"Now, Herr Baron. I'm following the river. We keep Manaus south of us. Poor Manaus, once so glorious. Our own town of O Linda reeks of poverty. No one wants rubber any longer, and we own the gold mines. Our estates—there are twenty of them—form a half circle from one point on the river, up into the hills, and down again to another point on the river. All the estates are connected with tunnels. We have bodyguards, small armies of trained Indian warriors, and river patrols. The town is in the middle. Your estate, Herr Baron, is of great interest. Willi had it built for the Fuehrer, and it had been waiting for him." He sighed. "We are delighted that you will occupy it. Still, it's very sad, is it not? He could have left, of course. We could have brought him out. Sad. He didn't need to die. None of us will ever understand."

"Hitler's dead?" I blurted out. No one responded.

There were no lights below and no lights above. No moon.

There was not a light below us, not a fire. No here, no there. No up, no down. The vomit of fear rose in my throat. No moon. I had always trusted the moon.

Dr. Hermann looked over his shoulder toward me. "Axel, in the daylight I will take you up in the airplane again and you can see the forest and the rivers. Do you like broccoli? The forest looks like hundreds of kilometers of broccoli. It goes on forever."

"Forever," Dietrich repeated. There was something despairing and final anchored in his voice. Dietrich cleared his throat. "So, Manfred, on behalf of myself and my brother and my family, thank you."

"Our honor, Herr Baron. Your house is almost ready for you. There is farming equipment waiting. Maria will run your house. Her relatives already work your fields. You have a gang of gauchos to run your buffalo herds. And a tribe of Indians to protect you in case there's an uprising. We've already planted acres of coffee for you. A major plantation. You are now to be a coffee baron." Dr. Hermann chuckled. "My little joke, not to offend. So, as soon as you feel settled, we will take you to O Linda. Our savings are stored in the basement of what looks like Willi's pawnshop. But it is much more. It is a safe place with a tunnel to the river. But, if there is a security issue we cannot handle, you understand, we will go to Willi's, through his basement, into the tunnel leading to the river. If necessary, we can even assemble there and barricade the tunnel until help comes. We also have an early warning system up the river. A Christian ministry. Pastor Ken and his wife, Kathy, befriend the tribes—then he tells us what they're up to. Husband and wife even teach some of them, convert a few, or so Pastor Ken thinks. We support him. So, you were able to bring money?"

"Diamonds."

"Oh, yes, of course. We'd arranged that for you. And there's plenty here for you. Excellent. Whatever we have, you know, it's yours as well. Actually, someday we hope that your boy and little Margaret, the daughter of our Willi…. We start our lives again with the children."

I sensed Dietrich immediately dismissing this proposal. This was not the kind of common blood he would choose for his progeny. "This is a good-sized plane, Manfred. What kind of landing facility do you have?"

"Actually, Mr. Ford built a fine concrete one for us when... when...." He choked and changed the subject. "We have a very effective cloud machine. We are well able to disguise our properties from the air. If need be."

"Who are we hiding from?"

"Americans, Jews, Nazi hunters. We can create and lift a cloud cover in five minutes or less. Excellent machine. In five minutes, we are virtually invisible."

I was sick to my stomach from too much candy. Luba was sniffling behind me. "I don't feel well," I said.

"Hush, *shluf*, Axel. We'll be there soon. Close your eyes."

Dr. Hermann went on. "The homes in the Occult Bureau Colony are in a horseshoe pattern. Magdalena and Karl— remember Karl? From Galicia? They have one end on the river. Your house is across from them, also on the river. My place is at the top of the horseshoe near the gold mines. There is an estate for you as well, Wolf. A fine house on excellent land, not far from your brother. There is plenty of rich floodplain for rice and water buffalo. Willi paid a provincial mayor someplace to remove O Linda from the maps. So, no schools, no priests, no outsiders. The boats no longer stop here. Actually, it is no town at all. We call it No Linda." Dr. Hermann laughed at his joke. Dietrich did not.

"Who teaches the children?"

"There is only Willi's Margaret and now yours. The others are sent away to schools and safehouses in Germany. The *Cabloco* children? 'Cabloco' means river people, mixed. Sometimes a matron, Doña Brianca, teaches them. We gave her a projector and movies so they can learn English. The river people have some kind of language, tribal, and some speak Portuguese and now some English. This Doña Brianca also preaches a little. If the townspeople want to, they can go downstream and go to market. But no one comes here. No mailboats, no cruise ships, nobody at all."

"And medical?"

"We fly to Rio. The river people use the chief, Okok. Tiny little fellow who heals with plants. People come from town and wait for him. They call him a *vegetalista*. I don't know what he does, but it seems to work. For them, not us. We fly out weekly for supplies. You must let me know what is needed. You will have your own plane. We've hired Grevaldo to fly you. He's from Venezuela, but he trained in Detroit in small engine repair. But no one goes anywhere unless Willi gives permission. There are people already looking for us. Do you wish to fly the plane now, Herr Baron?" He turned over his shoulder to me. "Your father is one of the finest pilots in Germany."

"Was," said Dietrich.

And then, because I could no longer contain my thoughts, I yelled over the noise of the engine. "My mother jumped overboard and killed herself."

Very evenly Dietrich said, "Quite enough, Axel, enough stories. Go back to sleep and let the grown-ups have their conversation."

Mama had disappeared from our lives and was not to be discussed. I was being urged to forget about her, but that wasn't possible.

Dr. Hermann turned to look back at me. Dietrich stood, took a seat next to me. Dr. Hermann, who continued to watch us, cleared his throat. "Well, this would interest you, Axel. You have your own Indian tribe living on your land."

"She killed herself," I insisted.

Dietrich squeezed my hand until I thought it would burst like a fruit. Finally, he spoke. "Well, now, Manfred, who does all the work?"

"The Indian men are fully armed warriors. And native women plant and provide their food. Some work in the fields. We've taught your tribe to repair batteries. We are always in need of batteries. The Cablocos—we bring them up from O Linda to work in the houses. I personally have *Kupis*, the fiercest of tribes. I need them to control my miners. They'll fight alongside your Indians if needed."

"Aside from Americans and Nazi hunters, what is such a danger here, Dr. Hermann, that you need armies?"

"Oh, the miners get drunk or crazy on drugs or just brawl because they're bored. We send whores up there, but sometimes they raid the town or try to take the Indian women on our land. And we have Commie organizers who try to get our workers to strike. Sometimes there's a shoot-out. Sometimes a forest Indian wanders near the borders. A forest Indian will kill for an empty soda can or steal your children. Rualdo is O Linda's police chief. Everyone fears him because he is a stupid kid who thinks he's Wyatt Earp and loves to shoot."

Luba yelled from the rear of the plane, "Would the forest Indians take Cecilia?"

"Dr. Hermann, you're scaring the children. Your stories are as distressing as Axel's."

"Of course. So sorry, Herr Baron. Actually, no one has ever been stolen. None of us has ever been shot. I didn't mean to frighten you, children. I want you to feel safe. We are here to make your lives safe. Please understand that. So, Herr Baron, do you yourself have any plans?"

Dietrich released my hand. "You would know that better than I, Manfred."

"Hitler would have loved this place. Don't you think so, Herr Baron?" Dietrich grunted, meaning nothing, which allowed Dr. Hermann to continue. "Remember when we were at the Berghof how the Fuehrer would go out at night and look up at the stars for hours?" As young as I was, I could hear deep sadness in his voice, an old man reminiscing of lost loves, of homeland, of the magic and power of Hitler.

"No, I do not remember."

"Oh, he did. It was after Hess betrayed him and flew to Glasgow. He'd lost his energy. But he'd look at the stars and then he'd burst back in where we were sitting, watching a movie, so many movies we had to watch. The Fuehrer would wake us up with a grand idea. A grand, mad idea—rockets to the stars, rockets to Sirius, spirits, ancestors, the hallowed earth, the spirits…just like the Indians around here."

"That's quite enough, Manfred. It's late and we are all extremely tired."

"Remember how he claimed he spoke with spirits, old gods, just like the Indians here, old warriors, old ancestors, emperors, and then he'd come in from watching his stars and announce a new project…like yours?"

"That's enough, Manfred!"

Under the whine of the engine, I could hear Uncle Wolf singing a marching song, beating his feet on the floor of the plane.

Broccoli sounded benign. The forest, the Indians, the police chief, and the miners did not. Luba sniffled behind me.

"Manfred," my father asked, "if one were to leave to go to Rio, for example, one needs Willi's permission?"

"Oh, yes. Willi will know when it's dangerous. We can't expose ourselves, of course."

"Are we then your prisoners as well?"

Laughter. "Don't be foolish, Herr Baron. What will imprison us are the Jewish spies. Not each other."

℘

At Dr. Hermann's darkened home, Luba carrying Cecilia, who was almost too big to carry—and certainly much too old to nurse—me following; we were led through a long hallway and tucked into one bedroom. Indian women came to help us undress and wash. We fought them off.

I heard Dietrich's laughter somewhere in the house.

Sitting on the edge of a bed, I watched Luba brush Cecilia's hair.

We slept in our clothes. Luba climbed into bed with me, and I lay there hoping that someday my poor little member would find its way, now that I had long pants and plenty of food. In the meantime, I buried my head between her breasts, and we cried on and off until falling asleep. Someone came during the night to lower the mosquito netting tied up over our heads.

Chapter Eight

That first morning, in Dr. Hermann's vast house, I lay disoriented under a cloud of netting in a great bed. And under a puffy cloud of white hair, Mrs. Dr. Hermann, which is what the servants called Dr. Hermann's wife, was talking to me, rubbing my hair, pinching my cheeks.

"Good morning, Young Baron. You wake up now and we will bring you a nice breakfast. Good boy. Your little sister is out taking a walk with your friend. They'll be back for lunch. Come now. There's so much to see. A new world for you. A good world. Come."

A tawny woman with a flat head, squinted eyes, and high cheekbones brought me hot chocolate and buns. I think she might have watched us through the night.

❧

Lunch was an elaborate undertaking on a porch with white furniture. We were in a grand house overlooking the Amazon, on a bluff with a patchwork of planting fields climbing the hills above us, with servants, horses, peacocks, and endless panoramas of coffee and fruit trees.

Dietrich and Uncle Wolf seemed too happy, too sociable among the many gathered. Dietrich wore a new white linen suit. I found him shockingly handsome and rugged. Uncle Wolf, surrounded by women, was even more astonishing and alluring than Dietrich, although both were pale and thin and angular in the company of these corpulent, ruddy Germans.

Luba remained silent. She would not speak with me nor meet my eyes. At that moment, I hated her. She looked like a clown in a wide dress of magenta flowers and blue birds pulled tight across her breasts. The fabric would have better upholstered a sofa.

On the porch, Mrs. Dr. Hermann told me she was a distant cousin of my mother's, descended also from the Hapsburgs, that her grandfather had been the gamekeeper for King Leopold of Austria, that she had been for a short time—she told me as she gave me a chocolate-drenched puff pastry—the chocolatier to the Fuehrer. She took me to the kitchen and showed me a green, glass bottle. In it, she said, was the water she washed her hands with after she shook his hand. "Now where is your mother, my cousin?"

I could only cover my anxieties with a shrug and run off.

Wandering outside, I saw an Indian with feathers on his head, a rifle in his hands. He smiled at me. His teeth were black and pointed. Earlier, I had watched a pig roasting outside on the patio, watched its mouth turn up in a smile as its skin tightened. It arrived at the table still smiling, carried by Indian women and surrounded by pineapple slices. I had never seen either Indians or pineapples in Germany.

Unfortunately, because of the amazingly humid climate and the ridiculous dress Luba had been forced into, the numbers on her pale, white arms were exposed. While seating us at the table and noticing this, Mrs. Dr. Hermann, hand to her mouth, eyes opened wide and round, very blue, muttered something about the sun and the mosquitoes, of which there were neither on the porch, sent a servant for a lace shawl, and sat Luba at the far end, away from us.

I could see that Luba was terrified. Her eyes were fiery opalescent gemstones under her plush black mane of curly hair. I didn't know how to help her with her pain. She was so beautiful. Her pain made her even more beautiful.

Dietrich requested a lemon for his tea. A small woman came from the kitchen in response to the ring of Mrs. Dr. Hermann's tinkling bell. The woman was dressed in a black-and-white ruffled maid's uniform with a wide skirt and a lacy apron. She wore long blonde braids that bounced on her breasts as she approached Dietrich. She laid the lemon on his saucer, bowed, turned.

Shocked at the sight of her, I dropped my fork. It clattered.

Everyone was staring at me but smiling at my dismay, for the woman was two women, or one woman with two tops and one bottom and four blonde braids and four arms. When one turned away, another woman looking exactly like her was facing me, smiling at the joke before curtseying to Dietrich.

I felt my face burn. Everyone watched me. Dietrich showed no surprise, but nothing surprised him. Dr. Hermann left his seat and stood behind me, his hands on my shoulders. He leaned down to me. "This is an experiment that failed. But not so bad. One bottom and two tops."

The deep voice of a man called Siegfried Putz called out, "Better than the two-headed sheep you came up with." He laughed. Mrs. Putz did not.

Dr. Hermann turned to Dietrich. His voice dropped but I could hear, "Double duty in the kitchen. She can wash dishes and cook at the same time. And double duty in the bedroom. Very naughty."

"I can imagine."

Unlike Dietrich, I could not imagine. She curtsied and turned, and the other of her curtsied again, giggling. Her other self looked at me over her shoulder, winking at the big joke.

I whispered to my father, "He made a two-headed sheep?"

Dietrich patted me hard on the shoulders. Too hard. I had moved into a dangerous emptiness and was to back away.

After the big and embarrassing joke on me, Dietrich, in measured tones, as if he had rehearsed this conversation, which well he might have, held forth to those gathered at the long table, mourning the loss of his wine cellar and poor Violet, his giraffe. He did not mention his wife, although, by the way I was coddled, I was certain everyone knew my mother was somehow lost. Dietrich had the undivided attention of everyone but me.

My eyes were fixed on the wall of the dining room where an enormous painting of a goddess and a swan commanded the room. Cold air from behind its heavy frame blew on my face. I'd seen copies of that painting in books in our home.

When Dietrich noticed that I was staring, he shook a warning finger at me, then went on with his recital. Talking much too fast, my father explained that Luba was the unfortunate daughter of intellectuals. "Philosophers," he declared, and everyone except Luba nodded with understanding. "From the university." He added the death blow: "Political."

They smiled sympathetically at Luba for having chosen her parents so poorly. "Bolsheviks," someone muttered. Which I understood to be somewhat more acceptable than Jewish because after that people did try to engage Luba in conversation although she only stared at her lunch with the same tight smile of the roasted pig.

Dietrich's new friends joked. Uncle Wolf became quiet.

He and Dietrich had been quarreling over the double doors of my grandfather's castle. Dietrich had offered him the Madonna, but Uncle Wolf refused; he wanted his half of the door. The conversation rose and fell. Cigars were lit. Luba was excused. She was escorted upstairs. She had eaten nothing.

Willi hit a crystal glass with his spoon. When he stood, I saw that he was wearing leopard skin high heels. I would see him later in a dress and a pink angora stole.

Dietrich leaned over to Dr. Hermann. "The shoes are very strange, yes?"

"Yes, Willi indulges his fantasies, but don't we all? Actually, acting queer has been a fine cover for Willi. Nazis, of course, don't tolerate queers, which would mean to the curious he was not a Nazi. The men you are about to meet, the scientists, live in a complex on the hill with their studies and labs. They don't...uh...often mingle with the rest of us."

Willi was waiting for a signal from Dr. Hermann, who nodded his head.

"Years ago, when I had hair—" cautious laughter greeted Willi's pronouncement "—we formed a shadow Colony here, a safe haven. We have been successful in protecting some of the genius of Germany, some of our bravest thinkers. Some Occult Bureau members have been here for years. Others have just arrived. Now that we are all together, we are ready to do our work. It is time for the real introductions." Willi tapped his wine glass. "Gentlemen, we will start with...uh...the mystic. You will stand and announce your line of work. No names, please. A salute is correct." He pointed his chin to a scarecrow of a man. "Fortune teller, you go first."

The man leapt from his chair, barked "*Sieg Heil*," and thrust his arm into the air. "My work isn't work. It is a gift. I am a...I am *the* mystic, the teller of fortunes." He folded his arm over his waist and bowed to Dietrich. He had wild, rolling eyes, a huge head of curling, stand-up red hair that appeared charged, as if electricity were pouring from within.

It seemed deliberate on the part of Mrs. Dr. Hermann to again and again destabilize this impromptu Occult Bureau meeting. Her staff constantly interrupted the speakers with dessert and coffee, then cream and sugar, then a plate of fruit and gold foil bonbons, all of which seemed to arrive as each of the speakers stood and thrust their arms into the air.

Mrs. Dr. Hermann led a line of kitchen help bearing flaming puddings, which they dished out in globs just as Willi called out, "Refrigeration."

The refrigeration expert shot from his seat, unwittingly interacting with a tray of flaming pudding, thus knocking a quivering bowl of lemon sauce from the tray of a waitress, who attempted to wipe it up as he spoke. "My area is human refrigeration experiments," the expert called out. Some at the table applauded. "For the space programs."

"And Decompression," Willi proudly added. "Now, World Astrology, please."

World Astrology bowed toward Dietrich. "How do you do, Herr Baron. World Astrology. Welcome to the Amazon."

"Race and Resettlement."

"Selective Breeding program and I run the washing machine factory." There were chuckles at the mention.

Dr. Hermann leaned over to Dietrich, whispered. "Genius. He designed the race-based weapon, based on genetics. We start with insecticides that can differentiate between moths and butterflies, for example. Brilliant, race-based."

"Personal Astrology, please." Sitting just near me, Personal Astrology was not what I would expect an astrologer would look like: slick dark hair, a perfectly trimmed mustache, urbane.

"What's a personal astrologer?" I dared asking him. "Would you explain the difference?"

"World Astrology does floods, earthquakes, asteroids. I do people. Destinies."

The waitresses returned with coffee. When Personal Astrology sat after his introduction, he upended a steaming pot of coffee and failed to foresee it painfully spilling down his back.

Propaganda and Enlightenment stood just as his dessert plate was placed in front of him and, as he leaned forward to speak, one hand went directly down into the volcanic pudding, which splashed on his pants. He was licking his fingers while speaking angrily of professors who had to be reeducated about prehistory, about the proven presence of Germans at the dawn of civilization.

Others, one by one, presented themselves. Just as "Hollow Earth and Subterranean Cities," introduced himself, he farted.

Dietrich laughed loudly.

The list went on. Department of Prehistory. Race and Selective Breeding. Meteorology. Ancestral Heritage. Propaganda and Enlightenment. Rune Master. World Ice. Perpetual Motion Machine.

Willi explained to Dietrich. "The time-travelling bell. One has gone to Russia, one to Pennsylvania. What could we do? We're building a new one. And, last but not least, Akashic Records, the ancient history of the universe. Learning to tap into the Akashic records will give us access to all that has happened and all that will happen." Someone stood, sat down.

Willi smiled at Dietrich. "So, Herr Baron, this is our talent. And you will share your field of research with us, please?"

My father said nothing. Willi tapped his wine glass, repeated. "Herr Baron? Your field of research?"

Dietrich stood, turned on his heel, took my arm, and we walked out.

Dr. Hermann followed in our wake, entreating us to stop. "Baron, Baron."

Dietrich continued a brisk stride although we had no place to go. "I will have nothing to do with these crackpots. You've turned science into séance. Madmen all!"

Dr. Hermann held him by the arm. "Baron, there is a thin line between genius and madness. I control that line. If one out of the dozen comes up with an idea that will change the world, it is not worth the trouble? Of course, it's a gamble, this shadow Occult Bureau of Willi's, which is why your work is so important. You are not a gamble. You are a sure thing. Come back and smoke a fine cigar, and then we will let you nap. You've had such a terrible experience. It's over now. It's over. You are safe. Tonight at dinner you will meet the leaders. Lunch was only the talent."

Dietrich turned and thrust his face into Dr. Hermann's. "I've met enough of your puppets. I will dine alone."

"Herr Baron, you can choose the friends you want or none at all. Trust me."

Dietrich shook him off. "You, Manfred Hermann, are the last person I would trust."

Dr. Hermann drew himself up, stopped following us, called to Dietrich's back. "What are your choices, Herr Baron?"

☙

Within days, we moved into Hitler's house. Half palace, half fortress, it was far too elaborate for a working plantation at the end of the world. It was grander and much larger than Dr. Hermann's home. Of course, it was smaller than our German home, more open, with porches and balconies everywhere. With a Bavarian heaviness, every piece of furniture in the great room was upholstered in the same hunting designs of deer, men on horses, forests: sofas, easy chairs, wing chairs, settees. Shuttered windows, jalousied windows, heavy drapes of the same upholstery fabric were all drawn and closed against the terrible sun. The three-story house rose high with roofs of red tile.

The home was hot and dark, with high ceilings, heavy oak beams, and an overwhelming African collection of taxidermist art, exotic and sad, an indulgence of stag horns. Colorful flags of German cities hung from the rafters of the great room—official banners, melancholy and proud—painted with gryphons, lions, stags, and castles. Wiesbaden, Dusseldorf, Mainz, Kiel, Esse, Lumberg.

Cartons of new clothing waited on our beds. I determined not to tell Luba that the house had been built for Hitler although he'd never been in it.

"As far as we know, he was never here," Dietrich had mused upon our arrival as we strolled the grounds. "But when did

Hermann's wife ever shake his hand, then? She's been here almost a decade. So many secrets…. She confided to me that she thinks her husband is poisoning her." He ran his hand over the stone walls near the entry. "Eighteen inches. This is a fortress. I thought we were safe. So why would we need walls like this?" He glanced at me and looked away.

Although he maintained his arrogance and his distance, Dietrich was also a puppet. But I was able to reassure myself; as Dr. Hermann had asked, what choice did he have? Are Nazi hunters in the Amazon rainforest as dangerous as Russians in the Black Forest?

My father read my thoughts. "Axel, we don't know what the future holds, but at least we have a future. I can do my work undisturbed. And what red-blooded boy wouldn't want the good fortune of growing up in the jungle? Such an adventure."

"What about Luba? She's so frightened."

"Luba is lucky to be alive. And so are we. The world turns, Axel. Politics change. Don't let this worry you." He threw his arm around my shoulder.

Our lawns ran down to the Amazon. The rainforest began behind Hitler's house. The machinery of its sounds was deafening, demanding—not at all like the soft whispers of our pine forest in Germany. Here monkeys and frogs and God-knows-what roared, howled, chattered, scraped, screamed, buzzed, burped, and farted through the night.

Dr. Hermann assured us that eventually we would become oblivious to the sounds. Three arched and elegant wrought-iron gates—flotsam from a Portuguese past—marked the entrance to our lands. An orange windsock, phallic, swelled and collapsed at the gates, which attached to nothing, simply stood there in the wilderness, an unkept promise. A long row of royal palms lined our driveway, which was long enough and wide enough to serve as a landing strip if need be. The path to the river was also lined with palm trees. We called it Palm Alley. Amazingly, the coat of arms doors from our German home were already installed into an immense entryway. The entryway was covered by a pergola that opened to a central courtyard with a fountain and a fig tree that could easily have been the oldest and largest in the world.

Dietrich, sucking on a juicy fig, joked, "Since this is Paradise, the tree must be Adam's tree." He dropped a handful of figs into my hand. "Here, take these to Luba."

Maria, our new housekeeper, her head no higher than my chest, sweet-faced, mostly Indian, braids down her back, stood with three young, swarthy girls who looked very much like her. Smiling, they watched us from the kitchen doors. These river women were hairy, with faint sideburns, braids down their backs, hairy legs and arms. Maria had astonishing cheeks, fat as a squirrel storing a winter's worth of nuts. Not fleshy fat but full, with a bow of a mouth and glittering brown eyes under a single fused eyebrow. One of the girls with Maria had the same full cheeks. It was her daughter, Maria, whom we would call Also Maria.

Maria and Also Maria would eventually come to know everything about us: Everything we did, didn't do, should do, shouldn't do, shouldn't have done, needed, didn't want.

Maria reached up to pat my head, then gave me a plate and a napkin to take with the figs to Luba. Shteinberg in a different skin.

Chapter Nine

Soon after our homecoming, Dietrich accepted Dr. Hermann's invitation to visit Willi in O Linda. Not, of course, because he wished to socialize with either Willi or Dr. Hermann, but he wanted to examine Willi's bunker and the layout of the bragged-about escape tunnel described by Dr. Hermann. Dietrich was already considering his options. I, of course, was thrilled to go on the river, to see the town of O Linda.

"O Linda will be a disappointment," Dr. Hermann warned us as we left our dock on his yacht, heading downriver.

"What does it look like?" I asked.

He spoke over my head to my father. "Have you ever seen an American cowboy movie? That's what it looks like. Almost a ghost town now. First the town grew prosperous. The money came from rubber, then gold, then oil, then us. This was a major rubber station, with a fine dock, a counting house for gold and rubber. Now the river's width at O Linda is five or six kilometers. It shifts, the banks shift. See over there? Cinnamon Island, because it smells like cinnamon."

As we passed, the island exploded with crocodiles, hundreds, thousands, alarmed at the noise of our engines. Dr. Hermann plowed right through them. "They nest here. The river people eat the eggs. It's a floating island, a grass island. It's been here since the thirties, just arrived one night and decided to stay. These islands come and go. Look." The island had trapped a dump of gigantic trees, old boats, siding, pipes, fish nets, balsa. "They sometimes find corpses there when collecting the crocodile eggs."

"Isn't that dangerous?" I tried to fill in my father's sullen silence.

Dr. Hermann shrugged. "They like the eggs. I tried them. Good only with ketchup. If it wasn't for ketchup, I'd be a vegetarian. I used to be. Hitler was, of course. Now here the channel on the far side of Cinnamon Island is deeper than the O Linda side, and we've seen to it that there's no reason for anyone to stop at O Linda, the river—there, here comes a riverboat. Watch. Listen, they shoot off rockets."

Three rockets whined, screamed, landed on the stretch of floodplain.

"Every boat shoots rockets off to honor their St. Benedict. O Linda was his home. Even though they have Christian churches, Old Benedict is a Black saint. Very pagan. The Catholics tried to dress him up and claim him. Didn't work. We'll stop here until the boat passes by. They don't need to know about us."

Dr. Hermann pulled his yacht into the foliage of the island, turned off his engine. Hidden as we were, I couldn't see the riverboat but heard its churning and steaming. I watched an army of crocodiles slither onto the island from the water. Some prodded our bow with their monstrous snapping jaws. The riverboat churned into the channel beyond Cinnamon Island. When it was out of sight or we were, Dr. Hermann pulled back into the river. At another area of trees and dense green, he steered the boat into a small slip, anchored, and again hid the boat.

We rolled up our pants, took off our shoes, and stepped into filthy water, walking toward O Linda's broken dock. Garbage floated beneath it, reeking of sulfur and urine.

A single potholed, muddy street led from the dock past two small, square, dilapidated churches, once painted blue. There was a three-story mansion in even worse shape than the dock, two reasonably modern cinderblock square buildings, as well as three old houses that once had been fine and ornate. Beyond the old houses, huddled at the eyebrow of the forest, were tin-roofed shanties. And beyond them, thatched huts, and beyond the huts, gardens of manioc and banana palms. Then, the forest wall.

On a sloping porch were three men, small, brown, flat-faced, foreshortened as if the Amazon had rolled over them, crushed them. Wearing only loose short pants, more like underwear, they stood listening to a soccer game from a radio broadcasting static and shouts, nodded at us, grunted. One rearranged his testicles, methodically coordinating with the announcer's shouts.

"They're Cablocos—river people of undetermined race," Dr. Hermann explained. "A few handfuls of mixed breeds still live here because there's no place for them to go. I've experimented on them." He shook his head apologetically. "Not a drop of Aryan blood, the lowest of the races. Now down over there by the river. To the left. That used to be the counting house. Fancy Greek pillars, from the rubber wealth. Now it's half a mule stable and half a convent for a bunch of rabbit-brained nuns and river bastards. You can still find gold dust under the feet of the mules. That cement block building on the left of the big building? That's Sheriff Rualdo's jail. You'll meet him. Rualdo has only one cell. If he has to arrest a second person, we think he kills the first one to make room. The big building is Mohammed's Hideaway, our bar and hotel, and that cement block structure to the right of the Hideaway is Queer Willi's Pawnshop, which we'll visit after we have a drink. And there you have No Linda." Dr. Hermann slung an arm around my shoulders and squeezed. "Does your father let you have beer yet? Maybe we celebrate."

Music and laughter floated from the Hideaway. A generator buzzed. Behind the Hideaway, like beacons, and perhaps they had been, the sun flashed on two towering pyramids of liquor bottles.

I followed Dietrich and Dr. Hermann into the Hideaway, sat on a stool in a cool and dark room with a silver chandelier hanging over the long bar. Sultry laughter of women drifted from above.

"Second floor for whores," Dr. Hermann said and went on with his history. "Americans came in the early thirties looking for oil, but they were massacred by the Indians. Then we took over. We'll meet Mohammed, and of course Rualdo, our psychopath sheriff, and Doña Brianca, who sometimes teaches the river kids, whose son Luis, our local Communist, I will someday murder. Brianca has an old gold harp in her sitting room—one of those mansions. Her great-something was an American colonel in their civil war, and he escaped here. Made a fortune. Her redheaded son, by the way, is a dead ringer for the Irish priest who left O Linda and eventually became a bishop in the Vatican. He supports the family.

Which explains that big generator in their backyard, a fine little boat, nice clothes. Brianca considers herself white. She used to be pretty good-looking."

My father looked up at the bar mirror, into Dr. Hermann's face. "You've spent a lot of time here, Manfred?"

"Back and forth. Mrs. Hermann's been here since '36. Of course, now....Everyone is related. They all look alike."

The Germans had clearly redecorated the barroom; three walls were filled with shelves of beer steins, plaques of little blonde girls tending sheep in the mountains, porcelain platters of our Black Forest, even one of my family's ruined fortress.

"Hey, Mohammed, company." Dr. Hermann banged a fist on the bar. Bottles shook and clinked. "This is Mohammed. He sleeps in that hammock above the bar with a couple of guns to protect his liquor bottles. The whores upstairs take care of him. They winch him up on pulleys at night. He pees into that beer keg below the hammock. Double woven on butcher hooks. Great contraption. When he wants to sleep, he pulls on a rope so his hammock swings."

Mohammed appeared through faded, black velvet drapes at the end of the bar wobbling on two canes, virtually crippled. As he worked his way toward us, Dr. Hermann dropped his voice. "Mohammed's the ears of the forest. He knows everything. Three hundred pounds on the stable scale behind the convent. Still the best trader up and down the river. Emeralds, slaves, diamonds. If you want emeralds, Herr Baron, this is where to get them."

Mohammed was huge, sensual, swarthy, Middle Eastern, avuncular, perspiring, smiling. Flesh hung, swung from his arms. Sweet-faced, bearded, heavy-lidded, with a nose curved inward toward his upper lip.

He leaned on the bar. Wearing a kaftan, stained and dirty, he smelled not unlike whatever floated beneath the dock. He dipped a heavily ringed hand into a large glass bottle and tossed a handful of olives into his mouth, leaning toward me. "So, Young Baron, look carefully at my nose. It's shaped like a number nine. Know why? It's an old desert nose. I'm an old Phoenician with an ancient nose so sand doesn't go up it." He barked out a laugh. As I was soon to learn, he laughed often and smiled always.

Dr. Hermann ordered three beers and asked Mohammed to send one of the pretty young women to find Sheriff Rualdo.

When she sprinted from the Hideaway, Dr. Hermann winked at me and said, "She's Chinese, God knows where she came from." She did not return.

A small native woman served us. She was as flat and foreshortened as our house servants. The beer was cold and delicious. Volker, our barn man, had given me beer, but it was never cold.

Willi came in from the light of the street, nodded at us. "No one can find the little shit Rualdo. Do you want to see the bunker now, Baron? I think Rualdo's sleeping it off someplace. Or screwing someone."

Dietrich looked to Dr. Hermann, returning to a previous discussion topic. "What happens during these uprisings you referred to, Manfred?"

He wiped the bar in front of him with his handkerchief, spoke in that thin and dreamy voice, "Oh, Indians get riled up, or drunken miners, Nazi hunters."

That got Dietrich's attention. "Nazi hunters? They've been here?"

"We're prepared. We've been prepared." He nodded to confirm the preparation to himself.

"Mohammed, if Rualdo shows up, send him over to Willi's."

Mohammed waved off Dr. Hermann's offer of money. "You come back here, Young Baron. Anytime, you come back. I have treasures to show you."

"Mohammed—" Dr. Hermann took him aside but not far enough. "If you ever hear of a half-white, half-Indian woman, that's what I'd like to do experiments on."

"Who wouldn't?" I heard Mohammed's laughter from the street.

At Queer Willi's Pawnshop, I followed as Dietrich strode past paltry shelves of dust-draped guitars, radios, record players, boots, belts, hats, watches.

A refrigerator door disguised an elevator to the lower level, which was filled with sandbags. With his hands clasped behind his back, Dietrich followed a narrow path between great masses of sandbags piled along the convex steel walls.

Willi was right behind him. "Mr. Ford was kind enough to build all this for the South American operation long before the war. Very sophisticated. That door leads to the convent. We go through the convent to the tunnel, right into the river." Willi pulled at my sleeve. "Have you ever been inside a submarine, Young Baron?" Young Baron would become my name.

I shook my head.

He grinned. "Well, you are in one now." Dietrich swiveled around in surprise.

Dr. Hermann caught up to us. "This is ingenious. Under the elevator is a rocket engine. Forward are steering and sea engines; below us, whatever a sea-going submarine needs. The whole thing is on tracks. They run through the convent and into a large, dredged area in the river. Is this not amazing, Herr Baron? If we ever need to escape."

"But if a rocket were used, wouldn't you blow up the town?" Dietrich patted the sides of the walls, which indeed were concave. "And the convent?"

"Well, it would only be a final, desperate measure."

"I see. And these bags?" He pointed. Piled against the walls were masses of burlap bags, some big, some small. "Do you have much flooding?" asked Dietrich.

"Flooding?" Dr. Hermann squinted his eyes in confusion, then laughed. "Dietrich, those are teeth from the camps."

"My God!" Dietrich said.

"Worth billions," Willi added proudly, taking a folded paper from his shirt pocket. "Maybe nine billion, at present count. We won't lose the next war." Willi gave Dr. Hermann a sly glance.

He smiled. "There won't be a next war. Now that we have the good Baron aboard."

"Of course." Willi went on. "We melt down the gold teeth when we need cash. Whatever you need."

It might have been at that moment, in the chill of the underground, under the sweating overhead piping of Willi's bunker, against the walls of hundreds of burlap bags, when at last I knew who these people were, who we were, who Dietrich was, and why they and we were hiding.

Willi smiled at Dietrich with that huge mouth full of teeth, too many for his mouth, and said, "Those over there came from the Pappendorf Foundries. Wait. There are other surprises." Willi pressed a button, pulled a lever. A steel door slid open at the end of the space we stood within. "And the tunnel? Isn't this impressive? You wish to—"

"We've seen enough." I realized Dietrich had become afraid of what else I might see or hear.

"That room is the communication room, worldwide."

"And the art collection," Dr. Hermann suggested. "Perhaps you'd like—"

"No, no, that's alright. It's becoming too cold down here."

❧

Back on the yacht, moving upriver, out of anyone's earshot, Dietrich said to me, "A man must do what a man must do. They died, Axel. What were we to do with their teeth? Orders." He turned away, and we watched the wake of Dr. Hermann's boat. "Don't be afraid, Axel. It's only a matter of time before we get out of here."

Dr. Hermann wiped sweat from his forehead and called out, "Why don't we stop at your village and take a look, meet your Indian tribe?" He put his arm around me. "I'll bet you'd like that: real Indians. Try not to make eye contact right away, as they are very shy." We docked at a clearing and walked a substantial wooden dock into the village. "Your house is just a half mile away from here. We built this additional dock for you. The big house right there is the men's house. It's the size of an airplane hangar. First we'll find Okok. He's the chief. And he gives permission to visit." Dr. Hermann shrugged. "Okok might be tiny, but he's as powerful as six men twice as large."

Pot-bellied naked children and ragged dogs raced away as we approached. "You see that woman over there by her hut?" said Dr. Hermann. "Negroid features. And next to her in the garden? Asian, particularly around the eyes. I've done work on their babies. Amazing assortment of inferior genes, the flotsam and jetsam of mankind. Nothing Aryan here at all."

The Indians here were even further foreshortened and flattened than the Cablocos we'd seen in O Linda. A pig snorted at us, charged, changed his mind, and labored after the children. Rows of thatched huts faced each other, each with a kitchen garden and a garbage pit. The men's house, the community center of the village, was a vast, shadowy, woven dome. Three young women in skirts and blouses held infants in their arms. They were villagers, *Riberinos*, not Indians.

"What are they doing here?" my father asked.

Dr. Hermann shrugged. "Okok heals everyone, villagers, other tribes up and down the river. They come here and wait, sometimes for days. He uses plants and chants." He winked at me. "That's pretty good, yes? Plants and chants."

We bent low and ducked through a small opening into a smoke-filled room.

My father and Dr. Hermann paused before a rack of long wooden pipes. "Musical instruments," Dr. Hermann said. "Don't touch." I had already seen a small, sturdy-looking man, wearing little more than a red beeswax cap, surrounded by the smoke, sitting by a central fire and reading a newspaper.

Upon seeing me, the man crumpled the paper and tossed it into the fire. There were other men in shadows. I did not understand until much later that Okok hid his ability to read.

"Okok," Dr. Hermann called out. "Visitors! The Baron and his son, the Young Baron."

The village chief, a knot of a man, earth-sprung, Okok, was all muscle, not even four feet tall, with a smooth and gentle but unsmiling Buddha face. He motioned that we should go out into the sunlight and fresh air.

There, obviously intrigued with Dietrich's cheek-to-jaw dueling scar, Okok ran his finger over his own cheek, drew the shape of the scar, trotted back into the men's house, trotted back with his own instant cheek-to-jaw scar painted in black dye, the same dimensions as my father's dueling scar.

Dietrich smiled, amused for a beat, then understood. With an elegant appreciation of Okok's silent language, my father bent down and touched Okok's cheek, demonstrating without a word their equality as warriors, as tribal brothers. From that moment on, there would never be any question of the loyalty of Okok and his warriors to Dietrich.

Okok shouted into the men's house. His warriors, heavily muscled, beautiful, gleaming, smooth-skinned, with long black hair cut to their shoulders, their bodies painted in vegetable dye, came out, preening in the sunlight. Whatever Okok said to them, they turned back into the men's house and emerged in moments with dueling scars painted on their cheeks.

Okok led us through the village. Imperious, majestic, towering above the Indians, a colossus among them, my father strode through the filigreed light of the rainforest into the village clearing. Women raced into their huts. Children ran toward me, touching and pulling at my clothing and blond hair, then dashed away, screaming with excitement.

Protecting me, Okok took my hand. His was strong but small, like a child's.

His Indians allowed me to wander in and out of their huts and thatched overhangs. I watched women and children grating manioc, frying cakes, scraping flesh from enormous turtle shells. I squatted next to a few women and young children restoring batteries.

Dr. Hermann explained, "Inferior races, frozen in time. Looks like a museum exhibit, doesn't it? The women won't look at us. Now this battery rebuilding is a simple and small business but necessary in these places where goods are scarce and the forest eats every-thing."

Okok released my hand, following me as I wandered, leading me now and then, blocking me now and then, explaining, choosing words carefully, even hesitantly, but well able to speak. He had, after all, been reading a newspaper, so the broken language he offered might have been a cover-up. He did not speak to Dr. Hermann or my father but rather held me aside and explained that I had to avoid the huts where the girls coming of age were in seclusion, where a husband whose wife was giving birth suffered her labor pains, where young warriors were isolated and tortured. We were mutually shy and curious.

When we left, he touched my hand. "Come back. Be our friend. I can teach you about our forest." It was a glorious invitation.

Chapter Ten

Deep in the rainforest, our stated goal was to discover the language of Babel, with which we would be able to hypnotize the world for the Fourth Reich. As hot as it was, I woke up every morning with fear in my blood coagulating into ice, my heart racing.

Dietrich set about to organize my life with three disciplines: remain fit, learn, and at all times remember who I was—as if at that stage, not even sixteen, I was anything but his reluctant cipher.

Now and then Dr. Hermann visited on horseback, drank coffees, examined our coffee fields, bit into a coffee bean here and there, told the terrible jokes he took from an American jokebook because he was, he assured us, going to take over. When he relocated to America, he wanted to sound like the real McCoy. "What do you call a fake noodle, Axel, my boy? An 'impasta.' Ho ho ho."

And then in his deceptively dreamy voice, Dr. Hermann would ask how Dietrich's work was going.

Dietrich, devil that he was, invariably answered in the same tone, "Four or five years, Manfred. You don't need an entire alphabet to give commands. A few letters will suffice to cast a spell, to hypnotize. Begin with our seed letters, the ancient letters, and place them within the commands. It will work subliminally."

The real joke, my father told me, would be when Dr. Hermann found out he couldn't hypnotize the world. We would play along until Dietrich found a way out or the avenging Jews found us.

One afternoon, with the servants taking their siestas, I found three men sitting in the sunroom. Beside Dr. Hermann was Graf, the wooly-haired, wild-eyed astrologer, and next to him a large, redheaded man, bearded, with pointed ears and a twinkle in his eye, a devilish elfin face.

Dr. Hermann stood when I came into the room. "No one answered our call. We came to see your father, but no one answers. Knock knock. Who's there? Spinach. Spinach who? Spin itching all day. Get it? But come, Young Baron, sit with us."

"I'll get my father." I sniffed. Dr. Hermann still used baby powder in his shoes. Wherever he walked, I saw dustings of it on our floors.

"No, no wait. You will remember our astrologer Graf. And let me introduce you to Horst, one of the leaders you met when you docked."

Redheaded Horst pumped and repumped my hand. "Special Projects."

I itched to run from the room.

Horst cleared his throat, flattened out a roll of blueprints on the piano top, found two heavy, silver cigarette lighters, positioned them to keep the blueprint flat. "Come, look. Someday you'll play a big part in this. We want you to understand."

The blueprints were detailed designs of a rocket ship. Running up the side of the paper was the word "Sirius" in proud, cursive flourishes.

I rang for Maria. Her eyes widened at the sight of these men. A teaspoon trembled in her hand. Her people knew how dangerous they were and of the work they were doing. "Maria, these gentlemen wish to see my father."

The three of them stood when Dietrich arrived in his bathrobe. "Yes? What can I do for you gentlemen?" He gave me a steady look, which meant he wanted me to stay.

"We've been admiring your well-mannered son. And he looks just like you, Germany's finest." Dr. Hermann, dreamy-voiced, motioned everyone to take a seat as if it were his home, not ours. Graf and Horst dropped like broken marionettes into their chairs. My father and Dr. Hermann remained standing.

"You know, Dietrich," Dr. Hermann opened, "you and von Braun have much in common."

"Is that the occasion for this visit?"

"Yes, as a matter of fact." Smiling, Dr. Hermann leaned forward. "You are both barons, both geniuses, both apolitical, although you, at least, didn't defect. Both of you are more interested in your own work than…than who you work for. And, also, you and the other baron tend to leave things behind."

Dietrich stiffened, tightened the belt of his bathrobe. "I burned everything in Kashmir. I'm a military man, Manfred. I was very careful. When I left Germany, I took everything else with me. You saw the boxes on the ship. But what is this about?"

"Sirius."

Dietrich leaned over the blueprint. "*Hah*. I had no idea. Sirius. Wernher and I spoke once. He wasn't interested in my work. Nor I in his."

Dr. Hermann stretched a finger out to my father's chest, not quite touching, but jabbing nevertheless in the air. "I believe you did have an idea. You knew about dark matter, about Sirius B." He nodded at Graf, who stood and recited almost to the word, certainly to the meaning of what I'd heard from the window seat so long ago, what Uncle Wolf had recited about the rocket ship.

"Sirius B." Graf spoke in a flat voice while studying the ceiling. "One of the stars in the constellation of Sirius. The Arabians called it *Wazn*, which meant it was very heavy. It weighed one thousand camels. A teaspoon of its matter weighs a ton. An African tribe, the Dogon, knew of its existence long before telescopes even though it is invisible except by telescope, which they did not have. The Africans say it is the star wisdom came from. Hitler told me it was the star the Aryans came from." He sat down.

Be still. My mother had spread the curtains of the window seat so long ago, her arms filled with Uncle Wolf's gardenias, and hissed. *You have heard nothing*.

My father knew about Sirius B, the Dogon. He had been lying to Dr. Hermann when he said he didn't.

Dr. Hermann unlocked a briefcase, pulled out a piece of crumpled paper torn from a lined notebook, laid it on the coffee table before my father. I remembered my mother tearing pages from his notebook, crumpling them, the pages swept away by a wind into the parade grounds next to our house. Dietrich's eyes narrowed; I felt ice water in my veins. He remembered as well.

"Let me read this to you, Dietrich. 'Serious is the same word as Sirius, and Sirius is a heavy star, heavy with gravity, dark matter, and a grave situation is a serious situation, and a grave is where the old gods go, the grave. Must follow s-i-r. Important. Look up the word 'grave' in Tamil.' Somehow you left this fragment of paper behind. And we found it."

"You were at my home?"

Dr. Hermann continued without answering, "If you didn't know our plans, how would you explain these notes, Dietrich?"

"Wordplay. This is how I work. I examine mutations of words. Resonances, resemblances. As if they were living creatures. These are very old words, ancient and original words."

"It is very interesting that both you and Wernher were so interested in Sirius."

"And Hitler," Graf interjected. "Sometimes that's all Hitler talked about. For days, he would talk on and on about Sirius."

"Thank you, Graf. So, Dietrich, this dark matter. It is not something we wish to be known."

"I talk to no one. How can I talk to anyone? I can't even mail a letter."

"Be cautious, Dietrich. Please focus on that, on *your* own work, not ours. Please continue with the alphabet."

As though he were a schoolboy with the correct answer, the astrologer waved his arms in the air.

"Graf, did you want to add something?" Dr. Hermann, annoyed, put his arm around him. This astrologer was a loose cannon.

Graf, agitated, faced Dietrich. "You are like a Ouija board, Baron von Pappendorf. Your mind. Whatever comes up, just comes up. He is a Ouija board." And then Graf grabbed the cigarette lighter from the piano, lit his hair on fire, and ran out of the room toward the river, hair flaming.

The blueprint rolled itself up.

"What can I do?" Dr. Hermann spread his arms, shaking his head sadly. "Dietrich, please send someone to see to him."

Horst fell into his chair, ran his fingers through the ringlets of red hair, shook his head. His curls danced. "War takes its toll. But poor Graf is invaluable. He invented the race-based powder.

Race-based, like insecticides. Kills beetles but leaves the butterflies. Great man, Graf. A genius."

My father and I could not look at each other, could not acknowledge this new horror. We watched as a pair of our gauchos galloped toward the river.

Dr. Hermann turned back to Dietrich. "Poor Graf. He is afraid to swim but he wants to swim. So he sets himself on fire, then he has to swim. By the way, you are not to leave unless Willi knows and has given you an escort." Again, he poked the air at my father's chest. "Our safety is fragile. You are my genius and countryman and I must protect you. In a sense, we are all prisoners of our destinies. Now I wish to examine your study."

"It isn't ready...I..."

Horst close behind, we followed Dr. Hermann up the stairs. He knew the house well. Clouds of powder puffed from his boots. In my father's study, he stepped over piles of paper, stacks of books, strewn notebooks, looking up, shaking his head. "*Gott im Himmel. Saustall.*"

Dietrich had rigged fans above, adding word fragments to their blades. Attached to these blades were colorful tentacles of yarn reaching towards each other, connecting words and languages.

In apparent awe, Dr. Hermann said to Horst, "This is where our words are born."

"It will take years," said Dietrich. "Straw into gold, Manfred."

"I see." He did not. "This is very exciting. Is Sirius up there?"

"Oh, yes, Manfred, front and center." Dietrich pointed with a broomstick to the SIR fan.

"I take it the Aryans were the first born, at the dawn of civilization?"

My father shrugged. "Well, someone must have been. We know that."

Dr. Hermann offered up his *Ho Ho Ho*. "Good man, Dietrich. I am very happy with your progress. You cut up all these little papers by yourself? Why didn't you tell me? We will order you whatever you need...labels, thread, wool. Anything. Horst, you will find out whatever is needed by the Baron."

ॐ

After they departed, the dripping becalmed mystic in tow, Dietrich strode in circles under his fans, his hands behind his back, smug, self-satisfied. "The more I tell him, the less he's able to understand. Last week he came to me about a question in English. He wanted to know why Americans say a car goes through a light? Why don't they say it goes under a light? Hermann plans to take over the state of Massachusetts, so he's very serious about his American English. And why is the yellow part of the egg the yolk but the white part is called the white? Hermann is strangled by his logic. I answer him in Mobius strips, around and around, have him skating in figure eights on thin ice, wondering where he's been with no idea as to where I'm really going. I overload him with information so he thinks he's getting his money's worth." Dietrich stopped pacing. "We're going to get out of here, Axel, believe me, on my terms."

"Papa, did you get a good look at the blueprints or was that a trick? Were they real?"

"Very real. I've seen them before. Von Braun worked with rockets. I worked with words. We were going to the same place. And your mother, may that stupid woman rest in peace, nearly ruined us with her page-ripping temper tantrum." He threw his head on his desk, covered it with his arms. I thought he might bang his head on his desk, but he did not.

"No one asked *me* to defect," he said bitterly. "The Americans wanted the rockets. They had no use for me. So von Braun lives in American luxury, protected, maybe even worshipped for his genius, famous. And I live here like this. I can tell no one of my discoveries, no one of our origins, no one. I should be lecturing all over the world, my boot on Darwin's neck. Gentlemen of the Royal Astronomical Society, this evening I will introduce to you information that will overturn everything you know: the origins of consciousness. Gentlemen, we have here…"

I felt deeply sorry for his frustration, for his dreams, grateful that he would share them with me. "It isn't fair, Papa."

"No, it isn't fair."

Dr. Hermann wasn't such a joke. My father was in danger. I had always seen my father as a fearless, strong, determined force to be reckoned, having a core of inner strength, but that view was changing.

I had to do something. I had to help. I had to write a letter to the Royal Society. If the honorable Baron von Pappendorf can lie, so can the Young Baron. Within a year, I would find a way to mail that letter. I would find wax to seal it. I would find my father's signet ring and would copy my father's signature. My hope was that the British would come and find us with a helicopter. They would whisk us from the jungle, and my father would live in luxury, protected, admired, famous.

Everything was simple when I was young, especially as I was younger than I should have been. Everything was possible. If I wanted something enough, it would happen.

Chapter Eleven

Declaring I was too weak, bemoaning my ignorance, my father intensified my regimen of physical and mental fitness. It was time for me to leave behind my effete childhood.

We ran barefoot on the floodplain along the river in an apricot fog as the sun rose over the Amazon. Frigid fog wrapped reality, shivering on the water's skin. My father had enormous endurance. A fine physical specimen, as usual, he ran ahead of me, arms pumping mechanically, shouting syllables at me, words, connections. As he was never behind, he did not see my growing braid. Thin and blond, the flag of resistance bounced on my neck in purposeful contrast to his cropped Teutonic cut.

I, breathlessly, repeated his shouts sentence by sentence. My chest ached. As I did too often, I fell behind.

Dietrich slowed down, not to allow me to breathe but to ascertain that I was still within hearing distance. I was expected to recite on the way home what he had told me on the way out, to make notes of what I heard when I returned, exhausted, home.

He surprised me this day by collapsing on the riverbank, head in his hands. He lamented that he was unable to sit in the Widener Library and read the Berossus fragments in the original. If only he could get his hands on the originals.

The Babylonians, the Egyptians, Sanskrit!

Lying beside him, splayed out on the floodplain, the sun struggling to break through the fog, I awaited his first morning lecture.

"Up, up, up, Axel." And again, we began running. His mind connected what seemed to be random concepts. Later, when I put them to paper, they would make sense.

"Take a note for the lecture file. Please entitle 'Opposites Attract.' Ready?

"Gentlemen, I propose that atoms are like tiny solar systems, and Sirius is an atom in another greater solar system. Little wonder Hitler wanted to go there, to get a piece of it. Imagine splitting *those* atoms. Proton and neutron. Resistance holds them together. This force must exist to support the opposites of Not and Is. Resistance between the two holds the universe together. There, Axel, soon our lecture file will be a fat one."

I was not happy. Nor was he. As my teenage years passed, the less happy we were and the more he disciplined himself and me.

ᘓ

That same day we ran past Okok and a young warrior. They carried armloads of plants, vines, and twigs. I stopped. My father ran on, lecturing all the while, fading into the early fog.

Okok laid his bundle down and took my hand, leading me to the river. My toes sunk into the sand. Gentle waves lapped at my feet.

"This river, *Barozhinoa*," he told me, "this river is not the Amazon. This river is the Solimeos. That is what we call it, and before Solomon came here to teach us, it was the Para. But those who listen call it Solimeos. You understand? Those who can hear. Someday you will have ears. You will hear and understand."

"Was Solomon here?" Was it possible the Israelite king who built the first temple at Jerusalem had travelled to the Amazon?

"He is still with us. We sing his chants, we heal with his plants."

"Solomon. My father would be so interested—"

"This is our secret, Barozhinoa, not his. And now your secret, yours."

Suddenly, my father was upon us. "Where the hell have you been?" He pulled me away by my arm, roughly. "I wasted all this time lecturing and you heard nothing. Nothing. Come."

My father regularly warned me to stay away from anyone who might endanger us, if not by intent simply by gossip. "The servants tell everything from household to household," he would say, "God knows how because they aren't to use the telephone system."

∽

At twilight, I saw the smoke of Okok's fire from our dock. I walked the beach and found him sitting by a fallen lighthouse tree, a tree stripped and brilliant white. He smiled and took my hand, patting the sand next to him.

"Young Baron, trust that you have ears to hear even that which is not said, and you will hear. Trust the forest." This was my introduction to the old language of the forest, the unspoken communication used by these native peoples. Okok spoke to me of his plants, which he treated as kindly as he did me. I loved hearing him sing to them. For a time he did not speak, but his presence remained sympathetic and calming. His hand patting the sand had been an invitation to another dimension, something ancient, what I would think of later as the heart of the forest magic.

On later visits, he would offer me a sip of that, a sip of this, a sniff, a taste of a leaf. I politely refused, not because I wasn't curious but because I didn't want my father to smell anything on my breath.

One night, when I was sixteen, Okok spoke again to me of Solomon. He gripped my hand and led me to the river's edge, water covering my boots. I heard the low music of the river and then actually saw the outlines of the golden fleet with proud prows, the waves lapping at their sides, bronze men shouting with joy.

I saw what Okok was seeing. I stepped from the water onto the bank, dizzy prows cutting through the fog. I heard shouts of discovery.

Okok nodded as if he knew what I was thinking, as if he saw clearly what I saw.

These regular talks of ours often ended with Okok suddenly standing. "The spirits of the plants speak to me. They are now ready. We must go. I will look for you again."

☙

At seventeen, my life changed yet again.

Walking upstairs at mid-day, Maria handed me a plate of food and asked me to take it to Luba, an unusual request. Was she ill? I knocked on Luba's door.

When she opened it, her eyes were red, her hair uncombed. She still wore her pajamas, which were printed with brown bears on a pink background. I recall those pajamas clearly because it would be the last I would see of her for a long time.

"I'm sick," she snapped as if it were my fault. She held an Eskimo Pie ice cream bar in one hand, grabbed the plate I carried with the other, and kicked the door shut. Luba stayed in her room most of that day and the next.

Then that night she appeared before me, standing over my bed.

"I am being sent away," she said. "I'm going to have a baby again, and he doesn't want to see it because I get so sick. It disturbs his work and his sleep. I'm going away until the baby is born."

I was shocked. "But you can't go, Luba!" I couldn't hold back my words. These days Luba and I spent less and less time together, but the knowledge that she was nearby sustained me.

"I'm three months pregnant, so I'll be gone at least another six months. He didn't say where I'm going. I don't know what's to become of me."

"I hate him."

"Don't be stupid, Axel. He holds our lives in his hands." She took my hand for a moment, then dropped it and left the room. The scent of coconut oil lingered.

I barely slept that night. When I came downstairs, Luba was gone. I wanted to attack Dietrich for hurting her, for sending her away, for touching her.

With Luba, I'd had a human connection. Other than Okok, I had no one to talk to. Without her presence, I felt bitterly lonely and lost. There was only my father, ever demanding, ever controlling: "Take a note, Axel. Take a note."

☙

Cecilia acted out the betrayal I felt. Seven years old, she still wanted to nurse. Maria brought in a wet nurse from the village, but Cecilia bit her breasts. It was not unusual for my little sister to hit and bite and scream.

In Luba's absence, I helped Maria force baby food into Cecilia's resistant mouth. My fingers were notched and nicked, scarred from our mealtime duels. Cecilia bit both Marias viciously. She wouldn't let them comb her hair. She found a purple blouse Luba had left behind and would wear only that. No one could get close enough to snatch it off her to wash it.

Maria took Cecilia to Okok, who, I was told, blew smoke into her nostrils, chanted, gave her a tea that Maria called magic tea. Cecilia, who had never grown normally, then agreed to eat baby food from jars.

She would never thrive. Even full-grown, she would always be a small person with narrow bones. And often mean of spirit. Visitors to our house ignored the wrath of the gloomy child, then cooed and gooed over my perfectly Aryan golden self, now in long pants and approaching adulthood.

ɣɔ

I eased the torment of Luba's absence with my imagination and my hand. I didn't know if my hand or my member would be calloused first. Or my mind. Whatever the external events, Dietrich continued his work. "Axel, where are you? I have a lecture. Og, gentlemen. Og."

I didn't think of him as a bad man or as a good man. He simply was not present, immunized from emotion by the logic of his work, by his obsession. Humbled by his intellect, I could not follow. When I tried, I was not stepping in his footsteps but on his toes. He could bear no competition. Utterly alone, my father struggled at the edge of tightening, enlightening circles, to Sirius, to an unknown universe.

He set about to educate me as his shadow. I translated hieroglyphics, ancient alphabets, scratchings, runes. If I leapt ahead in a lesson or an idea, he would burst out in fury or stomp out of the room. My lessons were fraught with dread. I would never be good enough. I didn't think he was teaching me so much as cloning himself so he would have someone to work with. I thought it was a selfish act. But everything he did was selfish.

"Alright, Axel," he would start, "Gentlemen, gentlemen, from serious to Sirius. Where to begin? It is as circular as the orbits. First, I must suggest the real Exodus was not from Egypt to Canaan but from Sirius to Earth. The desert they crossed was space, their spiral path unwinding the original egg of creation, the path of conscious-ness. Its path is still in the neck of the cello. That is its geometry: the seashell spiral neck of the cello, which gives forth the sound of the numbers of creation through the shape of a woman…the hole in the center of the instrument, under the bridge. *Pluck.* That word again, that oc. A fecundating word, if ever. Og, oc, uc, fuck, ugh, ouch. You will never look at a cello innocently again."

One night—three months after Luba's disappearance—Diet-rich banged on the jalousies of my room. He was on the balcony connecting our bedrooms. "*Naga* in Hindu and in Mayan means 'snake.' Write that down. How did the Hindu word get to South America? How did the South American word get to India? Come into my study and take notes. I'm ready to lecture."

"It's late—after midnight. I was sleeping."

"What if I forget this? You can sleep in the morning."

My father rubbed his hands together and addressed the Royal Society. I suppose if I could make believe I was kissing Luba, he could make believe he was at Oxford in a great room, wearing a gold chalice and a white robe, with an overhead projector and a long wand. That's what I saw. "Gentlemen, with reference to one-legged gods. Please recall Yahweh on the Masada coin with his snake foot…."

What finally alleviated some of Dietrich's anxiety about losing a thought, missing a connection, forgetting, God forbid, one of his Royal Society lectures, was the installation of five even larger ceiling fans in his study. He had me order cartons and cartons of white silk labels, marking pens and yarn.

When at last one morning Dr. Hermann called to report the cargo plane from Miami had arrived, we abandoned breakfast and raced to Dr. Hermann's airstrip.

Dietrich drove a transformed 1936 white Cadillac convertible. Civilization was creeping ever closer. After Dr. Hermann's Kupis had cleared a road through the forest, Dietrich acquired the clunky Cadillac and converted it into a *Gasogeno*: a vehicle fueled by charcoal. He had attached an old charcoal burner to the rear and pipes to the engine. I'm not certain it was his idea, this boiler on the rear end, but my father treated it as if he had invented it and was enormously proud of solving the problem of gasoline shortages and expense on the river. Unfortunately, it didn't work that well.

Dietrich was ecstatic on the drive. "Now the real work begins," he shouted over the engine of the car. Slamming his foot down on the gas pedal in his zeal to begin his life's work, we sped down jungle roads. His life's work would become my life's work. I would be labeling silk strips and tying his yarns into immense patterns forever. I shifted in my seat.

We drove onto Dr. Hermann's airstrip. The Miami plane was on the runway, unloading. Dietrich dug into my shoulder and held me until we parked in the shade of the plane's wing. Jubilant, he leapt out to claim his yarns, marking pens, and silks and, remarkably, Luba's Hebrew National kosher hot dogs and Eskimo Pie ice cream in dry ice.

"Are those for her? When is she coming back?"

He shrugged, ripped my heart out. "She ordered the ice cream and hot dogs before she left. I forgot to cancel the order." I got the impression that giving me pain gave him power.

ͼͽ

Alienated by Luba's absence, I felt increasingly disaffected with my father. One day in his study, I dared to announce to him, "I have a lecture. Will you listen?"

"To you?"

"I always listen to you."

"Do you mind if I do my push-ups while I listen?"

"Yes, very much."

"Alright then, lecture." And instead of push-ups, he lifted his fists to his chest, dancing around me, shadowboxing in my face. "Go on. Gentlemen…"

"Gentlemen, there are two languages." I wanted to punch him in the face but forced myself on as he circled and twirled and feinted and came too close, threatening. Uppercut, right hook, lunge, squat, hop. I so wanted to punch him; he wanted to shut me up. "One for the people and one for the kings. All the earth was one speech and one language. That makes two. Because the noble written alphabet came from the stars. Because the stars are fixed, and the orientation of the earth periodically reverses, every place read the stars and saw the same constellations, making up the same names and stories, making up the alphabet. The moon moved through the constellations and wrote the alphabet." I could hit him. I could trip him. I was on the roof and I was right. "And the clusters of letters and animals in the zodiac, like the letters K, L, and M, appear everywhere, the same zodiac. Because it all comes from the stars."

"That's it?" He dropped into a desk chair.

I was so angry I could barely breathe.

For my insolence, I was punished with the longest lecture he'd ever had me record for him. It was so long my mind and my hand were paralyzed, to say nothing of my heart. I hated him. I would understand much later in life that Dietrich despised me because what he had to struggle for word by word I understood without work, without walking his endless paths. *Snap.* Understood. Stars. I was the one with the Ouija Board.

I learned to avoid conflict by keeping my mouth shut. I was his shadow no more.

ౚ

His mind floated to the ceiling, his thoughts captured in the wools and silken labels on his fans.

A gleaming ironwood ladder was installed in his study, upon whose platform two iron German eagles served as grips. He rolled his ladder about the room, climbed it, arranging or rearranging the words and connections. "Seminal, Axel. These words inseminate each other, descend from each other." He would reach into his quivering wooly heaven, pluck a word, add a word, tie one word to another. When he touched one hanging word, the entire ceiling trembled. There were so many lengths of yarn and snippets of labels, one could barely see the dark beams of the ceiling.

I was often sent scrambling up the ladder to find a word, to add a word, to attach wool. I sat for hours with a large-eyed needle, sewing wool onto the labels before Dietrich marked them and I hung them into the trembling, quivering heaven of words.

"Go there, to the Egyptian fan. There is an ancient connection between the Egyptian and the Mayan. You see S, B, and K? Crocodile in both languages." Dietrich strode around the room, his head in some vast and distant arena, hands folded behind his back, vowels broadening into High English, voice deepening, even more pompous. "Lecture now, Axel. Sharpen your pencils."

"Dietrich, it's past lunchtime. That's four times Maria has rung the gongs. Can we please stop to eat lunch?" He was making progress, but I needed to eat.

"Lunch. Yes, lunch. Someday, Axel, I won't be lecturing in the wilderness to imbeciles." I was sure he meant me.

❦

The spiderweb of ceiling words grew denser, more intricate, more complex. Climbing the ladder, armed with his broomstick, he had me push him around the room under his ceiling of words, around and around, dizzy and crazy, spinning.

Sometimes I pushed him in large circles, sometimes in tight circles, sometimes in Mobius strips. He preferred to be pushed around on the ladder in the figure eight. "Stop! Go to Nox, *aah*. Nox. Add obnoxious. Now tox, toxic, all Og, Oc, ox, octave, eight, Oxford. All go back to Oc. Good. If Oc is the God, then not-Oc, noxious is the invisible power." Dietrich's mind must have resembled that ceiling: One clue burst into five more and each of them again produced more and more connections.

"It's alive, Axel. Language has the same reproductive structure as life. Reproduce, mutate, all of it. Look at that: ten words on purple silk. Hermann would give his eyeteeth for these. He'll never get them. He wants an alphabet. Oh, we'll give him one, but he won't know what to do with it. It will take Hermann's people years.

If ever. History is forgotten. Politics shapes lives. Friends become enemies, enemies friends. It will happen."

One day we heard Cecilia sniffling outside the door of Dietrich's study.

"Axel, send her away," said my father. "I can't think with that little cur around."

I was on the ladder, tying new words. "What do you want, Cissy?"

"Nothing," she mumbled through the door in her tiniest voice. Eight years old but she still acted like a baby.

"Then go away," Dietrich said.

I climbed down, opened the door, and took her small hand. "Do you want to come in?" I asked. The door locked behind me.

"I want to ride the ladder."

"Just don't let her touch anything," Dietrich said.

"I'll watch her."

I finished tying his words on fans as Cissy walked around his room, her hands stuck deep in her apron pockets. I did not like the way she was smiling. Watching her wander Dietrich's library, I realized there was nothing absentminded about her. There was something fanged about her smile. Her hands were safely in her pockets. Her face was unreadable.

"Now, ladies and gentleman, honorable colleagues," Dietrich continued. He bumped into Cissy. "What the hell are you doing here?"

"I came to get a ride on the ladder. Axel said I could."

"*Shh*, Cissy, he's lecturing." Cissy stood silently beside me, tugging my sleeve. "Okay, if you climb the ladder, I'll push you."

I helped her onto the ladder, held her hand while I gently pushed the ladder. "Now you point, and I'll push you in that direction." She sat on the platform, gripping the eagles as I rolled her around the room. Her eyes were wide. She pointed to the window, then to the central fan. I rolled her there. She looked up into the brain of words, the tethers and ties of language—indeed, of consciousness.

"Axel, I need these pencils sharpened," called Dietrich. "Mus, messiah, mistake, mess, music, mushroom, mister, sister, Ishtar, mystery, history, hiss...snake."

Volker, our barn man in Germany, always told me bad things happen in threes. If a cow died or a dog ate her puppies, I would wait in alarm for the next disaster. Interesting word: dis-aster, a problem in the stars. Luba's leaving was the first disaster. I braced myself for the second and third disasters. But perhaps things don't happen in threes; things just happen, and we think in threes because of the fairy tales we were raised with. And then and then and then.

The pencil sharpener was in a closet. When I came from the closet with a clutch of sharpened pencils, Cissy was on the ladder, blowing on and fingering the labels of the Mus fan, smiling her fanged smile as they fluttered.

Mus, muse, amuse, misdemeanor, mis, music.

My back turned, I heard Cecilia scratch a kitchen match against the grip of the eagle on the ladder and light the Mus fan on fire. It took me a beat too long to register that this was the second disaster. I smelled the sulfur of the matchstick and the smoke of the flames. And then. And then I heard Maria frantically ringing the breakfast gongs although it was well past morning.

And then.

Number three: Dr. Hermann was outside the study door, calling in: "Knock, knock, who's there? Spinach. *Gott im Himmel*. I smell smoke. *Ach du liebe*. Open the door!" The outside was locked. Volker may have been correct about threes: Luba, Cecilia, Dr. Hermann. And then.

Oblivious to Cecilia, Dietrich thought only of Dr. Hermann. "Hermann must not see the purple words." My father grabbed my arm, pointing above our heads to the ten purple words—his treasured originals. I hit the wall switch that turned on the rotating ceiling fans. This caused the fires to spread. It danced on the ceiling.

"Open the door, Baron. I said open—"

I opened the door for Dr. Hermann as the ceiling fans circled, flaming chandeliers above our heads, crackling.

I yelled, "Get water, Dr. Hermann! Get help."

He ran off, shouting for water. Cissy jumped off the ladder and fled the room while we stomped on the wriggling fire. Dietrich pissed on the burning labels. I followed suit.

He zipped up his pants and stood in front of his smoke-filled room, considered the scorched ceiling, the embers of red and white threads on the floor, curled like worms, said very clearly, "I will no longer put up with the intrusion of madness in my home!"

The pilot Grevaldo and two barn men arrived with buckets of water, Maria with a rolling pin and a pistol. My father's work was destroyed.

Dr. Hermann stomped up the stairs. "What about the words, Dietrich?"

When his answer came, his voice struggled for strength. "We begin again. I know the direction now. It should take less time." And he would say no more until Dr. Hermann left.

Soon after his departure, Cecilia came out of my bedroom, slid against the wall, and crept downstairs into Maria's arms.

"Twisted mind to match a twisted body!" Dietrich shouted after her from the doorway to his study. He turned to me. "She is as vindictive as her mother and as insane as Wolf. Occam's razor, Axel. Entities should not be multiplied unnecessarily."

"You care more about your words than your own child!"

He snapped to attention, walked to the window, swung around to me. "Cecilia is not my child. She is my brother's child. Wolf's child."

Cissy might have been Uncle Wolf's daughter, but she was of the same twisted cloth as Dietrich. A man who doesn't care is more dangerous than one who does.

My mother's curse pounded in my heart, in my heat: *Maybe you should remind yourself who your father really is, who you will become.*

The floor was carpeted with flickering ashes, and the beams and ceiling fans were stripped of his words. Dietrich stomped around the room. "We'll get this cleaned up straightaway and begin again. But you remember much of this, and you still have your notes, don't you? Go to your room and write down everything you remember. We will begin again in the morning. This time we can be more certain of our connections. Take the ruler back to Maria. Ruler." His face froze. "Solomon knew the measurements of the universe and built his temples accordingly. The ruler."

Nothing further was said about Cissy. I left the study as if I weren't in a hurry.

A few days later, kicking and screaming in an epic tantrum, my sister Cecilia was taken to the convent in O Linda, to tend to river orphans and be an orphan herself. Within weeks, Uncle Wolf accessed his Nazi riches and had the convent restored. Dietrich installed the Madonna on a new altar and paid for a dozen new mattresses.

Cecilia was, we hoped, happy, but I doubted it. Happiness was not in her.

∞

Later, as she grew, she sometimes came to visit our housekeeper Maria and Also Maria, still small-boned, thin, sullen, empty. I would find the Marias in the kitchen teaching Cecilia how to darn socks, how to knit, how to fine-stitch and crochet.

As the years passed, she began to look more and more like our mother: small, bird-like, intense, with blinking eyes. When she visited Maria, Cecilia would look up at me with a blank face. I left gifts for her: chocolate bars and hair ribbons for her braids. She took them but said nothing. Maria and Cecilia ate from a large wooden bowl filled with a slurry of tapioca and Pepsi-Cola. Cecilia wore strange, loose dresses and aprons sewed by someone in the convent. She became gnome-like and secretive. She was no longer like us, if she had ever been.

"Now Jesus loves her," Maria assured me.

We were sad, relieved, confused. We were safer away from each other. But I had no place to escape to. After Luba's disappearance, Cecilia's was even more disconcerting.

How I longed to find another self, a braver self. I envied Cecilia that at least she had escaped, that someone loved her, even if it was only the distant Jesus.

I wanted to find another self, or my own self. From my bedroom late at night, I heard Dietrich whistling Strauss and lecturing to the Royal Society. The wooly heaven of fans in his study would be reinstalled. Nothing troubled him.

Chapter Twelve

It had taken an unusually long time, but, from weak roots, I had sprouted into a tall exemplar of Aryan manhood. My father approved of the parts of me that resembled his younger self, but he hated my braid—now down to the small of my back.

At Willi's request, which could not be easily refused, once a week I dressed in white pants and a white shirt, climbed into the motorboat with Grevaldo, and headed downriver to O Linda to visit with Willi's daughter, Margaret. Willi—our erstwhile spymaster and with whom she lived; in some undefined way, her father—would send Margaret and me from his pawnshop to visit in the dark recesses of the Hideaway just next door.

Sometimes Mohammed asked us to sweep the floors or count liquor bottles. He told us tall tales of the forest. He stank of turtle oil. He ate countless fish fried in the stuff, as well as formidable amounts of olives from the great glass jar on the bar. Even though he offered me a handful, he himself was so dirty, I knew better than to eat any.

One melancholy day when Luba was still away, as Margaret counted bottles, Mohammed gave me a beer; then, instead of into the olive jar, he shoved his hand between my legs, squeezed, smiled. "Well, Young Baron, so now you are a big Baron. Manhood has arrived." He released my privates, leaned on the bar, "Listen to me. Stay away from your father's woman. Don't touch her. Don't go near her. You hear me?"

"I have no intention—"

"Of course you do. We all do. A prick has no conscience. You been laid yet?"

Mohammed unlocked for me the rigid barrier between past and present, between if/then and what if. He gave me a hunger for wonder. The world I had come to know in his dark rooms was a mysterious, remarkable world, awaiting discovery and understanding. The hunger that drew my father to his words drew me to Mohammed.

When the bar emptied that day, Mohammed locked the front door and led Margaret and me into his bedroom at the rear of the barroom. It was an exotic space of fringed hangings, rich carpets, velvet pillows, incense, and minor-keyed music on a gramophone.

On his knees, damp and stinking, in the hot little room, he opened one sea chest after another, with pride showing us ancient clay figurines, rough emeralds, diamonds, fistfuls of gold. The figurines had men's bodies, elongated skulls, and snake faces.

"I'm Mohammed the Phoenician, do not forget what I say. It's important to think *maybe*. It's important to think *what if*." While he spoke of the mysteries in his chests, I was thinking of Luba: maybe, what if.

Margaret and I helped him from the floor when he closed the chests. We steadied his massive bulk into his hammock, turned the winches, pulled the ropes until he swung above the bar. We took turns rocking him until he slept.

When he was sleeping, Margaret pulled me into Mohammed's room behind the curtains and kissed me. I was repulsed, took a beer by myself, rinsed my mouth, and spat her out. Margaret was as obsessed with me as I was with Luba, and for that I pitied her. She suffocated me. Love seemed a pain.

As much as I wanted to be within the wonder of Mohammed's, I finally refused to go. It made me feel too empty inside as we crawled around Mohammed's bedroom, Margaret stroking my hair, touching my face, asking me to tickle her places I considered dirty. She had her fantasies as I had mine.

෪

Had I been laid yet? Of course not. Finally, it was under the amused guidance of Grevaldo that I came of age, so to speak.

Grevaldo had a mousy wife and three young children. He was young, short, slick, muscular, almost as short as his shoulders were wide, and wore tight blue jeans. He strutted when he gave orders and constantly adjusted his testicles. We sometimes rode out, inspecting the field workers, the harvests, the machinery. He spoke with me as if I were an equal.

"The time has come. How about sex? This here is a condom."

I shrugged. I suspected sex was my next assignment and Grevaldo had been placed in charge, which made sense. Grevaldo oversaw insemination among the horses and the water buffalo. He had let me watch as he collected sperm from the male or received a steaming canister from a distant breeder. With a gloved arm, he thrust it—much like the salute I'd seen among Dietrich's friends— into the cow or mare.

Grevaldo took me to the Indian village and introduced me to sex in a hammock with a naked, giggling girl whose brown body was flat, squat, with fat calves, breasts too wide apart, eyes too close together. In the same hut, not inches away, a young mother lay in a hammock nestling a brown baby. Much of me wanted to be that baby, not the man I was to become. Nevertheless.

It was sudden and swift and world-shifting. I tried to make believe it was Luba beneath me. It wasn't. The next day I rode a horse down to the village, smiled at Okok, who smiled at me, accepted my box of Whitman's Sampler candy, held my hand, trotted beside me, took me to a thatched hut where the same girl waited.

The young mother in the other hammock smiled at me, hummed to her baby. I wondered if my mother had held me, hummed to me. Manhood drew me. Relief and pleasure were only a half mile down the road in the village. Each day I lingered longer in the hammock after my native uprising moments. Moments, plural. I was welcome, but also watched…carefully.

Eventually, audaciously, I took our pickup truck and parked it without shame on the dirt in front of the men's house. The girls giggled, circled me, pulled on my hands. I brought boxes of Nabisco

Sugar Wafers or Vanilla Wafers, took young boys for rides in the pickup, bouncing along the flatness of the floodplain, returned for a second hammock roll, drove home, changed, charged with pleasure, greedy for pleasure, hungry, so hungry.

Maria yelled at me for going to their village, but it didn't matter. I was almost a man. That is, if being a man meant thrusting my swollen self into the nether parts of a small stranger whose stunted body could barely accommodate my manhood.

I could not forget that night on the roof with Luba when she took my hand and pushed it between her legs. "This is the triangle, stupid. This is the trinity." My native uprisings did not rise to such a universal wonder. That little bang of ecstasy was not the Big Bang Luba had promised. It was not the universe. It was more like a rocket ship to nowhere.

❧

One day, Okok waited by my pickup truck, touching me lightly on the hand. "No more. No more here. Go to the girls in O Linda. These girls become the wives of our warriors. This is what white men do—not you. For me, you are not a white man." In my head, I heard him say, "Be like us, our brother."

In the furtherance of my enthusiastic education, Grevaldo, who never participated, invited me to drive into O Linda with him. We parked at the Hideaway, drank a beer. Mohammed winked at me but treated me as a customer. Grevaldo examined his watch again and again, then signaled that we leave. We walked to the floodplain. Two mahogany coffins were set upright to serve as trysting sites. There we waited for a Cabloco woman to arrive.

Grevaldo seemed so much older than I was, but there was only a six-year difference. "How do you know about this, Grevaldo?"

He smoked a cigarette. "Mike. Mike set it up."

"Mike?"

"Maria's son—the one who drives the field bus. He set it up."

Grevaldo was not alone in orchestrating my coming of age; Maria was also involved.

Having been introduced to this new and generous and far more responsive universe of grown women, night after night I waited within these purloined coffins on the floodplains. Grevaldo stood watch, smoking cigarettes by the river. The women drew lots, taking turns to satisfy my desires. Sometimes they'd fight for turns, a mother shoving a daughter out of the way.

"Our monkey boys, they giggle in the hammock, but, Senhor Axel," one whispered to me, "you are good. And so tall and pale and handsome." But none of these moments were significant. All I wanted was gone. All I wanted was Luba.

⁓

It had been much longer than six months when a mountain of gleaming pigskin luggage preceded Luba's return. Soon after, I was summoned to the sunroom and self-consciously stood before her, examining my fingernails.

Dietrich stood behind her. A huge new yellow diamond flashed on his ring finger, but I only had eyes for Luba.

She had a new face, straight hair, and a new body. She also had a new name. "I'm called Raven now," she told me, her eyes on the ceiling. Our eyes would not meet.

I had come bearing a gift: a candleholder like the one she had made for Hanukah long ago. "Here, Raven, for you." I did not question the new name but held the rough candelabra out to her. "Here, Shamash."

Raven threw her hands over her eyes, bursting into gut-wrenching sobs. "You are so stupid." Frowning my way, Dietrich led her upstairs to his bedroom.

No sooner had his bedroom door closed, then he was back at my side. "What is this thing? Shamash. What are you talking about?"

"She made something like this in Germany to celebrate Hanukah. Shteinberg beat her for stealing the candles. Luba said she wanted a party, so I was celebrating her coming home."

"But 'Shamash'—what do you mean?"

"The tall candle is Shamash, who lights the small candles. The small candles are the planets. He's the leader, *uh*, the watcher. But it's not something religious. It's not Jewish. She said it's older than being Jewish."

"The word 'Shamash' is synonymous with the constellation Sirius. You do know that?" I didn't. Maybe he'd already told me. The veins on his throat pounded, twitching. "Shamash was the god of the sun. I think Shamash was the father of the son God. Our sun was his son." He struck a match and lit the Shamash candle, then the shorter one next to it.

"What happened to Luba's baby, Dietrich?"

"Shamash means firstborn, Axel. It means Sirius." He had no interest in answering my questions. Instead he continued speaking, "I'll be damned. I'll bet our alphabet will really take us to Sirius. Hermann is going to be so excited. But then eventually he'll find that the trail does not lead back to Aryans but to…a certain kind of people who are the firstborn, indeed, the chosen, indeed, the Jews. First born on Earth, those who descended from the star. The star Sirius." He suddenly focused on me. For a time, he'd forgotten I was there. "It was kind of you to make this candleholder. I'll take it to her. Maybe she'll accept it."

With thumb and forefinger, Dietrich snuffed out the candles.

"We were married in Rio." He shook his head. "Shamash! Amazing! Now I will go upstairs and perform my wedding ceremony."

❧

Luba was Raven, the Baroness von Pappendorf. She was no longer my beautiful voluptuous Luba. She was thin and angular, still stunning but sharper. The cleft in her chin was removed, her nose was smaller, breasts smaller, body slender and muscular. I didn't know this could be done.

She fastidiously obeyed a personal calendar, wearing a different scent each day. Just by sniffing her as she arrived—Ishtar, descending in her state of perfection into the netherworld of the breakfast table, perfectly coifed and bejeweled—I would know the day of the week. Tuesday was lavender; Wednesday rose, and so on, daily.

Dietrich and I would sit at the table, drinking coffee, listening to her footsteps above us: back and forth from bedroom to bath as she prepared for her morning debut. I thought of her as she had been at the castle when we were young, when she wore the stiff, Jewish-starred pajamas of her slavehood, and I forgave her for the delay in preparing herself, now that she was the master. When she arrived at the table, with a few polite grunts, we all bent to eating.

It struck me that she didn't know who she was and had to define herself by odor, by clothes, by exterior. Narcissism indicated pride, but her beauty protocol didn't mean pride. It meant lack of identity, covering herself, not knowing her real self. Her bedroom was no longer the nursery. She slept in Dietrich's bed.

In a flash, she had become Mrs. Baron, a lady, haughty and unapproachable.

Luba, now very much Raven, would have nothing to do with me. Now that she was someone else, the daily anguish of loss became even more exquisitely painful than the months of emptiness when she had been gone. When she arrived downstairs, she made no attempt to speak with me and sometimes turned her back or closed her eyes when I addressed her. I was nearly invisible.

Maria took me aside one morning in the kitchen. "You must be kind to her, to this Raven. She lost a baby—maybe two. They were born dead. Sometimes you put two people together who shouldn't be together, they have not-so-good babies."

Given the nature of my mother and father's hatred for each other, I wondered if I were, as Cecilia had been, also a not-so-good baby, if something dreadful was wrong with me. I had more questions to ask Maria, but she shooed me and a bevy of recalcitrant chickens from the kitchen and busied herself, unreadable, peeling potatoes.

❧

The new Raven was, I would see by the way men watched her every movement, a great and seductive beauty. One day I heard her buying polo ponies from traders who came to sit on the porch, drink cold beer, and bow to her, the new Baroness who handled the money, the business of our estate.

Dietrich begged her to be pleasant to Dr. Hermann during his unannounced visits, as he was, after all, our host.

"Host?" she snapped at him. "He's our jailer." Where had she found this self-confidence?

Even so, at Dietrich's insistence, she descended one day to the sunroom, perching like a butterfly on a chair for a moment, lighting a cigarette and gazing into the distance. There would be no eye contact.

At her appearance, Dr. Hermann said, as if she were not there, "*Aah*, Dietrich, to have such a beautiful, fiery woman. I have a house frau, a good cook, a fine manager, fat and boring. Not like this woman of yours. Keeps you young, does she?"

Dietrich shrugged, dismissing Dr. Hermann's envy with a look at Raven. "Not, however, particularly good-natured."

She stubbed her cigarette into an ashtray. She enjoyed her power. Dr. Hermann turned to watch her undulating body as she left the room. We all lusted, everyone undressing her, a weapon herself.

Chapter Thirteen

Year in, year out, Raven limited our interactions. She didn't need me.

Despite the age difference, I'm sure Dietrich satisfied Raven. I could feel the sexual tension between them. Dietrich and Dr. Hermann, as they aged, boasted of strange things to keep their young wives happy. I had heard the two much older husbands joke about monkey glands.

Sometimes Dietrich would reach behind himself and, surprising Raven, pinch her just around her bellybutton. She would slap his hand lightly, giggle.

Soon after Raven's return, Mrs. Dr. Hermann, née Hitler's chocolatier, became ill and abruptly took her cloud of white hair to heaven. I recalled Dietrich telling me of her concerns that her husband had been poisoning her. Had Mrs. Dr. Hermann been correct?

Soon thereafter, there was a new and much younger Mrs. Dr. Hermann named Bebe. Bebe had long, dark hair and a beautiful rear end, firm enough, Grevaldo said to me, you could crack an egg on it.

❧

Raven was a poor sleeper. She had frightening dreams and dozed and then dreamed again. She told Maria her dreams, and Maria told me. In her dreams, Raven saw lines and lines of dead people in white gowns, slowly walking away. Some would turn and look back as if waiting for her. Some carried Jewish babies. Raven was afraid to sleep.

Secretly, so Dietrich wouldn't prevent it, Maria took Raven to Okok, who blew special smoke into Raven's nostrils and gave her good dreams but also a message from a living child who said she needed a name. Someone in the forest who was lost and living and had no name.

Maria said that Raven dreamed of this forest child and heard her voice but that it was friendly and soothing. A lot goes on in the forest. Spirits, ancestors, telepathy. Maria was upset, but Raven seemed to forget about it, or, at least, as in most other things, she didn't allow it to surface into reality. She slept better after Okok blew his smoke into her soul.

❧

Many times a day, Dietrich would brush past me, snap at me, wait impatiently as I opened one journal after the other, wrote carefully, my fingers squeezing the pen. He was driven and he drove me.

"You know what I imagine?" he said one day in his study. "I imagine when I give Hermann the original alphabet, he'll give it to the astrologer, and the astrologer will grow a little toothbrush mustache and become the next Hitler. Actually—" he gave me a strange look "—I think Hermann has his eye on *you* for that role." He laughed. I didn't think it was funny. "Alright, to work. Moses. Look at the syllable Mus. Moses as a serpent? Mus, mess, messiah, muse, music, *miskeit*, which means ugly in Hebrew. One can always trust the Hebrew. That story of Moses coming out of the bulrushes in a basket. Twisted. He was an amphibian, an ugly, an Ugh *carrying* a basket with civilization in it. Just as the other fish kings did, just as the Babylonian founding father, Oannaes, half-man, half-fish, carried a basket. Fuxi and NuGua, snake creators. Moses, Mus, messiah. Mos-Is. Snake of Is, of Ishtar who is Isis. Do you have that? Ugh. Reptiles. Tails. The Chinese founders had tails. I think that entire Exodus story is a code, a code for something else." We added Ugh to the ceiling fan. Our plan was to give them enough truth to confuse them, and certainly the letters would have no order.

One day, rain beat at our windows and rushed from the roof. The water buffalo had been driven up to the hills as the river was threatening. In his study, Dietrich was hunched over a thick, yellowed book, the Nazarean Codicil.

"Look at this, Axel. The word in Greek for HaShem is never—"I remember the word *never* hanging in the air because as I walked into Dietrich's study, a very large snake was hanging from a fan directly above his head, corkscrewing downward toward his shoulders.

It was a three-foot-long pit viper, as lethal as they come in this deadly jungle, and, before I could speak, it descended within a foot of his head, ready, I thought, to strike, death hanging over Dietrich's head, weaving destiny.

Never, not. Should I interrupt?

"Dietrich, very slowly roll your chair back toward me. Snake above you. Pit viper, move."

He started rolling and looked up, stopped. "*Ach du liebe*." He was scared. Dietrich hadn't spoken a word in German for years. "Axel, it's a sign from the gods."

"Dietrich, come on, for God's sake." My father was now enamored with the snake.

"*Ach*, Axel! Oc. In German, the name of the great god. On my tongue all my life. And I never realized...*Ach* is the name of God."

The snake rose in the air and explored the ceiling. Words on paper fluttered to the floor, onto Dietrich's shoulders. Dietrich shouted, "Oc. Oc!"

My legs filled with ice water. Blood rushed to my heart. I didn't think I could move, but I had to. Or did I have to? Perhaps it would be best to just stand still, give destiny her moment. It would be so easy. Allow the snake his wrath. My father dies. At twenty, I was old enough to marry his wife. So easy.

"Dietrich, roll over to me." I pushed the ladder toward him. The corkscrew movement lessened. The snake turned my way, thinking: Which one should I attack? "Now, Dietrich."

The snake snapped, lengthened, plunging poisonous fangs into the Nazarean Codicil, which fell heavily off the desk onto Dietrich's velvet mules.

"I daresay." Dietrich pushed off and rolled behind me.

I shoved the ladder against the snake and pinned it to the wall. I pulled Dietrich and the chair from the room, slammed the door, shouting to Maria to find Grevaldo and men with guns and hatchets.

Grevaldo and three gauchos ran past us, weapons ready, the swarthy pilot with a gunnysack and a hatchet. "Grevaldo, the head!" I called. "Its head stays alive over an hour and can bite even after it's cut off."

Dietrich looked back at me over his shoulder. "An hour, decapitated? You really are half savage, aren't you?"

&

It took two days for the rain to end. The river receded. The water buffalo herd thundered past our home and into their pens in the river.

As he did many evenings after dinner—long, silver cigarette holder, black satin smoking jacket, the velvet mules—Dietrich spread his emerald collection out on the dining room table and, absorbed, examined his precious gems with a jeweler's glass.

Raven slipped into a barn jacket, kissed Dietrich on the top of his head, and left.

I was certain she was meeting lusty Grevaldo. I imagined the entire episode in the hay. I worked up the courage to follow her. I was still the spy I'd been in the window seats.

She held a lantern. I followed its light into the barn where her horses were stabled. Standing deep in the shadows, I watched as she kissed each horse good night, told them to sleep tight, promised them they could play as soon as the sun rose. I heard a whinny. She cuddled her palomino's head as the other beasts snorted and whinnied. Raven's Violet.

"There you are, my darlings. Sleep tight." It was the palomino she loved.

&

I was looking for more—more of what I didn't know. One afternoon, I went to the Indian village and found Okok in the men's house, making arrows. I sat on the floor with him. He nodded, said nothing. For weeks that followed, Okok allowed me to sit by his side as he made arrows. He taught me sentences in Kupi that need not be uttered aloud. *How are you? I need meat. Where are you going?*

Then one day he passed me an unfinished arrow point and a large and stony scale from a fish. This was the first of many days he allowed me to work on the arrows. Time passed unnoticed as we sat together in great peace, sharpening the points.

One languid, humid day, Raven playing Mah-Jongg with her friends in the sunroom, Dietrich tying bits of words to his ceiling, I sat cross-legged in the great, smoky shadows of the men's house, under its vast, curving ceiling.

A fire burned sullenly in the center of the house. Its smoke rose to a small hole in the ceiling. Okok squatted across from me. We were shaping arrowheads. Finally, after watching me closely, he smiled a sly smile and took away my arrowhead.

"Look up, Young Baron," he said. "Look up to the sky hole. Watch how the smoke from our fire goes to the sky. This sky hole is our path to our ancestors. From this they watch us. From this, they watch you. They say it is time to give you a gift."

He stood, moved behind me, put his hands on my shoulders. I could feel his breath on my neck. He was breathing with excitement. I knew something important to him was about to happen to me. He slid a necklace over my head: a stone hung on a strand of gut. The stone felt cool on my chest, flat and cool and smooth. I felt Okok's small hands fumble with the gut, tie it securely, tight, double. I shivered at his touch. Then he stroked my braid.

"You are a beautiful man, Young Baron, a giant. Beautiful. You are a friend. You will be a great warrior. This stone, Young Baron, is for hunting, to bring you much meat. But you do not hunt for meat. With this stone, you will hunt for your heart." He held onto my braid a brief moment longer, as if reluctant to release it. Then he came around me and squatted before me. He grinned.

"First, you must find your heart. Then you will be ready to go into the forest. Find your courage, then go. Trust the forest. You will need this stone for courage and good luck. If on the way, a tapir comes to you and offers herself to you, well, then you will share her fine meat with us, your people."

"Are you my people?" I asked, astonished.

He smiled his sly smile again and did not answer.

I stroked the stone, cupped it in my hand. "Thank you."

"Not me, Young Baron." He pointed to the sky hole. "Them."

"Them," I repeated. I repeated breathlessly because I felt exactly the same wonder as I had felt on the roof in Germany watching the stars, reading the moon.

છ૭

I spent as much time as I could with Okok, then with the young warriors.

At first, the warriors had laughed at me because I wore my boots and my shorts. I finally learned to leave my boots behind, thus avoiding blisters and mold. It took longer to divest myself and my privates of my shorts. At last, I was offered a fringed breech cloth, which, to everyone's great amusement, was far too short.

I often saw tiny Okok wrestle the largest and strongest of his warriors to the ground. He taught me to wrestle, to shoot an arrow, to skin a peccary.

The young warriors invited me to wrestle. Though I was larger, they were stronger and quicker. Kindhearted, they sometimes let me win. Fighting was friendship. We swam in pools, in the river.

It took months before the warriors invited me to walk naked with them into the forest, to hunt with them, and, finally, one night they invited me to dance with them.

Okok painted me. He rubbed *genitap*, black and tarry, on my chest, my back, my belly, and told me he was painting the song of my soul on me. And then the warriors, shouting, drew me into the square before the men's house and invited me to dance.

Our feet pounding the ground, our hearts pounding in the same rhythms, the barriers between us were loosened, and we were, on the dust of the ground, as one, connected by the beat as I had never connected with any being before. I collapsed upon daylight.

I wore the paint under my clothing and prayed Dietrich would never see my Indian soul. As long as I completed my studies with

Dietrich, wrote in his journals, read the books he assigned, finished the research he demanded, my time was my own. I was learning to be an Indian. Distanced from my blood, I was motherless, even fatherless—an orphan.

"No, Young Baron," Okok sympathized. "You are the son of the jungle. You and Okok."

I grew to love Okok deeply. He'd stretch his arms for me to lift him up, and we'd walk into the forest or along the river, and he'd tell me his truths—never a lie, never a deception, never an exaggeration. I learned that my truths were not his truths, but that they were both truths.

Chapter Fourteen

I did not think of Dietrich as a war criminal. As years passed in the jungle, there was more news of the outside world. I knew, for example, that the Jews now had their own country. With this link to civilization came more knowledge of the past, no longer actively hidden from me. I believed then that war was war and there had been atrocities, and, as Dietrich had pointed out to my mother just before we left Germany, if Germany had won, he'd be a hero with an Iron Cross. But we lost.

I remembered him lying on top of me, bombs crashing around us as we were escaping, and that he said, "I am not like other men." He certainly was not like the men we knew in O Linda, neither the mad scientists nor the portly, pork-faced, bejowled leaders we briefly saw at parties. And certainly, if one added our own elevated ancestry, I was content in the belief that my father was not like other men. He would tell me of archeology digs looking for Rosetta stones, codices of lost languages, the heat in the desert, sandstorms, and adventures on camelback.

One day after siesta, Dietrich told me to get dressed to go into O Linda for a meeting at the Hideaway. It was late afternoon, and banks of clouds boiled over the river. The sun gripped the horizon, blazed low through the palm trees.

Mercedes lined our driveway. Their drivers swam in our pool. Their owners played Mah-Jongg with Raven in the sunroom, drinking margaritas and chattering of men and shoes.

We were taking the undependable Gasogeno into the forest because, I was certain, Dietrich preferred the challenge. And I think this particular evening, he needed the flamboyance of the Gasogeno because he suspected what his hosts were planning at the Hideaway.

Grevaldo's men filled milk cans with charcoal and piled the cans in the back seat over blankets. We had a case of Coca-Cola and baskets of bananas and bread with us, as well as blankets, flares, and guns. O Linda was thirty kilometers away and, in 1952, we still had to take a logging road through the forest. It was a filthy trip, but even so I had been instructed to wear a clean white shirt and long linen pants. Dietrich, who wore the same, also flaunted a neck scarf printed with American flags: his joke. We both covered ourselves with dusters.

He rarely went to town and certainly not in the evening because animals prowled the road to town after dark. And Dietrich also infrequently wore a clean shirt and linen pants. He preferred to be seen by the Cablocos as a hardworking rancher rather than the gentleman, scholar, nobleman he was.

Something was wrong. I sensed it in the muscles around Dietrich's mouth. There was a threat to be addressed, and perhaps, now that I had reached my majority, he wanted his son by his side.

Stopping in the village, Indians surrounded the car. Everyone wanted a ride to town. Since we might need strong pushers, I chose two husky young warriors I knew well and, of course, Okok, who enjoyed any car ride.

He rode on the hood of the Gasogeno, clutching the Cadillac's hood ornament: a silver woman with a rocket ship body, which I'm certain was one of the reasons why Dietrich was attracted to the vehicle. How little Okok didn't bounce off I will never know. Since our trip was downhill in daylight, there were few delays.

Lining the road on each side were deep, dark ditches filled with caiman and python, anaconda, unfriendly Indians, and devils. We could not afford to break down in the open car. We urinated into a hole Dietrich had drilled into the floorboards. Now and then we made swift pit stops as the Indians removed a log in the road or refilled the charcoal.

When we finally reached the edge of the town, Dietrich and I slipped off our dusters, directed the Indians to line the milk cans up on the side of the road so we wouldn't rattle as we arrived.

Okok yelled at Cabloco children surrounding the car, "No touch, no touch!" He shot his rifle above their heads.

In front of the Hideaway hotel, two drunken miners were unsuccessfully trying to fuck an uncooperative donkey. Women stood on their broken porches to see the Baron and his golden son. I was hot with embarrassment.

Rail-thin, a shadow of himself, Uncle Wolf stood in the road, waiting for us. Dietrich and he shook hands, muttering something to each other.

Uncle Wolf shook my hand as if I were now one of the men. His skin was yellow. So were his eyes. "How's the heir to the throne, Venerable Nephew?" He didn't wait for an answer but headed inside.

Lights went on next door in Queer Willi's Pawnshop. I ignored Margaret as she called out my name.

Dietrich motioned me to sit in the back of the Hideaway's dark, timbered meeting room. "My brother is now an alcoholic," he said, "and he probably has malaria. He squandered his heritage, the purity of his blood, his nobility. Polluted. Take a good look." I could not.

One wall toward the back, mostly unlit, was covered with glass. I'd never looked closely at it before. Behind framed glass, tacked onto a faded and singed American flag, were hides painted with circles and triangles, the same designs I had been painted with by the warriors when I was invited to dance: These were the songs of their souls.

I stiffened. Were these hides of men?

And then, because there was nothing more to do with the thrust of this realization, trembling, I traced the songs on the hides into my own chest, silently singing songs of souls of warriors who screamed as white men skinned them. And as I sang their songs, I heard their screams, wires pulled through my veins. In my head were their songs even as Dietrich called me forward to stand beside him. I had to grasp the edge of the table I was so weakened by my horror.

In my mind's eye, I had seen what happened. The Indians burned a flag. So they were skinned. Revenge.

Here and now, a dozen men, including Dr. Hermann and the astrologer Graf, were drinking beer from their own personal steins and trying to teach a green parrot named Helen "*Ach du liebe.*"

Helen the parrot screeched, "*Ach, ach.*" My father smiled at me: our secret word, discovered when the pit viper nearly did him in.

The men guffawed and let Helen the parrot drink beer.

Mohammed shuffled over to us on his two canes, put one down to shake Dietrich's unwilling hand, then mine.

Redheaded Horst threw his arm around Mohammed's shoulder. "This man is a Jew, Axel. You have never seen a Jew? They are very rare now. Mostly in landfills. Aren't you a Jew, Mohammed?"

Some of the men laughed, Mohammed loudest of all. "On my mother's side. If my father had three dollars more, I would have been a Christian," he explained to me. "Just a joke, kid. You know I'm a Phoenician." There was more laughter.

Dietrich leaned over and whispered that Mohammed was saying his mother was a whore and that Jewish whores were cheaper than Christian whores, which, he added, was probably untrue or extremely rare. "For example, Raven is the most expensive woman I've ever known."

Mohammed winked at me. "Hey, Baraozinho, give me a hand with this pitcher. Save me some steps, yes?" I carried a pitcher of beer over to the club. Dr. Hermann rubbed my hair, messing it. That annoyed me. I was six feet tall.

One of Dr. Hermann's colleagues pulled me away, sticking his finger into my chest. "Some handsome son the Baron has. Oh, how Hitler would have loved him. Now this is breeding. This is selection. This is our goal. The size of him, the muscles, the blue of his eyes. Look at him. But the braid. Get rid of the braid, son. It's a woman's foolishness. You are even better looking than your father, Young Baron. Already a lot bigger."

At the roar of a pickup truck outside the bar, Dr. Hermann leapt from his chair to the door. There were gunshots. Dr. Hermann turned back to the group. "Two of my miners were down here, dead drunk, messing with a mule. Now dead, thank you very much."

There were murmurs of admiration.

Dr. Hermann cleared his throat. "All right, gentlemen, back to business."

Uncle Wolf sat slightly away from the others. Willi, thin-lipped and narrow eyed, had moved toward the back and was reading a newspaper. He wouldn't be involved in what was coming. Dr. Hermann had Mohammed take Helen the parrot back behind the bar. Then, with his little fat hand, he smoothed a wax-sealed, weather-beaten envelope on the scarred table.

The envelope. I froze. I recognized it.

"We have given you your privacy for all these years, Dietrich, and allowed you to work without interruption. Everyone has been patient and supportive. But now…" With a gesture of his other hand, Dr. Hermann invited Dietrich to sit beside him at the table.

Dietrich refused. He looked confused. "You confiscated my mail?"

"We haven't opened it." Dr. Hermann displayed the intact wax seal. This was my letter, sent many years ago to the Royal Astronomical Society, somehow returned, somehow found. I was para-lyzed with fear. What had I done?

"Our friends in Para were kind enough to send it to me. What would you tell us about it, Dietrich?"

Dr. Hermann should have addressed him as Baron. This was intimate, lacking in respect.

Dietrich was ramrod stiff. My blood was ice. My chair wobbled under my shaking. The screams of the skinned Indians were still in my gut.

"It is a letter to the Royal Astronomical Society. Within it…" This was my letter. Even though five years had passed since I'd written it, I realized that I'd made a grave error trying to send it. It had been intercepted. Oh, God. I felt like a child again. Dietrich grabbed it from the table, cracked the wax seal with his teeth and tore open the envelope as if he could rip its heart out. "Within it is…and I shall share it with you. 'Your excellencies…'" He looked at me. I held my head in my hands, covered my eyes. "It has come to my attention that Brazil holds the key to an ancient Mediter-ranean-New World connection, a Mideast weapons monopoly. I have in my possession a particular emerald stone with deeply incised early Semitic letters on it. This stone was found layers deep in a gold mine. I believe…'" His voice cracked. He stuttered, then caught himself. What had I done to my father? "Sea kings," he mumbled. "The same men who named Para named the Euphrates and Ophir, the gold. This was the secret Paradise. King Solomon was here." He glanced over to me.

I could not meet his eyes. My limbs went limp and cold.

Dr. Hermann stood, leaned forward, his knuckles on the table. "You have more letters? If you have more letters in the alphabet of Babel, they are ours."

"Just scratchings," Dietrich lied, "symbols, nothing conclusive, not letters."

"By sending such a letter, you subject all of us to scrutiny we cannot afford. Need I say more?"

Without looking up, Milos, an electrical engineer from Peenemünde, said, "Endangering our safety, our dream, our anonymity. We have sacrificed so much to live here without…" He left the idea unfinished, muttered: "You, more than most of us."

There was a sympathetic nodding of heads and a silence then among the creaking of bedsprings above our heads. All these men were guilty of acts the world had deemed criminal; all of us were criminals in hiding.

Dr. Hermann stood at Dietrich's side. "Calling attention to us is too dangerous. We understand you have other information you wish to share with the world. But that will have to wait until we have our letters. Do you understand, Dietrich?"

My uncle pulled a chair out from the table for Dietrich. From behind the bar, Helen shrieked, "*Ach, ach!*"

Dietrich sank into the chair. I leaned up against the hides, tracing their designs with my fingers, shrieking within myself. I supposed the oilmen who had built the bar had done this. Dietrich put his head between his hands, then lifted it, accepted the beer Dr. Hermann offered. Finally, he said, "I am sorry."

Dr. Hermann "patted" my father's hand. "Dietrich, why don't you read the rest of the letter to us? Tell us, Dietrich."

"Semites were here. There is a current in the Atlantic that moves from North Africa to Brazil, something of a conveyor belt. A river in the ocean. Sea kings crossed the Atlantic on the ocean currents."

"Sea kings," Dr. Hermann repeated and looked around the table. Clearly, he was being patronizing. He didn't believe Dietrich. "Imagine!"

"Jews?" Milos questioned.

"Semites, Hittites. Phoenicians, Northwestern—"

Horst threw his stein to the floor, shattering it. Beer foamed onto the palm boards and spread out. "Jews!"

I stood by Dietrich. He raised his arm and held my hand. I dropped my hand onto his shoulder. He squeezed my hand as if drawing courage from me. He stood and took a deep breath. He wiped his eyes with the cuff of his white shirt, then he let them have it. This was Dietrich, the Baron, the great grandnephew of an emperor.

"Ignorant peasants!" he shouted. "You will not take my dreams!" He grabbed me by the arm, swept the pieces of the letter into his pocket, and pulled me out the door.

❧

Dietrich sat silent and rigid in the driver's seat of the Gasogeno as our men pushed the car out of town in the torpid night heat, out to the road home. He ignited the charcoal and at last, after numerous pneumatic attempts, started the car and reloaded the milk cans. In moments, we were deep in the forest, our designated pushers riding joyfully on the running boards, screaming with laughter when a wheel hit a rut and tossed them off. Dietrich never slowed down. They ran alongside and hopped aboard.

"I am so sorry, Father. I did something so stupid. It was a long time ago. I was a kid. I only wanted to help."

"You're still a kid. When will you ever grow up? And the road to hell is paved with good intentions."

"I was trying to—"

"Enough. Whoever mailed that letter for you knows we want to escape. I have told you time and again that you are to tell no one, involve no one, trust no one in our work. Ever. Until we have proof, tell no one of Solomon."

"But Okok says there are relics of Solomon up and down the river. Why don't we—?"

"We'll find our own. You nearly had us killed when you sent that letter. Do you understand?"

"Yes, it was foolish. But if we could find relics of the Jews' King Solomon—proof that he really was here in the Amazon. Then you go to the Israelis and trade that monumental piece of Jewish scholarship for amnesty."

That quieted him for a time. The car hit another bump; Okok screamed and nearly tumbled off. "You may have stumbled into something resembling a good plan," my father said, eyes remaining straight ahead on the road. "Of course, but no one else can be involved. For God's sake, Axel. This is not a boy's game. We can trust no one. I can't even trust you."

Dr. Hermann's friends and the departed American oilmen had made Indian skins into wall hangings. There was much in Dietrich that was like these other men who skinned human beings. I reminded myself that Dietrich's mind was at the edge of the universe, alone in his intellect. He remained necessarily at a distance from others: without pity, but not evil, unless being without pity is evil.

The car's engine faltered, wheezed, coughed, sputtered, stopped. Dietrich and I took off our clothes and climbed out to push. We did not take off our boots for fear of snakes crossing from one bottomless ditch to the other. I remember the silver shining of the Gasogeno, Dietrich's flat ass white, pale in the night, the deep, strange, embryonic crack of his center, distant and alien from me, even more so now that I'd put his life in danger.

Rather than look on his nakedness, I imagined him dressed in the suit of armor from my grandfather's castle, that heroic metal no longer rusted, and thought of Dietrich in another century—a more appropriate one—on horseback, the huge melancholic mustache, the burning blue eyes, the deeply cut dueling scar, the flat skull, the flat little ears, the thick neck, the wide shoulders, the narrow hips, slashing pitilessly at the infidels in Wagnerian fury, the blood of the emperors raging within him. I watched him on his horse, his sword slicing and gashing, his great head without helmet, his neck thick with fury and pounding with the soul of the Aryan race.

My stupidity had nearly done him in.

The Gasogeno struggled uphill, died, coughed, resurrected. Unnatural lights flickered in the trees: imagined eyes, beings, the *bopes* or spirits of the Indians, cannibal Indians, white-hater Indians, witch doctor Indians, head-shrinker Indians. The moon, then many moons, winked behind the trees as we moved.

Dietrich jerked his chin to the front of the car, handing Okok the rifle. I wondered why, at that point, Okok simply didn't shoot Dietrich and run into the forest. Okok did not know he could do such a thing as turn on this naked god of a man. Nor did I. Okok climbed on the hood and shot happily upwards into the night sky. A snake stretched across the road.

"Goddamn it! You! *Untermensch*!" Dietrich shouted at Okok. "Get off the car and watch the road, not the sky. One more snake..." He shook his rifle at him.

Okok slid off the hood and took up watch in front of the car. "Snakes in sky too."

"One more snake, Okok, I shoot you. You understand?" Dietrich shot into the air over his head. It didn't matter that Okok had a rifle. Monkeys screamed and chattered, filling the night. "Hear that, Axel?" my father said. "The smaller the creature, the louder the noise. Remember that."

He stopped pushing the car, and it rolled backwards. I leapt out of the way and wondered if it were intentional. But no, Dietrich had just vanished into himself. I was no longer present.

The men pushed the Gasogeno. Okok shot imaginary snakes, heavenly and otherwise. The road flattened. We poured more charcoal in the burner and climbed into the car. The Indians took their places on the running board. Okok shouted. We stopped the car again.

A large snake was crossing from ditch to ditch, her body completely stretching the width of the road: a small anaconda, six feet, eight feet, no more. Plants grew on her back. Some had pale yellow blossoms.

Without thinking, I shouted to Okok in his native tongue. "Be careful, Okok."

Dietrich swung around, sneered. "What did you say? You know their language?"

"A few words."

His face closed. "I am not bringing you up to be a savage."

"Didn't you? To live among men like those at the Hideaway? Aren't you the savages?"

He swung about, his face stone. "You dare accuse me. A man does what he must. I've told you that. So, my Judas son. How did you mail it?"

"I met a cruise ship and gave it to a crew member to mail."

Dietrich cleared his throat and spat into the night.

With pointed sticks, the Indians pushed the snake toward an empty milk can Dietrich provided. The Indians laughed. Dietrich laughed. Was I forgiven or forgotten? I wondered what happened to the donkey at the hotel.

The snake caught the sticks, tried to wrap around them. Then, thinking the milk can to be a dark hiding place, just as we had thought Brazil would be, allowed herself to be prodded into the can, thinking she was safe.

The men, chattering, shouting with excitement, dropped the cover over it. The can, too quiet, as if calculating, sat in the back seat with the other milk cans, and the Indians, much to their delight, were allowed to sit on top of the milk cans until we arrived at their village. I don't know what they did with the snake, but Dietrich allowed them to keep it.

Chapter Fifteen

Just as my father withdrew further into his study with his phonetic fossils, as my twenties progressed, I withdrew into the forest. Okok became my master; his warriors, my brothers. I would find him trotting beside me, smiling, watching, directing me into the forest to this plant, to this vine, to this tree, to this snake, to this fear.

Those first years of going barefoot took courage, my stomach was in knots, my chest frozen. Eventually I walked with my warrior friends in the very pulp of creation, naked and barefoot.

On one such excursion, when I could go no further, Okok sat me by an anthill, then took his place beside me, and for the next few hours, sitting perfectly still, we watched the ants' determined comings and goings. "In the forest," he told me, finally, "there is a little spider who is always frightened. Always, like you. And here she comes. The enemies of all spiders are the ants. So when this little spider finds a dead ant to eat, he pulls it over his back. I've watched him on the forest floor. Sometimes he drops the carcass and goes about his business, but he always returns to it, picks it up. He hides beneath it to confound his enemies, the ants. The spider's fear is his burden. This is what I wished to tell you: Drop your father's carcass, Young Baron. Remove the black ant. Become yourself. Oh, poor, brave Baroazinho, your father is your carcass."

A brilliantly colored black-and-red spider scurried over his hand, then dropped to the ground. I watched as it somehow managed to pull the body of a dead ant over her back before disappearing into the brush. "Your father is your dead ant. You

cover yourself with him. You hide under him. You must get rid of
the dead ant, get rid of your fears, be who you must be. Now you
are ready to become a warrior among warriors. Next moon you
will come into the forest with us, with the warriors, and we will
teach you."

⌾

When Okok introduced me to the brotherhood of the vine, I had
to quell both my fear and intellect. On this day, thick with heat
and moisture, I carried Okok on my shoulders. The forest changed
under our feet as we went deeper into it. Everything, vine, root,
leaf, became something other than what they were at the moment.
As I did. Noises that leaped around and within me, strangled me,
were finally silenced by the forest as it entered me. Rain came
from every leaf, from another time. I could hear a deep breath,
the terrible black and velvet breath, that of beauty and danger and
death, the song of the rainforest. My blood sang with it. A snake
danced before my feet, painted her name on the floor, raised her
head and looked into my eyes. Roots of trees as thick as ten men
arched over our heads.

  We walked from dawn to dusk. When the forest dimmed,
thousands of birds swarmed above, shrieking, cackling, calling as
they roosted in the trees. Day was over. The termite hills gave off
faint lights. We rubbed the salve of night vision into our eyes and
dragged ourselves on. Finally, at dark, when we could go no further,
we lit a fire, ate handfuls of manioc.

  Okok placed his hands on my shoulders. "Young Baron, you
will be fine. I am with you. Only when dark comes will you see the
stars. Now we go to see the stars."

  He stirred a vile liquid in a stone pot, nodding happily, swaying
back and forth, singing to the mix, singing, he said, the songs of
Solomon. Who was I to question? Other young warriors eyed me
carefully, curiously. I trembled with fear. No one else did. They were
ready for danger; they were ready for dreams. I was not.

  "Look and watch, I bring to you a vision of the condor," said
Okok. "See the condor, Barozhinoa? This is an ancestor, not a

condor. She chatters. It means she loves you. Pay attention." He turned from me to the others. "Now we will go to the pink crystal city on flying saucers."

Flying saucers, my intellect interfered and questioned. Would Solomon know of flying saucers?

"Stop thinking, Young Baron. Listen." Okok tugged my ears. "Have ears, listen." He passed a bowl to each of us. "Ayyn, Ayyn, let the visions begin." Okok stood watch as we drank his ayahuasca, the drink of the vine.

After we had retched, shat, emptied ourselves of everything except the vine, Okok waved branches over us and chanted *icaros*, magic songs, as we dreamed, the warriors and me, our feet touching as we travelled to kingdoms and stars on spaceships, for that was where the ayahuasca vine took us.

My first night of ayahuasca, I travelled with them to the star Sirius. We left behind our bodies, crossed the Great Gate, and became spirit. At times we stood at the river's edge and watched Solomon's graceful ships sail past; we visited cities real and unreal, there was no difference.

What astonished me about the drinking of the vine was that all of us—no matter who we were, what our blood was—had the same dream, orchestrated by Okok's icaros leading us into other dimensions.

A breeze picked up. I returned, remembering, changed. Arrows of light cut the night into pieces and served it up to the trees. I heard the pain of a howler monkey that had lost its mother. His mother screamed, and his howl shrunk as he flew to her through the trees. I remembered my mother's ghost whisper, "Wolf, Wolf, where are you?" Something feathery danced across my foot, exploring.

Night slept longer in the forest. Our dream over, the lights of the spaceships faded, failed, becoming the lights of termite hills, which then disappeared into morning fog. We returned to the dimension of matter. The warriors stirred. The trees dripped night water onto our fire. It hissed as it died.

By my mid-twenties, I was fully accepted by both Okok and his warriors. The secret initiation rituals were challenging and torturous. I lived two lives. In one, I was an Indian in the forest; in the other, a self-indulgent playboy.

☙

With Willi's approval, I took a mistress in Rio: an unremarkable but pleasant Ukrainian woman who seemed to know Willi quite well. I saw other women in the city too, many of whom looked faintly like Raven when she had been Luba.

Each month Dietrich and I journeyed to Chile, had dinner at the La Familia Restaurant where the waiters—who looked very much like myself—showed Dietrich great respect. On these trips, while Dietrich sat in meetings with dark-browed men, I dallied with waitresses.

I turned down numerous invitations to visit and stay in what, from the physique and discipline of the waiters, seemed to be a warrior training camp for young Nazis.

Admired and desired and mired in the doldrums of pleasure, I dreamed the old dreams of leaving, but there was no place to go. If not for Raven and the promise I made to the ghost of my mother to care for Dietrich, I would have left. However, if I were to race cars from Paris to Dakar or sail a catamaran from California to Mexico, I would—given that I had become a larger version of my dashing father—be recognized. I would draw Nazi hunters home to Dietrich.

And if I were to marry, would I have not-so-good babies with Dietrich's genes? Maybe this was a good enough reason for putting off life.

☙

For the most part, the forest had been quiet since we'd arrived, no burnings, no kidnappings, no murders. What happened within the tribes was their business. The settlers, our Colony, and the miners were safe. But as oilmen and lumber titans advanced deeper into tribal lands, there were increasing reports of mayhem: the murder of a missionary couple and their children, babies stolen, the burning of farmers' houses, killing of rubber tappers, nut gatherers, an oil rig operator, a road engineer. The Colony began to fortify itself against the forest.

Dietrich ordered Okok and his best warriors to guard our house from the roof. And so at dusk every night, Okok and his men, two and three at a time, ran up the latticework and vines, up to the balconies, to the roof where they sat with hunter's paste on their eyes to give them extraordinary vision. From this roof perch, they watched the river, the woods, the gullies, the driveway. Dietrich purchased four large searchlights for each corner of the house, but the warriors insisted their hunter's paste was enough.

Okok knotted a rope ladder for me so I could climb to the roof with him. The warriors, with their oddly opposed big toes, could climb anything: vines, latticework, drainpipes. I sat with them, taking turns walking the roof line.

When I was off watch, I sometimes stayed on the roof and slept under the stars, my back against the largest of two sleeping warriors so I wouldn't roll off. On my back I dreamed boyhood dreams and read the moon. The stars were different below the equator, but the same moon of my childhood still moved through them. Thousands of birds roosted at twilight, then through the night came a cacophony of frogs, a scream here, there, too close, far away.

Only once did Okok's warriors spot a war canoe moving swiftly past our dock. We shot guns into the air. They moved on, but they could have stopped. They could just as easily have landed, shot fiery arrows into our windows, set our house on fire, and murdered us as we ran out.

❧

As I learned more about World War II, World War III raged in our house. There were great and electric tensions between Raven and Dietrich, tensions I dreamed would eventually separate them and throw Raven into my arms. One evening I heard Raven shouting and weeping from the sunroom, and I ran down to find her in tantrum state, throwing things at Dietrich. Luba, with all her demons, still existed, deeply buried. And Raven, for all her airs and acts and power, was still driven by Luba. Raven was vulnerable.

Dietrich stood before her, hands spread, not knowing what to do. "I thought you would..." he stammered, a crack in his armor.

"It's red, Dietrich. The shmata is red. Shmata, shmata!" She pulled it from the box and threw it at Dietrich. "Don't you understand? What do you want from me? What do you want?"

Maria held me back. "Your papa sent for dresses, beautiful dresses," she told me. "Grevaldo brings them back to the house. Mrs. Baron opens the box. She throws it to the floor. Look at your father's face. It is white."

On the floor in a pile was a red-and-white houndstooth coat-dress with gold buttons, epaulettes, and a luxurious red chiffon scarf. Lifting it from the floor, Dietrich spread his arms, said apologetically, "I ordered it from Paris for you. It's very fine, Raven. For the races, when we go to the races in Argentina. You'll look wonderful in it."

"I don't wear red," she shouted at him. "You know that. If I wear red I'll fall down." She held herself. She was quaking. The terror that she lived with, that she'd known. "What will become of me? Where will I go? Keep your shmata, Dietrich. Keep it!"

I remembered her, on the roof, watching the war in the sky, shouting.

Dietrich grabbed her arm, twisted her toward himself. "What is that word? Shmata. What is it?"

Raven looked, at that moment of exposure, two-dimensional, paper-faced, something startling and burning and terrified in her eyes. "Take your hands off me."

"Just tell me what *shmata* means."

"It means *rag*!"

He released her. Raven, exposed, weak, vulnerable, took a step back. Dietrich folded the dress and its stole, placed them carefully back into the shipping box, passed it to Maria. No one looked at each other; nothing was said. Then Dietrich put his arms around Raven. "That's all right, Raven, you don't have to wear it. We'll keep it. Maybe someday you'll like it." He turned to me. "Please look up the origin of the word 'shmata', Axel. It sounds original."

For a brief second, Dietrich had been present as a human being. "Raven, my dear. Look in the bottom of the box."

"No."

"Yes, look. It's alright. You can look."

Raven pulled out a tiara, a queen's ransom tiara. Very gently, Dietrich placed it on her head. "There, isn't that nice? Go look in the mirror. You are the Queen of the Amazon. Go look at yourself, how lovely you look."

She did. She was able to. She had become Raven again. Entitled, manipulative, greedy.

Later I said to her, "Raven, is that why you don't wear red? Because you have no courage?"

Very lightly she touched the top of my hand with her forefinger.

"I am afraid to wear red because they will find me. I am afraid. We wore yellow. Yellow stars." I had no idea how deeply she'd been damaged.

"I know how to get up on the roof here," I told her. "Come up with me. Come dream and count the stars with me. Come, Raven."

Her eyes softened. She managed to smile. "That's crazy."

"I could help you climb."

"Oh, Axel." And then she shoved the tiara on her head and ran upstairs to look, I was certain, in a better mirror.

"Axel, the word shmata, please. Axel!" Dietrich yelled.

"It's Yiddish. An insult to the old gods. Shmataii means two rags. The early meaning was two goddesses of the constellations Sirius, sisters. Isis was the goddess of retribution as in nemesis. Isis's sister was the dark goddess, Nepthys, the dark star who is Sirius C, orbiting, the invisible star orbiting around Sirius. Two sisters, two rags, rag as insult. Shmata. Two sisters, two rags.

"Shma equals Sirius. Equals Sirius. That's an indisputable connection. Schma, HaShem, Shamash. Shomah means soul, doesn't it? Sirius, where souls go." He shook his head. "What an astonishing letter. HaShem takes us back to Sirius, takes us back to the Jews. Poor Hermann. He made a terrible bargain. He's not going to find Aryans at the dawn of civilization. He's going to find something resembling Jews. Serves him right."

Chapter Sixteen

Headlines trickled in: Physicist Albert Einstein turned down the job of president of Israel, West Germany joined NATO, Stalin was replaced by Khrushchev. Wars were smaller but not over. Meanwhile, hidden in the jungle, the people we lived among had parties all the time, celebrating even as there was nothing to celebrate.

Party-givers Magdalena and Karl Meyer lived in a ridiculous, orange-stone gingerbread house. Aside from its spectacular dock, one of the house's distinguishing features was a large, glittery mirrored ball that Magdalena had acquired from a Manaus dancehall. Hundreds of small mirrors reflected the deep unhappiness below as the ball swung in the river breeze, looming over the Colony's heads in multiple fragmented magnifying reflections of the pain of exile, the shame, the pride, the ambition, hope, hopelessness, fury, and fear. One night I overheard host Karl Meyer, a man I barely knew, tell another, "Maybe five hundred thousand. Some I killed personally...."

Karl Meyer grew pineapples and hops and brewed beer in his basement. We learned about the beer that evening because there was a deep-throated explosion just before dessert.

The man who had killed half a million somethings leapt from the table and ran to a kitchen door.

Magdalena ran after him. "Karl, Karl!"

All the men drew their pistols until Magdalena explained her husband's beer barrels were exploding.

I told myself he had killed half a million snakes in his hop fields.

When he was introduced to me again later that night, Karl was sweat-soaked and excessively cordial. Four or five more barrels had blown throughout the evening, and everyone was able to cheer and laugh at Karl's problems with his hops.

The event around which Magdalena's party grew was the annual visit of a plastic surgeon from Rio—the same one, it turned out, who had reorganized Raven's face and body and had excised the slave labor numbers from her forearm.

Now she was having her eyes done. "They need to be widened," she had explained to Dietrich and me. "Your face starts deteriorating when you hit thirty."

The surgeon arrived every year on his fully equipped hospital yacht. He brought with him technicians and an anesthesiologist, remained a week, charged a fortune while making virtually the same improvements on each of the old, thick, lumpy wives who had, over the course of his visits, begun to look very much alike: noses, lips, hips, bottoms, bosoms, eyelids, faces. Magdalena had the longest dock and, since the surgeon's yacht was larger than anyone else's, Magdalena achieved the honor of hostessing.

While I had driven the pickup, Dietrich and Raven had sailed there. Visiting yachts were moored up and down the river. Dr. Hermann had arranged a cloud cover of fog dropped over them. Small planes landed at his airstrip, and partygoers were driven down the mountain to Magdalena's estate.

She had arranged for the surgeon to bring with him a psychic communicator—

Madame Wanda—a Hungarian, probably a gypsy, who it was said had been doing extremely accurate readings with the dead for Magdalena's cousin in Paraguay. Madame Wanda was to be that evening's entertainment.

Some guests had flown in from other parts of South America, mostly Chile and Argentina. Like other similar parties, this event had been organized with safety as a priority. Bodyguards surrounded the house, patrol boats moved up and down the shoreline. After everyone's arrival, the landing lights on Dr. Hermann's airstrip were shut off, the boats and planes covered in camouflage netting, the cloud cover established.

Some of the guests I knew; others were unfamiliar. Some were Nazis; others hadn't intended to be Nazis. Some hated themselves and hated Hitler. Others worshipped him. Our mutual exile and deep longing made us companions.

The guests arrived early in the evening, drank heavily, talked loudly, and were excited and rather silly about the psychic. A handful wore Waffen uniforms with an array of medals. My father sulked, arrogant and distant. Raven circled around him, chatty and charming. Surgeries were planned for the next morning, and the five female patients had been told not to drink.

We took seats in the back of Magdalena's large dining room, which was more of a hall.

Dr. Hermann tapped a whiskey glass, welcomed the crowd, then complained that a yacht had left its lights on at Magdalena's dock. "We have been secure here for years. No one has bothered us. But we cannot afford to let our guard down, ever. I thank you for your continued attention to our safety."

At the front of the dining hall, Madame Wanda sat in a straight-backed chair, smoked steadily, wore black clothing, scuffed white high heels, and a flowered stole. She had electric, flyaway hair—long, almost kinky—very poor teeth and a gravelly voice. I kept staring at those teeth. They were large and yellow, like old piano keys. She seemed shy and would not meet my eyes.

Magdalena's maids passed trays of candles in crystal tumblers. Magdalena curtsied to my father as she gave him his candle. Dutifully, everyone lit their candles and she turned out the lights.

"I am not a psychic," Madame Wanda began. The red tip of her cigarette moved in small circles as she spoke. Placed beside her was something she described as her "spirit horn." "I do not read minds. I am a communicator. Spirits speak to me. I just tell you what I hear. I take no responsibility. I don't fabricate information, and, after, I don't remember what I say. If it comes into me and it is wrong, it is most likely another voice, the wrong voice. Spirits are very anxious to come through the channels. They mass up and everyone yells like schoolchildren. I know none of you. I know nothing about you except that you live well and are all very anxious. Please try to be quiet. So—" She stubbed out her cigarette on the sole of her shoe, folded her stole, laid it on her lap, clasped her hands over it, closed her eyes. Her chest rose and fell.

The room was utterly silent. We held our breaths.

"Wait your turns. Speak louder. Someone has a black-and-white kitten. On this side. The kitten says she can't wait to get to heaven so she can have a cigarette. And there's a child in the forest—a girl—who says she needs a name."

Where had I heard that? A child in the forest who needs a name. Then I remembered that Okok had told that to Raven who told it to Maria who told it to me.

There was nothing on Raven's face. The assemblage looked around at each other. The candles made monsters of us.

Madame Wanda closed her eyes, pinched her forehead with forefinger and thumb, concentrating. "Someone says to me, 'I wanted my pocket watch to go to Norman. Why did it go to Niklas?' Is there a Norman in the room? Someone, Frank?"

Embarrassed, we looked around at each other.

From the back of the room, Uncle Wolf said softly, "Hans Frank, the Butcher of Poland, had a son named Norman."

"Shut up, Wolf." My father leaned toward Raven. "Does this worry you, my dear?"

"Who was Hans Frank, Dietrich?" Raven asked. She looked worried. Why was that?

"Inner circle, governor of Poland," said Dietrich. "Two sons, Nicholas and Norman."

"Oh God, Dietrich."

"Don't be afraid. She's a phony. She probably has notes on the bottom of her shoes."

From the rear of the room, a woman called out, "There was a problem with the Frank sons. I knew them." Someone else told her to shut up. An odd mix, I thought, of the curious and frightened. The past loomed up dangerously in that glittery, grim room of candlelight and shadows.

Magdalena passed around a silver bowl of smelling salts, but no one wanted them. There was not a sound in the room. Candles flickered.

"Someone here should not wear red," said Madame Wanda.

I took Raven's hand. It was cold. I knew Madame Wanda meant Raven. After being forced to wear that ugly, bulky, diamond-smuggling vest upon our arrival in Brazil, Raven had refused to wear red. She'd told me, "If I wear red, I'll fall down."

Now she said, "I don't want to believe it, so I won't." Even so, she sat on the edge of her chair, leaving her hand in mine.

Madame Wanda paused, lit a cigarette, inhaled deeply, exhaled, brought her spirit horn up to her ear. "Oh, yes, darling, don't be afraid. Someone wishes to…Violet. Does anyone know a Violet?"

Raven pulled her hand from mine and clutched her husband's. "This is nothing, Dietrich. Someone told her of the giraffe." I, too, moved closer to my father. The muscles on his neck tightened, pulsed.

Raven ripped her hand from mine, hissed at me. "You told her about Violet?"

"What are you talking about?" said Dietrich. "I never saw the woman before in my life."

Raven turned to look across the table at Uncle Wolf. "Someone did."

"Maybe not, Raven," I said.

"Don't be stupid."

"You sound just like a girl I used to know. Her name was Luba."

"Keep your mouth shut."

Madame Wanda banged the spirit horn on the floorboards. "I asked you to be quiet, Missus," she addressed Raven. "Oh my! This voice comes like thunder, like a tornado. Above the other voices. Be quiet. You in the audience, also be quiet. It's a man."

My father gripped the edge of the table. There was nothing on his face. Magdalena crossed herself.

"Very intense," Madame Wanda continued. "He says…'I regret that I didn't give you a gold medal. You deserved a gold medal.' Does anyone understand? For Poland." She put the large end of the spirit horn to her mouth, blew through it as if cleaning it.

"It's him!" Horst shouted. The old "Special Projects" Nazi ran to Madame Wanda, lifting her from the chair, shaking her, as if to shake loose something or someone from her.

Weeping and blubbering, Horst shook Madame Wanda too hard.

"Ask him why he led us into the wilderness," he said, looking at her desperately. "Ask why he took us to Russia. Ask him why he ruined Germany."

Madame Wanda scratched Horst's cheeks, trying in vain to free herself from his grip.

I jumped into the fray, struggling with Horst to protect Madame Wanda, finally pulling him away. Others who didn't understand were laughing but some were not. I was not.

Madame Wanda collapsed back into her chair. "I refuse to work like this. Take him from the room or I leave."

A few others helped me settle Horst outside by the pool. I loosened his tie, his pants. A surgeon present came to listen to his heart. Among continued sobs, Horst struggled to find his breath. Our hostess Magdalena fanned his face with her large hat.

Inside, Dr. Hermann took a seat next to Dietrich, and I joined them.

Madame Wanda snapped her fingers. She held the spirit horn to her ear, cocked her head. She looked around the room. "Now he says to...*uh*...*uh*...Dieter." She spoke to the air as if calming it.

"Dietrich?" Dr. Hermann offered wryly. "We have a Dietrich."

My father snuffed his candle with thumb and forefinger. Dr. Hermann leaned over and relit it with his own flame.

Madame Wanda continued in a flat tone that wasn't her own. "'It is the curse of the great that they have to step over corpses to create new life.' That's what *he* says, not me. Madame Wanda says nothing."

Raven shivered. The room was deathly quiet. My father stared steadily at Madame Wanda.

"Ghost," Dietrich mumbled. "Ghost, host, guest. Write this down, Axel. How does the host of the communion relate to the ghost of this party? Host, guest, ghost, visitor. Who is our visitor? Who is our guest? Who is our ghost?"

Madame Wanda bent forward. She pointed the spirit horn at my father. "He congratulates you and promises you the recognition you deserve."

My father sat ramrod straight, an iron composure. "Magdalena, get her out of here," he said calmly, but I heard the panic just underneath.

Madame Wanda stood behind her chair, continued in a small voice, not her own. "One more thing, Baron. Violet says she loved it when you kissed her eyelids."

The assembled laughed and hooted at the thought of the upright Baron having a mistress. A few stuck their pinky fingers into the sides of their mouths and whistled harsh taunting notes. My father got to his feet, correct and upright, and faced them down. They fell silent.

Magdalena begged all of us to be still. We were ruining a lovely evening. Out of respect for Madame Wanda, who came all this way to entertain us with her gift, we should remember our manners.

Again a man yelled, "Ask him why the hell we went into Russia."

My father's face was white with anger. He stood, moved forward, hand raised to slap Madame Wanda. His fury and arrogance were palpable. "I will not have this...this gypsy insult the Reich!"

Uncle Wolf did not cause the trouble. My father did, but Uncle Wolf capped it off. These days, people in our circles had begun calling my uncle Wolf "that Wolf." He'd become a jackal, wandering as he did at the edge of our lives: hungry, ill, self-destructive.

Madame Wanda stood, expecting a blow from my father, but she went on, "He says, this voice like a tornado, 'You will get what you deserve.'"

At that, Uncle Wolf jumped from his chair, which went crashing to the ground. He ran to my father and, before anyone could stop him, broke one of Magdalena's crystal tumblers on Dietrich's forehead.

The wound filled with blood, then bled profusely.

Magdalena fumbled against the walls for the lights, turned them on. We blew out our candles. Some guests ran from the room. Others surrounded my father, helping him lay on the floor. People held napkins to his wound.

He pushed them away, waved his arm toward Madame Wanda, who sat shaking in her chair. "Get her away from me. Get her out of here!"

The surgeon bent over my father, plucking a sharp piece of crystal from his forehead. "He's fine. This is just minor. Surface. I do need more napkins, please."

The surgeon's assistants tried to lead Madame Wanda from the room. Part of the crowd followed her, pulled at her clothing, grabbing her arms. "What else did he say?" a man asked. "Is he coming back?" a woman asked breathlessly.

Raven leaned closer to me, said, "He's still hypnotizing, even while dead. These pigs are willing to believe anything."

"Remove her!" Dietrich shouted in a battlefield voice. "Remove that gypsy now. Out!"

❧

Early the next morning, I caught up with Raven as she hurried from our yacht on a path through palm trees outside Magdelena's orange gingerbread monstrosity. "May I walk with you?"

"I have no time to dally," she said. "The doctor's beginning right away."

"You think that was Hitler last night?"

"Some people did." She touched the cuff of my shirt, admitting, "I did. I was scared to death."

"So was Dietrich."

She drew me toward her by my wrist. For the briefest of moments, I watched her consider the possibility before dismissing it. She put her arms around my neck, speaking into my chest, "Forget about Dietrich, Axel. Find yourself by yourself, not through him."

I felt her against me, a flash of comfort and excitement. And suddenly it wasn't about Dietrich. It was about her arms around me and mine around her. "For what it's worth, Luba, I'm still here."

She looked away, mumbled. "You were a little boy when you slept with me. You cried and shivered, and I held you. You were my only friend in the world. The world burned and bled, and we held each other. I imagined your breaths were palm trees fanning me on a tropical island, warm and sweet. It was a terrible time, but we had each other. Now we avoid each other, which is as it should be. Try to leave me alone. Let me forget. Remembering only makes me lonelier. Your friendship only makes it worse." Her face hardened. "And don't call me Luba."

I could feel the knot of my sex unwind and press into the hollow of her crotch. I could feel her press against me. "I want to kiss your eyelids."

"I know."

"I will never leave you, Luba. Never."

"We were good friends, Axel. And now we are not." She drew away but only slightly.

"But you come to me when you're scared."

"I go to Dietrich when I'm scared. I come to you when I'm scared of Dietrich."

Footsteps approached, crunching in the loose stones of the path. Willi stood beside us.

"Little accident here?"

"Remind me, Willi, never again to wear high heels on these stones. Thank goodness Axel was passing. Stupid. And now I'm late for surgery." She leaned on Willi, took off her shoes and tossed both of them into the river.

℘

From Magdalena's, I drove to Uncle Wolf's house. One half of our ancestral doors leaned against the entryway. Uncle Wolf was in his underwear, which hung, stained, loose, and gray on his hipbones. "Good morning, nephew. Your miserable father had the door sent over this morning. I think Hitler scared him into doing the right thing. Your father must be apologizing, which is strange since *I* hit *him* on the head."

"Maybe he recognized he shouldn't have kept both halves. That half was yours. I planned to give it to you when he dies."

"Oh, he'll never die. He's made of concrete." He draped a thin arm around my shoulders. "Dear, weak-kneed, Venerable Nephew. I would like to give you courage, but I have none to spare. Give me a hand. I'll get some tools."

I helped him replace his door with his father's door. Uncle Wolf said, "This door that divides brothers, this door that bears our family's arms, the arms of generals, ambassadors, colonial governors, the scandalous lesbian poet, the aristocrats of Pomerania, these doors, this door is mine. The inner circle of Hitler's Berghof, the…I am happy to have my door."

I was twenty-seven years old, a scholar of antiquity, supposedly a man of the world. Even so, I had massive gaps of knowledge.

I painted the door with linseed oil and had a beer with Uncle Wolf, although there was already an open bottle of rum on the kitchen table. From the kitchen, I saw into a living room. There were murals of Germany on the walls, mostly unfinished, in shades of brown and green. I recognized a face.

"Why is my mother's face yellow?"

"I used chicken shit to paint her because she was a coward to jump overboard. A chicken shit coward to leave me."

There was more—enough, I thought, to make my uncle a lunatic. Maybe all of us.

Chapter Seventeen

In all these years, my father managed to produce just six letters for Dr. Hermann, all documented with origins, examples, connections, resonances, resemblances.

Dietrich led expeditions into the jungle, searching for Phoenician letters carved into caves, into rock formations, into anything. He explored the forests and the rivers: this Lost City, that stone with footprints, this cave with carvings, that column with ancient letters. Here and there he found a trace of Phoenician script that had no meaning, which might have been an errant plow mark or an ancient boundary marker. Most of what he found were marks, not sentences, not words. He kept careful notebooks, methodical, diligent. With a tape recorder and bags of Nabisco Sugar Wafers, he collected stories from tribal elders.

Dietrich found accurate flood legends and reasonably familiar creation myths. But the myths, mangled and mingled with the present, ranged in credibility from an astonishingly familiar creation myth—how the creators made woman from a bone—to how the harpy eagle became a sewing machine. The further he dug, the worse it became. Not a fertile field. Or perhaps like the forest: too fertile. Still, he kept to his schedule, hung his labels, and continued dictating to me.

Dr. Hermann didn't seem to mind these field trips. Willi bought us a larger yacht. No one understood what my father was doing, but they dared not ask, dared not offend. Years passed quickly, days slowly. We found an extraordinary carving, writing of the firstborn of Jethel, giving us confidence in our suspicion that Solomon or his cohorts had been to South America.

Doña Brianca bought a larger television set and played it turned to the street so everyone could watch soccer. For weeks, O Linda was paralyzed. We nearly lost our coffee bean harvest because the field hands didn't show up. We finally used the gauchos and the Indian women of our village to complete the harvest.

Our landholdings expanded to the edge of Dr. Hermann's gold fields. Our water buffalo herds multiplied. We hired dozens of gauchos and field hands. Raven and Grevaldo spent long hours keeping the books, the records, sending out invoices, organizing what was becoming a successful operation. As long as Grevaldo was with us, Raven admitted me to her company; otherwise, she would not.

Raven was Mrs. Baron, and I hated her for it. Dietrich collected emeralds, she collected power. Dietrich gave her more responsibilities. It didn't take long for Raven to start running the estate with an iron hand, leaving Dietrich to work in his study.

When I watched Raven and Grevaldo ride off in the morning to inspect a field, its harvest, the loading of barges, the unloading of barges, I bitterly imagined them as lovers.

☙❧

Dietrich had more royal palms transplanted into Palm Alley, which led from the house to the river. At the end of this alley, he had a platform built with a roof supported by Doric columns.

There were steps leading down to a pier. Our veranda was furnished with Venetian lamps, painted posts, lawn chairs, umbrellas, spittoons and stemmed ashtrays, aluminum and shining.

He had expanded Palm Alley for Raven. She walked it every morning in her robe, either a pale blue one with red poppies or a white with daisies, holding her coffee mug to her cheek for warmth.

One morning I watched her from my bedroom balcony. She went down to the river, dipped her feet, washed her face, sat, and watched the sun rise. Clumps of cotton fog drifted away. A great sun licked the horizon, emblazoned the river orange.

She didn't hear me as I descended the stairs. She was crying into the hem of her nightgown, shivering in the morning's cold, her nipples hard and swollen. I dropped my windbreaker over her shoulders. She wiped her nose with my sleeve.

"Good morning, Amazon Queen."

"What are you doing here? Just go away."

The water buffalo were penned near us in the river. The rising sun glistened on their crescent horns. Mud was clotted to their heads from digging in the river bottom. They were mean and ugly, not like our sweet cows in Germany. No lowing, gentle sounds. They sounded more like the scream and scrape of gears as trucks downshifted on their descent through the hills of tailings from the gold mines. Dangerous beasts, profitable beasts. I didn't leave.

Raven sipped her coffee. "Today is my sister Dorie's birthday. I hear her calling me from the forest." She spilled the remainder of her coffee into the river, flung her cup after it. The water buffalo grunted, mooed, moaned, stomachs rumbling as they tore at the rice shoots, vast hulks in the fog. Cotton fog, cold and dense, floated over the river. "They never came back for me."

There was nothing to say. I dared to take her hand. Easily, she curled hers within mine. "I want to see my sister, Axel. But if I look for her, they'll find Dietrich and kill him. Maybe after Dietrich is dead...maybe then I'll go look."

"Perhaps they're in Israel."

"They're probably dead, all of them. Dorie was going to be a doctor. Daniel played the piano, a genius on the piano; Frederick wanted to be a psychologist. I...I wanted to be a singer. And my brother Ruben wanted to be a sandwich, and they all froze to death in the Alps. I was going to be a princess. And look, I'm a baroness. Look."

"A sandwich?"

"I'm trying to be funny."

"Maybe they're still looking for you, Raven."

"And if they find me, then what? Dorie, this is my husband. Remember him? He owned the factory. We were his slaves." She knotted her hair with a diamond clip, stood. "A sandwich." She laughed. She frightened me. I watched our reflections in the movement of the river and imagined us drifting away in each other's arms. "If they were alive, by now they would have found me. I should have gone with them over the Alps. I should have just gone to sleep in the snow with them. Forever."

"C'mon, Luba." I imagined the possibility she would slip into the river and give herself to death just as my mother had slipped into the sea. I took her hand again, held it tight. "Luba…"

She tore her hand from mine, pulled off my jacket, and threw it at my face. "There's a shipment of water buffalo going out this morning." She stood and walked away. "Stop remembering," she called over her shoulder, taking long, angry strides toward the house.

ɘↄ

Old Maria died. It was a quick death. One morning she failed to wake up. Her lungs were filled with fluid. Her daughter Also Maria became Maria. Pastor Ken and his wife, Kathy, sailed down from the mission to conduct a proper Christian funeral. Death was an ordinary event on the river. Young Maria recovered rapidly.

But Raven did not. It seemed she mourned more than Maria.

The evening after the funeral, we found her sitting on the floor of the living room, a single candle lit, rocking. She refused to go upstairs to bed. She told Young Maria she was sitting shiva for her family. Nobody challenged or questioned her.

After two nights, Dietrich knocked on my door for help. Raven still refused to come to bed. Sleeping on the sofa, she spent much of the night sitting in the center of the living room with a lit candle, not eating.

I dressed and joined her downstairs, asking if she were mourning.

"No," she said, looking up from the flame with gorgeous, tormented eyes. "This is sitting shiva. I'm sending their souls to heaven."

"Whose?"

"Everyone's."

It lasted a week. Maria brought her food, mostly eggs and crackers. She ate the eggs. Dietrich damned Okok's "mumbo jumbo" again and again. We tiptoed around Raven.

Dietrich reminded me the word "shiva" was the name of the Indian god Shiva who was Sirius, and that Sirius was the gateway to death.

☙❧

After finishing her first meal back in her dining room chair, Raven sent Maria for ice to put into her water glass. Her glass was a delicate, crystal, fluted red goblet. It had an edged art deco rim of gold. I'd put the glasses on the table as a gift for Raven. They had been purchased at my latest mistress's gallery in Caracas.

Raven twirled the red goblet in her hand, held it up to the light. "It looks like a flower, doesn't it?"

With sugar tongs, Maria dropped the cubes in one by one. They tinkled as they hit the crystal and each other. Raven spoke but didn't look up. "When the Nazis took our house, they threw our piano off the balcony. It sounded like this when it fell...and even a little longer after it fell." Playing with ice cubes with her spoon, stirring them, she asked me, "What's the difference between ice and glass?"

"Ice melts. And glass is made of sand." I answered. "Do you like the glasses?"

"I love them. Their stems, the blooms." She twirled a goblet in her fingers, holding it up to the light. "It's lovely, a lily." Her hand was shaking around the glass, the ice cubes tinkling the music of fear. "Why doesn't glass melt?"

"It does," Dietrich acknowledged. "In the heat."

"Do you think the sand feels pain?"

Dietrich and I dared not look at each other, dared not acknowledge her suffering.

"You make glass with heat," she mused. "And ice with cold. Someone made this, didn't they? Imagine making something as beautiful as this from sand. I would like to make glass. I suppose I'll need ovens. And we'll need to do construction to build a studio, yes, Dietrich? Blowing glass—what do you think?"

"Hear, hear." Dietrich tapped his spoon on his juice glass. "From facelift to forklift."

☙❧

Dietrich rarely questioned Raven's extraordinary expenses, but he soon turned against this new one. Diamonds, clothes, and horses were acceptable; glassblowing was not.

But there was no stopping her.

Within a month a German engineer arrived with his crew, the equipment sat on the dock, instructors were scheduled, the odd tools from another age (Roman, I thought) were laid out in a new metal building that went up in a day. A wall of blowpipes, a great stainless-steel oven, worktables, fans, a cooling oven all arrived, then were installed. The ovens were as advanced as the tools' designs were ancient. Dietrich tried to dissuade her, but to no avail.

Dr. Hermann dropped in, admired the newly arrived ovens. "We never had anything so nice. Is your wife getting ready for another Holocaust, Dietrich? Ho, ho, ho. So, what is your wife building here?"

Dietrich and I could only watch in amazement, and, of course, as with everything Raven took on, there was a nagging concern that this new hobby was a sign she might soon slip over the edge to madness. We held our tongues until one morning she joined us at breakfast with a thickly layered, red-stained, gauze bandage wrapped around her hand.

"I take it the ovens are working," said Dietrich.

"Yes, I'm very pleased."

"Are you bleeding? Why is the bandage red?"

"It's tree sap. Not blood. Heals overnight."

"How can you hold anything if you're shaking so? It's dangerous and highly unnecessary."

Raven closed her eyes. "And going into the jungle looking for artifacts isn't?"

"That's my *work*. This is not your work."

"I am working on my soul, Dietrich."

He raised his eyebrows in his nastiest supercilious presentation of disapproval. "And when are we going to see *those* results?"

"There's a load of glass rods arriving this morning. I have to go to the dock." She left without eating, defiant, stomping off like a child.

❧

Dietrich moved from being annoyed to being threatened. I was, however, fascinated by the changes in Raven. She stopped her routine of a different perfume every day. Her hair was singed. She had to be flown into Rio for a burn on her forehead. She was in her studio at sunrise. Grevaldo's jeep was parked outside. He was the only one allowed in.

She began work in her studio at dawn, long before Maria rang the breakfast gongs. Then she'd rush from her studio into the house, upstairs to dress. At the breakfast table below, we listened to her showering and running barefoot around her room. When she finally sat down with Dietrich and me, her hair was still wet and tied back with a ribbon. Which then became a rubber band.

Within a few weeks, she didn't even change her clothes but rushed in directly from the studio, smelling of chemicals, her face flushed with heat, smudged and sweaty, her hair plastered with sweat against her brow. She was carving out a territory apart from us.

Some mornings she skipped breakfast. More and more of her day was spent in the studio. She was carving out emotional territory as well. She developed a swagger in her step, something I'd noticed in the gauchos' limps, a male motion, as if she had big testicles.

At last, one day when Grevaldo had to take a barge of water buffalo to Manaus, Raven invited me to help her in the studio. Gleaming steel, aluminum, the two ovens, searing heat, no windows.

"Over there are some balls of glass. I'm just not ready to make things. Yet."

I examined a wizened vase, a leaning cup on a shelf, an unsteady wavering platter. The platter rocked when I set it down. It was misshapen, irregular, and pocked. "That's all you've done?"

Smiling as unsteadily as the platter, Raven turned her back, threw on a face shield, slipped asbestos mitts over her hands, and opened a fiery oven. "They call this the glory hole." She shoved a globe of glass on a long rod into the oven, twisting the rod.

She'd begun just three months earlier, but already her actions appeared fearless, accomplished, tranquil.

"When you blow on the pipe to shape the glass in the oven, don't you burn your lips?"

"Not yet."

"But no results, Raven? No glass?"

She moved the orange molten glob of hot glass onto a table, rolled it, shaping it, pressing it into the table's surface, had me pour water from a garbage can over it. Her capability and focus didn't surprise me. But her tranquility did.

Her hands were steady. She was getting better.

She was so focused on shaping the hot glass, I thought I might be able to talk to her, and I was correct.

"Do you think he ruined your life as much as he ruined mine?" I asked her.

"Who?"

"Your husband, my father, Dietrich. Do you think he's human?"

"Oh, him." She laughed. "Fill that garbage can over there with water. I've seen indications. Mostly after the sun sets, when he goes into the nightly rut. Here, keep this steady while I put it on the table over there. Steady. Twenty-three hundred degrees. If the definition for humanity is feelings, he's lacking. Love isn't rut. Rut is attack and conquer. It's hard work, every night."

"For whom?"

"For me."

"You don't ever refuse him?" I dared.

"If I do, and a couple of days go by, he's a real son of a bitch. Then I have to defuse him. Refuse, defuse. Sometimes I punish him. I make him stand on one foot in the hallway for an hour. Turns him on." She laughed again, wiped her forehead with her mitt. She was offering me intimacy and laughing at Dietrich. And at herself. More than her perfume had changed. Her language had a rough, tough edge. "I know his every move, Axel. Don't forget my life depended on him. That's where *I'm* coming from."

"Well, certainly, not where you're going."

She looked up at me sharply.

"Am I like him, Raven?" I asked.

"You have more feelings. Too many. That's why I must avoid you."

"And your feelings?"

"I keep them tucked away where he can't get to them." She flipped her face shield in place and mumbled behind it. "Tuck them away. The anger keeps trying to escape. Here, that cup-like tool over there. I need…yes, that one." I watched as she flattened one side of the hot glass on the table. "Now take some of that water from the garbage can and pour it over this. You see, the process is what's important, not the things. It's somewhat alchemical."

"And when you tuck them away, your feelings, do they fester and burst? Is this helping, Raven?"

She carried the fiery globe on a long tube, opened an oven, pushed it in gently. She was careful and in control. "I'm healing myself, Axel."

She moved from the oven into my arms, whispering into my shoulder. "Straw into gold. Sand into beauty. Raven into…"

"Luba?" I ventured.

"Luba was a child. Look in that garbage can, Axel. Those are my failures. All the garbage cans. I want you to dump them in the river."

The garbage cans were filled with broken glass in a painful rainbow of colors.

"Is there any chance for us, Raven?"

"There is no us. And anyway, this is about me, only me. Ovens," she watched me carefully, took my arm. "I'm making babies, Jewish babies. I'm reversing history. Taking Jewish babies out of the ovens."

For a moment, I was astounded. "Oh, God, Luba, is this what you're doing?"

She bent to her knees and blew air into the hot glob of glass and brought out babies. She was making figures of babies, turning the ovens back in time, forgiving deaths, bringing containers for the souls of the dead who went into the ovens. Making glass babies.

"I thought you'd understand."

"I do, Luba."

My heart leapt from my chest to hers. I was overwhelmed with love for her. It spilled from every cell, every organ, every breath in my body. She ignored me until I left.

❦

Finally, one morning, Raven, with a shy smile, laid a small, undulating shape of shell-pink glass on the breakfast table. A translucent baby sparkled from within.

"Emeralds," Dietrich pronounced unkindly, "cost less than that thing."

I put out my hand. She placed it in my hand.

"I feel as if I've given birth," she said.

I passed it back to her, trying to let her know I understood how precious it was.

There would be others on the dining table, or sometimes catching the morning light on a coffee table or a windowsill, or dancing in the light of the chandelier. The colors changed, the shading more complex, but the undulating form stayed the same. Maria made a theatrical show of dusting the babies, fondling them, holding them up to the sunlight.

Soon they were everywhere in the house. Maria bagged them and decorated the fountain, planting some upright around the fig tree roots, hanging others from limbs of the fig tree. Maria thought they were dolphins and said they reminded her of her sister, Esmeralda, who had died. Maria believed Esmeralda had been reincarnated as a pink dolphin who would often appear to her.

Sometimes Dietrich filled his pockets with Raven's glimmering, shiny glass creations, a dozen at a time. He used them on his jungle expeditions as gifts for Indians.

Chapter Eighteen

Raven's bold initiative encouraged one of my own. One morning I brought Dietrich coffee in his study and announced for the first time in over a decade, "I have a lecture for you. I've been working on something important."

"I'm in the middle of something, could you...?"

I rolled his chair toward me. He turned it away from me. Even so, I cleared my throat just as he would and began.

I knew he listened because his shoulders tightened with unforeseen anger. I should have known. "Dietrich, this is entitled 'From Coin to Cohen.' Alright." I shifted my feet. My voice was higher, nervous, unsteady. I went on, fired by my own correctness. "The word 'numi' in Egyptian means 'money'. In the ancient Dogon religion, the *Nummos* were the creator gods, eight of them, who descended to civilize mankind. The coin is a replica of the god. His face is on the coin. From coin to Cohen. God, coin, replica, imprint. Numismatist...stamp. Just as the priest is a copy of the god. For the Jews, the priest is a Cohen, a coin of God, a stamp, an imprint. All the Cohens have the same genetic code, the same genetic imprint. The rest of the Jews don't. The priests are in the image of the Nummo. 'Numi' means money and God. *Nun-me* in Sumerian means Star of Wisdom. *Nummi* means those who hold the plan of creation—the numbers. Numi, number. Nummo—numinous means divine, does it not? The divine Nummos came to Earth to imprint their genetic code into the rude life, to imprint themselves on their Earth-born nurslings. They came before creation. They were the creators.

Numbers or Nummos came before creation. There is a great carved
stone in Lepenski Vir in the center of a Neolithic village. It is the
face of a fish, obviously an object of worship. And isn't Pluto God
of the Underworld? And isn't a plutocrat a wealthy man? What
is this connection of God to money? God and wealth, God and
money. Many more secrets are held in these words."

He scoffed. "That's it? You interrupted my work for that drivel?
I could go from dog to hippopotamus in six words. Meaningless
connections."

I would not be stopped. I addressed his back, as with a shotgun.
"Alright, what about the frog prince? And your Og. Frog Og. I
suppose you're able to go from Og to frog. Dietrich, listen to this. I
want to tell you the story of the frog prince."

I stuttered here and there but forced myself forward. "Alright,
here is a children's story alive with our prehistory. When the princess
kisses a frog, he turns into a prince. You don't kiss a horse or a camel
or a pig and get a prince. Only a frog. Fr-Og. I'll suggest that the 'FR'
means brother. Brother Frog. Our brethren. The royal nature of the
reptilian. In a tantalizing fragment, the Babylonian historian Berossus
described these ancient creature ancestor-teachers as repulsive. He
called them *annedoti*, which probably means old for *anne* and *doti* for
the duad. Old creators. He called them Mus. Musara. That's a core
fossil, Dietrich. Mus. Ugly. Which we will get to as we orbit Sirius.
The royalty. According to Manetho, the Egyptian historian, the reign
of the gods continued for 13,400 years, until the reigns of the human
kings began with Menes. King Menes, Manetho wrote, was the first
to assume human form. Who or what reigned earlier that were not
human? Reptilians. 'That the sons of God saw the daughters of men
that they were fair,' Genesis 6, verse 2, Dietrich. That's what it says.
They created giants who ate people, demons, kings, ogres? Ugly and
wise and very dangerous firstborns. Sires from Sirius, Dietrich, Paris,
river of Is. Prague, river of Og."

"I expect better from you. They are cities."

"P and R, Dietrich, always meant river before 4,000 BC. They
are cities on rivers, Paris, Prague. And I expect more of you, Dietrich. I of you."

Then, remembering my promise to my mother to take care of
him, I stopped talking.

That night Okok spotted a war canoe moving slowly near our dock. He sounded the alarm, and Grevaldo turned the searchlights on. Night became day. The war canoe sped away.

After that, our warriors thought the searchlights were miracles and turned them on and off for hours, laughing, focusing the beams on each other, playing, dancing with their shadows. I joined in and targeted them as they ran around the roof, sure-footed as goats. Then they froze. Someone was climbing the rope ladder.

With dart guns ready, we stationed ourselves at the lip of the roof. I swiveled and turned the searchlight on the roof's edge. In seconds, Raven's head appeared. I turned off the light and hauled her up the rest of the way. The warriors giggled with excitement, then moved to the far side of the roof to leave us alone.

"So this is what you do all night?" she asked.

"Better than listening to you and Dietrich in the bedroom."

"I would think so." I imagined her smiling as she said this. She took a seat beside me.

"What brings you here, Raven?"

"You, what else?" I felt her stretch her legs out, settle in close to me. "Old times, on the roof, yes?"

"Nice night," I stupidly said after a long and—for me—painful silence. I wanted to say everything. All at once.

She pulled me down to her. I lay there with my hand in hers, our shoulders touching, her head on my shoulder.

I was paralyzed. A butterfly had landed on my heart, and if I were to move, it might fly off.

We were surrounded by stars. But of course these stars below the equator were different from those of my childhood. The stars of my alphabet in Germany were the stars of Solomon's in Israel. Here they created a different alphabet.

With Raven on the roof, past and present disappeared. No burden, no baggage. No husband, no Indians, not even memories, just a morphic resonance, just us, what I had longed for, where I wanted to be forever, in a space that existed between us and nowhere else on Earth, with no one else in the world.

"Your father's exile is geographic. He is in no place emotionally, nor has he ever been. I feel I've been brave, very brave, daring even, dangerously so, doing things well, meeting challenges, doing everything perfectly, even the terrifying house parties, polo, horses, clothes, jewelry, everything, meeting the challenge of this destiny of mine but nevertheless always pretending. And waiting for the ship to return and rescue me from the cold and wind and the fury of the storm. I always thought in some deep, dark, secret place that you, Axel, would come get me. That's the word: get. That if you had the capacity to 'get' me, to see me as a whole person, not as a woman, I would finally be home."

"You're waiting for me to understand you? Is such a thing even possible?"

"I waited for you to grow up. You grew older in years but have no courage." She wasted no time twisting the knife in my stomach. Her voice changed. She was Raven. "I understand you had a falling out with Dietrich this morning. He regretted it and asked me to speak with you."

"Come on, Raven, that's bullshit. I told him something he didn't know."

"He said you were cocky, arrogant, and insulting. He feels that you are competing with him."

"He's correct. I want his woman. How can you let him touch you? How can you forget?"

She sat up. "Axel, if you're staying around because of me, don't. Not long from now you will be thirty. It may be time for you to start your own family."

"I promised my mother I would take care of Dietrich. That's why I stay."

"That's a worn-out excuse. Make your own way. I'll see that you have plenty of money." This was not Dietrich's message. It was Raven's message, telling me to leave.

Anger forced me to stand up. I tottered, pitched forward.

Okok caught me. Raven took my hand to steady me.

"I will never leave you, Luba. Never. That's another promise I made…to myself. You know I love you."

She pulled me down next to her and curled up. I felt her knees against my thighs.

I closed my eyes. As long as I could feel her breath on my cheek, her hand in mine, our thighs touching, as long as the stars shone.

"Poor Axel. You think no one loves you. Your father doesn't love you. I don't love you. There are many different kinds of love, and they are all profound. Don't make daisy petal judgments: He loves me; he loves me not. Your father loves you deeply and terribly. He also needs you to love him. He doesn't need you to challenge him but to help him move forward."

"I was correct this morning, Raven, and he would not acknowledge it."

"You overwhelmed him so he's jealous. That doesn't surprise me. So what? But you must work with him, with devotion and kindness, to illuminate his work. We'll all be happier. We have to make this work, Axel. We have no other choice."

"Raven, Luba, for me there is only one kind of love. I pity you that you can convince yourself you love him."

"He saved my life, Axel." She sat up. "Okok, please help me down the ladder."

She was right. I was a grown man in a cage because I loved her.

Chapter Nineteen

There was a note from Dietrich pinned to my door the next morning. "Axel, it is time. Tell Hermann the letters are ready. We want passports in return. Ask for an extra one in case Raven wants to take a servant."

I hadn't been to Dr. Hermann's house in years. I drove over in the old pickup.

Although Bebe, the new Mrs. Dr. Hermann, had attempted to lighten up the place with cabochon rose upholstery, the rooms were still overpowered by dark woods, stag horns, bear heads, boar heads, German flags, tapestries, and exquisite oil paintings stolen in Europe.

Willi, eating a chicken salad sandwich at the kitchen table, greeted me with a mouthful of pumpernickel bread and offered me a half. Dr. Hermann sat next to him. "So, Young Baron, some good news! We're getting close to operational."

"Operational?"

"The Fourth Reich."

"Yes, yes, of course," I said, taking a seat with the two old Nazis and filling them in on our developments. "You don't need the entire alphabet to demonstrate its effectiveness, Dr. Hermann. We're ready with enough letters to do that. You only need a handful for a sentence. Just something like a chant, something subliminal."

"A hypnosis. Of course."

"More like a spell. You chant the correct letters. You speak the command. We have six. If you use them subliminally—"

"Yes, yes…and give a command in any language and be well understood—is that correct? Slovenian or French, it doesn't matter? That should be a pretty good test."

I already had a plan on how we would demonstrate our alphabet's effectiveness. I would assemble a handful of Indians and Cablocos who also had a deeper sense of hearing, who had "ears" as Okok would say. Dr. Hermann would give his spoken commands, Maria would speak to them in the "old language," using telepathy, and it would appear they understood his letters. I knew it would work.

"I will give you six cards with the letters," I told Dr. Hermann. "I'll bring in some Indians from our village. All you have to do is chant the letters and give commands."

"It's that simple?"

"Why not? Bring our passports, Dr. Hermann."

Willi slapped mayonnaise on his second sandwich—a great deal of mayonnaise. With a surgical knife I would see again, he cut a thin, translucent slice from a red onion and laid it neatly on his sandwich. "Nothing happens quickly, Young Baron. Finding new identities may take a bit of time. And where do you think your father would like to go?"

"He has said Oxford, as I told Dr. Hermann."

Willi looked at me skeptically. "We can't really approve sending him out until we're fully operational. I'm afraid that would be awkward. And dangerous for us. We are considering New Zealand or the Orkneys. Until we're fully operational, we must remain quiet, and then, by God, he can go anyplace he wants and say anything he wants. The world will be ours. We will never have to hide again. Congratulations, Axel. Your news is very welcome. This is an important moment in the history of Germany. Do you have the letters with you now?"

"Next week we'll meet at our house and run a test. I'll bring the letters. Willi, bring your camera."

☙

I explained what we were doing to Maria, who immediately understood. She laughed and said, "That Senhor Hermann, he believes in himself so much, he becomes stupid."

She and I drove down to the village, where she silently paid respects to Okok.

Then she silently asked him his name, and he silently answered.

How did I know this? I could hear them. She nodded to me, and we walked into Okok's house. Two of his four wives were also able to hear. Okok led us to Has Sores, who was thin and shrunken, but she could hear clearly. Okok summoned his warriors from the men's house. Only three of them could hear, and another small boy could also hear.

The next week, our field bus brought Okok's people up to our house. Maria silently explained to the villagers that they should sit in the shade by the pool, that there would be men arriving who would talk to them, but they were not to listen. They were to listen only to her and do whatever she said. But they should also pretend they were listening to the men. And then we would all have cookies. She instructed them to sit, cross their legs, and listen. They smiled. They were going to trick the *Viracochas*, the garbage from the sea.

❧

Dr. Hermann and Willi arrived at our house wearing their ridiculous uniforms. They assumed this was a historic day, an indication and good sign of their faith in Dietrich's alphabet.

Dietrich and I sat in deck chairs. Willi carried a clipboard. I gave him my three-by-five cards. Willi put his arm around my waist and had Dr. Hermann take a photograph of us. With a flourish, Dr. Hermann laid out four passports on an empty deck chair. Maria sat down in the group. Willi waited for a signal from Dr. Hermann, who nodded.

To my horror, Willi hugged me. Another camera moment.

Willi shuffled the cards I'd given him and intoned our letters.

I interrupted. "Make your voice lower." As if there were a protocol in the mystique.

Unnerved, he began again and dropped his voice. "Ik, Og, Is, Nummo, Mus, Shma…"

Dr. Hermann had neglected to count but gave his order in a faltering French. To my relief, he had chosen to speak in French. "Clap your hands."

I silently translated for Maria. The Indians followed Maria's instruction and clapped.

Dr. Hermann turned and looked at Dietrich, raising his eyebrows in startled excitement. Dietrich smiled, put his thumb in the air.

"Stand up!" Dr. Hermann shouted.

Everyone but Has Sores, who could not, stood.

Willi passed a bag around and distributed thin, surgically sharp knives.

Maria looked at me.

I met her eyes steadily and told her in the old language: "Stay with it. You give the commands."

"Now," Dr. Hermann barked, "cut off your finger."

Dietrich jumped up. "No, Manfred, no! I will not allow you to harm my people."

"They must do something they don't want to do."

"No, I insist." Dietrich's lips were white. I saw that he was genuinely afraid of Dr. Hermann.

"You wish to leave O Linda, Herr Baron? You want your passports?"

Dietrich, defeated, fell back into the deck chair.

Maria looked steadily at me. Everything depended on Maria.

Again, Willi intoned the letters of the stars. I heard the old language. I heard Maria tell the Cablocos and the warriors, "Cut off *their* fingers."

At Maria's command, three warriors leapt on Dr. Hermann and Willi and, with their knives, chopped Willi's forefinger in half and clipped off the top of Dr. Hermann's pinky.

I covered my face with my shirt as Dietrich did, in mock horror. We were laughing at Maria's brilliant joke. Willi leapt into the swimming pool, a thin trail of blood following him. Dr. Hermann stood, stunned, wrapping a white handkerchief around his damaged finger.

"I only lost the tip. It works, Dietrich! I knew it would. Did I say *your* finger or *a* finger?"

"You must have said *a* finger."

"It works. Savages, get rid of them!" Dr. Hermann had his arm around Dietrich, blood trickled onto Dietrich's shirt. "Do you know what this means? You did it, Baron! I knew you would."

Willi climbed from the pool and grabbed his camera, taking more photographs of Dr. Hermann, Dietrich, and me. Strolling casually to the empty deck chair, my father slid the passports into his pocket. "Maria, get some towels."

She giggled as she ran by us to the pool house.

"Everyone on the field bus." I called out.

"This is an enormous day for the Fourth Reich," Willi said, his drenched Nazi uniform stained with blood. Smiling at Dr. Hermann, he said, "I knew it would work. The world is ours, Manfred."

"Ours," Dr. Hermann repeated.

❧

Much later that night, Dietrich knocked on my door and whispered, "Daddy?"

It was a word origin test, and I replied, "The eight Duads, ogdoad."

"Nu?"

"Creation."

Dietrich laughed. It was an exultant laugh but a laugh, nevertheless. "Ha! Good work. Now we're just waiting for a relic from Solomon. With such a discovery, perhaps we gain a destination for those passports."

"I don't trust Dr. Hermann," I said from my bed. "How can he let us go?"

It was quiet outside the door, then he said, "Yes, I don't think that is his plan."

Chapter Twenty

Midway up the northern flank of Dr. Hermann's mountain was a grassy straightaway—something of a causeway that ran a few kilometers from the mountain toward the river. At its widest, the track was a good dozen feet. As it narrowed and dropped toward the river, it disappeared in washouts and creek beds. Raven rode her palomino here often, working young horses on it or racing with visitors. Even though this strip of land belonged to the Occult Bureau Colony as a whole, Dr. Hermann controlled it and let us know when he didn't want us on it.

Along the causeway were piles of square stones that may or may not have been cut. Something was artificial about their fractures, pressure bulbs on them from hammering, but since there was no apparent carving or writing upon them, and since we had many other forest sites beckoning us, Dietrich and I had ignored the site.

Until one day when my horse pulled up a divot of grass and unearthed a large round stone with an iron ring in it. As soon as I told Dietrich, he understood its significance.

"Ballast stones from the People of the Sea. Solomon's ships were here! Goddamn you, Axel. I work a lifetime for an idea, and you go for a horseback ride and stumble on it. You sit on the roof and figure out how writing began…and you…the universe just gives to you." His laughter was greased with an odd mixture of joy, incredulity, and cruelty. "You do recall, of course, that Plato wrote that the gods purposefully chose worthless people as agents of their revelations? They did this in order to make it plain that the revelations must be of some other origin than human contrivance. So they told a stupid man." He threw the stone at my feet. "We'll dig where the road hits the flank."

I didn't respond to his words, focusing instead on the ballast stone.

Without informing Dr. Hermann, we took a team of Okok's warriors to the causeway and dug holes along its grassy upper bank. On the first day of blazing sun and dust, digging and pounding, we removed numerous blocks of solid rock before opening a small crack on the flank behind the ballast stone.

Cold air escaped from the gap. Dietrich, along with the warriors, pulled away more rock and dirt until there was an opening almost large enough for a man.

Clawing ferociously, Dietrich burrowed partially in on his belly. The Indians backed away, leery. One by one, they disappeared into the wall of nearby forest.

I caught up to the last one and asked why he and the others were leaving. He explained in one word: "Charged." They felt a dangerous power. For any further digging, Dietrich and I would need to bring our Cabloco gauchos in from the high fields.

Dietrich was struggling to wedge his shoulders in and out of the maddeningly unreasonable hole when Raven raced her palomino up the causeway. "Axel, exactly what is your father doing in there?"

"He's always looking for something. He has a hungry mind." I pulled my father out by his boots.

Dietrich stood, wiping sweat or tears from his eyes. "The Sea People—"

"Manfred Hermann's at the house with guests," Raven interrupted. "I told the creepy old Nazi you were out hunting. He's with one of your generals and someone from Chile who doesn't speak, wearing a Savile Row suit. They're smoking your cigars, sitting in the sunroom waiting and..." She raised her voice. "And my house stinks from their cigars. Manfred's pacing back and forth and has asked Maria to show him your study again."

Dietrich moved quickly. "Axel, put rocks in front of that hole. We'll need a half dozen gauchos tomorrow." He wiped his forehead with his arm.

෫෨

At lunch, except for a few random conversational grunts, the Savile-Row, pockmarked Chilean remained silent. Dietrich, Dr. Hermann, and the general chatted about commodities, one of which seemed to be women. After the meal the four men returned to the sunroom, closed the French doors, and lit up another round of cigars.

Raven and I sat in a parlor just beyond the sunroom. In the doldrums of the afternoon heat, she sipped iced tea through a candy-striped straw. I watched her lips, considering the difference between the words doldrum and tantrum.

"Must you stare?"

"I'm watching your lips. I'm wondering…your…"

"Don't be stupid." She snapped the straw in half. "Can you see anything from where you're sitting? I don't want Manfred to see me spying."

"From here, I can see something being exchanged from Dr. Hermann and Dietrich to the general and the Chilean. Dr. Hermann passed them a burlap bag. The general looked inside, smiled, nodded." I got a sick feeling. I remembered those burlap bags in the tunnel under Queer Willi's Pawnshop: They'd been filled with gold teeth.

"Can you see what's in it?"

"Coffee beans?" I said. I didn't want to distress Raven. "It's a coffee bean bag."

"More likely gold—protection money. Disappearing is expensive. These payoffs. It would be the Colony's money, not ours. What is this business about Solomon? More than scholarship, I take it?"

"Dietrich's plan is to find relics of Solomon—proof that the Israelite king was here in the Amazon. Then he'll go to the Israelis with the discovery and trade this monumental historical discovery for amnesty."

She slapped her knees, laughed. "Sweetheart, Jews don't care about Solomon. Dietrich's truly mad. Will you go with him again tomorrow when he goes back in his hole in the ground?"

"I certainly cannot let him do this alone."

She shook her head. "I'll pack fruit juices. Make certain he takes plenty of liquids. Don't let him get heat stroke. So, I hear you have a new mistress in Rio. A fat one."

"Yes. Fat and jolly. She cooks and reads romance novels, as in *rock-hard, throbbing member* romance novels."

"And she cooks as well. How terribly exotic."

"Cabbage rolls. With a sweet and sour tomato sauce. I think she's Russian."

"You *think?*"

"We hardly talk. Mistresses who don't talk are more expensive than ones who do." I looked at Raven's face. "That's a joke."

Raven turned away and pulled a tissue from her pocket, blew her nose noisily into it. "My mother made cabbage rolls. She wore a house dress and sang '*Träumerei*' and made cabbage rolls."

The visiting war criminals were readying to leave. To avoid getting caught spying on them, Raven and I moved to another room and continued our conversation.

"Raven, please tell me you're jealous."

"Of your fat mistress? No. Of your cabbage rolls? Yes. My mother…" Instead of finishing, she sauntered back into the vacated sunroom, opening all the windows. I emptied ashtrays behind her.

"Men and cigars," she muttered.

"Seriously, Raven, if you want me to bring back some cabbage rolls, decide soon. My mistresses usually only last about six weeks."

"No, thank you. She sounds, somehow, unclean."

I stepped on something, lifted my foot: a gold tooth. I picked it up and tried to hide it from Raven.

There was something desperate in the speed with which she plucked the tooth from my fingers. She placed it in the palm of her hand, curved her fingers around it, and stared into her hand. She let out a deep groan. "It's Dorie's tooth."

          &cº

Raven ran from the room, from the house, toward the river.

"Dietrich, Maria, come quickly!" I called before running outside in pursuit, my voice echoing in the house. "She's going to the river! Raven's in trouble."

I was halfway down Palm Alley, sick with the knowledge of her pain, still yelling for help, yelling to her.

"Raven, it's okay. Raven. *Luba!*"

She stopped.

I caught up with her at the stairs leading to the river. She was shaking like a jackhammer. "Luba!"

"It's Dorie's tooth."

"Your sister was a child. She didn't have a gold tooth."

"Then it's my mother's, my grandma's, my grandpa's, my uncle's."

She struggled to pull away from me. Her body shook in a storm of terror. I held her tighter, pried her fingers open, grabbed the tooth, popped it into my mouth, and swallowed.

"And now it's everyone's tooth. I swallowed your pain. Alright? Now I have your pain. It's everyone's tooth. There, Luba."

Her body eased against mine. I spoke into her hair. "We could leave, Luba. We could hitch a ride on one of the tour ships, give the ship captain a pile of cash, let him hide us, drop us off in Miami. We could."

Her eyes widened. "I can't stop trembling. Hold me, Axel."

Like the anaconda in the milk can, hiding, calculating, my rock-hard, uninvited, throbbing member whom I shall not refer to by one of my mistress's pornographic metaphors, found its way into the hollow of her crotch. Raven, aware or unaware, leaned into me, pressed against me.

Dietrich's shouts rumbled down the Palm Alley. "Raven!"

And then everyone was upon us, and Raven flung herself into her husband's arms.

"Oh, my poor darling, those men frightened you. That's a good girl. They'll never come back here. I promise. You'll never see them again. My poor little girl. Come now. You'll be safe, I promise."

Dietrich clasped her around her waist, held her tightly. She leaned into him, looked over her shoulder at me in a way that might have been meaningful, but I was unable to attach any definable meaning to it. I was incapable of knowing the margins of Raven's fear, her deceptions, her madness. Dietrich led her up Palm Alley to the house. I burped, belched over the journey of the gold tooth through my esophagus and into my bowels.

ↄↄ

Raven was still too upset to come to dinner. Maria stayed with her in her room. After a silent meal, I invited Dietrich for a cigar by the pool. Frogs were frantic with mating. We lit up and waited until Raven's bedroom lights went on.

"That shaking, Dietrich. She shouldn't be left alone."

"Do you think I just fell off the turnip truck, Axel? Manfred used poor judgment coming over here today with the payoff. I had forgotten about our appointment, and he was, as usual, wildly impatient. Since I didn't show up at his house, he brought the teeth over here."

"Pretty bad, Dietrich. Ghastly."

"Those teeth helped make the Colony operational. It would have been foolhardy to bury all that gold with its owners." He flicked ashes into an azalea bed, turned to me. "You know what Raven said earlier tonight? She said war is like a member of this family. In our own separate ways, we all live with it. She also told me Maria brings her tea from Okok. That it calms her down."

"She needs more than being calmed down. Do you think she really might kill herself, Dietrich?"

He rubbed his chin. "She loves herself too much. Not like Berthe. Berthe..." He stopped himself. "We absolutely cannot, cannot leave her alone even for—"

Above us, Raven suddenly flung open the balcony doors, and we jumped.

Light discovered us, poured over us.

"Pergamon, Dietrich?" she called down. Maria stood next to Raven, her arm around Raven's shoulders, supporting her.

"What about Pergamon, dear?" Dietrich's voice was disgustingly mellifluous, revoltingly patronizing.

Raven's was not. "Dietrich, when Axel was a boy, did you ever take him to the museum in Berlin to see the Pergamon altar?"

"Perhaps his mother did. I didn't." Quietly, he said to me, "Told you so, Axel. She's ratcheting up for an attack. Anger. Pure anger."

"No, Dietrich," I said. "Pure sorrow, pain."

"My father took us every Sunday," Raven said from above. "Every Sunday we stood in front of that Pergamon altar and he lectured us. He said the old gods are fighting with new gods, who had no pain on their faces. No pain whatsoever. In fact, no feelings on these Nazi faces. Did you ever see that altar, Axel?"

"I never left the forest, Raven," I replied. "I went from Forest A to Forest B."

"There's nothing on the faces of the new gods. My father took us there and said to us, 'See? Those are the Nazis. No feelings.'"

Dietrich sighed, sucked on his cigar, as if thoughtfully. "Of course we had feelings, Raven. Loyalty, bravery, devotion."

"I said *feelings*, not your asinine codes of honor!" she shouted. "You know nothing about feelings."

Dietrich shook his head in dismay, as if he didn't know what she was talking about—a definite possibility. Or perhaps he just didn't want to hear.

"And by the way, Herr Professor, the old gods…all had snake bottoms. All reptiles on the bottom."

That caught his attention. "Really?" His eyes widened. "Gods with tails. Pergamon, you say? The Chinese had tails, Osiris, the old gods. She's right." He said to me. "Snakes, reptilians—you'll find the references please, and, Axel, we must continue the dig before Hermann gets wind we're up there." He stomped out the flame of his cigar and was off to his study, leaving me in the shaft of Raven's bedroom light.

She leaned over the balcony railing.

"Thank you for swallowing the tooth."

"I didn't know what else to do."

"Sorrow, Axel. Deep and terrible sorrow."

"I know. I've always known. Raven—?"

"That's why I keep you here."

Chapter Twenty-One

At noon the next day, Dietrich and I continued the search for Solomon on Dr. Hermann's mountain, along the old roadway down to the river. For two hours, Cabloco gauchos, my father, and I grappled with stubborn rock. They were still at it as Dietrich and I sat in the shade of a small tent. Pouring water over our heads, we drank greedily, watching Okok and the miniature donkey Raven had given him make their precipitous way toward us.

Okok wore a large and frayed straw hat, as did his donkey. He carried a satchel of books, a guitar, and our lunch. Smiling, he took off his hat, passed the satchel to Dietrich, who seemed to be expecting it, and said, "Mrs. Baron has drunk the tea. She slept for hours, then ate a fine breakfast, which I did also, and went back to sleep. I set up a hammock in her bedroom. Maria rocks her. The shaking stopped. I do not know if it is ended. Maria sent this lunch." From the donkey's saddlebag, he produced paper bags of sandwiches.

Okok settled himself in the shade of his donkey, which shook off his straw hat and proceeded to eat it. Okok offered me a fruit juice, patted a place under the donkey for me, and said softly, "Sit with me, Young Baron." In the shade of the donkey, Okok lay back, his hands behind his head.

I sat against the donkey's rear legs and brushed flies from his belly.

Even as he wolfed down his sandwich, Dietrich tried to watch every stroke of the men working in the stone hole. When they finally finished, he dropped into the hole. From where I sat, I could see him examining each loosened stone, tossing them off the causeway. I wasn't needed.

When the donkey had finished eating his hat, Okok lovingly scratched the stiff hairs between his donkey eyes. The donkey let loose a series of snorts and whinnies and wheezes. Okok laughed. However, when he looked up at me, he sighed. "This Raven. Her spirit is trapped in fear."

Dietrich shouted, his voice crackling with excitement. "Look what we found! It's a factory. A goddamned factory, a foundry. This is incredible. Axel, come!"

Okok and I followed Dietrich's voice into the now-larger hole. We wriggled into a lit stone tunnel, then joined my father in a vast room. He was ecstatic. "Stairways, catwalk, columns. What's this? It's a building, not a mountain. Or perhaps a pyramid. The jungle hides many. Great cities everywhere. We may well be inside a pyramid!

"Capstones, cornices!" Dietrich shouted as I regarded the room in awe. "Perfectly fitted. No mortar. Worktables. Not a mine. It is a factory for thousands. Look, it goes on and on. Axel! A hundred furnaces, sulfur, fire. Ankle chains in the walls. So they had slaves." Dietrich held up a sheet of metal in a large, oxhide shape.

I knew what it was: ancient money. Hundreds were stacked in a herringbone shape, laid out on brushwood. "This is for trade," Dietrich said. "Oxhide because each is worth the value of an ox. And we know who Ox is. What was it the ship's captain said about the conveyor belt? The current?"

"If someone left Spain, they would arrive at the mouth of the Amazon."

Dietrich waved his lantern at the wall. "Writing, Axel. Phoenician, Hebrew. Get over here and make notes. On this wall, we have a bill of lading in clay. Yes." He wet his finger and licked the clay. "Here we are: Phoenician!" he shouted, exhilarated, as he stumbled over the letters. "My God! Six hundred bronze chariot wheels, four spokes, helmets, bronze, ten thousand shields of bronze, weapons of bronze, forty garments, sleeveless, linen." Dietrich challenged the ceilings. "Does anyone have any further doubt that Solomon's ships crossed the Atlantic?"

Okok and I followed Dietrich into an immense, vaulted, circular room, all stone, with capped doorways, a dozen of them leading out from the center, wheel-like, vast, into further rooms. The floor was studded with stone hammers. I felt cold air from a ceiling of rock: ventilation. In the center where we stood, astonished, were lines of stone worktables constructed of a horizontal slab with two uprights.

Dietrich's footsteps echoed on the hard clay floor, his voice, in all his sepulchral glory, booming through the darkness. "Drainpipes! Ventilation! More oxhides of copper. Oxhides, the coin of the god Og."

"Are you feeling all right, Dietrich?"

"Never better. What a discovery. Furnaces everywhere!" Dietrich led us into a larger room with curving ceilings supported by enormous stone columns. "On that wall, a sacred ibis. Egyptians were here too." He picked up a hammer, passed it to me. "Soil pounders of the Bronze Age. Look at this. They have found the same hammer all over the world." He turned away into another curve of whatever we were in. "Skeletons everywhere. Human bones with human teeth marks." He lifted a femur, thrust it at me. They buried their dead in their bellies." I jumped backwards into the dark. "Victory, victim, victual. A simple food supply: Work slaves until they die, then feed them to the remaining slaves. We never went that far."

Okok and I followed Dietrich from room to room as he worked his way back along drainpipes. I was frightened; Dietrich was fearless.

I felt my heart pounding in my neck. Or was it a reverberation from the stone hammers of the slaves who had worked, suffered, and died here?

We approached an inner wall and found an anomaly. This wall was man-made, with square bricks. "Dietrich, these bricks...they are the same as our house." As we felt along the wall for an opening, Okok came up from behind, startling us.

Grabbing our lanterns, he snapped them off and pushed us down to the floor with great force. Alert now beyond the strangeness of the interior wall, I became aware of the smell of smoke and the sound of chanting.

"Indian ritual?" I whispered to Dietrich.

Okok twisted my head to the right, toward a light flickering through a crack in the wall's mortar. There was another cavern just beyond. "Your people," Okok said to me in the old language.

On our bellies, we crawled to the light and peered through the crack.

The light came from a large, round, high-ceilinged chamber. I remembered Dr. Hermann saying all the houses were connected by underground tunnels. This must be one of them. Staring through the crack in the wall, I did not want to see what I saw.

⇽

Torches burned in wall sconces. Twelve figures in masks and black robes in a ring of polished stone chairs. And in a stone pit before them, in the center of the room, was Dr. Hermann's two-headed waitress, her four braids now growing iron gray with age, her four arms outstretched as an Oriental goddess, standing, spinning, spinning, and speaking in strange voices, many of them male, all in German.

Two masked figures lay inert on the chamber floor, perhaps dead.

The dozen masked figures chanted. I smelled incense on the smoke, or drugs. A faint ring of light increased in brightness and form, circled the pit, hung above it, growing brighter and brighter, then defused. The chanting stopped.

Still, the two-headed waitress turned and spoke in voices not her own.

Finally, one of the men stood and moved to her, ordering, "Stop."

"It's Dr. Hermann," I said to Dietrich. "I recognize his voice."

"Willi, the sacrifice, please." Dr. Hermann moved forward, intoning in a deep, resonant, and cadenced voice, his sincere voice, not the dangerous singsong: "Get up, oh son of the Aryan race. Wake up the strength of the god who sleeps in your interior. Defy and get over the curse of the world."

Dietrich sighed. "So, it's gone this far. Where will it sink to sleep and rest, this murderous hatred, this fury?" I knew Dietrich was now speaking of the Furies' rage, the rage of Achilles. He dropped to the dirt floor.

Willi, unrobed, unmasked, in uniform, wearing leather jodhpurs and a cluster of medals on his chest, dragged a screaming girl into the chamber.

I grabbed Dietrich's collar and hissed, "They have a girl." I squinted to see better. "She's a white girl. Where did they get her?"

Dietrich scrambled back to our viewing point. "What's this? Who is she?"

"Numi, Awa!" the girl screamed.

Okok pressed his face into my back. "She calls for Numi, Chief of the Shamburo tribe."

Light-skinned, the girl wore a small breechcloth and many red and yellow woven bracelets around her wrists and ankles. She was young, slim, innocent, barely curved. Her breasts in the flickering candlelight seemed like small buds, flowers. I couldn't see her face.

"A slave," said Okok.

Dr. Hermann pulled her down to the floor of the crypt and sang out: "Release the Aryan blood by the sacrifice of…of this girl."

Dietrich was next to me, pressing against my shoulder, gripping my arm. "Do not try to save her, Axel. Do nothing stupid."

What happened to "A man does what a man must do"?

As if someone had opened a window, a wind, a storm of wind, blew dust into our faces, and, quicker than a heartbeat, one of the masked men in black screamed, clutching his heart, falling over in his chair.

In the melee, a warrior wearing a majestic crown of yellow feathers leapt into the crypt. He took the girl in his arms and carried her away.

"Awa," Okok whispered with fear. "That is Awa, Numi's son."

Oddly, none of the men in their chairs moved or reacted to the attack. They must have taken heavy drugs. Only Dr. Hermann and Willi were active and upright.

Dr. Hermann scrambled to the inert figures laid out on the floor, tearing the mask off one. I recognized the face of the "Refrigeration" specialist. Dr. Hermann lifted another hood. It was a woman with yellow, piano-key teeth.

Madame Wanda, with a yellow feathered arrow in her chest.

Dr. Hermann took small Willi by the shoulders and, with the back of his hand, chopped him across the face. "I told you I need a Jew. This won't work."

"You achieved the ring of light, didn't you? Didn't you?"

"How can I release the power of the Aryan blood unless I kill a Jew? How can I contact Hitler?"

"Where am I going to find a Jew for you in this jungle?"

I heard a sharp intake of breath from Dietrich. My blood turned to ice.

In the dark, barely breathing, we crawled back toward the exit, Okok leading.

Chapter Twenty-Two

Numbed by our singular realizations, we emerged into the sunlight and sank to the earth, our heads in our arms, bent by the brutality and lunacy of what we'd seen. Sweat, dust, tears rolled down our faces, striped our shirts. Now we poured water over our heads as if to cleanse ourselves.

"Evil, evil," Okok intoned. "They make holes in the sky," he called as he left us to go sit under the shade of his donkey.

"Poor Madame Wanda," I said.

My father's head fell to his chest. "Hermann must have known about that cavern. He bricked it off from the tunnel. In his quest for his damned Aryan language, what other momentous facts has he hidden from me? We're as doomed as that damned gypsy. My work will be lost. These madmen will never let me go."

"Dietrich, there is something…. This cavern and its ancient writing show we are following the right trail."

"My lectures," he muttered, and I knew in his head he was picturing himself a scholar being admired and lauded. He lifted his head sharply, focused on some distant spot while his mind filtered my idea. Then he turned to me. "Ask Okok where we might find a remnant of Solomon."

"He called the Amazon Solimeos."

"Just so. We'll fight madness with madness."

Okok, out of deference to us, remained under his donkey, covering his eyes with his hands, pulling down his frayed straw hat. I beckoned him to rejoin us and explained what it was that we sought.

"Ah, *Solomao*." Okok paced before us, rubbing his chin. "And with this relic of Solomao, you will then leave our land? Could such a treasure draw the Nazis out of O Linda? That would be a good thing for all the jungle people. First, speak with Numi. That is no easy task. His tribe is isolated, scorning any contact with outsiders. Even so, there is little that Numi doesn't know." He spread his arms over us. "You will find something. Solomao is everywhere. Maybe your Hitler too."

I was not about to dissuade him that we had meant the relic was only for the three of us: Dietrich, Raven, and myself. But I intuitively knew that, if we escaped to Israel, Dietrich would turn the Occult Bureau Colony over to the Nazi hunters. He would identify and locate them not because of venality or morality, but absentmindedness.

So perhaps, ultimately, Okok could be correct that he would be getting rid of all of us. A relic of Solomon could rid O Linda of Dr. Hermann and his men, as well as the von Pappendorfs.

I helped Okok onto his donkey. "Will you come with us to find Numi?"

"Young Baron, wherever you are, I am. But Mohammed knows the way best. Ask Mohammed."

"Mohammed can't walk."

My father spoke up. "We can carry him!"

ↄ৴

Okok was arranging the expedition into the forest to see Numi. Since it was the rainy season and the forest was flooded, travelling by canoe was faster and safer than trekking in. At my father's behest, I drove to the Hideaway. Inside, the bar buzzed with fans and flies. A handsome native warrior, dripping in orange beads and painted in an elaborate mosaic of black paste, sat cross-legged in the shadows, against a wall, drinking a Coca-Cola. He glanced up as I came into the room, then looked away as if I were toxic. Helen the parrot presided over the bar.

A massive, nearly naked Indian woman, her body shaped in inner tubes of gleaming fat, was leaning into Mohammed's hammock, washing his feet. I was surprised to see an Indian woman inside the Hideaway.

I stood over Mohammed, cleared my throat.

Mohammed held up a chubby finger as the woman finished his big toe and moved away.

When I had his full attention, I shouted to him over the loud hum of fans that I'd come to invite him on an expedition to an uncontacted tribe deep in the jungle. It was believed they had emeralds and diamonds. We sought a relic of Solomon's.

He was less surprised by our quest than I had expected. "When I was trading on the river, I heard stories of Solimeos—they even call the Amazon that."

"Yes, I know. Okok told me. He also said you are the best guide we could have."

"True, to be sure," said Mohammed, "but I can't walk." He signaled the woman to turn down the noisy fans.

"Okok is making arrangements," I said. "Kupis will carry you in your hammock. Name your price. Dietrich says he'll double it. He agrees with Okok, says you're the only trader on the river who can handle a wild tribe."

"In the jungles are many isolated, uncontacted tribes. They can be pretty dangerous." Mohammed closed his eyes. "Tell your old man I want enough money to get out of here, to buy a small place in Rio and get medical treatment. Have my stomach stitched up." Mohammed took my hand in his beefy paw. His camel eyes were dark, limpid. "Hey, kid, do you think I can trust your father? I've had dealings with him in the past. I'm not so sure."

I didn't know what I should say so I said nothing.

"Here's the story," Mohammed continued. "I won't go if Dietrich goes. He'll bring trouble. His eyes…you know his eyes, there's nothing in them. Nazi, not see. How's that? Nazi, not see. Jungle people will surely kill your father if they see what I see."

"Alright," I said. "Let's say Dietrich doesn't go with us." That may be preferable, I thought. "How long would it take?"

"I'd say about two or three days, rowing above an old rubber station. Now, while the forest's flooded, we could sail up to a river station, hire dugouts and rowers, then row in easy, couple of days. So, Young Baron, where are we going?"

"Shamburo. Numi."

"Jesus, Young Baron, that's dangerous. Numi's okay, but his son Awa is a cannibal. Very dangerous, but they cannot be described as *uncontacted*. Who said that?"

"Okok."

Mohammed laughed. "Numi trades goods with Pastor Ken, though he is also too proud to let anyone know he's made any kind of deal with the hated white man." Mohammed lifted up on an elbow, blew his nose into a red silk handkerchief.

The nearly naked Indian woman ran to pick up the handkerchief and give him another as he continued, "At least a dozen or more years ago, it is said that a white woman in the forest had a pair of twin girls. Twins are very dangerous. Bad luck for the tribe. They must be killed. One died right away, but the other lived. Pastor Ken somehow got hold of this girl baby. Numi said she was theirs, but Pastor Ken and his wife, Kathy, wouldn't give her back to them. Awa brought a war party to the mission. Pastor Ken didn't want to give them the baby. Finally, they made a deal. The Shamburo got the baby girl, and somebody got a yellow diamond the size of a spotlight."

Stunned, I remembered the diamond flashing on Dietrich's hand soon after Raven returned, saying she had lost her baby.

"Awa agreed to keep the baby alive until she was full grown, and in return Pastor Ken would send rice and pots and pans and knives and chocolate. Pastor Ken gave her lessons too, I hear. She read Charles Dickens novels and the Bible, so she speaks English.

"I've had emeralds from that area, big, gorgeous ones, six, seven carats. So we take the yacht up river into the Saudade, then get to an old rubber station and hire rowers and dugouts and look for a white cliff. That's Shamburo territory. The white cliffs are about two days' sail from the last rubber outpost. That's where I traded in my glory days, at the rubber outpost. Nothing surprises me on that river. There are creatures we don't know wandering deep within. Who knows what they are, where they come from? Everyone's been in and out of here for thousands of years. You go deeper, you find huge villages, roads, bridges. Civilized. Thousands, maybe hundreds of thousands of people. Cultivated fields, cultivated forests. That's why all these tribes speak different languages. They come from different places. Blue eyes. Jews, Greeks, Irish. This was the garbage dump. Slaves, all that shit, colonies. You hear this stuff up and down the river. Everyone's got stories. Listen, up in Titicaca they have the same reed boats as in Mesopotamia. A tribe north of here has two-nosed dogs. Won't sell them. Tried to buy a bitch and a dog. Double-nosed Andean Tiger Hounds. This is God's kitchen, and he cooked up some real messes."

"Two noses, Mohammed?" I challenged. "Come on."

"I'm not shitting you, Young Baron. Snakes have two pricks. Why can't dogs have two noses? Why do women have two breasts and not one big one? Or an extra one on their backs for dancing? And why two noses? Why two balls?"

From the bar, Helen echoed, "Two balls!"

Mohammed looked her way. "While we're gone, Maria will have to watch my parrot. Take Helen back with you today. Axel, you know where my trunks are? Go in and get this little khaki bag. It's got my trade stuff in it…rings and bottlecaps. And put more bottlecaps in it. Jungle people love bottlecaps. Before reaching Awa, we will have to go through the territory of another uncontacted tribe, very small. Shouldn't be a problem. Except you need five more men beside the Kupis."

೧⁊

After convincing Willi I was looking for emeralds and Mohammed would come along because he was the only one who could deal with an uncontacted tribe, Willi granted us permission. He issued me an odd handful of travel documents, all meaningless but impressively official.

We prepared to go into the forest, this time with Okok, a half-dozen Kupi warriors to protect us, and five more men to carry Mohammed.

The Kupis, teeth newly sharpened and blackened, hair long and thick with grease, bodies painted in reds and blacks, boarded our yacht. They carried baskets of meat: monkey, parrot, snake, otter wrapped in shiny banana leaves, all ritually cleansed by shaman chief Okok. They hung calabashes filled with manioc around the deck, hammocks in a spider web configuration between upright pipes in the engine room. The Kupis walked around the yacht like jaguars, with a peculiar forward roll, a bend to their shoulders, a dance in their feet, the heels hitting the ground first, that sullen, wound-up, almost four-legged gait, a lethargic stalking that might instantaneously launch into animal speed. Whatever happened, we would be safe with them.

Unless, of course, they turned on us.

Mohammed arrived at our dock, a grand potentate in his hammock, in a shimmering, white silk kaftan, clean, and, extraordinarily, the skin of a black jaguar thrown over his shoulders, its legs looped in a knot on his chest. Incandescent, a great gleaming moon god, he was larger than life. I expect he would stun Numi's tribe. Beneath him four Kupis struggled. A fifth Kupi carried Mohammed's olive jar and two canes.

He took a seat next to me, and I heard irregular rattling in his chest, blockage in his airways. I could only hope Mohammed survived this journey.

Okok came up from behind me and patted my back. He gave me a leaf to chew. He inhaled a pinch of something from a monkey fur bag hanging at his waist.

Maria's son Mike was our driver, taking the yacht as far upriver as he could. When we passed the mission, Pastor Ken's adorable, bland, blonde wife, Kathy, blew us a kiss. "Pastor Ken's in the back," she called out, "tending to his flock of asparagus. Stop on the way back. I'll have plenty for you. Safe trip. God bless."

Mohammed kept pointing and waving us on until we came to the truly decomposing trading post from the years of the rubber boom: a shack, a sinking dock, roofless storage outbuildings, a handful of Yama men smoking and watching us. Mohammed was tense, flatulent with excitement.

We offered the headman a small amount of money for three dugouts and five rowers. The steely-eyed Yama and his boys jumped into a dugout. After we lifted Mohammed into the sturdiest of dugouts, Mike tied up the yacht. He'd stay behind, with two armed Kupis guarding the boat.

၅၇

Our party turned into the forest, into a dismal dawn. We removed guns from waterproof cases and laid them on our laps. The Kupis were ready with their bows, I with my dart gun. The forest was flooded to a depth of thirty feet. Hundred- and two hundred-foot trees stood knee-deep in these invasive waters. We paddled under giant, arched roots.

I sensed Okok's suspicion. He didn't like what he saw behind the eyes of the Yama rowers, but we had no choice. As soon as we completed a curve in the river, two Yamas in our forward dugout jumped overboard, swimming back toward the trading post. I managed to shoot two small crocodiles just before they snapped jaws on them, but other brutes soon followed in their wake. The two Yamas disappeared in a crocodilian kill roll.

"Good sacrifice," Mohammed said with a nod. "Should be lucky for us."

We moved further into a melancholy twilight of enormous trees, twined curtains of thick ropes. There was little light, no wind, little air, a stink of molds and sponges. Except for pinpoints of light where a giant tree had fallen, the canopy blocked the sun. The water was without movement; a terrible silence. Occasionally we heard a scream, a hard-metallic sound, a crash, the cough of a jaguar, the slap of a fish hitting the surface. Every sound seemed to mark another death somewhere in the forest.

Okok shook his head, shrugging his shoulders, and mumbled, "Spirits." Sometimes the Yama rowers stopped, waiting, shoulders dropped low, heads hanging. They wanted to go back.

We switched from oars to poling, which meant that three Yamas had to stand for hours. I saw them shave bits of wood from the poles, mix the shavings with river water in the palms of their hands, and drink the potion. They took turns, poling or sleeping.

Okok teetered precariously on the prow, slashing at thick, twisted knots of lianas with a machete. Now and then, he tossed a length of neon-pink surveyor's tape over a limb to mark our path. The water was dark with leaves and muck. Great snakes hung from trees. Fish leapt into the air around us, snapping fruit from trees. The rowers and the Kupis plucked fruits and nuts from low-hanging limbs. Through olive waters, we saw tree roots deep beneath the surface. We couldn't see the forest floor, just gigantic roots, like aqueducts of ancient cities, here, there, vanished. Terrifying, dim, pathless, a shadowy netherworld of stink and splash, created over time.

Our own sounds were eerie: lonely, hollow, too human. Snakes slithered beside us on the water. A large female tapir and her baby swam past. The mother glanced shyly over her shoulder at me and swam on, breathing hard. Everything was muffled, unclear. No one dared ask if we were lost. The sun dropped. The water deepened. The rowers shifted from poles back to oars. We put up our oars, slept on the dugout floors, sandwiched between mats. Okok chanted his icaros, fast and nervous.

Chapter Twenty-Three

On the second day we set off before dawn. When the dugouts scraped shore at the still-moonlit white cliff, I knew we were in Shamburo territory. Mohammed reached his hand out for a piece of the cliff, then licked the chalk.

"Seashells," he pronounced. "The ocean was once here. The Amazon Sea. The earth shifted. The sea became a river, and they called it the Solimeos. And this dike? Pure vitrified glass. This one horizontal layer...beneath it, fossil shells and bones. Above it? Nothing. A line of death."

As dawn crept closer, we climbed a soft, crumbling path winding from the water up and around the limestone cliff, the Kupis laboring and groaning under the great burden of Mohammed in his hammock. Before us the forest sprang up forever.

Okok and I knelt behind trees under the canopy. Ahead we saw a fire in a clearing. The forest was quiet. Every creature listened, waiting for us. The warriors found their bows and arrows. Someone was nearby.

Okok lifted his arms up to me as a child would, asking to be put on my shoulders. Up there, while I clasped his small feet, he tasted the wind with his tongue.

We heard a girl's melodious voice. "Come."

Looking around, we saw no one.

"Be cautious," she sang, "for the forest is a creature." Words lilting, her voice got closer. "The forest, wild and rapturous, black and green, obscene as the droppings of a spider, as the placenta of a dog birth. It is the mind of the tribes, this forest."

Spotting her in the dusky columns of early forest light, we approached. It seemed she wasn't speaking to us as much as reciting lessons. Under the buttress of a great tree, we stood and watched as she pulled a pale young vine from the arching tree and wound it around herself in a pirouette.

Was this the girl rescued from Dr. Hermann by the cannibalistic Awa? We hadn't seen her face then, but she'd had blonde hair and looked about the same height.

Okok slid off my back, dashed between my legs, and turned to stand in front of me, his finger pushing into my chest, into my heart. He looked at me steadily, excitement in his eyes.

A stroke of sunlight lit the girl's face. She looked like an adolescent, blonde, blue-eyed Raven. Was this the girl in the forest who had no name?

Hand raised, her fingers long and translucent, she signaled us to follow. Bracelets of live beetles flashed on her wrists and ankles.

When she saw me looking at them, she smiled. A forest creature herself, she had Raven's legs, too long for her body, and the high waist, the tiny cleft in her chin. And those eyes.

"Soon the arrows of day will enter the forest," she said. "Numi waits to welcome you."

In the opal flesh of morning light, past the black holes of garbage pits, she led us toward the village clearing but then carefully away, in a large arc, from its center—hiding us, I thought. She was so evanescent, I thought that at any moment she might disappear. I wanted to hold her, to make her real, to keep her safe.

"These are the manioc gardens of the women. As I am a twin, I am not allowed in them." We circled the gardens. She pranced in front of us like an excited puppy.

Outside a hut, a bent and twisted old woman waited, like an eel ready to spring. "Die, twin!" she said with an upturned lip.

The girl stopped, laid her hand on my chest. "I had no name but Twin, but Pastor Ken gave me one: Rainflower. Isn't that pretty? Still, because I'm a twin, children hide from me. Women flee to their huts. Only Numi loves and protects me. When Numi dies, I will be killed because a twin brings danger."

There was something both hopeless and magical about her. She stopped and laid her hand on my arm. "I talk a lot. I survive by telling my story." She turned on her heel and we followed.

"Rainflower," I called, "if they have to kill you, why did they save you?"

She smiled at my ignorance. "For the tribe. I cannot die until Numi dies, and then the tribe will have good fortune." With hands floating at her sides like butterfly wings, in a cadence of movement and words, she spoke from memory, rehearsed. She reminded me of my father—her father?—lecturing, wandering through his broken landscape of ideas.

"Numi said they traded a yellow diamond for me," she said. "My baby sister died. They were going to kill me too—to bring the tribe better luck—but Pastor Ken stopped them. He would teach me and give our village rice and guns and candy but no bullets every year for the rest of my life. Numi agreed, as long as he could get cookies and Hershey bars. He promised to send me to the mission for lessons. So Kathy and the ladies at the mission made me dresses and Pastor Ken taught me words. Tura took me in the boat every day. Numi came to love me." She held a strand of her hair next to my head. "Do I look like you? Your eyes..."

"No, you are beautiful."

She nodded. "What is your tribe?"

Before I could stammer out an answer, drumming began behind us. It grew faster, louder, filling my chest. A brilliant pair of red-and-blue macaws flew over our heads, swooped, dipped, and called out. "*Nga, nga.*" A cloud of saffron forest light wove itself into the fine fog.

We followed Rainflower around the periphery of the village. I heard drunken men snoring and retching, a baby crying, a woman singing. A dog barked a thin, sickly bark.

She looked at me gravely, peering through the filigree of light as she took my hand. "I tell my stories to the birds. But they fly away and take my words with them. It is too late. Numi grows older; soon they will kill me. I speak my words to you because you have kind eyes. Maybe you will take my words away with you." She laid a finger on her lips to quiet us and led us to a large hut. Her pain pulsed in my chest.

Okok hissed. I slipped my hand from hers.

"And here is Numi's hut. He has four wives and many children. I sleep next to him. His feet are swollen like gourds, and his banana is the size of a grub, yellow and folded, and his voice is thin like air, like mosquitoes, and he talks all day. I am safe at his side. I clean him and stroke him and bring cool river water to him and manioc beer. He drinks and talks to me about the wind, the stone-mouthed fish, the green stones, the great mother snake at the bottom of the river. Even as he lives in this time, his head is with the Creators. I have crept behind him in his jaguar nights, quietly, softly, on my hands and knees. My hands curl under and become claws. It is true. In the morning, my knuckles are stained with the birth colors of the forest floor. Numi says we are all things. Do shamans come to you? Numi is an important chief. Many shamans come to heal him."

"Do they ever speak of Solomao?" I asked.

"Oh, yes, of many things. Numi will tell you what you want to know." She put her hand on mine, a spidery touch. She drew a little circle on my skin.

I was shocked by this child who had so much to teach. I asked, "Is it true that when you know how and when you will die, then nothing frightens you?"

"Yes, that's correct."

I thought of my experiences in the jungle with ayahuasca. "Do you drink from the vine, Rainflower? Have you seen spaceships flying above?"

"Spaceships?" She looked at me quizzically while uttering the word. "On the river?" She didn't know what they were. "I've seen pink cities of coral under the river. And palaces of green stone. When I lie on the hammock beside Numi, he pulls me toward him, laughing. He wants to hear words I learn at the Mission. 'Radio,' I say. He wheezes with laughter, and I hear the rattle of the demon beetles that invade him." She turned to me and placed her hand on my arm. Bracelet beetles danced on her wrists. "Do you have a name?"

"Axel."

"Mr. Axel, do you know Mr. Charles Dickens? Does he live in your village?"

A small pig rushed past us, screaming. Dogs woke and barked high-pitched alarms. People stumbled from their huts, rubbing their eyes, scratching themselves.

"I must wake my grandfather, Numi. Sit here." She disappeared into the hut.

There was no question who she was. I didn't know how I could save her, but I knew I should.

❧

An arc of thatched beehive huts circled the plaza. Overshadowing the other structures was a looming men's house. Which meant there were many warriors, but we saw none. We sat on an apron of hard-packed soil against the side of the men's house, our weapons across our knees. Okok gripped my arm.

"Her face is yours, Young Baron," he said.

I could set the forest on fire, and white men up and down the river would be massacred.

Okok heard what I was thinking. He shook his head sadly and spoke slowly. "Everyone goes where he belongs. Rainflower belongs here. Leave her." Okok squeezed my arm. "Remember why we are here. Signal Mohammed to come in."

After they'd rolled Mohammed out of his hammock and stood him upright on his canes, the warrior Kupis moved well behind us, crouched, invisible, available. The carrier Kupis stood around Mohammed, leaning on their guns.

The plaza was empty. The world held its breath.

Mohammed stood in full view, vast, magical, breezes whipping his kaftan about, swirling, shimmering, larger than life, immense, wavering on his canes, the fur of his great cat shining on his shoulders. He called out his greeting, "Ho!" Again, "Ho!" and, bending over, managed to lean on a cane and blow the trumpet of his nose into a fire-red silk handkerchief. He swayed back and forth. His unsteadiness made him seem even more unworldly—as insubstantial as he was substantial. He acted with such abandon and titanic madness, the poor Indians, I'm certain, wouldn't be able to identify him as enemy, victim, or a great and gleaming moon god.

He had become Mohammed again and knew how to trade and terrify.

"Ho!" he called again. "We arrive as friends, seeking answers." It was unclear how many hidden people were watching. "We're okay, Young Baron," Mohammed said to me. "They would have killed us by now."

Surrounded by his Kupi guards, Mohammed tossed bottlecaps and dime-store jewelry to the ground. Women and children peeked from their huts, found courage, and scrambled for Mohammed's treasures, then raced back to their dwellings.

A dog sniffed, growled at me. I knew Shamburo warriors were fully armed someplace in the rear shadows of the huts, ready.

Another red-and-blue macaw swooped across the dance plaza, and when I turned to watch, four warriors appeared, stone-faced, with bow and arrow aimed at us. Asian-eyed, thick-lipped, long-eared, their faces painted in swastikas, circles, dots, stripes. Small but fierce. Their leader was the man who had saved Rainflower from Dr. Hermann.

Okok whispered, "Awa. Cannibal. Son of chief."

He was magnificent, knotted with muscles, smooth, laden with jaguar teeth, shells, bracelets, as beautiful as a jaguar itself. He was short but so powerful he filled the space of a man twice his size.

He walked directly to me, energetic hatred flashing in his eyes, a rictus grin on his face, part greeting, part bite. He stamped his bow on the ground, dropped it at my feet, and ran counterclockwise around the dance plaza again and again. His warriors cheered. Then he stood before me, chin in the air, challenging.

With no tricks at the ready, I laughed and ran clockwise around the dance plaza. The dust of my steps erased his, and he was furious, leaping in the air, shouting. Unwittingly I had erased his magic.

Everyone observed our display. Awa shook his green, woven penis shield at me. It was the size of my index finger. I grinned at him.

Okok tried to tell me something, but it was too late, for, thinking this was a play motion of friendship and manhood, I had already drawn my relatively exemplary penis out of my pants and shaken it at Awa.

Infuriated, he jumped me, knocking me to the ground and pinning me in place.

Using a move Okok had taught me, I surprised him and was able to roll away and pin him to the ground. Shamburo warriors moved in to protect his honor, their arrows pointing at us.

Okok pulled me toward him as four women rushed into the plaza. On their shoulders they carried a small, nut-brown, wizened man who wore a red beeswax cap, little else. The old man wielded a large palm club that he swung expertly, hitting his target with such force that he himself tumbled off the women's shoulders.

But the old man had managed to knock Awa onto the plaza floor. "Numi," Okok said to me in the old language.

Numi locked eyes with me, pointed to the men's house, and I heard his voice in my head. "Be careful. My son is a good son but a bad man. You are not safe here. Go into the men's house."

I assigned four of the warriors to remain outside with Mohammed. He was too large to carry into the opening to the men's house. Mohammed, glorious, was soon surrounded by women and children; he tossed them more bottlecaps.

I had promised Dietrich to also ask for emeralds when I spoke with the chief. I would not.

Four wives carried Numi into the hut. They gestured for us to sit on woven mats. Numi sat higher on an ironwood tree stump. Smoke coiled and rose into a hole at the top of the house.

Rainflower wandered into the smoke. Now she wore a flour sack muumuu and carried a young caiman in a basket on her head. The caiman's awful claws were caught up in her hair; its tail flapped on the back of her neck; its ancient, corrugated head dropped over her forehead. Rainflower sat beside Numi, the caiman now in her lap, her arm around Numi's insect waist.

The four solemn wives brought us bowls of something black and bitter.

Numi cleared his throat. The drumming ended. I could hear his wheeze although I was a good ten feet from him. The wives sitting around Numi fanned him with palm fronds as he rocked back and forth, reciting singsong in the cadences of Rainflower's stories.

He sat before me, eyes searching mine. I reached my hand toward him, looking steadily into his eyes, as steadily as I could. It was like looking into the smoke hole of the men's house, the hole from which our ancestors watched, where the spirits descended.

Just as cautiously as I had, he reached out and grazed my knuckles with his. A shudder moved up my arm and through my body. And then Numi approached and poked me hard in the belly and again in the chest. He wanted to see if I was real. He thought we were ghosts. He reached toward my boots, touched them, nodding, I thought, in approval.

I wanted to touch him as well, to hold his hand, but was worried that might alarm him. Reading my thoughts, he took my hand and held it against his cheek for the briefest moment. I smiled.

Standing for that brief moment in the aura of humanity, he gripped my arm, squeezed it again and again, and smiled with me, pumping my arm, unblinking with those smoke-hole eyes searching me, I knew, thinking of me, validating me as I had never been before, validating us, connecting me with his power, offering himself to me.

Even though I had been standing in what I had considered a primitive landscape with a primitive being, it was I who had just advanced, I who had leapt across an abyss of time into an expanded consciousness.

I felt lightened, enlightened, and deeply connected. I had to wipe my eyes with my sleeve. I wanted to give him something. What did I have to give him, not to trade but to share? In my back pocket was a soggy postcard of the shoreline in Rio: the beach, the hotels, the high-rises, the umbrellas, the sea. I handed it to him.

He turned the limp postcard upside down, over, around, up, and down, as if perhaps there were something inside it. He could not understand buildings, what he was seeing, if there was something perhaps within the cardboard. But he passed it to two of his wives, who also turned it upside down, around and around, and over, not comprehending what they were seeing.

Sitting beside him, Rainflower listened to Numi, then spoke his words for me. "There are only a few of us left in the forest—a small tribe, once great. My people are weavers. Plump and brown like tough birds, they wear string on their groins, feathers in their noses, needles in their lips and cheeks, and weave what is not to be worn nor sat upon nor slept upon. We weave our story in three layers. The outside layer tells the future. The under layer tells the past, which is not unlike the future. Between the two is a secret layer, one that is never seen. That layer is the real story of our lives, the true secret of our creation, our center that binds.

"We live not to offend, not to disrupt the harmony, the uneasy balance between our tribe and the forest, between our tribe and the animals, between our tribe and the Mother River. Do not disrupt our lives, our harmony."

Awa burst into the hut, standing before his father, muscles twitching, his back to us.

Father and son argued, voices rising and falling as Awa jumped up and down, twitching, shaking his bow in the air, punctuating his anger. Turning toward me, he glared with hatred. The wives pulled him away. He squatted before his father, made two fists, and pressed them into his eyes. I believed it was an apology.

Okok spoke to Numi, who nodded his head in understanding.

Awa swiveled around and looked directly at me, then said, "Yes, I will find something of Solomao, and you will remove the white men from the forest."

High above me on the roof of the men's house, black-and-white orioles flitted in the smoke of the fires. The parrots called and sang and cackled and swooped with my own exhilaration. *Solomon!*

I told Okok to tell Numi we sought a solid object from Solomao that we could carry away when we departed his lands.

Awa nodded his understanding, but there was something so murderous in his eyes my fingers shook. He pulled at my braid, brandished a knife, cut off four or five inches, and held them above his head—a trophy. Next my head, I knew. Next me.

Even so, Numi spoke to Okok. "My son and his warriors will go to friendly tribes seeking Solomao. And they will go to tribes who are not our friends. We will find a thing for you. Now, run!" Numi said, although he said nothing aloud. I heard him in my head. "Leave now!"

We ran. I lifted Okok onto my shoulders and carried him down the path, out of the village and onto the pulpy floor of the forest. The four Kupis had already vanished into the forest with Mohammed.

Rainflower stood at the tree where she had first wound the vine around herself. I reached for her.

Okok pounded my shoulders. "No. Don't touch."

"Come, come home with me," I said to her.

Rainflower did not answer, only turning away and heading back to Numi's hut.

$\wp$

Rain fell in fat drops. We rowed with every iota of strength we could muster. There were no sounds. Mohammed said he heard nothing, that Awa and his men weren't following us, he didn't know why. "Maybe they aren't hungry."

After we arrived at the rubber station and transferred into the yacht, our driver Mike paid off the Yamas with pots and pans. He turned the yacht into the river. Upriver there had been a powerful, damaging storm. The river waters had turned from jaundiced yellow to amber, murky with sediment, the legs of her long banks open to the garbage of the forest, murdered trees, mercury from our gold mines, dead fish.

The waters churned mud and vegetation; the boat humped and bucked, arched and dropped. Blood-red lightning cells burst to the north. Thunder rumbled, still distant. We were forced to drop anchor in a bay as turbulent skies and churning waters threatened.

For two long, tense days, we slept with our weapons. Finally, Mike announced the storm was retreating and we were heading out.

But no, scars of lightning closed in on the booms of thunder as we neared the mission.

I heard Okok's bare feet pounding on the stairs down to my room below deck. He knocked on the open door, jerked his chin upwards, tossing a pile of horse blankets into my arms before saying, "It's Mrs. Pastor Ken! And Mr. Pastor Ken! Quick. Guns! Awa."

Blankets went over the railings to protect us from arrows. On deck, with rain driving against us in horizontal sheets, the boat jumped under my feet as Mike tried to hold it in place. It took me a few moments to understand what I was seeing, a few heartbeats to realize that Pastor Ken's mission was now a pile of rubble with smoke rising, hissing in the rain. And on the two lampposts on the landing were Kathy's head and Pastor Ken's head.

Even through the rain, I could see the horror on their faces. What kind of God allows goodness to merit such cruelty? "Mike, take the boat up to the dock."

Okok said, "No. Too dangerous."

"There might be other people at the mission still alive. We must."

Okok and I draped the blankets over the railings, passed rifles to me and his warriors. Ken and Kathy's faces were contorted, frozen in astonishment. Or did Pastor Ken greet martyrdom as a step in the right direction?

Awa appeared between the lampposts, arms raised, a palm club pointing to Pastor Ken's head, the tip of his bow pointing to poor Kathy's head. He wore his great crown of yellow feathers, my braid attached. Warpaint blackened his body, a sheath of arrows on his back: powerful, frightening. A generator of evil, the other side of Paradise.

I felt as if I were in the quicksand of evil, a horrible connection drawing me to what he was. Enough to fog reason, enough to make my fingers tremble on my gun and my limbs turn cold because my blood had moved into my heart as my last defense. He was half my size. And thousands of times my strength. Paralyzed, I heard the thud of an arrow on the horse blankets damp with rain, a hiss as the fire sputtered out. Murder, hot and swelling, rose in my throat.

Awa shouted a word in anguish. "Tun! Tun!" This was the real heart of the forest, the horror, the inherent cruelty of nature.

Okok yelled across to him. Awa yelled back. "Tun! Tun!"

"He wants twin. He says you have twin. White girl from forest."

I yelled to Awa. "Awa, I don't have."

"Tun. Tun."

"His girl ran away to the mission, said she would not return to their village. So Awa burned the mission. Now he thinks we have her."

Okok shouted in some atavistic *lingua franca*. Awa yelled back.

"I tell Awa, 'Go sit in shit until your nose falls off.'"

Awa shouted back, let loose another arrow over our heads. "Tun. Tun!" Demanding, furious, desperate, his yellow feathers vibrating with anger.

Okok told him, "What have you done, Awa? You put the Shamburo in danger from the white men."

Awa stamped his foot on the dock. "They steal from me, I kill them. You steal from me, I kill you."

Okok spoke, then told me, "I told Awa that we will look for her. You give him the girl, he gives you Solomao."

Awa stuck the tip of an arrow into a pile of ashes. It came up burning. He placed it in his bow, held it toward us, threatening. It sputtered in the rain.

Mike and Okok let off a barrage of gunfire over his head. We did not want to kill Indians and bring on a massacre of white men.

Another fiery arrow hit the blankets. Awa backed into the forest.

We crouched behind the blankets. I called to Mike to anchor at a distance for twenty minutes longer, to turn the radio up as loudly as he could. We watched and waited for any sign of survivors on shore. Someone might have escaped the fire and still be hiding in the forest.

Through spaces between the blankets, guns ready, we watched the trees around the mission. Samba music filled the forest. The rains eased. The river slowed. We had anchored out of the mainstream of garbage floating in the angry current. Still the boat bucked and swung and creaked.

I heard the thin, high whistle of an arrow, felt it part the air and penetrate my leg. I fell back on the deck. My destiny, hot and ferocious, quivered in the calf of my leg.

Okok grabbed a gun and shot where Awa had stepped back into the vegetation.

He sniffed my leg, sniffed the arrow, sniffed its feathers. "Maybe curare, maybe not." He blew his powder in my face, mixed salves and lotions, gave me something to drink, held my head on his naked lap. He prepared a paste of salt and rubbed it around the arrowhead. He poured a salty drink into my mouth. "Salt helps."

There was no getting the arrow out. I felt Okok tug gently. I howled and forced myself to think through the pain. Okok touched the feathers of the arrow, smelled them, listened to them, whispered to them. Heat rose in my leg. Okok blew smoke in my face. He'd lit a fire in a pot and was blowing something dizzying in my face, something sweet and penetrating. Even so, I could feel the burning of the arrow all through my leg, up into my hip. Very gently, Okok removed my boots. My feet were swelling. The poison was spreading.

Mike and Okok tried again to pull out the arrow. They couldn't.

The pain was excruciating. Okok threw something else into his pot. With both hands, he lifted the smoke toward my face. The pain receded. Everything receded, blurred.

I watched the condors. I flew with a squadron of red-eyed males and flew from one double helix to another, from one ladder of braided snakes to the other, spiraling upward, widening as they lifted me toward a street of towering clouds, heavy with tears. I might die. "What a pity," I told the lead condor, "that I'm going to die before making love to Raven."

He seemed to understand because he laughed.

Curving from thermal to thermal, too low, skimming my own great bird-shadow over my river, my mind unfettered, I sailed into great answers and knew everything. "Bananas, Dietrich. Forget words—trace bananas across the continents. Bananas."

I came to consciousness as another fiery arrow hit a horse blanket. A blanket next to it was on fire. Okok threw the blanket into the water. I crawled behind the cabin. The warriors and Okok kept shooting. Mike was shooting from the wheel.

"Is it just Awa? Or a party?"

No one answered. No one knew.

Two small and pale hands clutched the edge of the deck, then disappeared. I pulled myself over to the water. The hands came up again, nearer the prow. I slid towards them, in agony, grabbed one, pulled.

Rainflower was very light, very small. I pulled her easily up over the railing and into my arms. Slender and slippery, something aquatic. Even in my arms, even pressing her flesh and bone against my chest, even then she became something else, wavered between reality and hallucination.

I leaned against the cabin wall. Her hair smelled of smoke. Her mouth trembled. She'd seen the massacre. "Okok," I called. "She's here!"

"Very bad." He swung around, tossed a blanket to us. "Now Awa follows us."

Mike called down. "Too dangerous. He's shooting fire-tipped arrows, and the rain's stopped. They could ignite the fuel tanks."

"Okay, we're out of here," I said. "Okay, Okok, moving out."

We were underway, crashing wildly through a blockade of limbs and lumber and crocodiles, submerged trees and palm fronds, crashing through them, driven from behind by them.

"*Nga! Nga!*" Macaws vanished into the sun to dip their feathers in its blood. A band of howler monkeys screamed, shrieked, flung themselves into the ceiling of green.

Mike carried me into the cabin, laid me on a bed. Rainflower was on the other bed, breathing heavily, curled up like an animal.

I watched her chest rise and fall. I wondered how many breaths I had left. My head spun. I needed an airplane to get me to a hospital. They were all in Rio.

Okok again tried to pull on the arrow, smelled it.

"If I go septic, Okok, take Rainflower to the convent, to my sister Cecilia. Make certain. Only to Cecelia."

As I turned, I hit the arrow on the soft edge of the blanket. I screamed.

Rainflower uncurled, sat up on the bed, stared at me, bent toward me. "Numi Chief tells me I must take the arrow from your leg."

"Don't touch it! No! Stay away from me."

"Mr. Axel, Solomao told him so. I hear him in my head."

"Don't you dare touch it! You hear me?"

"I'll just speak to it. Numi says I must." Rainflower jumped off her bed and stood over me, folded her arms across her chest, tucked her hands into her armpits, dropped her head, and sang in a monotone. "No bite, little dog.... Come to me, little dog...."

I felt the arrow topple from my leg and fall to the floor. She was singing to the arrow. Dogs obey. I had never heard an icaro sung in English.

Okok, watching, nodding, took the arrow from her, stuck it in an open cereal box.

"Why did you run away from the Shamburo?" I asked Rainflower.

"I had to be with you. My spirit guide told me so."

Puppyish, Rainflower crawled into the bed next to me. Rainflower, a child, a small, sexless Luba, curled up next to me in my narrow bed. She held my thumb with her entire hand, pressed her lips against mine to speak. "I will sing the songs of Solomeo that have come to us through our ancestors. Numi sings with me."

I had come close to the core of forest magic but was too late. The dark side of it was killing me cell by cell. "Go ahead. Sing."

"Numi will tell me how to help. I won't let you die, Mr. Axel."

"Sure, Rainflower. Just don't touch my leg."

She cocked her head, listened to the wind, sniffed. "Awa follows. I must make you strong very quickly." She whispered, sang, chanted into my mouth. Her breath was clean and sweet. It smelled like daisies in wet soil.

Time stood still, and I entered Rainflower's forest. In spite of everything I knew and trusted, something small and weak in me hoped she could keep me alive. I could feel poison burning in my gut.

She closed her eyes, rocking back and forth. "Your spirit says she did not come here to die from an arrow wound. Numi says you should trust Okok. He is a good shaman. You will live."

௸

By the time we got to O Linda, I was feeling better. Mike took Rainflower to the convent with my promise that if Cecilia could temporarily shelter and protect her, I would build her a new sanctuary. Nearly twenty but old beyond her years, bossy, wealthy Sister Cecilia had taken over. She now ran the convent as she pleased.

Chapter Twenty-Four

The house pulsed with anger. Dietrich and Raven had been fighting. My leg throbbed as I entered the dining room for breakfast. I could feel the tension climbing my spine. They were both dressed smartly: Dietrich in a fresh, white silk shirt under a paisley smoking jacket, Raven in a black kaftan embroidered with pearls, her hair done up in a great bun, held with diamond hairpins.

I was the guest, the joker before the king and the queen. Both acknowledged me with a brief nod and continued sipping coffee. Each had a folded newspaper at which they glanced from time to time. The outside world got closer and closer.

Neither looked my way as I lowered myself to the chair, careful to avoid hitting my tender leg on anything. I had returned from the expedition the day before.

Raven rang her silver bell. Maria appeared. Raven held the coffeepot out for refilling. Maria dipped her head and left. Not once had Maria raised her eyes to look at us. I felt a deep shame. We sat politely, as if a normal family at breakfast, as if the temperature of the coffee was important.

Dietrich refolded his newspaper. "Axel, tomorrow Colony members will be flying to Rio together, for fittings and so forth in preparation for Raven's birthday party. I'm assuming you don't feel well enough to join us."

"It's *your* birthday party, darling," Raven said. "Celebrating sixty glorious years."

"My dear, it may be my birthday, but it will be your party."

"Dietrich, enough. And I'm not going to wear your damned cross at the party. You hear me? No." So that was the matter at dispute.

"Do you want me to leave?" I interrupted.

Raven patted my hand. "Oh, no. Please stay. It might get better. It can't get worse."

A large crystal vase containing an arrangement of birds-of-paradise sat on the table between me and Dietrich. Maria would have done this purposely, so we didn't have to look at each other. I bent a few stalks sideways to see my father. He pushed the flowers upright, covering his face and, of course, mine.

He cleared his throat before speaking to his wife in a clipped tone. "I only request that you wear a cross so you will be safe in the time we have left here. Axel has arranged it so the Shamburos are searching for a relic of Solomon. When I have it, I will trade it with the Israelis for amnesty…for our amnesty."

"Not ours. Yours. You may have forgotten I am a Jew. I don't need amnesty." Raven closed her eyes. "Are you serious? You think you can turn yourself in and lecture around the world? Solomon? That's your bargaining chip on this suicidal ego trip? Jews don't care about Solomon. They want to watch you squirm in the witness chair, to hear the bones snap when they hang you. They want sweet pure revenge, *mein herr*."

Dietrich walked around the table, standing over her. "Goddamn it. You had better *listen*." That's when I saw long scratches on his cheek, deep scratches.

She sighed, shaking her head. "Alright, Baron Dietrich von Pappendorf, I am listening." How had she made our name sound like an insult? She poured another cup of coffee, twisting a spoon of cream into it, watching the cream circle.

"Soon we will have proof that Solomon and his ships visited the Amazon. With that, we shall make ourselves known and negotiate our freedom. Then I will rearrange the history of mankind, the origins of consciousness, the source of civilization, the connection between language and the genetic code, the mutation of genes, the mutation of words."

"And with whom do you intend to make these arrangements?" asked Raven. "Perhaps you could wear a sandwich board and walk around Rio. Wanted: Israeli Nazi hunter. For a good time, call. Details on rear."

Dietrich retook his seat, then smiled crookedly at us both. "How I adore this. Have you ever taken a Jewish mistress, Axel? Well-advised. So much Jewish passion."

Part of me wanted to hear everything. Part of me wanted to hear nothing. It invariably thrilled me when Luba made the occasional appearance, coming alive, swollen with anger, like a tick on Dietrich's blood.

She threw one of her sparkling glass torso babies, a red one, at Dietrich. "I'm not leaving," she said. "I've put my life into this place. You haven't so much as touched a coffee bean or a centavo. Grevaldo and I have made this enterprise into a great success while you were playing with yarn in your study. Language and genes. Who cares about any of that? I care about this place and my life here." She leaned back in her chair and closed her eyes. "You know, Dietrich, Bebe tells me everything…everything. And who Willi really is. Everything, Dietrich, because Hermann knows everything. He tells Bebe. Everything, Dietrich. And she tells me. As in Chile. As in the Fourth Reich."

"These things are in the past. I have no control. Willi is in charge—"

"Don't 'Willi' me, Dietrich. I know what's going on in Chile, for God's sake. They're training an army of Nazis. Hard not to notice all the gorgeous Aryan waiters at La Familia. You think they're really waiters?"

My leg throbbed. I excused myself and headed to the safety of the bathroom. Their words trailed me down the hallway. I heard shouts and the crashing of china through the walls.

Okok's chants and plants had helped. Raven was no longer shaking.

"Don't think I don't know who you are and what you did, Dietrich. I was there. I can bear witness. I know how many Jews you killed."

He choked, coughed, laughed. "Don't be a fool. That's ridiculous. You would never testify against me."

"And do you know what your dear Colony will do to you if they find out you turned yourself in? They'd hunt a traitor like you down.

You were the handsome aristocrat in their inner circle, an Aryan pilot flying to the glorious music of Wagner. A big-time, dangerous, murdering Nazi. But not just a Nazi, a criminal. You were one of Hitler's madmen!" Her words echoed throughout the house.

"You bitch," he shouted. Something dropped heavily to the floor. Dietrich shouted, demanding, "Axel! We have work to do. What's taking you?"

"And you can shove your cross up your ass," said Raven. "I'm not wearing it. I'm a Jew. Don't forget, Dietrich!"

"Axel, what the hell is taking you so long?"

Leaving the bathroom a minute later, at the foyer I smelled baby powder. I stopped in my tracks. Had Dr. Hermann been here and let himself in? My fears were confirmed when I heard a horse outside galloping away. What had he heard?

Ten minutes later, Raven found me in the sunroom, collapsed in an armchair. I wasn't quite ready to head up to work in my father's study.

"Are we even sure that Dietrich is actually a wanted man?" I asked her. "What if he turns himself in and they don't want him?"

"Then we have a hanging party. I'll take you to the Swiss Alps. *You* are very wanted."

She laughed a ragged laugh. She stood and walked around the room, breaking dead leaves from a ficus tree, crushing them, putting them in her pocket. "You know what I don't understand, Axel? Why didn't he change his name? Why did he insist on remaining—" she dropped her voice to a lower register as if announcing his entrance "—the Baron von Pappendorf?"

"It's his heritage."

"Stupid."

"It's who he is."

She spun around to look at me. "Is his work...*uh*...essential, in any way?"

"What are you thinking?"

"Wernher von Braun and his rockets are seen as critical, needed, important. The Americans protected him, gave him an entire agency, made him a hero. Are your father's studies even remotely as essential to, say, scholars as Wernher von Braun's work is to science?"

"If he's correct about Solomon, he will turn history upside down. If he's correct about language and genetics—well, there is no telling what other scholarship will follow, building upon his research. The problem is how to get it out to the world. That's why he wants to turn himself in. Of course, Dr. Hermann thinks Dietrich's alphabet work is essential to the Fourth Reich so they can rule the world. Dietrich devotes maybe ten minutes a day to Dr. Hermann's work, a lifetime to his own. He is conducting his own origins of consciousness work."

"Malignant narcissism. I am, at least, only narcissistic. Axel, I saw Hermann's horse from the dining room. What was he doing here?"

"I think he came in, heard the argument, and left politely."

"Manfred Hermann is not polite. Do you think he heard Dietrich say he was turning himself in? What if he heard me say I'm a Jew—I don't need amnesty? Oh, God!"

I stood and put my arm around her shoulders. "I don't know what he heard. But it may be yet another reason for you to leave this place."

Chapter Twenty-Five

In Hitler's house, Dietrich, exiled genius, yearned for recognition. His son, an Amazonian Teuton, half Indian, half German nobility, yearned for the genius's wife, certain that he would find, deep within her vagina, a golden homunculus who would tell him who he really was. Meanwhile, marvelous Raven, erstwhile wife, hid from history and pain, covering herself with jewels as if their glitter would blind others to who she really was.

That evening, Dietrich and Raven were to fly out with other members of the Occult Bureau Colony to Rio for haircuts and gown fittings in preparation for Raven's vast extravaganza—Dietrich's imminent birthday party.

It was midafternoon. Dietrich was upstairs; he had slept most of the day.

Maria had dyed, curled, and pinned Raven's hair into a gleaming black chignon, which, stuck as it was with her diamond-tipped hairpins, looked like a star-studded night cloud, pubic, silken, easing the growing ferocity of what was, after so many surgeon visits, Raven's sharp Inca profile.

She wore a handsome, white silk suit with black piping on the seams, sitting at her bridge table in the main room, dealing out endless games of solitaire, turning the cards face-up, bending the corners unnaturally slowly, as if she were a fortune teller teasing a client. Sliding them into their columns until, annoyed at losing, she began slapping the cards hard on the bridge table. Her long fingers drummed on the speckled surface of the bridge table. Her rings flashed.

I lay silent on a plush sofa nearby, content to be alone in a room with her.

"Everyone's talking about your fat mistress," she said after a few minutes.

Sperm boiled up within me and became venom. Or was it the other way around, venom preceding sperm? "Gossip travels fast."

"Why can't you just find someone pleasant and fashionable and get married for God's sake?"

"Who do you know who is pleasant?"

I accomplished the dubious victory of having her look directly at me. "You seem different. What happened in the forest, Axel?"

I had yet to tell her about Rainflower and was reasonably certain this was not the time or place to do so. I was terrified of how she might react and what she might do when she found out the truth but decided to make a start: "We are on the trail of solid proof that Solomon was in the Amazon, and, oh yes, we saw a girl living with a group called the Shamburo. She's very beautiful, with very sweet, intelligent eyes. The Shamburo are going to kill her as soon as she comes of age. She's bad luck for the tribe."

"That's terrible, Axel." Raven looked at me, waiting for something. She was not a person I could hide secrets from, I should have known. "You're not telling me everything."

"That's correct."

"Is there something I need to know?"

Dietrich arrived in a maroon velvet smoking jacket. Raven lay her cards down, stood, greeted him with a kiss on the cheek. "Well, look who's here. And none the worse. You slept all day."

Dietrich took his place in a winged chair. "How is it that shrewish rhymes with Jewish?"

"Silence, Baron," said his wife.

Dietrich rattled his paper. He read slowly, holding his head at odd and awkward angles. From my vantage point, all I could see of him were his black velvet mules and one long, elegant hand tapping out the rhythm of the words he read, tapping on the arm of the wing chair, a hand with an enormous, yellow-diamond ring, the size of one of Raven's Mah-Jongg tiles, the stone of which he had himself, he said, dug from a dry bed somewhere near the mouth of the Tapajos, which was a blatant lie.

Howler monkeys stole figs from the tree in the courtyard. Shitting, roaring, they raced above us along the roofs and the balconies. Under the howler screams, frogs riveted the ever-virgin forest with their demands. In response, Dietrich rattled pages of his newspaper. Raven slapped her cards.

A stream of urine splashed onto Dietrich's newspaper. A howler monkey scrambled along a beam above us.

Dietrich pulled a pistol from the pocket of his smoking jacket and shot him.

The monkey, a small one, dropped to the floor.

Raven rang a bell for Maria. She entered with her head down. Dietrich pointed his soiled newspaper at the dead monkey. Maria, accustomed to the monkey invasions, kicked the carcass into the kitchen, wiping her hands on her apron. She returned with a bucket and a mop, scrubbing up blood.

From the kitchen, I heard Helen call, "Monkey see, monkey do." Mohammed had yet to pick up his dreadful parrot.

ভ৩

We swung, this happy family, on a pendulum from pathological to normal, exhibiting the finest of manners between swings. I listened to Dietrich's heavy footsteps as he trod up the stairs, then waited for the slam of his bedroom door.

At her table playing cards, Raven listened also, eyes shifting.

"Raven," he called from above, "where are my cummerbunds? I can't find them."

"Top left drawer of your dresser, in a long brown box."

Words exploded from my dream world. "I want to feel you under me," I told her from the couch, sitting up. "I want to see you throw your head back in ecstasy. I want to hear you groan my name. I want to feel you come, Luba."

She swept her cards into her lap, and they fell between her legs under the bridge table. "Pick them up," she whispered, closing her eyes.

I dropped to the floor and crept around, ignoring any leg pain, picking up Raven's cards, resting my hands on her knees, which opened for me.

"Tongue," she commanded, pulling off her loose silk trousers. Tongue, I did. I was at ecstasy's gate.

She snorted, breathed, heavily, came almost instantly.

I scuttled about under the bridge table, picked up the remainder of the cards. When I had a full deck, I tossed them onto the bridge table and crept as fast as I could toward the sofa. I rolled into its crewel plush pillows to conceal, as they would say in my latest mistress's romance novel argot, my throbbing member.

When I was again presentable and dared to look over my shoulder to see a room empty of Dietrich, I observed Raven still playing her cards like a fortune teller with her pants pulled up, rearranging her destiny. I kept my voice low. "Let him go to Israel. You go free. Get out of here. I'll go with you."

"Why I stay here is not your business. Why don't *you* leave? You're a little goose-stepping rubber stamp."

"How can we so love each other as much as we do and be so cruel?" I asked.

It was a long time before she answered. And when she did, it was not Raven but the small voice of Luba, the wet nurse in my grandfather's castle, of Luba, sitting on the roof at night with me, watching stars, watching the red blood of war in the sky. "Where would I go? I've been safe here, Axel."

"Remember, in the forest, in the war, once, on the roof of my grandfather's house. Remember when we were watching the cities burn in the sky, you said that. 'Where will I go? What will become of me?'" I sat beside her. "You were Luba. What happened to her?"

"Tucked away. She's too sad. She remembers the stars, Axel. You made an alphabet. She remembers the moon rolling through the stars and writing stories. I don't want to remember her."

"I loved you even then."

"We were children. I was all you had. It's different now."

"You said Dietrich had blood on his hands. Back then I didn't know what you meant."

"You do now, don't you?" she snapped, her voice again Raven's. "Axel, there are two ways to survive. One, keep revenge burning in your heart and live on its fires. Two, try to forget and take the best of what you can. I have one hundred polo ponies, a closet full of designer clothes, furs, diamonds. And I control all the money. Luba grew up. It's better to forget."

"What about Dr. Hermann?"

"Dietrich will protect me."

But she had not seen what I had seen: a stone pit surrounded by twelve demented men in robes. In a fiery circle, with Dr. Hermann chanting his magic and a knife held at Raven's throat, could any of us save her?

ℰℐ

Dietrich returned from upstairs, oblivious to any lingering heat in the room. We took our places: Dietrich in his wing chair, me on the sofa, Raven at the bridge table with a new box of cards, starting a new game, shuffling cards.

From the depths of this chair, Dietrich announced, "First Eichmann—now this! The paper says Nazi hunters have caught Karl Steinmetz."

Raven held her cards in midair. "Oh my God, where?"

Steinmetz had spent time at the Colony, though he preferred Rio and his family lived in Buenos Aires. I took the newspaper, read out loud. The paper was two weeks old. "Scheduled for heart surgery, Karl Steinmetz was taken from his hospital bed in Buenos Aires at gunpoint. A high-level member of the *Kommanderwerks*, a Slovenian industrialist, expert in water energies, a suspected former Nazi, Steinmetz will stand trial in Israel for war crimes."

Dietrich's hands shook on the armrests of his chair. "Poor Karl. His family."

I stood over Dietrich's shoulders. "What did Steinmetz do in the war?"

"Ran factories, just as we did. Steinmetz was also a subsidiary of Thyssen. Water, heavy water."

Bright red spots painted Raven's pale cheeks. She had given up her life to be safe, and she was no longer safe. Her cards slapped harder and faster.

"He'll die in jail," said Dietrich. "He should have stayed here at the Colony. He would have been protected. But he wanted to live in a city and play his cello."

"They'll take everything from him, won't they?" Raven asked.

"Everything he has. How much do we have in Amsterdam, Raven?"

"Quite enough," she answered offhandedly.

"We have weapons, Raven, and small armies. No one is going to come this far yet. That's why I want to dictate the terms of my surrender before. Until then…we…you…are safe."

Raven didn't answer. A king, four kings, *slap, slap*, harder and harder.

Dietrich mixed a whiskey sour. His hand shook on the tumbler. "They hunt us like animals," he said.

"You *were* animals." Raven replied, head still bent. Her clubs were falling into place easily. "And you know why they really killed us?" Dietrich now safely behind his paper, she turned to me. "Not because we killed Christ. They didn't care about Christ. Not because we had money. They had more anyway. Or because we were smart. Because we are the royal blood of the house of David. Did your father ever tell you this, Axel?" Raven set down the cards. "No medieval kingdom could legitimize its reign without someone from the House of David, someone with Jewish blood. The Pope had his own Jew, of course—Jesus. So, his antagonist, Charlemagne, needed a Jew to legitimize his kingdom and his fight against Rome; he imported Jews from Alexandria, or was it Constantinople? The Jewish armies fought the Papal armies. Which was funny because the Jews wouldn't fight on Saturdays. That Lion of Judah on the British flag is no lightweight decoration, Axel. Everyone was claiming descent from the chosen ones. House of Hitler versus House of David. It was a war of blood." Raven slapped her knees in some kind of stinging finality.

She resumed her card playing. "Look at that!" She had brought all the clubs out and was down from ace to two of clubs. "I can't remember the last time this happened so fast." She turned to look at us, a frenzied look in her eye.

"They won't find us," Dietrich reassured her. "Karl didn't protect himself. We are well-protected." He stood behind Raven's chair, placing his hands on her shoulders. "Don't be afraid."

"The Germans were crazy," she said to him in a deep and ragged voice. "Maybe the Jews are crazy now."

"The Germans weren't crazy. They were hungry."

That halted the conversation.

"Well, enough of this," said Dietrich. "Axel, call Hermann. I assume he already knows about Karl Steinmetz but make sure. He'll let everyone else know. And call Rualdo. Tell him Nazi hunters might be around. Tell him to be very cautious. Damn. Do you think they took Karl before surgery or after? Hopefully, he'll die in jail before the trial, before they drag survivors out to accuse him. He was too kind. He left too many alive."

Frightened, Raven had grown more aggressive. "Well, in that case, Dietrich...you must be quite safe."

Dietrich joined me at a window, looking toward the swimming pool. "Damn frogs. A plague of frogs." Dietrich sighed. "The winners write history, don't they? I never killed the way the others did."

"Your father is incorrect, Axel. Extermination through labor kills two birds with one stone. Efficient amortization: the debt of death."

"I did precisely what I had to do. Perhaps if they take me, Raven, you'll come and bear witness."

"I've sacrificed my credibility. I've slept with the enemy."

"Shrewish Jewish fishwife. Enough of this. Axel, please come with me. And," he called over his shoulder, "Raven, the black cummerbund or the plaid one?"

"Black. We're not going to a party in Rio. Is that really necessary?" Still the wife.

❧

When I phoned Dr. Hermann, he grumbled at the mention of Steinmetz's capture. "He was a weak man—good organizational skills but lacking in character. No backbone. He may have talked about O Linda. They've never come this far, but who knows? The sword I once thrust hangs over my head."

Nonetheless, Dr. Hermann decided the party-prepping Colony members could still leave for Rio.

That evening, Grevaldo held a black satin coat for Raven, who, with a lovely make-believe smile, slipped into it. I held the front doors open for her and Dietrich. Like two small children lost in the darkness of their lives, they held hands as they walked toward a Cessna waiting in the driveway.

She called over her satin shoulder, "Axel, make sure the water buffalo are brought in if the river rises." It was as if our conversation had never happened, our card game had never been played.

ᐰ

I settled into Dietrich's chair, finished off the whiskey sour, tapped my fingers on the upholstered wing, listening as Grevaldo revved the engines.

I heard Dietrich's plane clear the driveway, thrust itself into the air. Others followed. Finally, in the distance I heard the roar of Dr. Hermann's Heinkel, the last plane to take off. That made ten planes. I picked up Raven's cards, slid them back in their Bicycle box, finished her iced tea even though it had too much mint, licked the rim for her taste.

I heard Maria singing to her animals. Dozing, I sensed Maria tiptoe into the great room, felt her removing my boots and socks.

I took her rough hand in mine.

If only Maria were beautiful and didn't eat live flies, I could fall in love with the sweetness of her. I handed her the king of hearts. She slipped it under her shirt, between her breasts where it would melt and enter her. Smiling at me, Maria covered me lightly with a blanket and kissed me on the forehead.

If she knew how I'd misbehaved under the card table that night, she would have spanked me.

Chapter Twenty-Six

Toxicities—from the poison of Awa's arrow combined with the hallucinogens of Okok's potions—left a thin film over my mind, as if I had a foggy camera lens. Nonetheless, I managed to warn Rualdo about possible external threats. I phoned and checked on Rainflower, cared for by Cecilia and her sister nuns.

The following day I rested my leg and edited Dietrich's lectures.

Raven and Dietrich returned from their shopping expedition late in the evening. From my bedroom I heard the plane land in the driveway, the front doors open and shut, Raven's quick and Dietrich's tired footsteps, Grevaldo's grunting as he carried their luggage up the stairs.

Minutes later, Grevaldo and Raven spoke softly as they descended, light-footed. Then their voices rose from the courtyard. I slipped onto the balcony and watched them in broken moonlight slanting through the fig tree. They sat on the stone bench of the fountain, apart from each other. The fountain was an oval with two-star points in its center. Grevaldo sat on one point, Raven on the other.

"The Baron is fine, Mrs. Baron?" Grevaldo asked.

"Probably already asleep," she answered. "He took two sleeping pills."

They leaned across the pool to tap their wine glasses together.

Jealousy flared at the thought that I was about to witness the intimacy between these two that I'd always suspected.

"Your party will be incredible, Mrs. Baron," said Grevaldo. "You will be much admired." He read from a pad of paper he held up to the moonlight. "The boys will arrive early. They'll need two field buses for the food and instruments and serving tables. Did you hear something in the tree, Mrs. Baron?"

"Damned monkeys. The figs must be ripe. More monkeys. Make certain you have some Indians up here with slingshots while we're setting up tomorrow. And get the horrid agoutis out of the kitchen, no matter what Maria says. Rodents are unwelcome. They can go in the barn. I already told Maria. The chickens should be out of the kitchen *and* the courtyard."

A fig dropped heavily into the fountain pool. Limbs creaked; more figs dropped. Raven looked up. "Eat the figs, already. Stop throwing them! These monkeys. Maybe we should put dear Dr. Hermann in charge of a monkey extermination."

"You need anything else, Mrs. Baron?"

"No, that's it. Get a good night's rest, what's left of it." She stood and kissed Grevaldo on the cheek.

❦

Minutes later, Raven shouted from the kitchen, and I ran downstairs.

She was banging a broomstick on the ceiling beams. Feathers floated around her head. Between her feet, squawking chickens ran, retreating to their nests. She paused with her broom midair.

"I have two hundred people coming to a party in two days, and I will not have chicken shit in the kitchen when the caterers arrive! I told Maria last week to get every animal out of the house." She picked up a handgun from the counter and aimed. Three shots rang out with no success.

From her cage, Helen squawked, "Shoot to kill!"

Raven looked up and aimed the revolver at Helen. I grabbed it. "No," I said, laughing. "Mohammed would be very upset."

"Are you sure about that?" asked Raven. Smiling crookedly, she pulled back her weapon and handed me the broom, indicating with a nod that I should use it to whack a chicken off the beam above.

There had been intense moments like this before, when we found each other alone in a room, on the roof, on the dock, a breathless parenthesis of time. I knew if I were to say something truly kind, even loving, she might close the space. I was as afraid of stepping into that moment as she was. We knew the quagmire love could be. When we were on the roof together in Germany, it hadn't mattered.

Violence stirred our blood. I knocked a frantic chicken off the beam. Raven tried to shoot her and missed. We laughed, then choked on our laughter.

"Axel, someone's outside in the tree. Sounds a lot heavier than a monkey."

I sniffed a vegetable sulfur scent. Awa.

Trembling, Raven tried to slip the bolt on the kitchen door but couldn't. I pushed her aside, bolted the door. We rushed from the kitchen to the center hall to the gun cabinet. I pulled out a pistol and a shotgun and we ran upstairs to their bedroom.

With Dietrich obliviously snoring on the bed, we crawled to the windows, rolled the jalousies closed, pulled the interior shutters together, bolted the doors.

"Get under the bed," I said. "Dietrich!" I shook him, pinched his hands, his cheeks.

From under the bed, Raven said, "His pills! Nothing will wake him up."

Yet he stirred and growled.

"Dietrich, Indians! You must get under the bed, Dietrich. Arrows, blow darts. Get up!"

He rolled off the bed, and I was able to shove him under, still asleep. I gave Raven a second pistol, pulled blankets from the bed, covered her head with a pillow to quiet her.

"Raven, be still!"

Monkeys scampered across the roof. We heard the soft, stealthy scrape of other feet above our heads.

Raven's voice was thin with fear. "He's listening. He's looking for us."

"He's not looking for us. He's looking for the girl, the unlucky one from the forest. Raven, for God's sake, I beg you, be quiet." I put my arms around her, ignoring Dietrich's presence. "This is how you kept me quiet in the war. When the soldiers were outside," I said softly. "It will be all right, little Luba." I pressed my hand over her mouth.

The Baron snored. I was able to press my fingers over his nostrils. Raven lay between us, oddly, as if our child. I kept my hand over her mouth to keep her quiet.

Bare feet ran across the roof, then on the balcony outside the window. Our breaths rose and blended. She whispered, "He's down by the kitchen. He's rattling the door."

"Stay calm. Think of the stars."

Dietrich growled. "Quiet, you two. I'm trying to sleep."

We heard scratching on the window. Raven stiffened.

"Me, Mrs. Baron. It's Okok."

She let out her breath. "Okok! Thank God."

"Awa is gone. My warriors are here."

From below, Grevaldo called, "Stay where you are until we check the barns. I came at the gunfire, then saw someone on the roof. Anybody hurt? Who fired the gun?"

"That was me," said Raven. Then, looking my way, she let out a hearty laugh. "Maria's damned chickens saved us!"

❧

The night before the party, I lay in my bed, willing myself to sleep, distracted by worry.

In the hallway outside my door, I heard endless footsteps, Dietrich and Raven and Maria and others, scurrying this way and that in preparation for the festivities, moving with a purpose I lacked.

Dietrich's footsteps approached my door. He knocked.

"Come in."

The light went on, and I opened my eyes. At my desk, Dietrich lifted my crystal paperweight, examining snow falling on miniature mountains. I imagined Raven's family lying frozen in the Alps.

"Axel, how is the leg?"

I sat up. "Still sore and a bit swollen."

"Will you be able to dance at the party tomorrow? I need you to make a small toast. I have pain pills if you need them." He got up, paced the room.

In the jungle with Numi, I had dipped a toe into the infinite, touched the immortal. Here and now, with Dietrich in my space, inspecting my belongings, I felt great unease.

He took a seat on the edge of my bed, tugging the collar of his shirt, adjusting, loosening, then tugging his cuffs. "So, I am sixty. This party of Raven's reminds me that I am less than immortal. This morning I was thinking that I will have to die of something and wondering what it might be. I was thinking of the arrow that nearly killed you. I was thinking of crashing in my airplane. What do you think I'll die from, Axel?"

"Shame."

He laughed. "*Ha!* The shame of the Great God Shamash, leader of the planets. Shamash is Sirius. Oh, yes, add shaman to our Shma list. Brilliant, *eh?*"

He stood again, rubbing his hands together. Inwardly I groaned. A lecture was coming. "If I am to die in an untimely manner, there are certain things I wish you to fully understand. Our work was spiritual alchemy on a grand scale, Axel. It was a new religion. We would become half-gods and half-men on our Earth. We would storm heaven. No longer would man struggle with the dead weight of matter. We knew its secrets. There was no room for others or for other ideas. Everything had to go toward transmuting to the new race. Everything and everyone. Which is, of course, what the unawakened world called murder. It was not."

I wished I was asleep. My father was not unlike Dr. Hermann, after all.

My mind raced into corners with more pressing issues, like Rainflower and Awa's readiness to kill for her. We would not acquire a relic of Solomon unless we handed over the girl—an impossibility. I knew better than to share this quandary with Dietrich. Instead we were talking about the war, which was long over and had become less relevant in relation to the immediate dangers surrounding us.

"Axel, what the world considers murder was ritual."

I listened for a note of sarcasm or sorrow or pride. No, there was no emotion. The frozen Pergamon faces of the new gods. He paced the floor, circling my bed. I put the pillow over my head. He didn't notice, or perhaps he'd forgotten me.

"Hitler pursued the same goal in two directions. One was world conquest through industrialization, which of course required slavery. The other was world conquest through the creation of the master race, which also implies world slavery. Nazism was an occult religion. Both the occult and the world conquests had as their goals the creation of a new man, a new god-man of Aryan perfection. Now I've written all of this down in my notebooks. If anything happens to me—death, insanity, Jews, Nazis, drowning, and so on—you are to publish my lectures. Do you understand?"

I saw snow falling on the Jewish baby in the woods next to Dietrich's factory. From under my pillow, I said, "You believe this, Dietrich?"

He pulled away my pillow and resumed pacing. "This is not belief. This is knowledge. By sacrificing millions of beings, they released the energy needed to cause a mutation in mankind, a mutation that would lead to god-men: a new race of Aryan giants, the pure. Himmler was looking for giants in Tibet. He spent years measuring Tibetan noses. Do you have any questions?"

"I suppose. Why didn't it work?"

He rubbed his chin. "It almost did. Someday it will. It has nothing to do with war or politics or geography. It has to do with Hitler creating a new order built on the Aryan model, but vastly improved. If necessary, Hitler would have killed Germans if he needed the fuel of their souls. Remember this: 'So, too, the evil Tiamat and her brood, sharp of tooth, unsparing of fang, with venom, the begetter of the great gods.' You see, killing begets the gods. It is so important that you understand this, Axel. I don't want you to think of these people as murderers."

"More like priests who make sacrifices? Like Dr. Hermann and his crew?"

"I wouldn't go that far. Personally."

"War as ritual." I wasn't agreeing; I was leading him on. "The Incas knew that. They fought wars to control the movements of the stars."

He nodded approvingly. "Yes, this was a new religion. We sacrificed others as well as ourselves. Hear the Och in Moloch? Moloch, the god of sacrifice."

"I cannot say I understand, even as I follow the logic. In your scheme of things, I am one of the unawakened. There is a great deal to think about. Murder is a secret act. Yours was public. I don't know what to call it. A crime against humanity, I suppose."

Dietrich moved around the room. "A crime against humanity. That's what the *honorable* judges will say." He punched the palm of one hand with his other fist. "But it was *for* humanity, to achieve its destiny."

The lecture was over. I felt as if the black hen had been sitting on my chest, a nightmarish worldview filling my lungs with pestilence.

Except for one muscle trembling across his temple, Dietrich stood straight and still. This is how he would look before a firing squad. "I had better let you rest," he said. "Please remember to prepare a birthday toast to me for tomorrow evening. Maybe one for Raven as well."

He stood—momentarily forgot, I think, who I was—clicked his heels, and said, oddly, "Thank you for your time. Please rest."

I was just about to dismiss him as totally nuts when he suddenly landed in the neighborhood of stark reality. "Oh, about your visiting savage? I've put warriors up and down the waterfront and around the perimeters and along the driveway. I've stationed Kupis near the house. Our guests, of course, will have their own guards. We'll be well-protected."

He paused, his hand on the doorknob. "And don't think I don't know about the girl you sent to Cecilia's. The sooner she goes back to the forest, the better. Maybe we could even trade her for something of Solomon's. Look into it. You don't think I want this party, do you? I detest parties."

ex

In the twilight of falling asleep, bits and pieces left over from the day bombarded my head. Words, phrases, combinations of words that meant nothing, unfinished business kept me from full slumber. "You should have…" or "the end of the pencil." Sometimes, when they seemed to have the possibility of meaning, I jerked myself awake. But there was rarely any meaning, and by the time I attempted to examine these connections, they'd already vanished.

But that night, hours after my father's visit, I heard other sounds. I felt a ping in my cheek. *Ping.* Shteinberg coming home with the pigs and the cow? No.

"Help. He is here." The voice echoed in my consciousness.

Something bit me on the cheek. *Ping*, again. I wiped my cheek. Nothing there. A bat? Was I imagining Raven calling for me? It wasn't until I heard a singular word—*Awa*—that I was awake enough to orchestrate words into meaning. I shook my head.

"Awa shot the wood lady."

Startled, I threw off my covers, pulled off the mosquito netting. It was Rainflower's voice, crying for my help in the old language of the forest. I had ears. I remember Okok telling me just that.

"Awa shot the wood lady."

Dressing quickly, I threw open my door, only to find Maria about to knock. "The girl in the convent," she said.

"I know. Get Mike. Get Grevaldo." The wood lady was the Madonna statue at the altar of the convent. It was real. Rainflower was speaking to my mind. *Ping*.

"Please," called Rainflower.

"You hear?" Maria called out to me as she ran down the stairs. "You hear too?"

I didn't answer Maria, but instead called "I'm coming!" to Rainflower. "Talk to Numi," I told her. "Tell him to help you until I come."

Just before I rushed out, Cecilia called on the house phone, shrieking at me, "The alarm we installed in the Madonna? If someone moves in front of her, she sings *Ava Maria*. It went off. There's an arrow in her chest, and you know how we sprinkle cornstarch at night on the floors, so no one steals food? I saw footprints: a forest Indian, opposable toes. You better get here fast, or I'll put this little ragamuffin outside."

Mike, in khaki boxer shorts and flip-flops, helped me to the river, steadied me as I climbed into the motorboat. Grevaldo came running down Palm Alley, jumped in. We roared over the river to O Linda.

Mike yelled down to me from the wheel, "What are you going to do with her?"

"Protect her from Awa. His people want to kill her. Then maybe get someone to adopt her."

"Take her away from the forest? That would be wrong, Senhor. Very. You can't change them. You think you're going to scare Awa away? I hear that guy can turn into a jaguar."

When we reached the convent, Cecilia, surrounded by three of her fellow sisters, let us in. She held a torch, leading us into the convent.

"I can't find Rualdo, little fool that he is. Your father should fire him."

"Rualdo and Willi are out looking for Indians."

"They should be here. Look." She flashed her light at the arrow in the Madonna's chest and turned to me as if I'd shot the arrow, then showed me the route of Awa's feet in the cornstarch. His footsteps led to the row of bedrooms that had once been stable stalls. They led to Rainflower.

She was cowering under the bed. A nun slept atop it, holding a club. The cell's windows were covered with strong wire fencing. Rainflower's ankles danced with light. I snuffed the lights out.

I sent Mike and Grevaldo to stay in the main hall, sent the nun away, and pushed the bed against the door. I climbed into it.

I heard rustling in the bougainvillea, Cecilia grumbling, Rainflower breathing softly. I heard an earth-rattling scream, the zing of an arrow, running footsteps.

There was a gunshot, two, three, then footsteps on the roof and rustling in the bougainvillea.

Grevaldo knocked on the door. "All clear."

"Did you get him?"

"No blood. Mike and I are going to sleep. Your sister gave us blankets."

Rainflower stirred, reached upwards for my hand. I held hers. "It was wrong to escape. I should let Awa kill me. I want to run into the forest and hide."

"Bad idea." But I had no better idea how I could help. Anywhere Rainflower went, danger followed.

❦

The next morning, in her office, I offered Cecilia a fancy new roof for the convent if she sheltered Rainflower a bit longer, at least until Dietrich's birthday party was over. In the meantime, Mike and Grevaldo and a half dozen of our Indians could guard the convent.

Cecilia shuddered, looked up at a leaky ceiling, and accepted the bribe.

Chapter Twenty-Seven

Months before the Baron's sixtieth birthday, I had listened on an extension while Raven hired a Miami party planner named Benjy over the phone.

His company, Food and Flowers, was, he said, internationally acclaimed and would bring everything by plane from Florida, even the musicians. Benjy—of the mellifluous, not-to-be-trusted voice, unctuous and suggestive at the same time, more theatrical than swish—enthusiastically embraced the idea of a Black Forest theme.

I was astonished to hear Raven confide in him that her husband's friends were old Nazis, peasants, bureaucrats, men with simple origins except for her husband and Dr. Hermann, that although they might begin with wine and go on to champagne, they would assuredly finish the evening with schnapps and beer dribbling over their leather jodhpurs. Many of them, she warned Benjy with a snicker, shoveled food into their mouths rather than eating correctly with a fork.

Raven planned a menu that would make the Nazis weep with joy.

Later I confronted her, forced to admit to my eavesdropping. "Suspicion is one thing, Raven. Stating it aloud is another. Don't you worry you're putting Dietrich in danger?"

She laughed. "Once Benjy arrives, he'll know anyway. The Colony fools will all wear their medals." She would be correct. "Remember, Axel, and you can tell this to everyone whose calls you are listening in on: no gifts and no photographs."

She chartered planes from Rio and Sao Paolo for her guests. She hired buses from Manaus to pick them up at Dr. Hermann's airfield since it could accommodate larger planes. I had a sickening sense that Raven was dancing as fast as she could before the music stopped.

"And no gifts, Axel," she stressed. "If anyone asks, I'm doing something special." Her extravagances were legendary.

Raven and her friends, financial predators all, vied for the high-water mark of conspicuous consumption, although sadly, only they could enjoy it among themselves, their only audience. Even so, competition was fierce. So far, Raven was the only one with a tiara, and it was well known that her collection of diamonds surpassed all others.

Enter Benjy, arriving on a field bus from Dr. Hermann's airstrip. I first saw him on the morning of the party. I was standing on our front steps. My heart jolted.

Benjy was elegant, muscular, smooth the way a racehorse is smooth, with a golden tan, full lips, burning blue eyes, tight white jeans, a French-striped boatman's shirt. Barefoot, he had a red-and-white farmer's handkerchief stuffed into his rear pocket and God-knows-what stuffed into his underwear.

Emerging from the bus, at the end of the line of white boys, were three elderly Black musicians descending down rusty stairs, clutching their instruments in aluminum cases, their clothing in plastic garbage bags, stooping, scowling, squinting with city eyes. They wore loose trousers, bright Hawaiian shirts, and shining black shoes. No smiles.

Benjy's cadre of talent unloaded food from a second bus as he theatrically hugged and kissed Raven. "Oh my God! You are even more beautiful than I imagined!" Our servants dropped their eyes at this display. Benjy stretched his arm out to introduce his boys, who at his signal stopped mid-task. He left his other arm around Raven's waist. "The Talent!"

The boys bowed with chorus-line perfection.

Benjy turned to me and grabbed my hand. "And this must be… why, you must be Axel. He is gorgeous, Raven. I don't believe you live with this man day and night without sinning." His grip was strong and firm, masculine, and a few squeezes too long.

"You shouldn't go barefoot," I said. "There are poisonous snakes."

"Oh my God. Of course. I keep thinking I'm going to the beach. Thank you, Axel. Raven talks about you to the point of boredom, and now I see why."

℆

On the long-awaited day, Benjy's boys quickly transformed the house, flitting to and fro like so many birds, squealing and giggling. Candles floated in our pool. Flowers sprung from every space possible. Bamboo torches marched through the gardens. The boys constructed outrageous pyramids of wine bottles and castles of bonbons.

The party began early, with cocktails at 5:30. Margaret, anxious, unusually cheerful, arrived even earlier, greeting Raven on a high C note. Because Raven's once-voluptuous body had been reengineered into that of a boy's, and Margaret's body having never matured to that of a woman's, Margaret was often the recipient of Raven's discarded gowns, usually worn just once before being tossed Margaret's way.

In shiny, pastel dresses, like a pair of long, thin, exotic fish, Margaret and Raven swam through a sea of tables filled with silver serving dishes, orchids, and birds-of-paradise.

The musicians, unfolding their music stands and tuning up their instruments, had hit a tuning fork note of A. In the forest, war parties and hunters signal each other in creature calls. I had learned to distinguish between the real call and the human predator's false call. The hunted creature cannot.

Around her neck, Raven wore an extravagant double strand of black pearls. She had not given in and worn the cross.

Margaret apologized to me for Willi's absence. He was indisposed; he had a weak stomach. She assured me he would arrive later. Willi, good old Willi, might wear leather jodhpurs and a tunic emblazoned with Third Reich medals, even though he'd spent the entire war in South America as spymaster. Or perhaps he'd give Benjy's boys a real thrill by wearing a ball gown and his pink angora stole. Without Willi, Raven's party would be just a bit duller.

Raven's friends arrived with squeals, among them dumb and innocent gossipmonger Bebe Hermann, of the long lashes and huge, moist, dreamy eyes. Bebe was surrounded by Benjy's waiters, who admired her diamond rings and the single large emerald swinging between two solid, squash-blossom breasts. In the main room, she maneuvered past her many admirers to present Raven with a small, red-satin box.

Raven kissed Bebe's cheek. "Naughty girl, Bebe. Didn't I say no gifts?"

"This is more than a gift," said Bebe. "And anyway, it's for you, not him. It's a souvenir."

Dr. Hermann followed in her wake. As he energetically shook the Baron's hand, he asked, "Why is a Shamburo looking for a white girl? Is there something I should know?"

Dietrich adopted a perplexed expression, looking from me to Raven. "I know nothing of it. Do you know anything about this, Axel?"

I scratched my head, shrugged.

Dr. Hermann looked from Dietrich to me, unable to make a judgment. "Let's work it out after the party, yes? I imagine you heard about Pastor Ken's mission. Heads on posts. Dreadful stuff," he said in his characteristic dreamy way. "I'm keeping my Indians armed. I noticed you have done the same." He bent to kiss Raven on the cheek.

She stiffened, lifted a wineglass from a nearby table, examined it for dirt, and left for the kitchen.

The Baron shrugged. "I doubt it has anything to do with us, Manfred. Sunoco just began blasting a new road through the forest. The attack on the mission was likely a protest. Or that little Commie Luis organized the Indians. I hear he's trying to organize the nut-gatherers."

"He touches my miners, he's a dead man."

"Dr. Hermann," I intervened, "you needn't worry about your miners. They couldn't give a shit about unions, politics, or a new world order. They want gold."

Dr. Hermann laughed, threw his arm around my shoulders. "Our coffee buyer in Seattle predicts in the next ten years or so, the price of coffee will go through the roof, and people will pay for it! They're starting to roast them with flavors like the Turkish do."

"There's that entire island on the river filled with cinnamon," said Dietrich. "Cinnamon coffee. But no, the island is crawling with crocodiles. We could go to vanilla or hazelnut." He looked over Dr. Hermann's head, repeating, "Cinnamon."

The word "cinnamon" had rocketed Dietrich back into the ether of the consciousness of early man. I could follow his thoughts. Nuts from sacred trees, Neith, nothing, dark stars, night, naught, Nishtar and Ishtar, the Is and the Not. Even as he was lost in thought, I heard the lecture in my head.

Dr. Hermann stood, patiently waiting for the Baron's attention, waiting kindly as one would if a friend were to stutter. It was a great effort for Dietrich to pay attention to the Dr. Hermanns of the world—in fact, to any of us. I elbowed Dietrich.

His eyes refocused on Dr. Hermann.

"Strange, isn't it, what we've become, Dietrich? Farmers. Imagine."

"Cinnamon, an old word, Manfred. Means 'with Amon'."

"Amen. How about that?" Both men turned to watch a buxom blonde girl walk by on Siegfried Putz's arm.

"Who's with Putz, Manfred?"

"She's from Chile. Miss Nazi 1960."

"Mrs. Putz doesn't mind?"

"It's her niece. What do you think of her, Axel?"

I tried to stay positive. "She has pretty curves, but her face doesn't quite match." She had a mass of long, blonde curls, which softened the odd effect, but it was unnerving that her parts didn't coordinate.

"That's right. I'd say monkey-ugly." Hermann slapped me on the back. "How's your lovely lady in Manaus?"

"Lovely."

"Same one?"

"Never, Dr. Hermann. Never."

Dietrich behaved as he must: polite, gracious, expansive, even avuncular, remembering children's names, inquiring after maladies, kissing the hand of Miss Nazi 1960, bowing toward her slightly.

But within his head, I saw snake-children, abominations, genetic engineering, and the roots of words, the names of gods. Og hammered within him, demanding to be known, partaking of many worlds.

Chapter Twenty-Eight

The grizzled Miami musicians played jazzed-up waltzes, rolling their eyes at each other as the overstuffed partygoers arrived and rushed to the steam tables. They lifted the hot covers, inhaling gastronomical aromas from their pasts.

With Bebe's package in her lap, Raven perched herself on the piano, sipping champagne while receiving compliments. The Occult Bureau Colony's inner circle huddled together. Waiters circulated with trays of undercooked lamb chops and apple pancakes.

However acclaimed Benjy may have been internationally, he did not have a handle on his finger foods. Bloody juice and grease dribbled onto the starched shirts and silken bosoms of the guests until everyone was forced to hold their hors d'oeuvres at arm's length and bend far over their waists to eat. Blood and fat ran down their naked arms or up their silken cuffs.

Emaciated Uncle Wolf, who hadn't stepped into his brother's house, our house, for years, bent over the steam tables set up at the window wall of the dining room. Long, thin, gray hair floated over a frayed and yellowed collar. He resembled an escaped prisoner wearing street clothes. Perhaps that's what he was; since there was no leaving and nowhere to go anyway, Uncle Wolf was on the Colony bankroll until he died, which seemed as if it might be any time.

We had tried to help him, but he refused. I was astonished that he had come to his brother's birthday celebration.

Uncle Wolf removed a silver lid from a serving bowl on the steam table. He covered his eyes with his great spade hands, standing straight over the steaming spaetzle, then, overcome with emotion, wept in mucousy gulps.

Guests near him tried not to notice the war hero crying over the smell of spaetzle. They understood he was weeping not over innocent noodles but for Germany.

I watched with pain, wishing I wasn't there.

Trapped at the edges of civilization, the Germans, with their unrequited passion for the past, ate and danced their deaths away. Do you know, Germans, that dancing is swimming? That you are celebrating a far older past, a Sirius past? The church didn't allow dancing because it was a pagan ritual, calling on the stars, an amphibian ritual.

Words flowed in my head, others on my periphery.

"What are you up to these days, Axel?" Someone caught my arm. "You know, Axel, we thought you might be our next leader. We thought…" I turned away. "We've formed an anti-communist military operation right here that could spread across the world. We're already in Spain. Very powerful potential, of course."

I approached the Queen of the Amazon, still perched on the piano. "How are you doing, Luba?" I asked quietly.

She grinned her neon grin and took my hand. "Dear Axel, do you remember when we first came here? The horrible luncheon with the smiling pig on a platter? And the first Mrs. Dr. Hermann had a pale-green water bottle with water she saved after she'd touched Hitler's hand?"

Uncle Wolf suddenly dipped, disappearing under the steam table. The white linen moved slightly as he breathed. Still crying, he didn't want to be seen.

"I'll get him." I moved to the back of the steam tables, pressed myself into a small space between them and the kitchen door, slid under, wrapping my frail uncle in my arms.

"A moment of privacy, Venerable Nephew." He buried his head in my shoulder, pointed at two pairs of boots sticking under the hem of the tablecloth, pressed his forefinger on my lips. We listened.

"Look, Manfred, weinerschnitzel. *Ach*." Memories were pain. Raven's buffet table steamed with pain. "Nothing I have ever eaten since has ever been this good."

"Take your finger out of it, Horst," said Dr. Hermann. "Someone will see."

"How much longer?"

"A year, maybe two." Dr. Hermann's voice dropped. "I'm worried the Baron might...*mmmm*...defect. Ultimately, our timing depends on his work."

I placed my hand tightly over Uncle Wolf's mouth.

"We watch him carefully. He's not one of us."

"I had a power outage last week, Manfred, at the washing machine factory. That was very close."

"You should have backup generators. Willi promised."

"He promised, but we don't have them. Do you think the Baron's alphabet will work?"

"Oh, yes, I know it does, but we could use more letters."

I placed my hands under Uncle Wolf's armpits and slid him out backwards toward the wall. Together we crawled through the tunnel of tablecloths into the kitchen until we could stand upright without being seen. I made a cup of tea for Uncle Wolf.

He drank it with shaking hands.

"What were they talking about, Uncle Wolf? What goes on at the washing machine factory?"

"You would be better off not asking." His fingers were long and graceful and tinged with yellow. "*I'm* better off." He was no longer a part of the Occult Bureau.

"You go sit in the sunroom. I'll send Margaret out to you."

Uncle Wolf wove through the clusters of guests toward the sunroom. I remembered him in his black leather coat with the red fox lining. I remember him carrying my mother up the stairs. I remember him whistling as he counted Jews.

After I spoke to Margaret, Bebe jerked playfully on the hair at the back of my head and asked me to waltz. She reached up to my face and tickled my upper lip. "There, how handsome you would be with a mustache."

"I'd look too much like Dietrich." Even though my leg throbbed, I wouldn't refuse the dancing. She was lovely to hold, chubby and sweet. Her solid breasts poked into my ribcage just above my cummerbund.

"Are you enjoying yourself, Bebe?"

"Oh, yes, Axel. Isn't that Miss Nazi ugly? And all those stupid blonde curls. Who in the world would want to be Miss Nazi? Except Margaret, who wants to be your Mrs. Nazi and make lots of little Nazis. You know, Mr. Hermann will never die, but if he ever does, I'm going to capture you."

"These men live forever. Dietrich's in great health."

Bebe giggled. "I think they take something from monkeys."

❧

Everyone sat after the Baron took his seat. He beckoned me closer. "Wolf is gone. Find him. Probably setting my house on fire. Runs in the family."

Uncle Wolf was in the sunroom. Box of tissues in hand, blossoms of used tissues on the floor, he lay with his head in the sequined lap of Margaret, who sang to him. She stopped short as I approached, blushed brightly.

Uncle Wolf went to wash.

I smiled at her. "You're a decent sort, Margaret. Perhaps you should find someone to care for. Maybe even Uncle Wolf. God knows he needs help."

"God knows. I was being kind."

"Yes, you were."

"Remember that, Axel. That I can be kind."

We, the three of us, made our way to the tables for dinner.

The Baron stood, cleared his throat. The men sprung from their chairs, clicked their heels, thrust their arms into the air, shouted, "Heil Hitler!"

My father raised his glass, and his world cheered for him.

Wriggling like snakes in heat, Benjy's Flower Boys carried in cases of Krug and filled countless glasses. There were eight guests at each table, perhaps two hundred celebrants. Uncle Wolf sat dour, sullen. Benjy, bubbling, on Raven's left; Bebe and Dr. Hermann completed the uneasy circle. The Baron held Raven's hand, now and then releasing it to pat it and stroke it, then held it again, in a demonstration I felt was for the benefit of his guests.

The Baron's friends toasted him, giving sloppy, drunken speeches.

Weirdly enough, I had never seen Dietrich so clearly. The shield of a face, the wide brow, the little ears flat against his head. He seemed to struggle to hold the great head up, to stand straight. A great and towering tree, I thought, rotting from the inside.

I imagined a young and hungry vine strangling him.

"Thank you for coming," said Dietrich to the assembled diners. "And to my own brother, Wolf von Pappendorf. Please, Wolf, please stand for a special welcome."

Uncle Wolf struggled to his feet and held his glass up to his brother but did not break a smile.

Raven elbowed me. "Your turn, Axel."

I lifted Raven's chin with a forefinger. She offered me her frantic neon smile.

On my feet, I lifted my glass. "To Dietrich, who saved the loveliest of them all: the Queen of the Amazon." Oh, God, what had I said?

As a group, the men stood, saluting Raven with their glasses. It seemed no one had noticed my use of the word "saved." Was I trying to liberate Raven's soul, or throw her into deeper isolation? I may have endangered her, exposing her to her enemies. I momentarily wondered if something within me was reminding her she was a Jew, and she should escape this hideous Colony.

Her face flashed fury, which disappeared just as quickly. Putting on a show, Raven pulled me down to kiss my cheek.

Dr. Hermann was leaning into Miss Nazi, smiling and enthusiastically nodding his head. He hadn't heard.

Dietrich complained, "The guests are sloshed, Raven. Stop the champagne and bring out the schnapps." He pulled his chair nearer mine, wearily holding his head in his hands. "Depressing, isn't it, growing old? If I don't find Solomon, if the Israelis don't forgive me, how will I ever be heard? Pride of my loins, you will become my memory. You become my reincarnation, my memory worm."

"God forbid. Is this belief or knowledge?"

"There is no room in my mind for belief. With you, believing is seeing. With me, seeing is believing."

☙❧

Raven gave orders to Benjy, who nodded, examined his watch, clapped his hands.

The waiters retreated to the kitchen and reappeared in long black kaftans embroidered in gold thread: hem, neck, and cuffs. The room hushed as they assembled before the piano, near the musicians.

A trombone player stepped forward and sang—in an unrelentingly chicken's cackle—"The Blue Danube": *Buck buck buck buck*. This was Benjy's Black Forest.

The guests guffawed, slapping their thighs and pounding the tables. They cackled along, kept time with their silverware. Maria watched through the kitchen doors, shaking her head disapprovingly.

The lost boys were having a good time. Here we were, rich, fat, drunk, and alive. Alive. Maybe we didn't lose the war. Maybe we won. Maybe we'll win again. Just wait. Yes, it had all happened. But how to erase the past and go on? Flatulence filled the air, belching, burping, laughter, catcalls. The guests were taking great pleasure in each other. They were like frogs calling in the night. Are you there? Isn't it wonderful to be here and drunk on the night and the music and the food and each other and everything German?

Isn't life grand? Inexplicably these people, these murdering peasants whom last week I had despised, reached into my heart. I made an error then, for I sought out Margaret, throwing my arms around her.

"I'm sorry, Margaret, that I can't love you. That you love me and I can't love you."

"What?" She burst into tears.

"I'm drunk. Never mind." I couldn't get away fast enough. I damned Okok and Rainflower. I would pay for opening my heart to the universe, segments of which were not quite ready to receive this new communion.

A dozen of Benjy's waiters stood in a chorus line and sang "Happy Birthday." Dietrich stood to acknowledge them. At the final, drawn-out "to you," the waiters bowed in perfect unison. Then they turned and bowed to the musicians.

I was looking down at my watch when I heard the room's collective sharp intake of breath.

The Flower Boys had cut round holes in their kaftans to show their behinds. The holes were trimmed with the same gold embroidery as on the rest of their kaftans. The Baron shot out of his chair, his face paled in anger. Except for Dr. Hermann, who was dozing in his chair, the other partygoers laughed uproariously, coarsely, shouting in German. "*Ach du liebe!*"

Raven clapped her hands, laughing too. Tiara or not, there was a clear streak of crudity running in the Queen of the Amazon.

The Baron hissed at her to stop the boys, but Raven continued clapping. "Look, Dietrich, someone just stuck a gold medal in that boy's behind."

The band played Strauss louder and faster. The bare-assed boys pulled women on the floor to dance. Dietrich dropped to his seat, and Uncle Wolf slumped next to him, his head into his chest, snoring, farting.

Disgusted, Dietrich punched him awake. Uncle Wolf staggered to the floor, grabbed a boy, and danced off.

Raven left and returned with shears, which she handed to Margaret. Benjy pulled Raven to the floor. She had indeed cut a hole in her gown, exposing her triumphant little ass as he spun her round and round.

Margaret appeared, bare-assed. They were destroying three- and four-thousand-dollar gowns. The shears were passed from table to table. Dr. Hermann danced with Bebe. Both bared their behinds; Dr. Hermann's was flat and withered, without flesh, Bebe's peachlike. Mobile gas units in the Ukraine, *eh*, Dr. Hermann? How much had he needed to drink in order to dance out there, exposing himself?

I saw Maria's face at the kitchen door, saw the shame.

Dietrich tossed his schnapps glass to the floor, then tottered to the dance floor, to his whirling wife. To everyone's vast and loud amusement, as Raven's behind was exposed to him, he spanked her.

She stopped for a moment, grinning, and said to Benjy, "We must do this again." She caught her husband in her arms and danced with him until he shoved her off and walked away, ramrod stiff as he took a seat alone across the room.

His handprint bloomed on her flesh. Indefatigable, Raven was soon on the dance floor again, this time with Uncle Wolf, who kept a stiff and straight-armed distance.

❦

Dr. Hermann dismissed the three musicians, waving them off with the back of his hand. "Enough, enough. No more music. Out. Go to bed."

Expressionless, they shook the spit from their instruments, folded their stands, and quickly decamped. Someone had brought a record player, and the first heavy-footed notes of "Bottoms Up Polka" shook the forest night.

Peasants, all, with great guttural shouts of pleasure and hoots, they took to the floor. The house rocked with foot-stomping, shouts, laughter. The serene Brazilian wives didn't polka. The old men of the club took each other's arms and danced with each other. "*Jägermeister! Jägermeister!*" they yelled, calling for Dietrich.

Dr. Hermann grappled with Dietrich, pulled him from his chair, and twirled him around the room. Dr. Hermann was a great mass. I moved in to free my father from Dr. Hermann and heard Dietrich say breathlessly, "Let me go, Manfred. For God's sake, let me go."

Dr. Hermann laughed. "Go where? Make me an offer, Herr Baron, a nice offer."

I pulled Dietrich away. Dr. Hermann continued to laugh, falling back into a chair.

Steins and a beer barrel arrived from the kitchen on cue.

Raven had orchestrated each moment. Taking up her piano perch once more, swinging her legs, clapping her hands, she had brought Brueghel to life in her living room.

"Make me an offer, Herr Baron. What do you have to trade?"

Oh my God, Dr. Hermann still needed a Jew. No, I was being paranoid. I tried to erase the thought. Too improbable.

Finally, the party calmed down. I sat with Dietrich and Dr. Hermann as they reminisced about childhoods in Germany, school days and circuses. They spoke of gold, the price of coffee, crocodiles on Cinnamon Island, and Miss Nazi 1960.

Dietrich leaned into Dr. Hermann's ear. "I want to leave soon, Manfred."

Dr. Hermann smiled, laughed, slugged a beer, belched, pressed his forehead onto Dietrich's. "There is unrest in Chile. Chile is impatient."

"Chile is not my concern. My work is my concern."

The hair rose at the back of my neck. I sensed something in the room, an odd sensation at a molecular level.

Awa stood framed in the light of the door to the terrace.

Chapter Twenty-Nine

Spectacular, dangerous, of course, but weaponless, painted, his jaundiced eyes black-rimmed with warrior paint, his body black, gleaming, Awa carried a package that he held out in front of himself, an offering wrapped in cloth.

As if a spell had been cast over them, the guests fell silent. Mrs. Putz fainted. Others backed out, trying to leave. Awa had no weapons. Hopefully, he did not have his ancestors with him.

The record player skidded to an end.

Benjy whistled between his teeth. "God, he's gorgeous. Look at the muscles. Who is he?"

"What on earth?" Raven exclaimed. Trying to save her party, she walked up to Awa. "I said no gifts!"

He didn't move. Awa's weird yellow eyes looked through her, searching the room.

The screen door to the garden slammed. The servants were running away.

Before I could prevent it, Raven pirouetted before Awa, inviting him to dance.

He stood immobile, not a nerve twitching.

I knew she wasn't that drunk. She put her hands on her hips and said again, "I said no gifts," then laughed at her joke.

Stupidly, Benjy reached out and touched Awa's naked ass. With an almost imperceptible movement, Awa threw him to the ground.

Benjy yelped, crawling slowly to the front door. Those of the guests who were able shrunk backwards toward the walls, toward the doors.

I stood between Awa and Raven, pushed Raven backwards, out of his way. Taking a deep breath, knees shaking, I spoke gently, "Awa."

He stared down at what he knew must be my still-painful leg, then his gaze darted around the room. His eyes were frightened and sincere, yellow and unfocused. He squinted into the lights.

Even as I could not hear what he was thinking, I announced to the guests: "He is not going to harm us. Be still."

Awa lay his cloth-wrapped package onto the table in front of me. The gift was for me.

"Don't open it," Raven said.

But I sat and took it in hand. Under the linen, banana leaves wrapped another object. Without realizing it, I had agreed to a trade.

Awa moved swiftly, grabbing Miss Nazi 1960, pulling her toward the front door.

Some brave guests held onto her as she screamed. Others scrambled into the kitchen. Horst, to no avail, broke a chair over Awa's head.

With an elbow movement, Awa tossed Horst to the floor. Then he held the blonde Miss Nazi 1960 in front of him. Looking into her face, he realized his mistake. This was not Rainflower. Shaking his head in confusion, he released her and loped out of the house.

Dr. Hermann was gone.

Dietrich was the first to speak into the vacuum of fear. "What's this about, Axel?"

"He's looking for the girl. He thought he could trade."

"What's the matter with his eyes?" asked Raven. "Is he *blind*?" She touched my shoulder. "Are you all right, Axel? What did he give you?"

"I'm fine. Just another shrunken head for Dietrich." Awa's package was a battered shrunken head, painted gold and filled with Pepsi Cola bottlecaps.

Dietrich took over. He was superb.

"He meant no harm," he announced to the alarmed guests. "He just wanted a beautiful white girl. And who among us doesn't? Can someone please help up Mrs. Putz, and attend to her niece? Raven, let's keep the schnapps flowing, my dear."

Dietrich sat, and I whispered to him, "This is what you have been waiting for."

His eyes widened, but he did not allow himself to respond.

I rewrapped Awa's gift in the banana leaves and cloth, took it to the kitchen, and stuck it into the freezer, wondering if indeed it might be Solomon's head.

ᘒᘓ

Grevaldo carried Miss Nazi 1960 up to a bedroom. Maria, crossing herself rapidly again and again, followed. Our remaining guests were shell-shocked, sitting upright, frozen in gilded chairs.

Raven hit a fork against a glass, raised her arms, spread wide to encompass everyone. "Next time, Axel von Pappendorf, I make up the invitation list. No Indians."

A few people laughed at her joke, were able to laugh.

The Queen of the Amazon was relentless. "Attention!" called Raven. "There are still fireworks. The servants, our warriors, and your bodyguards will escort you to the viewing area at the dock where there will be champagne. Grevaldo, light the torches."

I grabbed her arm. "Are you crazy? Awa's out there, for God's sake."

She continued. "After, we'll return to the house and…" She raised her voice into an exultant pitch. "Eat birthday cake!"

"For God's sake, Raven."

She would not deny herself her triumph. "And all of your bodyguards and our warriors will be escorting you to the river. If the gentlemen do not already carry weapons, we have extra. Please see Grevaldo for them."

I strode out of the room. At the front door, Bebe Hermann grabbed my arm. "So is she really a Jew, Axel?"

"Who?"

"Raven."

"Does it matter?"

"Yes. I would feel just terrible. My gift was the last bar of Treblinka soap Manfred had saved."

Behind us, guns were being distributed.

❦

Awa was out in the night, looking for Rainflower. He was nearby. The jaguar's cough, the castanet clicking of his ears, may have been Awa, signaling to Rainflower's jaguar self.

I felt too light, a speck of paper caught in a current, given to whatever direction the river took me. Too light, too vulnerable. I took a deep breath.

We had Solomon's head, but it was filled with Pepsi Cola bottlecaps.

Get through the night. Deal with it in the morning. I heard Raven's voice, trilling, cajoling, as she corralled the guests down Palm Alley toward the river.

The wind was mild and sweet with wild cinnamon. Chairs had been set out on and around the platform by the dock. The Baron sat among his Colony associates, Raven took her seat, Benjy next to her, whispering in her ear.

Fireworks? What was Raven thinking? I imagined the noise and light show rousing the sleeping crocodiles on Cinnamon Island, who would rush over and devour our overfed guests.

A magnificent chrysanthemum exploded, shattering the sky. Then an entire bouquet of chrysanthemums bloomed, boomed, sang, whistling above the river. Sky and river reflected each other, a puzzle in a puzzle.

The guests held their breath in amazement, then drunkenly clapped and cheered. Miraculously, the crocodiles did not attack.

After this spectacle, the various guests stood, some with naked behinds gleaming in the torchlight as they walked haphazardly back to the house. Raven shouted, "Birthday cake!"

Warriors flanked the party as they departed. As if she were taking her place in the society of which she'd been queen but no longer, Raven walked at the rear of the procession. Someone in the front of the somber line pulled up the torches and distributed them, and the party walked through the night toward the lights of the house. The black gowns and tuxedos vanished into another fantasy. Diamonds became fireflies: innocent, ethereal, bobbing like children's birthday balloons.

There was something infantile, childlike about all these exposed asses, so alone and brave in the raw and ugly night, perhaps pathetic. As I watched from the dock, I wanted to rescue the behinds from the rest of the dissolute minds and bodies, from the murderous hatred, the cold cruelty. I wanted to cut their bobbing asses loose and let them fly over the forest, a constellation of innocence, a bunch of balloons, freed from their awful history. "I've asked your asses to leave."

On the dock, the forest around me was silent and strange. Then the sky opened its arms and I became the sky. My condor swooped by, and I flew among the stars, escaping into the dark rift of the Milky Way. For a brief electric moment, I was no longer myself. I was the boy on the river with Okok, hallucinating as Solomon's ships sailed by.

❧

Halfway along my Palm Alley walk up to the house, I found Margaret, standing alone in her shimmering, pastel gown, looking at the stars. Had she seen me flying in the sky? I took the flashlight she offered and clicked it on.

Headed uphill, sometimes our elbows touched. Sometimes our shoulders touched.

"Why did you hug me?" she asked.

"To say I'm sorry I can't love you. You wouldn't be happy with me, Margaret. I'm not a nice man."

"Maybe I could make you nice, Axel."

There was nothing to say. I had hurt her enough. She kept rubbing the same spot on her arm again and again, in round tight circles. "I don't know where my father is. Have you seen him? He never came to the party. I phoned but couldn't reach him."

"If anyone around here can take care of himself, it's Willi." I offered a complete non sequitur. "Did you know that they make soup from tapir feet? It's good for hernias."

"Disgusting. What did the Indian give you at the party?"

"Just another shrunken head. They're big on shrunken heads." I put my arm around her shoulder. Among Margaret's flaws were that she loved me and she thought of herself as Willi's daughter. "Forget me, Margaret."

An idea came into my head sideways. "Margaret, have you ever considered as a possible husband O Linda's rabblerousing Luis? That man has vision. With your gold and his vision, you could change Brazil."

She stiffened and snapped away. "He's a half-breed."

"No. His mother's side goes back to the United States, an officer in the Civil War, and his father is Father Larry, who is now a bishop in Rome. But that shouldn't matter, he..."

She halted. Her eyes filled with tears. Her hands shook.

"I'm sorry, Margaret. I meant it with good intentions. Luis is a far better man than me. And he's the new Brazil."

"Shut up." She kicked her foot against the ground.

"Margaret, this business of blood, it's all wrong."

"We are *their* children. It's our duty to continue the race."

"Margaret, Dietrich says we're white because the Earth burned, because the deserts formed, because some of us went back into the waters for thousands of generations. When the Earth turned green again, we came out faded, pale-skinned, blue-eyed. It has nothing to do with anything occult. We chose to go into the water and the rivers. The others were brave and stayed on what was left of the land. They stayed dark. Dark people didn't go into the water. We're faded, not superior."

"I will have nothing to do with a lousy half-breed, thank you very much. And you can keep your insane ideas to yourself. You and your crazy father and his Jew ideas."

"What are you talking about?"

"She's a Jew, isn't she?" Margaret grabbed the flashlight, threw it at me, then ran up the hill to the house. Over her shoulder, she shouted, "What about the yellows? How did they get yellow?"

"Margaret," I shouted into the shadows. "This isn't about crayons." And then I knew something I had never known before but somehow would know forever. How I knew it, I could not say, but I understood that the rest of my life would be spent corroborating this instinctive knowledge.

"Margaret," I said, barely aloud, knowing she could not hear, "we are all from different planets."

Chapter Thirty

The party was over. I lingered in a comfortable lawn chair on the terrace and dozed off. Waking to the angry squawks of a pair of monkeys battling over birthday cake, I roused myself and headed inside to bed.

I had just stepped into the back hallway when I heard someone. It was Dietrich.

I remained behind a door. Rarely did I have the opportunity to observe him alone.

He removed three hats from the coat closet—a pith helmet, a rain hat, and a beret—then moved down the corridor, into the guest bathroom.

Following his path, I saw on the bathroom floor a laundry pile of lacy satin panties. He kicked some out of the way, muttering, but couldn't fully close the door.

Leaning forward, both hands on the sides of the sink, he studied himself in the mirror. He put on the beret, leaning again, studying himself. Then he tried on the ridiculous pith helmet, then the rain hat. The gleam in his eye suggested his mind was far away, but where? I couldn't hear his thoughts.

I stood behind him, my face appearing next to his in the mirror. I pulled my braid over my upper lip. We looked alike. He smiled at my reflection.

I asked, "How does Mengele's son look at himself in the mirror without seeing his father?" From the floor, I picked up a lacy pair of underwear.

He smiled again. "Why are underpants called *a pair* of under-pants, *a pair* of panties, when in truth they are only one item? A pair of trousers. Why isn't a brassiere a pair when in truth there are two parts? Foul peasants, Axel," he said, fingering a sky-blue fabric. "I am a scholar, a scientist, a nobleman. Because I wore the patch on my sleeve, they made my research possible."

"And the factory?"

"They needed steel." A pair of red satin panties went over his head and became a mask. He looked through leg holes, sniffed.

"And the Jews?"

Again he leaned over the sink and studied himself in the mirror. "We needed them."

"So you never hated?" I planted another mound of lace on his head.

After another wardrobe change, he looked at himself wearing a black lace mask.

"Jews? Slavs?" I asked. "You never hated them?"

"What's to hate?"

"Did you ever love?"

"Axel—"

"Did you? Beside your hounds and Violet?"

He dropped the underwear, kicked it away. Then he ran the water faucet, threw sleeping pills into his mouth, swallowed, pointing to his Adam's apple as the pills descended. "Adam's apple. God's gift got stuck in my throat. You know what your mother's doing? She's sitting in the kitchen, talking to a bar of soap."

"Raven is not my mother." I kicked the pile of panties.

His eyes remained fixed on a scarlet red pair. "Things of the past. Look at these. You know the old alphabet will never work for Hermann. But he believes it will...just like Hitler. Hitler may have looked into this mirror."

He picked up the red panties and shoved me from the room. "Go take care of your mother."

❧

"Oh! Senhor." Maria came from the kitchen. "She's in there. Please talk to her."

"What are you doing up so late, Maria? Isn't everything done?"

"I make soup for the morning. Mrs. Baron is not happy. You should talk to her."

"I will, Maria. Go to bed. I'll see to the soup."

Raven sat with her head in her hands, elbows on the kitchen table, the red satin wrapping of Bebe's gift spread out before her. She pressed the Treblinka soap against her cheek. She was wearing an old, black silk bathrobe of Dietrich's.

Near the worktable sat Helen's cage, the noisy parrot, shrouded by a rag, mercifully silent.

Seeing me, Raven burst into tears. "You know what this soap is saying? It's saying, 'Wait at the gate, children. Wait at the gate.' It's my mother saying, 'Wait at the gate.' Screaming. Here, listen." She handed me the soap.

I put it to my ear.

"Why did you tell everyone I was Jewish, Axel? I had the soap to tell me; I didn't need you." She sniffed the soap. "Exile, Axel. Dietrich's exile is only a matter of location. My heart is exiled. All this time, Axel, I've been waiting for you to come get me, let me realize my full self, be who I am, truly. But you didn't have the courage. We didn't have the courage. It's what happens when fear defines you. Or us."

I dropped my hand to the swelling of her breast, pulling Dietrich's robe from her body and tossing it to the kitchen tiles. It lay in a pile under the table like a black insect.

Something about that robe, black silk; something niggling at the back of my brain. The ant. Dietrich's robe was the black ant on my back. I had thrown it off. I had thrown off fear.

She was naked. Beautiful. "Don't be stupid," she said.

With my mouth, I explored her neck, her back. My hands caressed her, her body caressed my hands, I felt her crevasses as I had longed to for so long. She pushed against me, pushed back her shoulders.

Standing, she tumbled back onto the kitchen table. Her fierce eyes met mine, and she pulled her body up and offered herself to me. I entered her.

"Squeeze my tits, Axel. Squeeze my tits." I was, at last, Axel, not Dietrich.

Unfinished business between us was sated in thrusts and grunts. And when we were done, panting, she pulled herself away, put on Dietrich's robe, and left the kitchen.

"Axel, get me out of Hitler's house."

I turned off Maria's soup, covered the pot. The parrot scuffled around in her cage, kicking something out. I considered setting miserable old Helen free.

That black robe was the ant. My ant, my fear.

ဢ

I caught up to her on the stairs. "Raven, pack."

"What?"

"We can smuggle you out of here along with the musicians."

"I can't leave Dietrich."

"You must. You're in danger. Put your jewelry in a laundry bag. I'll send everything else. I'll take you to Dr. Hermann's plane."

"And you?"

"I don't know. Pack. Be ready to leave with Benjy's group."

ဢ

Benjy, his catering boys, and the three musicians were in an upstairs bedroom where Raven had set up cots. Dr. Hermann's plane took regular early morning flights, and Raven had arranged to get them out of the Amazon in a pre-sunrise flight.

Long after midnight I found Benjy upstairs, sitting on the edge of his cot. Nearby his bags were packed.

"I can't wait to get out of here. That Indian. My entire life, I've never been so scared."

"Benjy, we have problems you can't even imagine. Raven is in danger. I had an idea that we might get her out of here disguised as one of your musicians. Can you give me clothes and an instrument case? Take her with you and put her up until I can…help? I'll certainly make it worth your while. And Raven has plenty of money."

He hesitated only a moment. "Sure."

"Get her into something…some clothes. Just keep her with your guys."

Sleeping in their clothes, the musicians and Flower Boys woke, rubbed their eyes, peed outside, and climbed into our field bus. Head bowed, Raven climbed in with them, wearing sweatpants and a hooded leather jacket emblazoned with WANTAGH on the back in orange-and-gold letters. She carried a small laundry bag.

I took Mike's place behind the vehicle's steering wheel and drove the weary party through the forest, a too-bright moon flashing between dense branches arching over the dirt road.

Floodlights illumined Dr. Hermann's landing strip. I pulled in behind the hangar, turned off the engine.

The plane's engines were already chopping the air. The Flower Boys solemnly climbed from the bus onto the plane. The jazz musicians—now four rather than three—each carried a small suitcase and a tattered garbage bag packed full. I followed them onto the plane. A still-disguised Raven sat next to Benjy.

When she looked up at me, I felt an excitement, not in my groin, but just below my ribs. The feeling was entirely physical yet fully emotional. Something within me stretched out, reaching from my center, encompassing Raven, loving her, not needing or wanting or drawing her in, but sending something away with her. Never before had I come so close to love and sadness.

ॐ

Cecilia's convent sisters often flew back and forth on Dr. Hermann's plane to the Mother House in Miami, so it was no big surprise to see the convent's prewar Ford station wagon pull up under the plane's wing.

What I didn't expect were these three nuns climbing from the car: gray, hooded, one small captive between two larger ones. The middle nun struggled to free herself as they dragged her toward the plane's steps.

It was Rainflower.

The second she saw me, she began yelling, "Mr. Axel, help!" Her fury to free herself increased.

I hurried off the plane and caught the arm of Cecilia, one of Rainflower's tormentors. "What do you think you're doing?" I demanded.

"All of us, including Rainflower, will be much safer somewhere else, as long as that savage is chasing her. Go on," she ordered, "get aboard. Hurry." Cecilia shook off my clutching hand. "This was your father's decision—to send Rainflower to the Mother House."

The girl tugged my sleeve. "Mr. Axel, Numi tells me not to go."

Cecilia made a horrible face. "Axel, you have nothing to offer. No schools, no children, no family."

Rainflower looked at me for help. "I just want to say goodbye to Mr. Axel," she told Cecilia.

Cecilia nodded. The other nun freed Rainflower, who hugged me tightly around my waist. I stroked her head as she said, "Don't let them send me away."

Putting her on the same plane as Raven opened a floodgate. It was a chance I had to take.

Logically, the best thing for her—rather than spending her young life waiting to be murdered—was to get on Dr. Hermann's plane with her mother. "Rainflower, you can grow up safely and then come back. Return as a lawyer or a doctor and help your people. You can come back a writer and keep them alive by writing their story."

Rainflower yelled, desperate, "You promised!" She continued shouting as Cecilia and the other nun pulled her up the jetway stairs and onto the plane. "Numi!"

I followed her, walking past the Flower Boys, walking past the fourth musician, who was now feigning sleep.

The two nuns pulled Rainflower into a seat, sandwiching her between them. She sat with a hood draped over her head, softly crying. She sneezed.

Hearing her whimpering, Raven sprang up, then stood over Rainflower.

When the girl looked up, the Queen of the Amazon lifted the chin of this small nun who wasn't a nun at all. She was a blonde and fair girl. Raven stroked Rainflower's chin.

"You look just like my mother," Raven said quietly, as if praying. "The same chin, the same nose, the same eyes."

Rainflower reached up and touched Raven's shoulder, licking Raven's hand.

Cecilia tried to wrestle her away, but the distressed girl threw herself into Raven's arms. "It's me, Rainflower!"

"I know who you are." Raven didn't crumble or stumble from the shock of recognition. Instead she moved quickly, arms closing tightly around her daughter, half pushing, half carrying Rainflower to the plane's exit.

"Come on, Axel. Time to go."

Neither Raven nor Rainflower would be leaving with Benjy, who tossed a suitcase and the laundry bag after us onto the runway. He spread out his hands in a shrug of apology when the suitcase split and spilled out its contents. It had been filled with clothes.

Incandescent in the night, Benjy shouted, "Anytime. I'll always be there."

He wouldn't. But I would.

Wordlessly, Raven got in the bus's rear seat with Rainflower. From the driver's seat, I saw the plane's door close, Benjy waving goodbye from an oval window.

As the plane took off, its exhaust scattered Raven's clothes across the runway. I ran back to retrieve the laundry bag filled with Raven's jewels and American dollars, gathering clothes that hadn't scattered too far.

The Heinkel entered the night over O Linda, over the river.

Raven leaned toward the front seat. "Let's go home. I found my daughter." Weeping from fury and love, she held Rainflower close, rocking with her over the rough road.

I remembered Luba, not much older than Rainflower, remembered her rocking on the roof, watching the war. I drove slowly. Raven's voice was husky with passion.

"This is my baby. I saw her in the plane and knew. My blood knew. Her blood knew. She sniffed me. She licked me. She knew I was blood."

Raven and Rainflower blissfully clung to each other. I felt that same passage of bubbling energy stretching from my solar plexus to both of them, surrounding them.

"Your father was getting rid of her," said Raven. "Your father. He was getting rid of my baby once again. He killed my first child in the factory. Children are a nuisance. Jewish children are an unspeakable nuisance. Dorie said he threw my baby into the furnace. Then I had twins. I saw one dead baby," said Raven. "They told me that the other had been disposed of. I believed them." Her voice was more growl than speech. "The doctor told me how sorry they were."

෭෯

Once home, I pulled the bus off the driveway, away from the house, under a stand of palms. I saw Dietrich pacing before the sunroom windows.

Raven also saw him. "I can just hear what he is going to say. But if I can't keep her here, I'll leave, even if I have to kill him. I will kill anyone for this child."

Dietrich, framed by his half of the Baronial carved doors, stood in the driveway. "What are you two doing? What's going on?"

Raven opened the bus's door for Rainflower, helped her out. Approaching Dietrich, she said, in the deepest of voices, "I am no longer your slave. You are no longer entitled to me. Get out of my way."

He blocked entry, arms stretched across the door. "She's supposed to be going to Miami. She's not coming into my house."

He knew who Rainflower was. She was the yellow diamond on his finger.

"She'll stay," said his wife.

"Like hell, she will."

I shoved Dietrich out of the way, and he fell backward. Picking up Rainflower, I carried her upstairs to my bedroom. "Maria, come quickly!"

"Raven, Axel, I demand—"

"This isn't your house, Dietrich." Raven said. "It's my house."

Raven pulled back the covers of the bed. Maria ran in and out with warm drinks and bread and towels.

I found guns, gave one to Raven, kept one with me, lying on the tiled hallway outside my room through the night. Mother and daughter slept together in my bed. I heard crying and Raven's soft words, "Rainflower."

I fell asleep on the hard floor as she repeated the name.

Chapter Thirty-One

The Amazon morning came all too soon.

After a night of weeping lullabies, Raven and Rainflower were quiet inside my room. I heard the parrot Helen's screech from the kitchen. Her cry echoed through the cavernous house: "Squeeze my tits, Axel! Squeeze my tits!"

I heard footsteps from downstairs, lots of them, doors closing, shouts outside.

"Squeeze my tits, Axel! Squeeze my tits!" Helen, the parrot spy, was a canary, echoing back unleashed desire.

Still unkempt from the night before, I scrambled downstairs to the kitchen. It turns out no one was listening to the parrot. No lost language, this.

Grevaldo said to Maria, "No one knows yet. Keep this quiet as long as possible."

Something terrible had happened that had nothing to do with my spent passion for my stepmother. Maria dropped to her knees, praying. In the courtyard Mike shouted orders.

Helen the parrot was still broadcasting, "Squeeze my tits, Axel!" but no one cared.

I found her blanket and tossed it over her cage. Annoyed, Helen squawked unintelligibly from under the rag.

Grevaldo turned to me. "Your father is gone. Mike took him in the boat to Manaus early this morning."

Dietrich had left without us.

I called Mike into the kitchen. "Let's have it."

"The Baron told me the Jews were in Manaus, that they were coming for him, that it was time for him to leave. I took him in the boat to the Hotel Tropical just north of town. With just a briefcase and a suitcase, he walked in the water to a beach, then into the hotel's back door with the workers. He told me to wait an hour and leave if he didn't come back. He didn't come back, so I left."

I looked down at Maria on the floor. "Tell no one. No old language. Nothing."

Clutching my ankles, loyal Maria wept into my boots, covering her eyes with her hands as her lips moved in desperate prayer.

"Maria, pray later," I said, helping her into a chair. "Tell me what happened. Who told Dietrich about the Jews?"

She spoke through her hands. "Some lady calls on the telephone before sunrise. I answer. I don't know her. She says to me, 'The Israelis are at the Tropical. Tell the Baron.'"

Dietrich had not fled. He had gone to meet the Israelis.

"Was the woman who phoned German, Brazilian, old, young, American? What did she sound like?"

"I don't know. Maybe like you."

"Maria, don't tell Mrs. Baron. I'll do that when the time comes."

Maria sniffled. "Miss Margaret is here too, sleeping. She would not leave you, Young Baron, no matter what. She's skinny but would make a good wife."

"Margaret? Whatever you do, Maria, don't let her hear any of this." Why had Margaret stayed the night? And where was Willi?

Stripped of all but his knowledge, Dietrich was gone. It was what I wanted, what I didn't want. Had an invincible ego driven him so rashly into the arms of the Israelis? He had nothing to prove his Solomon theory—only his word, his logic, his reason, his goddamned righteousness, and the ego of nobility and genius.

Not enough.

Helen the parrot screamed, "Morning! Morning. Squeeze my tits, Axel."

Maria pulled her cover off, tossed it on the worktable behind me. A corner fell into a bowl of soaking string beans. I bent to pull it out and saw it wasn't a rag or dishtowel. I recognized it, but from where? It was a woven strip of fine linen.

A very fine, ancient linen with a prayer in gold filigree embroidered into it, a fabric that could be dated, a fabric joining ancient South America to Hebrews and Egyptians, perhaps others.

"Where did you get this?" The letters on the right side were something like Hebrew but not. Nothing I recognized.

"Maria, where did you get this?"

"Every day, I give Helen a fresh blanket. It's pretty for her. I take nothing good."

I flattened the cloth on the table. This historic fabric could enhance Dietrich's case for amnesty with the Israelis.

"I got it from the freezer," said Maria. "In the banana leaves, around that thing—that thing with the face."

"The skull with the soda tops?"

"Yes, with the face. No one told me not to take it. It didn't belong in my freezer. I thought it would be nice for Helen."

ༀ

Mike grinned at me as I jumped aboard the motorboat, bound for Manaus.

"What's funny?" I asked.

"Squeeze my tits, Baraozinho. You better kill that parrot." He winked at me in a fraternal way.

The shroud that had been around the shrunken head was a linen that could be dated. Taking a seat as Mike piloted us past Cinnamon Island, I lifted the cloth to the light and, through its gossamer, saw a pink dolphin dancing behind it. I wondered how the cloth had been preserved all these millennia. I no longer questioned the reliability of the Amazon pharmacopeia; their methods fascinated me. I would ask Okok what they used.

"Esmeralda! Young Baron! Esmeralda!" Mike shouted, slowing the boat's engine. "There she is!"

It was said that Maria's dead sister Esmeralda was now a pink dolphin. As the boat passed, the amazing creature danced backwards on her tail, chattering.

Even as he left Raven behind, left me behind, I couldn't abandon my father. I clutched his triumph in my hands.

ༀ

Mike docked the motorboat at Manaus and would wait for me there, keeping an ear out for local gossip or news. I joined a line of Cabloco girls and boys wearing brown uniforms and employee ID tags. A horn sounded, and we boarded the boat for the Hotel Tropical, something of a water bus with stiff wooden benches and loads of bananas. Three laughing young girls spread out on the bananas. We sailed into the wide-open harbor. The Hotel Tropical lay off a beach just upriver.

I rolled up the cuffs of my chinos, took my boots off and, when the boat scraped bottom, jumped into the shallow water with everyone else, wading to the beach. I followed hotel workers through a maze of dumpsters and garbage cans, past a sign that read "Old Wing." They entered a doorway into a kitchen area. A bit further on, I found a portico of marble, carved with vines and flowers, and entered the hotel.

Under brilliant light, it took a moment for my eyes to adjust to a long, wide, empty marble corridor. Another small sign read "Old Wing Pool." The newspaper kiosk was closed; an elegant jewelry store was open.

Down the corridor past the store's entrance, Dietrich sat on a velvet bench. He wore a white linen suit, a yellow tie, a blue dress shirt. His suitcase and briefcase were at his feet. His head was in his hands.

I took a seat next to him and put my boots back on. I put my hand on his shoulder.

He waved behind him. "They're eating breakfast, planning a trip on the river to our house. I can't bring myself to walk over to them, to introduce myself, to sit down with them under their beach umbrella and surrender. Axel, surrender isn't in our blood."

I handed him the ancient linen, an act of love or betrayal, I couldn't say. I just knew I had to give it to him.

He held up the fabric, carried it to the entry door, held it to the light. "Hibiru, Axel, the language of light, prior to Hebrew. Here is what it says: 'Bearded and breasted we came to your shores. Now abandoned and alone we watch the stars and wait.' My God, Axel."

Without asking where the shroud came from, as if he were entitled to it, Dietrich stood and headed toward the jewelry store, clutching his briefcase and suitcase in one hand, the linen in the other. "They'll have a loupe or magnifying glass to look at this closer. You're coming with me, of course."

He didn't mean into the jewelry store. I followed.

Glancing down, he said, "Your laces are loose."

I stopped to tie my bootlaces. Behind a column and a large potted palm, I had one foot on a marble bench. Dietrich moved ahead to the store's entrance.

From corridor's end, a figure stepped forward: Dr. Hermann, brandishing a pistol.

His voice was dreamy, signaling venom. "Where are you going, Herr Baron?" Wearing the same deranged, florid face displayed at the ritual sacrifice in the cave, Dr. Hermann's grin was a perverse rictus below narrowed pig eyes.

Spinning to face him, momentarily looking like a guilty child, Baron von Pappendorf took a split second to regain his hauteur. Standing straighter, he said, "I gave you your alphabet. I left the Jew for you. I'm leaving. What more do you want?"

Dr. Hermann looked over at the outdoor pool. Spotting four fit men in suit jackets and a curly-haired woman in a long ninja sweater, he knew.

From my vantage point, I saw Dr. Hermann calculating the odds. If he used his weapon on Dietrich, how likely was he to escape the clutches of five expertly trained Israeli Mossad agents? Germans are good at math. He pocketed his gun. Turning, he lumbered up the hallway and out the back door.

Dietrich, head held high, walked into the jewelry store. *I left the Jew for you.* My God.

Who had informed Dr. Hermann? Perhaps Margaret overheard what was happening in the house—the tumult would be hard to miss. Perhaps she'd finally reached Willi and told him.

In the jewelry store, a woman old enough and well-dressed enough to be the proprietress was bent behind the counter. With her back to us, she slid tray after tray of diamond rings from a safe. At her feet was a hound that reminded me of one of Dietrich's from our home in the Black Forest.

Dietrich addressed her matronly rear end. "I wonder if I might trouble you and borrow a loupe to examine a valuable object," he said, his voice croaking.

She continued her work but said, "Perhaps you need a glass of water."

Dietrich cleared his throat. "That would be most kind."

"One moment, please," she said. "I also have fresh coffee, acid-free."

"Yes, wonderful. You are generous."

She left, returning with a fancy cup and saucer. Hair gray, her cheeks were bright red as she held a Meissen cup before him. "Be careful, Dietrich. It's very hot."

There was a stillness in the air, a silence, a freeze around me. The only sound was the rattling of cup and saucer as he put them down on the counter.

Dietrich looked up, stunned. He faltered, steadying himself. "Berthe?"

I could hardly hear him. He turned to look at me, his face a mixture of shock and wonder.

"Axel, it's your mother." He struggled to speak. "Where have you been, Berthe?"

"Right here," she said, a loupe in hand. "Captain Kroening hid me, Dietrich. He hid me, and I married him. This is my shop, Dietrich. The captain gave me the money you paid him."

Heart pumping, legs threatening to fail me, I stuttered, "You were here, Mama? All this time?"

"Better to mourn me than hate me."

For a millisecond flash, I did hate her. And then I didn't. It had taken my mother courage to make her choices. And she had escaped Dietrich, a longed-for feat unaccomplished by the rest of us.

Tears ran down her face, and she ran around the counter to embrace me. She felt as soft and solid as my memories, smelling even more fragrantly beautiful.

Berthe turned and slipped her arm into his. She thought a moment. "Dietrich, I phoned your house to warn you, to tell you these Israelis were looking for you. What are you doing here? They're eating breakfast by the pool. Five of them. You could have hidden in the forest. Why did you come here?"

"I do not run, Berthe."

❧

After finishing his coffee and wiping his mouth with a napkin, Dietrich bent to examine the ancient linen through the loupe. It seemed to offer him comfort and courage. When he handed it back to me, he looked more resolute.

I walked behind my mother and father as they approached the pool area. Anyone else would have thought they were an ordinary tourist couple.

Berthe pulled me aside, said quietly. "I'll walk with your father. You stay inside just now. They need not meet you, and you shouldn't see this. Later there will be time for you and me."

Poolside, at the Hotel Tropical, Baron Dietrich von Pappendorf sat down with the Israelis at their breakfast table under the umbrella.

From the hotel entryway, I watched him introduce himself. All four men stood to greet him. There was no sign of weaponry or handcuffs. The woman fumbled in her pocket, then bent to inject something into his arm. As Dietrich's hand flew up, the female Israeli held him up just below the shoulders.

❧

I left my mother behind. She did fine all by herself, or she had all these years. She had been in Manaus, so close, yet she had never contacted me, for reasons I could not at this moment fathom emotionally. Perhaps down the road, there would be a more meaningful reunion for us.

I hadn't the time to consider this further just now. I needed to get home and take care of Raven and Rainflower, as well as fetch a briefcase of American dollars. As Mike docked the motorboat at our landing, I saw Colony planes—Hermann's Heinkel, first— flying overhead.

Back in Hitler's house, Raven and Rainflower were still asleep in my bed.

I woke Raven. I did not tell her that Dietrich had left her behind for Dr. Hermann or about Berthe, but even my redacted version of current events left her trembling and terribly scared.

We hadn't been this scared in a long time.

In the sunroom Raven and I met with Okok, Mike, and Grevaldo. To our relief, they agreed to stay on, running the household, plantation, cattle, until things settled down and Awa was somehow mollified.

Mike drove us to the landing strip. We'd fly to Rio. Raven and Rainflower would stay there, steering clear of Awa and any other malevolent pursuers. When no plan seemed a good one, this seemed the safest.

I assumed the plane on which they were transporting my father to Israel would also be leaving shortly from Rio. I would be on that plane.

Chapter Thirty-Two

I set up Raven and Rainflower in a high-security Rio high-rise, safe and sound with a spectacular beach view. Meanwhile, on our way to the promised land, we flew above the clouds, our route not unlike one Solomon might have sailed on the waves far below, were he returning to the Kingdom of Israel from South America's jungle kingdoms.

Through the plane's window, a tangerine-and-turquoise sunset tinted my father's face. He was still handsome, powerful, commanding. Tiny dream spasms twitched along his cheek-to-jaw dueling scar. The flamboyant, silver handlebar mustache lifted up and down as he breathed steadily in his sleep, his head resting against the shoulder of the Israeli agent sitting next to him. Mercifully, he wasn't snoring.

In the row behind him were seated two agents, male and female, reading documents. Two more sat in the row in front of my father. Turning in my seat, I looked up and saw the curly-haired female spy standing in the aisle. Our eyes met. Hers were dark and luminous. They looked directly into mine, unwavering, full of hatred. Finally she looked away, and I was suddenly irredeemably lonely.

Dietrich had been unsurprised to see me, but the Israelis were flabbergasted by my arrival at the Rio airport gate. They were wary, borderline hostile, purposefully difficult to read. It was unclear if they were pleased to have nabbed yet another jungle Nazi or annoyed by my interference. They were certainly irritated that I had managed to reserve an aisle seat just across from where they guarded my father.

First to Africa, then north to Israel; I would be in the Northern Hemisphere for the first time since 1945. My boots were under my seat because, if necessary, I was faster barefoot. In my pocket was a poison dart gun, with which I was, thanks to my forest warrior brothers, adept.

Maybe I would be coming back, maybe not. Uncle Wolf would have to watch over Cecilia, or more likely she'd watch over him as he degenerated even further. I wouldn't be surprised if I never saw either of them again.

Until this moment, flying across the Atlantic, I had been trapped in Dietrich's past, a jail made manifest in the jungle town of O Linda on the Amazon. Until Dietrich was jailed, executed, or pardoned, I could not fully escape. I had accompanied him on this journey to protect him, even if I might witness his end.

A plaid blanket was folded over his knees. His hands were manacled. A moment ago, he held up his hands and called across the aisle, "Axel, put this in my journal. 'Man' is the original word for hand. Manacle. Hand. Man. The designation for a creature with hands. Man is the word for hand. Manipulate, manually. 'Woman' means a creature with hands and a womb. Wombman."

My mind was elsewhere. Dietrich's contribution to the Nazi cause—steel for weapons from a factory of slaves—although pitilessly inhumane, would not have been deemed significant enough to warrant this intricate of a kidnapping. He was a relatively small fish in the vast Nazi sea of evil, hardly worth the effort relative to the dramatic capture of Eichmann or the hunting down of Mengele.

I wondered if perhaps the Jews had uncovered Dr. Hermann's plans for the Fourth Reich. Dietrich may have been kidnapped not for what he had done but for what he might yet do. Had Dr. Hermann bragged to someone about the Baron's linguistic crowd-control trickery?

In its final blinding fire before it set, the sun illuminated the airplane cabin. Window shades snapped down, one after the other. Its rays were incendiary now, a desperate farewell, a final flash. The plane bumped on something ethereal. It tilted, lifted, steadied.

Behind us, a dozen Jews in elaborate prayer shawls and skullcaps were praying, standing, rocking at the rear of the plane, long side curls bouncing as they rocked.

After more turbulence, an announcement asked us to fasten our seatbelts. A flight attendant came to the conclusion that the holy rocking could destabilize the plane. She asked the Jews to move toward the front of the plane or return to their seats.

Infuriated, convinced their prayers were keeping the plane in the air, they filed past us. One turned around, hissing at Dietrich, "Nazi pig!" spitting in his direction.

The Israeli agents sprung to protect Dietrich, shoving the prayer group forward. One of the agents wiped Dietrich's face. The Baron was too fine a prize.

Dietrich laughed. From across the aisle, he said to me, "Wait. They will come to me on their knees to hear about their wealthy wise Solomon, his visit to Paradise. They will be on their knees. And I will go free."

I responded in Latin, "*Cautelo*, Dietrich. *Cautelo*." But Dietrich was too elated to be cautious.

"Did you hear what the Jews said, Axel?" Dietrich said across the aisle a few hours later. I was grateful that most of the cabin's passengers were sleeping. The ones who weren't, turned. I looked at my watch. It would be a long trip.

"What?"

"The Jews, praying. '*Elohaynu*, king of the universe.'" He raised his voice. "Original word: Elo! In Akkadian, *elu* means lofty ones: gods. The origin of the word 'hello.' Write it down, Axel." He leaned across his spy, who scrunched back in his chair. "This is important. Words are the genetic code of consciousness, a living, evolving genetic code. It is the frame of everything we know, everything we want to know."

The two Israel agents in attendance looked at each other, raising their eyebrows. I buried myself in the safety instruction folder. Dietrich may be preparing himself for an insanity plea or spilling his seed because he knew he might soon die. In the lining of my jacket was the *pièce de résistance*: the parrot's blanket, Hibiru prayers bordered with something like Mayan glyphs woven in gold thread into its fine linen. He may convince his judges; he may astonish them; he may hang himself.

The female Israeli stands above me. "You are the son?"

I nod.

"I'm Thea, the doctor." She climbed over my knees and took the empty seat next to mine. "Don't talk to him. We don't want him disturbed. I have a pocket filled with syringes. I could use one on you."

"I'll talk to whomever I please," I said, slipping my dart gun from my jacket pocket. "And I could use this on you."

"What's that?"

"A marshmallow launcher." I laughed. She didn't. While she was very intense, I found her dark, wavy hair and flashing, disapproving eyes dangerously attractive.

The doctor studied me.

"What's the matter?" I asked. "You've never seen a Nazi before?" Not funny either.

"You look a lot like him, you know, but you need a mustache and a deep scar on your face."

"Is that an offer? The deep scar?"

"You don't have shoes?"

Two Israeli agents lifted Dietrich from his seat. His feet skimmed the carpet, did not touch the ground.

"Men's room," explained Dietrich's seat companion.

It would be humiliating and awkward for Dietrich, and I was sorry. Minutes later they returned. Dietrich looked around at his captors, politely nodding at them before collapsing into his seat, closing his eyes. He had distanced himself from the moment, somehow managing to retain his dignity. His ego drove him to this and was carrying him through.

Dietrich straightened, leaning toward me across his spy's lap. "Are we there yet?"

"Make sure his seatbelt is tight," I told his Israeli keeper. The man signaled Dr. Thea to give Dietrich another shot. After, he twitched, shuddered, closed his eyes. Snoring deeply, he shuddered, woke, and began speaking. Stronger drugs were needed.

"How serious is Sirius? Gentleman, no notes, no questions. Sirius B, the dwarf star circling the great star Sirius, is made of dark matter, the heaviest matter known in creation. The Dogon say Sirius B weighs one hundred and forty donkey loads. Modern astrologers say a teaspoon of Sirius B would weigh tons. That dwarf star is called 'Weighty' by the Arabs: *Al Wazin*, heavy.

The new word 'serious' is a description of the old word: the star. Heavy…grave. Sirius, the Egyptians taught, was where the dead go. Serious, Sirius, grave, gravity. All double meanings, jokes, puns. Initially, 'Sirius' meant death. Now the word is reduced to something important but not the most important. Just as 'martial' means 'like Mars,' 'serious' means 'like Sirius.' Consider Cyrus, Shirrush, the dragon on the Ishtar gates, the reptilian god from the heavy star. Heavy heaven. These words are in our DNA. Someday we will find that our DNA has the same structure as our language. Words inseminate each other. They have descendants. Og and Is, the father and mother of words, and Sirius, their star."

Dr. Thea returned to her seat, stepped over my knees. I felt the heat of her body.

"Who's he talking to?" she asked. "Is he crazy?"

I didn't answer.

She smoothed her skirt, patted the syringes rattling in her sweater pocket, and said offhandedly, "By the way, Pappendorf. How we found you? We have cousins in America, family. In the coffee business."

The right card in Raven's solitaire game. If you have the one right card in the right place at the right time, everything, all the other cards, line up neatly: spades for death, hearts for love, diamonds for wealth, and clubs for war.

"Everything going as planned, Axel?" Dietrich called out across the aisle. "How much time do we have?"

"Good as it gets," I told him. "Thirteen hours from Rio to Senegal. Refuel. Six hours to Israel. Pretty soon we should be approaching Africa's west coast."

"We need more time. Take a note, Axel. Zeus spelled backwards is Suez. Something important here. The river is the mirror of the god. Add J to Zeus and we have Je-zeus, son of. Perhaps son of a mighty conjunction of Zeus and Isis. Axel, are you listening? Do you have it all?"

Dr. Thea was scribbling my father's words in her notebook. "Hello, *Elohaynu*. He's pretty smart, Pappendorf," she said. "Actually pretty interesting. Nuts, but interesting. There's sodium pentothal in the shot…truth serum. You think he's right about this stuff?"

"Autodidactic. My father is a fine scientist, a man of extraordinary intelligence."

"Sure, many Nazis were. Some played the violin. That didn't mean they weren't monsters."

Still, hope rose in my chest. Maybe they would comprehend his potential value. My father's scholarly ideas traced a route all the way back to the reptilian origin of creation. He and I had dug out a cavern filled with Phoenician writing and ancient money in oxhide shapes, perhaps discovering Solomon's mining operation in South America. We had a golden skull full of bottle caps, and with me was an ancient linen, on it, Hibiru writing: "Bearded and breasted we came to your shores. Now abandoned and alone we watch the stars and wait."

More scholarship was needed, but we had uncovered an ancient transatlantic path, a trail worth following; these were the breakthroughs of a man more than half-mad in a Colony twisted by perversity and sadism. Had the world been wiser in Solomon's day?

❧

While speaking to the handsome man sitting beside Dietrich, Dr. Thea watched me. That Israeli was named Ari, and I thought he might be her husband. They spoke short sentences in modern Hebrew.

Ari ordered orange juice and dry toast for Dietrich. When the tray arrived, Ari fed him his toast bit by bit. He was exceptionally gentle with my father and courteous. These were strange spies. Ari checked and tightened Dietrich's seatbelt as one would for an infant. Ari wiped Dietrich's mouth, brushed crumbs from his shirt.

Dietrich leaned across him. "Axel, they drugged me." His head dropped onto Ari's shoulder, who stiffened anew at the intimacy. The plane hit an air pocket.

After it stabilized, Dr. Thea sat in the seat beside me and slapped a chocolate candy bar onto my tray table, startling me. "It is familiar?"

She tapped the wrapper, running fingers over a muted painting of the ruins of my family's castle in the Black Forest. I held my breath. She was interrogating me, perhaps trying to trick me.

"You see?" she said. "I've been there. I've been to your father's house, slept in his bed, ate at his table. It's a hotel now for hikers. Eat your candy, Pappendorf. I have more. It's not bad. They make it in your castle."

I folded my hands in my lap to keep them from trembling. They shook anyway.

"In your house, I met Mrs. Shteinberg and her daughter. The daughter runs the hotel. Her mother remembers you. She is very old, but she remembers you. You liked cinnamon cake. The little church is now a honeymoon cabin."

My eyes filled. "No."

"Yes. Mrs. Shteinberg said if you come home, she will make you a cinnamon cake. She said your mother came once to visit." I wanted to cover my ears. I wanted to hear everything. I wondered if Dr. Thea had injected me. "Your father's Jew, Senhor Pappendorf? Her name was Luba. You remember? What happened to Luba? She accompanied you when you abandoned your native land?"

"There is absolutely no reason for me to talk with you. Please leave me alone." I struggled to stay clear in my head. This woman had done her homework. They were looking for Raven too. For what? Treachery? Collusion? The Queen of the Amazon's riches were ill-gotten gains. She would not be betrayed by me.

Dietrich leaned across his captor, squinting. Half-asleep, he mumbled, "How much time do we have, Axel?"

"Almost to Senegal. Refuel. Six hours to Israel."

Dr. Thea stirred, reached into her sweater pocket, and pulled out a syringe, shook it up and down, wiped drops on her skirt.

"What are you doing?"

"Getting the air bubbles out."

"Who is that for?"

"Relax. It's for your papa. We want him quiet when we get to Senegal." She stood, climbed over my knees, and stabbed Dietrich in the arm.

He perked up at the needle's pinch, beginning mid-lecture, "Manioc, manna in the desert. Manna of Oc—"

"Would you also like a shot, Pappendorf?" Dr. Thea waved a needle my way, eyebrows raised. "Get a little sleep?"

"No, thank you. I'm afraid I wouldn't wake up. Are you a real doctor?"

"Yes, gastro."

"And your husband?" I nodded toward Ari.

"He teaches history at the university. And you, you know this stuff your father knows?"

"You are odd spies."

"Yes. And your father is an odd Nazi." Dr. Thea shifted in front of me to look up the aisle. Her long, coiled hair smelled good.

"Who is that woman?" she snapped.

"What woman?"

"In the red dress. She was standing there, by the curtain to first class. This is the second time she came and looked at your father. She looks like an Indian. And that diamond necklace. Did you see the size of that rock, Pappendorf? You must know her."

"I didn't see. I was dozing."

Dr. Thea grabbed my shoulder. "Of course, you saw her."

I pushed her hand off my shoulder. "I said I didn't. She could be anyone, someone who Dietrich knows from Rio. A lot of people know Dietrich."

"If she comes back, I'm going to…to wake you, and we'll go find her in the front of the plane and have a conversation."

"Leave me alone, all right? Or I'll turn you in to the pilot."

"There!" Sitting beside me, she grabbed my arm. "Look!"

I picked up a newspaper, shrugged to look beyond it. Raven turned quickly and was gone. I had not seen her wearing the color red since that awful quilted vest sewn with diamonds.

"Didn't catch her face. Maybe an old girlfriend of his."

My spy left me and conferred with her husband. Ari shrugged and went back to sleep, Dietrich's massive head on his shoulder.

If I went to first class to speak to Raven, would that lead Dr. Thea to Luba? The iciness of fear climbed from my ankles to my groin, to my stomach. Raven had been wily as ever, tracking my movements and making her own plans as I arranged for her lodgings with Rainflower in Rio. She trailed in my father's wake. Why she'd come I could not say.

Dr. Thea peeled the shell from a hard-cooked egg. "Who would imagine an egg could become a chicken? Now that's a surprise." She dropped the shell into the ashtray of the armrest, crushed the pieces so they fit, slid the cover over them, an act that struck me as significant. Even though Dr. Thea's cuticles were chewed, nails down to the nubs, I feared her. "Do you think the egg was surprised to wake up and find out it had become a chicken?" she asked no one in particular.

☙

I had no idea how to proceed. All I could be certain of was that coming events were unavoidable.

I drifted into an uneasy sleep. Mohammed's voice said, "It's important to think 'maybe.' It's important to think 'what if'." I woke at the cough of a jaguar. I sprung from my seat, out of my dream, grabbing for my blowgun, hitting the armrest instead. Instead I heard the jaguar's cough.

I reached down to a shape in the dark of the aisle, touching bare skin, not fur. There was the flash of a bracelet of night beetles. A week out of the forest, crawling on knees and knuckles, naked, the pale, unfinished body of a girl, crawling, coughing, looking for me.

I pulled Rainflower up into my lap, wrapping her in my blanket.

Captured, she growled until I uncovered her head. She touched my face, smiled gloriously.

"What are you doing here?" I whispered.

Rainflower stroked my face, touched my lips as I spoke, as if she could hear with her fingers. "Numi chief told me to become a jaguar and to find you and tell you I love you."

"Never take your clothes off like this. This is not the forest. These are not your people."

"Jaguars don't wear clothes."

Dr. Thea stirred, sitting up, alarmed. "What on earth, Pappendorf!"

"It's alright, Doctor," I lied. I talked too fast. "This is Rainflower," I attempted an explanation. "My girlfriend just adopted her, a jungle creature, a white slave escaped from the forest, now my girlfriend's. She's with my girlfriend up in first class."

"Was that woman with the glitzy diamond your girlfriend?"

"I told you I didn't see her. Listen, I have to go get Rainflower's clothes." I hoped to confuse her, to shield Raven from her. "Could you move over and keep Rainflower right here in the seat? I'll be right back. Rainflower, stay with my friend." I shook my finger at her. "Stay here. Listen, Doctor, right now she thinks she's a jaguar so hold onto her tight. I know this isn't part of your job description as a spy, but I really—"

"Why is she licking my arm? Does she bite?"

"Rainflower, do not bite this lady. Do not growl. Do not even lick. You are not a jaguar now. Stay here and be a girl, Rainflower, no matter what Numi tells you."

Dr. Thea moved over, putting her arm around Rainflower. "Numi is also on the plane?" she asked.

Rainflower looked up to Dr. Thea's face, touched her lips, sniffing her. "Numi Chief is wherever I am."

Dr. Thea reached into her knapsack. "Maybe you like chocolate? Black Forest chocolate?"

Rainflower reached up to touch Thea's cheek. "Do you know Mr. Charles Dickens?"

"I've heard of him." Thea unwrapped a bar from my grandfather's castle, from the milk in our cows, from the grass, from our bones. She broke off a piece and gave it to Rainflower. There was something kind and appealing about this spy.

Time slipped out of its niche. For a moment, in that dark cabin, I watched this forest sprite chew on my ancestors' bones. Molecules recycled, resurrected from our burial grounds, connected. No more solitaire. No more. On an airplane, in the middle of the night, over the Atlantic, Rainflower brought worlds together. Dr. Thea reached into her knapsack, retrieved a hairbrush, and brushed Rainflower's hair. Rainflower sat quietly, eating chocolate.

Dietrich sang out, "Chocolatl, Kwakiutl…Chocolate, accent the last syllable. Chocolatay. You get the names of the founding gods. The South American Kukulain, the Irish Cuchulain, the founding gods, the creators, the…"

"*Nu*, Pappendorf?" Dr. Thea said. "Go get her clothes already. Cuchulain," she called to Ari. "You know what a cuchulain is? A bungalow with a kitchen in the Catskills. The Baron is a nutcase."

I worked my way up the dark aisle to first class. I grabbed Rainflower's clothes, left behind in a pile on the seat next to Raven. Raven slept with her mouth open. I returned to my seat, clothes in

hand. It seemed out of context that my spy was brushing Rainflower's hair. What kind of spies were these?

Rainflower pulled at my sleeve.

"Just put on your clothes." Rainflower submitted to her underwear. I slipped the underwear around her feet, pulled them up to
her waist, patted her bottom. I recognized the embroidered roses of
the linen hand towels in the guest bathroom. Maria had been busy.
Thea and I pulled a dress and a sweater over Rainflower's head. I
recognized the blue-and-white seersucker of my pajamas. Rainflower took my thumb, wrapped her hand around it, and sang songs
of Solomon to me. After a while she fell asleep. I shook her gently.

She stirred. "I know more songs."

"Not now. Go back to your seat and stay with Raven. Keep
your clothes on."

"When I'm a girl, yes. When I'm a jaguar, I would look foolish."
She stretched her arms to me, and I lifted and carried her to Raven.

⚫

When I touched Raven's hand lightly, she opened her eyes.

"The Israelis are looking for Luba," I said. "Don't come near us.
You understand?"

"Why me?"

"I don't know, but they're looking for you."

She squeezed my hand.

Back in steerage, my father was addressing the passengers.
Most were ignoring him, though a few listened. "Solomon was
said to have a son, a reptilian monster named Ashmedai in a pool
beneath his castle, an ugly reptilian. A Talmudic commentary said
he was wiser than Solomon and more likely the true ruler. His
mother was raped by the god Baal...." Dietrich never stopped. His
energy was absolute. His mind drove his body.

"The great god Shamash became shame and sham. Insults. To
watch a word change: The word 'cunt' came from the word 'count'.
It became, oddly, a woman's burden. 'Sir' remained a word of respect.
'Mister' still carries respect, perhaps because it incorporates the word
'Ishtar'. And 'prick'. About 'prick'...Ik is an early word, an original.

Over the evolution of our consciousness, it has meant finger, point. Add the 'PR', which meant river, you then have a thing that points from which water comes. I daresay, prick, dick, Ik."

Chapter Thirty-Three

Beside me, Dr. Thea neatly piled her notepapers, put up the tray table, and stashed her documents in a bag below. She patted her syringe pockets—a nervous tic, it seemed. "Not far until Dakar, Pappendorf. Perhaps you should put on your boots?"

She jerked her seat upright, then slammed the armrest between us into position, dividing us. "My turn to tell you a story." She let out a big breath of air, raised her arms, and stretched. She was nervous or confident or something; I couldn't read this strange woman's movements. "But, Pappendorf, no questions or interruptions. You got it?"

My heart pounded against my ribs. My feet felt frozen.

Rushing into my head was the night we drove the Gasogeno back from the Hideaway, the night we caught the anaconda on the road and the creature was shoved into a milk can. I remembered that snake curling in that can, calculating, planning as Okok's warriors screamed with delight when she powerfully wriggled and shook the can on the Gasogeno's back seat. I remembered the pale-yellow flowers growing on her back.

Dr. Thea was the calculating snake in the milk can. Even as she allowed in vulnerability, she remained lethal.

Across the aisle, Dietrich started ranting about Og.

"Can't you shut him up, Ari?" Dr. Thea complained. "Wait a minute. I'll give him another shot." She climbed over me, bent over my father.

Ari tried to prevent this. "What he's saying is pretty interesting, Thea. Maybe leave him alone? I want to hear."

"Don't forget who he is and what he's done. Don't forget. Don't get trapped." With a look at her husband, she gave Dietrich the injection.

She took her seat. I tuned out Dietrich's fading lecture and listened to her story. "Once upon a time, my brothers, my sister, and I were taken to a factory in a forest. The night we arrived, you were there in pajamas and your mother's coat. Your mother's coat was white fox with a silver fox collar and silver fox shoulders and silver cuffs. We knocked you down and took your coat and pajamas. I was there, Axel. I hit you and took your coat. I gave the coat to Luba. I covered her. Your father saw her in the coat. He lifted her up in his arms and carried her away. We worked in your father's factory. In the mornings, young, strong men with chains on their ankles were taken into the forest to chop wood for the furnaces. Each morning, when they were gone, your father, the Baron, would come over to us and take my sister Luba by the hand, little Luba. Yes, Pappendorf, Luba." She looked down to contain her fury. "And he would pull her into his office. 'Take me, Herr Baron!' I once yelled because I could not stand her sorrowful eyes when Luba came out of the office. 'Take me! She's only a baby!' Luba came from the office, her hands over her face, and lay down by the furnace. What could we do? My little sister was silent. She grew fat. He was feeding her. We didn't guess she was pregnant. When she had his baby by the furnace, he brought her blankets. And like so many others, her baby became ashes. He killed her. And now I avenge Luba's death."

I was stunned. It was fuzzy, but I tried to recall with greater clarity the day she and her brothers appeared to us at the laundry line. I blurt out, "Are you—?" Catching myself, I said, "Are you going to eat that egg?"

"You want half?"

Logic receded, reeled. Should I trust the universe to work this out? Or had it already done so? I knew something terrible: Dorie had wasted her life hating, dreaming of revenge.

She wasn't done. "After Luba's baby was dead, Baron von Pappendorf had her put into a wagon and taken away. We found out she'd gone to your house. Months later he left and did not return.

His strange brother Wolf was put in charge. Then he left. One day there were no guards at our barracks. We looked around. We were free. My brothers and I hid in the woods behind your castle. One of your father's dogs bit my brother Daniel on the ankle. Finally, we saw you and Luba in the courtyard, hanging diapers on the line. She went inside and brought out a laundry basket. Under more diapers, she brought us knives and guns and bullets. She told us to run; she wouldn't come with us. She told us there was gold in the chapel on the hill. Gold and food. We waited until dark. My brothers went in. With the hunting knife, my brothers slit the throats of an old priest and a fat old lady. We wrapped gold plates and goblets and crosses and candlesticks in a sheet and tied the ends together. We took their chickens too, and ate them later. My brothers put on the priest's clothing, the robes, and I put on the fat lady's clothes. They were so big I had to tie a rope around my waist, but at least we didn't have yellow stars. I remember stuffing communion wafers into our mouths, filling our cheeks with them. We tried to eat slowly but couldn't. You cannot imagine how hungry we were. I wore the cross. We went from convent to convent to Spain." She pulled a three-inch cross from under her sweater, holding it out for me to see. It had a small ruby in its center. "This took me through Europe. Good luck, so I still wear it. Perhaps you've seen it before?"

"I saw their feet," I mumbled. "Feet and blood and wide-open eyes. Little feet and big, flat feet. We ate the two breasts that cross hung between. We, too, were hungry." For no fathomable reason, I took her hand. She allowed me to hold it. It was all I could do to remain quiet.

"We killed the fat nun and the little priest," she said. "You ate her. God help us all."

Dr. Thea, now Dorie, pulled her hand from mine. After slipping Sister Gerlinde's cross back under her sweater, she smoothed her skirt yet again. "And then we were finally in Palestine. I swore to give my life to revenge. I hunted your father because he made my sister suffer." Her voice dropped low, so threateningly low I momentarily thought she might be a man. Within Dorie, for that was again her name for me, there might be a strong and dangerous and righteous man, a man I would like to be. My mind raced. There were no corners in which any of us could hide. She kept her chin on her chest and spoke into her sweater. "Pappendorf, I have spent my life looking for your father. In another half hour, we are on the way to Israel. From her grave, Luba will have her revenge."

"Am I to understand this kidnapping is personal revenge? Not official?"

Her fingers tightened, whitened on the armrest. "For my sister's death? Yes, very personal, Pappendorf."

"You kidnapped Dietrich for making your sister suffer?"

"Yes."

I did not wish to laugh, but I laughed. I laughed at the universe and its jokes.

With horror, Dorie examined me. "This is not so funny to me, Pappendorf. This is not about your marshmallows. I have sacrificed my life for this revenge and justice. My life, my savings, my career."

And I've given my life to hatred. "So, *uh*, I take it this is a... family kidnapping?" I ask, as if this were a known category.

She waved at the other spies. "My brothers, Frederick, Daniel, Ruben. Ari is my husband, the professor. Of history," she added proudly.

"I see." I sat on my ice-cold, trembling hands. "What will you do with Dietrich once you have him in Israel? I mean, if it's not exactly official?"

"Turn him in, of course, and he'll have a trial. This is not just about my poor sister. They'll hang him or he'll rot in jail."

"Yes, a trial." I turned away. Something familiar, someone within me, someone who came with the vine, someone plant-like, someone universal, told me to reach, to stretch, to grow. And I was the lighthouse tree, the beacon. My brain was my crown, leafy green and moist and suddenly alive, flowering, blooming, bursting with information for my beloved Raven.

But how best to manage this newfound knowledge? I wondered how spies compartmentalized. What I now knew could bring joy, but there would inevitably be pain. I hesitated to cause it.

I heard Okok's voice. "Trust and wait, Baraozinho. Trust and wait." Okay, universe. You're on. Deal the cards.

Dorie tapped her fingernails on the armrest. "There, the wheels. After we refuel, we head to Israel."

Chapter Thirty-Four

Night struggled into day. The terminal in Dakar was a square cement block, mercury lamps crisscrossing its apron. Faint yellow lights strained through windows thick with dust. Thick sand blew across the runway. A small plane refueled from a yellow tanker truck. This plane, something like a corporate jet, and ours were the only planes at the airport.

Carrying a machine gun, a single soldier leaned against the wall of the tanker. Senegal lay empty, parched, barren.

"Look, Tuaregs," a passenger seated behind us announced.

Outside the terminal building, two men robed in indigo blue, heads wrapped, chins wrapped, sat across from each other on rough logs. Between these robed nomads, a pile of stones made a table.

"With guns," said another. "I'm not going out there. No way."

As our pilot deplaned and walked across the tarmac toward the terminal, the two Tuaregs moved to the other plane, squatting under its wing. They cradled rifles, smoked cigarettes, not even glancing in the direction of our jet airliner.

Our pilot returned a few minutes later with an announcement. In addition to refueling, maintenance work was required. Everyone had to leave the plane. The passengers revolted. They refused. Insisting, the pilot locked the restrooms and departed down the jetway stairs, perhaps headed to a terminal toilet.

Ari whispered into his wife's ear. He needed to take a piss. Jerking his head toward me, he requested that I accompany my father to the terminal. Together, Ari and I removed Dietrich's manacles, pulling his arms into the sleeves of a lightweight jacket.

As we left the plane, Dietrich clutched my arm, leaned heavily against me. Around us were Ari, Dorie, and their three other would-be spies, Dorie's brothers.

I sensed I was taking my father into dangerous territory but did not know how to prevent it. His un-manacled hand clasped mine as I led him to his dream or death. I could only hope Raven and Rainflower stayed on the plane.

Down the stairs and on the sandy tarmac, our small group passed the two Tuaregs squatting under the small plane's wing. We hurried through blowing sand to the pitiful terminal building, its outer walls acned with shells and bullets.

❧

Inside, sheltered from the relentless wind, a young Tuareg woman with an indigo mustache tattooed around her lips, upper and lower, swept the floor. She plucked a cigarette butt from an ashtray, dropped it into a fold of her robe, looked at her watch. *How odd*, I thought, *that she has a watch*, as if these people had no time. I had brought the forest with me. She smiled, welcoming us with an arc of her arm, bidding us to follow her to the VIP waiting room at the terminal's far end.

A platform rose at the far end of the waiting room. On it, painted bright and fresh turquoise, were eight seats lined up on a beam of metal, attached to each other, staring out at the terminal. The VIP space had a restaurant counter, a mirrored wall, cracked, red, leatherette sofas, and a row of turquoise chairs waiting for the curtains to part, the play to begin.

A religious Jew in a black suit, skullcap, long curls falling over his face, slept on a sofa, his suitcase a pillow, his briefcase chained to his wrists, his fur hat at his feet. I had not seen him aboard our plane earlier. I surmised he was a diamond dealer, meeting our plane to go on to Israel.

After Ari returned from the restroom, he took Dietrich's arm from me. "Come, Baron, come sit down." He helped Dietrich into a center seat, sat him upright, adjusting his jacket, putting his mana-cles back on.

The rest of our party took seats. Looking at their three hand-some brothers, I pondered the dilemma of Dorie and Raven. Would Raven want to be told first, before meeting her lost family?

Front row center: Dietrich's lids dropped. His chin fell on his chest. Ari lit a cigarette, nodded at me. He shook Dietrich awake, and my father took a few hungry smokes from it.

A thin Tuareg woman, pretzeled by pain and age, offered us a tray of bread, cheese, and coffees. The coffee was as thick as grease, the bread stale, the cheese hard. Ari and I gave her money. As he passed by, moving off and on the plane, the pilot said we wouldn't depart for at least another hour, maybe longer.

I felt a pounding at the back of my neck, a battery cautioning me, an alarm—a forest warning of danger.

Cigarette smoke filled the room. Toilets flushed. Other passengers exited our plane and joined us in the VIP lounge, usually after rushing to the bathrooms. The Jew I thought to be a diamond dealer had woken up, put his fur hat on his head, and was working the floor, hustling goods from an open suitcase.

Long, dark curls hung from under his hat. He pulled a tray from his briefcase, offered a glittery ring to a Western-dressed woman. Opening his coat, he displayed a vest sparkling with brace-lets and necklaces. I sat on one of the turquoise chairs and observed his showmanship.

Dietrich sat serenely, manacled hands in his lap, watching the mustached woman, now behind the counter of the VIP restaurant. "Axel?" he said. "Tuaregs: Berber, barber, barbarian, imberbe, not bearded. Berbe bearded."

The mustached woman approached us, whispered, "Private," and pointed to a separate bathroom behind the restaurant counter.

Using the old language, I sent Rainflower a message: "Tell Raven to stay on the plane."

In the reflected, mottled glass of the long mirror behind the counter, I saw Dietrich, his arms folded. The party of Israelis—Raven's family—looked strained, worried. Two brothers looked like Dorie, looked like each other, with thin and nervous faces, long, bony, a long, indented chin, dark eyes, sharp noses.

Ari had chosen a loose chair. He cursed and moved next to me, smiled as he took his seat. Dorie retrieved yet another hardboiled egg from her bag, crushed it, shook off the peel and dropped it into a green salad she had brought from Rio.

The pounding moved downward to my spine. If I told Dorie that her dead sister Luba was the Queen of the Amazon, that she wore a tiara, had more diamonds than anyone in South America, a closet filled with designer clothes, a barn filled with Arabian race-horses, a stable of polo ponies, a Shelby to drive around the estate, would she forgive Dietrich for Luba's suffering?

I moved next to Dorie. "You said there would be a trial. How does one arrange such a thing? Do I hire a lawyer for him?"

"Maybe this was the trial? Maybe we're the jury. On these turquoise seats." She spoke through her lettuce. A small, pale leaf rested on the corner of her lips. Something had hardened in Dorie's eyes, in her mind.

"But what would you do with him if he doesn't have a trial?"

"For what, killing a few thousand Jews? Ari, this guy thinks his father should have a trial for killing a few thousand Jews. You know how many Germans killed a few thousand Jews, give or take? Hey, Ari. We should put chicken fat on trial, right, Ari? Chicken fat killed more Jews than Hitler. Isn't that right, Ari?" They laughed at her joke. She was tormenting me. Now that she was closer to home, closer to success, she had become more contemptuous.

The curtains parted. The action began.

Ari watched the diamond dealer approach our row of theater seats. He elbowed Daniel, who also watched. The dealer came closer.

Ari leaned toward his wife. "You want a little something from this guy?"

"You're finally going to buy me a diamond, Ari?" She arched an eyebrow. "Maybe some earrings?" They allowed the peddler to come closer, although Ari strategically positioned himself between the stranger and Dietrich. The dealer laid his briefcase on the counter, opened it, and pulled out a tray of diamonds, a treasure of diamonds.

"Oy," said Dorie. "How do you choose? Maybe these?" She pointed.

Ari bent to look in the tray, no longer blocking Dietrich.

The dealer wore pink-shaded nylons under his trousers.

A beat too late, I recognize him as Willi. Slightly turning his jewelry tray, something erupted from it and sprang into Dietrich.

Dietrich clutched his chest. Looking for me, reaching for me, he slumped in his chair, croaking his last words or his first words, "Gentlemen, gentlemen—"

I didn't know whether to grab Willi or hold onto Dietrich. I held onto Dietrich.

Dorie's brothers wrestled Willi to the floor, beating him, kicking him, straddling him.

I didn't know what I could do for my father.

I looked to Dorie. "You're a doctor. Do something."

She didn't move. Her face was hard.

"For God's sake, do something."

Ari put his hands on my shoulders, said softly, "I don't think there's much she can do. I'm sorry."

I gripped her by the arm. "He's not dead yet. You're a doctor, help him. Now you've become the Nazi. To deny a person's humanity is to deny your own." She blanched, open-mouthed, as astonished by my words as I was. "You understand that, Dorie?"

She shook me off and dropped to Dietrich. She tore off her skirt, shouted commands, tried to staunch the flow of blood from Dietrich's chest. "Someone call an ambulance. I need more rags."

The tattooed woman ripped off her blue robe and gave it to Dorie. Underneath, the young Tuareg woman wore military gear.

Willi's hat was crushed. His fake long curls had flown off, lying disembodied on the floor. The brothers punctuated his life with angry fists.

"Enough," I shouted, pulling them away.

Daniel straddled Willi, who said to me through a tortured mouth, "I had to, Axel. Your father was going to ruin everything. The Fourth Reich. For our future, yours and mine, I had to."

To deny someone their humanity is to deny your own humanity. That had slipped from some other consciousness, not my own, but suddenly it was my own. I realized that most of my life I'd been denying Dietrich's humanity, such as it was.

Despite Dorie's efforts, I knew he was gone.

He told me so. It was the last time I ever heard his voice: "Keep making the connections. Make them with your feelings, with your excitement, with your love. Until you find your true being, your genius will be making connections."

I raised my head to the tin ceiling of the Senegal Airport Terminal. Okok had introduced me to my ancestor, the condor, and now I imagined I heard the rubbery flap of her great wings as she descended from icy peaks. I saw the shadow of her great, hunched, shaggy shoulders sailing above through the fog of ceiling smoke, circling us with her icy shadow, dropping down to Dietrich's body. She lifted his soul and carried him from dark to light. Was it too much to imagine? Too much to hope for? Her wingbeats and his heartbeats merged, lifted, and were gone.

❧

"Ari." When I got his attention, I pointed to Willi, now struggling for breath on the floor, wheezing under Daniel's weight. "That's the one you want. Hitler's spymaster for South America, chief architect of the Fourth Reich."

Ari examined me, numerous questions flashing in his eyes.

"A really big fish, much bigger than Baron von Pappendorf."

"He's ours." Ari manacled Willi, claimed him. "Get him on the plane," he told Daniel. "Clean him up a little first." The burly Israelis lugged Willi onto the plane like they were carrying a bag of soiled laundry.

I sent Rainflower another message. "Tell Raven to leave the plane. Tell Raven to say goodbye to her husband."

❧

She appeared at the terminal door in the red dress. Throwing herself on the floor, kneeling over Dietrich. Her hair draped his face, her face. Our worlds teetered on its cusp. Her life with Dietrich had ended. Another would begin.

"Rainflower said we must follow you," she said to her husband's dead body. I willed her to look into her sister's eyes.

Someone pounded my back. I turned to see who it is. No one was there. I stood and walked a few steps away.

The sisters who did not yet know they were sisters worked to revive Dietrich, hopeless as it was.

Wherever I turned, the pounding was still behind me. Solomon's head was trying to tell me something. Was this a universe I wanted to trust? The crazy universe that had sent Willi to kill Dietrich? Solomon's head pounded on my back, up and down my spine.

Over Dietrich's prone bloody form, the sisters' heads touched. Their hair blinded them to each other. Gerlinde's cross dangled from Dorie's chest, Raven's diamond heart dangled from her own, pendulums of Dietrich's destiny.

At last, Dorie stood. "I can do no more. He's gone. I'm sorry. He is your husband?"

"Yes."

"I tried."

Pushing hair from her face, Raven looked up at Dorie. In astonishment, the two looked at each other. Paralyzed, immobilized by what they saw.

∽

Dorie bit her lip, at last whispering, "What did you do to your chin?"

Raven gazed up at her from the airport floor. "It was too long."

"I looked for you all my life. Why didn't you look for me?"

"How could I? My husband... How could I? I'm alright," Raven added uselessly.

"You *married* that monster?"

"I am the Baroness Pappendorf, formerly known as Luba."

"He *married* you? I can't believe he married you."

Rainflower had followed her mother inside the terminal. The pretty girl touched her mother's back, and Raven stood up. While she clutched Rainflower, the two sisters stared at each other.

"This is my daughter, Rainflower," Raven said. "Say hello to your Aunt Dorie."

"Dorie," Rainflower repeated, touching Dorie's hand.

"This little jaguar?" Dorie bent and looked closer at Rainflower. She touched her exquisite face, kissed her forehead. "She looks like you, Luba. No, she looks more like Mama! The same chin."

Dorie reached across Dietrich, wiping tears from Raven's cheeks, then her own.

In a long, silent moment between them, the spaces of time and torture closed. Giving up revenge for love in a single moment was overwhelming.

⁊

A maintenance worker arrived and covered Dietrich with a brown tarp.

The sisters sat on the turquoise chairs, holding hands. Rainflower nuzzled against her mother's shoulder.

"We're middle-aged women, Luba," said Dorie. "Come live with us. Your brothers. That's Frederick and Ruben out there, Luba. And Daniel. Your brothers. Ari. Ari is my husband. We will take care of you. Come home with us."

"But Rainflower—"

"Your daughter is my family too."

Ari approached, offering Raven his hand. He pumped her hand, then shook his head as he glanced down at my father's corpse under the tarp. "Luba, you loved him?"

She looked to me. "We both loved him."

Ari's gaze turned to me. "Your father was a monster. All of them, psychopaths. It's incomprehensible what they did."

"He was a man." I thought of Dietrich's criminality, his cruelty, his brilliance, his incomprehensible monstrous acts, and, yes, his love. Ari and I shook our heads at the world's terrible sadness. I repeated: "To deny another being his humanity is to deny your own."

The sun broke the horizon. I heard a sound. The chord reverberated up my spine. I turned to Rainflower. "What's that noise? Did you hear that? It must be the plane engines warming up."

"No," she said, her blue eyes meeting mine. "When the sun rises, it sings. You hear the sun."

The stewardess called out, "Everyone on the plane. Please hurry."

THE END

Acknowledgments

Rhoda Lerman died in 2015 as she was completing Solimeos, the book she spent over ten years researching, writing, and revising, and considered her masterpiece. We, Rhoda's family, are grateful to Julia Coopersmith—the editor who discovered Rhoda's brilliance and published her first novel so long ago—for working with Rhoda on the manuscript in her final weeks. To Jean Stapleton, who brought Rhoda to the Amazon where she was inspired to weave this tale. To Laird Scranton and John Anthony West who spent long hours with Rhoda as the three shared their vision of the mysteries of the universe. Closer to home, we know that Rhoda would want to acknowledge her dedicated husband, Bob, of fifty-eight years who always said yes, her beloved twin sister, Judith Amster, for her love, support, and friendship, and her mother, Gertrude Marston, whose encouragement led to Rhoda's future and successes. Thanks to agent Murray Weiss for not letting this book die just because Rhoda did. The task of finalizing the manuscript and preparing it for publication was performed by Dana Isaacson in cooperation with Rhoda's family and Wicked Son Books. We wish to extend our thanks to both Dana and the publisher for their faith in Rhoda's work.